DEVIL OF THE NORTH

LINGUA MAGIKA BOOK 3

KAT ROSS

Devil of the North

First Edition

ISBN: 978-1-7346184-8-8

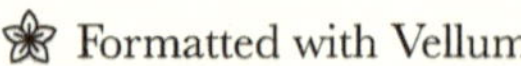

For Little Man

NORTHERN TERRITORY

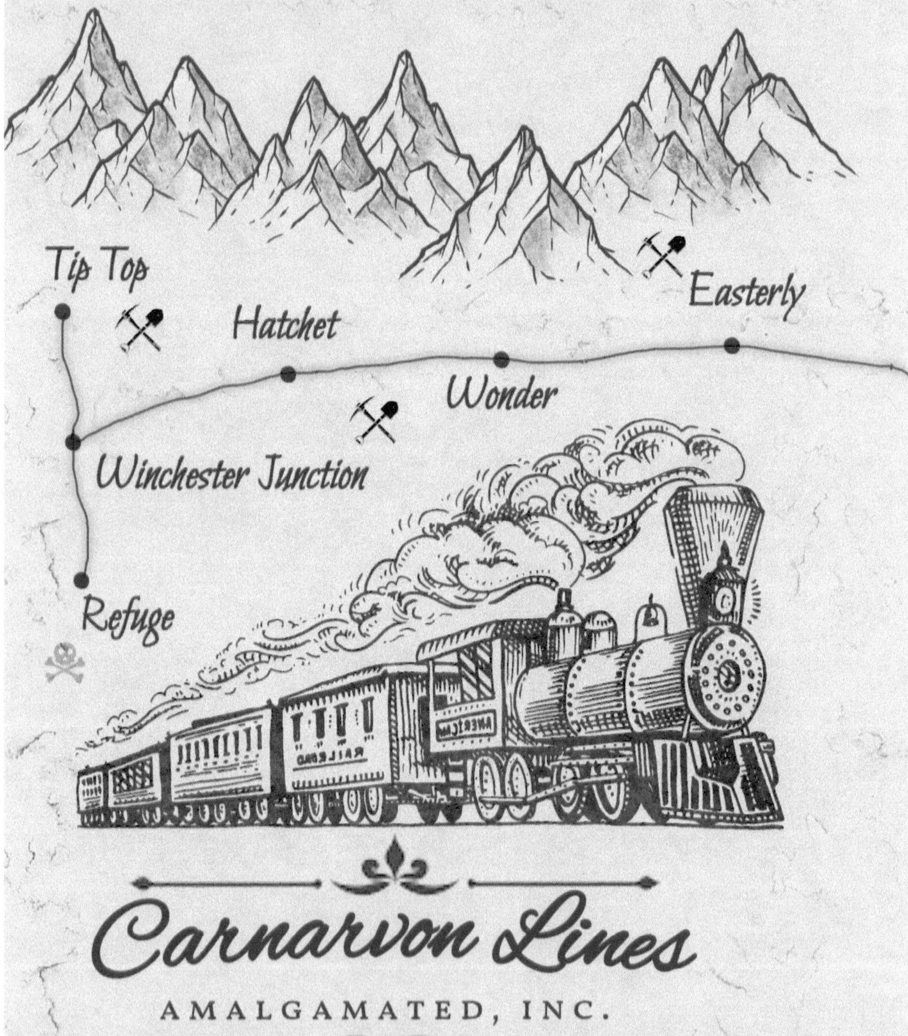

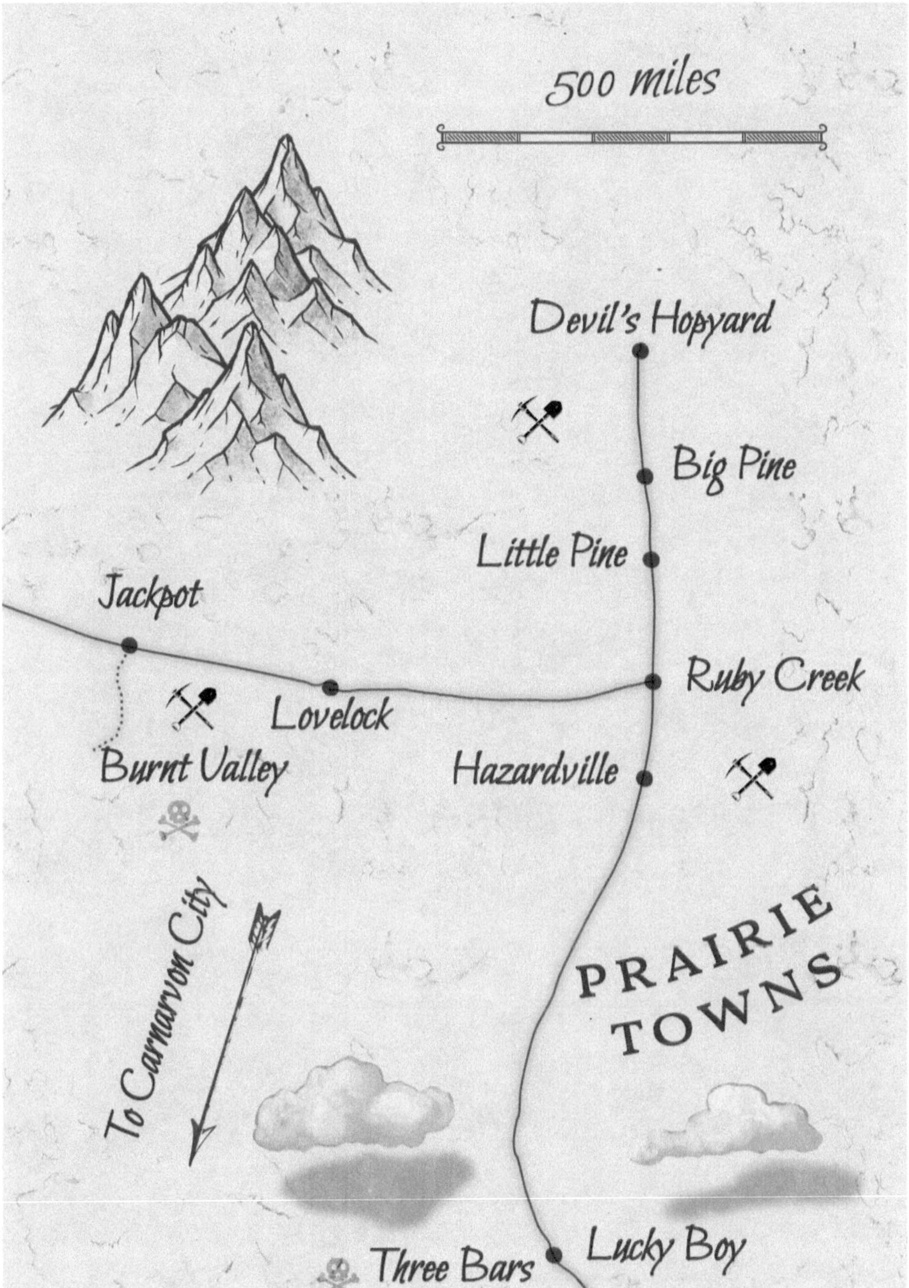

500 miles

Devil's Hopyard

Big Pine

Little Pine

Jackpot

Ruby Creek

Lovelock

Burnt Valley

Hazardville

To Carnarvon City

PRAIRIE TOWNS

Lucky Boy

Three Bars

1

Orville Royal Loving held strong views about the evils of sobriety.

"It leads a man astray," he liked to say. "Once you succumb to those temperance folks, it's ass over teakettle down the slippery slope to church-going and marriage."

"Amen to that." His half-brother Kirby Knox spat in the dirt to express his opinion of these institutions.

"Take you, Kirby. Ain't been sober a day in your adult life and here you are—a paragon of success in your chosen profession. I reckon that says it all."

Kirby wasn't sure what a paragon meant, but Royal had always been the brains of the family. He even read books sometimes.

"Damn straight," Kirby said.

It was their custom to stop at the local watering hole before robbing a bank, which is where they met Frank Whipple on a bitter afternoon in late October. Frank slouched on a stool at Brown's, working his way through a bottle of Forty-Rod. It was wicked stuff, made with raw alcohol, burnt sugar, a little chewing tobacco and a generous dollop of turpentine, but it did the trick. At least he wasn't cold anymore.

Frank had been born and raised in Big Pine, on the eastern spur of the railroad, but he still hated winter in the Northern Territory. It lasted half the year and never let up. If he had decent boots, the weather would be tolerable, but he'd just spent the last of his money on the bottle of Forty-Rod.

Frank looked up blearily as the two men entered the saloon in a swirl of snow. Royal had greasy dishwater-brown hair and a weak chin that he tried to hide behind an enormous drooping mustache. Kirby was tall and heavyset, with a curly red beard and wild curly hair.

Frank offered them a drink. The men accepted. Idle curiosity was frowned upon, and might get you dead in the street, so he kept silent and studied them from the corner of his eye.

"Have another," he said, sliding the bottle over.

"That's hospitable," Royal remarked, helping himself.

Frank recognized the pair. Their pictures were posted over at the telegraph office. He heard opportunity knock.

"Bank closes in thirty minutes," he said casually. "Friday hours."

Royal turned and gave him a hard look. "Did I ask you a question, boy?"

"No, sir," Frank said quickly. "Just thought the information might be useful."

Kirby glanced between them. "I reckon it is," he said slowly. "Seeing as we're in town to make a withdrawal from the Coffey Valley Savings Association."

Royal closed his eyes. He sighed and knocked back the bourbon. "What's your name, kid?"

"Frank Whipple."

"Well, Frank, it'd be impolite to shoot you after you bought us a drink, but if you don't keep your mouth shut, I might just cut your ears off."

The barkeep lowered his gaze and headed for the back room, muttering about clean glasses.

"Didn't mean nothing by it," Frank replied, slightly offended. "I ain't the law around here."

Royal studied him, unblinking, for a long minute. Frank's bladder suddenly felt heavy. He was about to stammer an excuse and flee for the outhouse when Royal grabbed the bottle and poured another inch of bourbon. "Where *is* the sheriff? Jail looked empty when we passed."

"Gone to Ruby Creek." Frank shrugged. "Some trouble up there. They say Winslow Cheever slipped the noose."

The brothers exchanged a look. "How'd he manage that?" Kirby wondered.

"They say it was snakes."

"What?"

"You heard me. A nest of rattlers was sleeping under the gallows. Got riled up when they tried to hang Cheever."

Royal burst out laughing. "God damn. You better not be having us on, boy."

"I ain't." Frank shot him a baleful look. "Bit the marshals all to hell."

"Lucky son of a bitch," Royal chuckled. "Well, that makes our job easier then. What about his deputy?"

Frank jerked his chin at a fellow who was face-down on a corner table.

"How fortuitous," Royal remarked. "Thanks for the drink, kid. Let's go, Kirby."

They slid from their stools and headed for the door.

"Wait!" Frank exclaimed.

The brothers turned back.

"I could be a lookout."

"What do we need a lookout for?" Kirby's gaze settled on the unconscious deputy.

"Sheriff might come back."

"In this weather?" Royal said dubiously.

"I jest want a leg up," Frank pleaded. "You two are ace-high in my estimation. I'll do what you say if you give me a chance."

"Ain't running no charity," Kirby muttered.

"I'm a wanted man, too!" Frank said, playing his last card. "Sheriff vowed to lock me up when he finished in Ruby Creek."

"What for?" Royal asked.

"Promiscuous display of firearms," he said proudly.

The only other patron at the bar leaned over, nearly falling off his stool in the process.

"Tried to shoot a rooster and the bullet near took his own foot off," he slurred. "Passed right between the second and third toes."

Frank reddened, glancing down at the hole in his boot. Royal started laughing.

"Come on, fellas," he muttered. "Just let me watch, at least. Learn a few tricks of the trade."

Royal felt a bit sorry for Frank Whipple. The kid reminded him of his younger brother, eager but none too smart. What harm could it do? "You ain't getting a nickel of the money," he warned.

"Didn't expect to," Frank replied cheerfully. "I only want a little excitement."

Royal looked at Kirby, who shrugged. They all headed out into the snow. Royal took a shotgun from his saddlebag and handed it over.

"Stand by the door," he told Frank. "Don't shoot anyone 'less I tell you to."

The Coffey Valley Savings Association was the grandest building on Main Street. It had a pressed tin ceiling and low wooden partition between the lobby and the manager's desk. The cashier sat behind a barred window. Six people waited in line to make deposits.

"This is a robbery," Royal announced, pointing his own shotgun at the manager. "Get yer hands up!"

Someone swore softly. Frank knew everybody in the bank, except for two. If he did good, maybe they'd let him ride along. He'd be a famous outlaw! Get his face on wanted posters, just like the Kid. No one in town had ever taken Frank Whipple seriously, but by God, they would now.

The brothers ordered the cashier, Amos Mitchell, to gather the money and silver and stuff it into a flour sack. They then proceeded to force Mitchell and all the customers against the wall.

Kirby started down the line, ordering people to turn out their pockets. He collected anything of value from the customers while Royal kept the gun on the manager.

"Come on over," Royal called to Frank. "Help him out."

Frank pulled his hat low and entered the bank, heart racing. Besides the cash deposits, they took spare change, watches and jewelry, tossing it all in a second sack.

"That you, Frank?" Mrs. Hoadley demanded, squinting. "When your mama finds out—"

"Pipe down," he snapped, conscious of Kirby's snigger. "Gimme that wedding ring."

She huffed but pulled it from her finger and handed it over. The last two in line were strangers. Frank swaggered up to the minister, who stood next to a tall, yellow-haired fellow.

"You don't want to do this, son," the minister said mildly, blue eyes twinkling.

"Shut up, preacher," Frank said. "Turn out your pockets."

"All I got is a Bible," the reverend said.

Frank looked him over. The man's coat was even more threadbare than Frank's and he exuded a fog of stale sweat that was potent even for the N.T. But the large leather valise at his feet caught Frank's interest.

"Then whatcha doing at the bank?"

"God's work," the minister replied serenely.

Frank shook his head, annoyed. "What's in the case?"

The reverend smiled. "See for yourself."

Frank lifted it up. It felt fairly heavy. Then the bag *moved.* He dropped it with a startled yelp.

"What the hell you looking at?" Frank demanded of the yellow-haired man next to the reverend, who stared at him without expression. Both Royal and Kirby were watching, and Frank flushed in humiliation when the man didn't answer. He leaned in.

"I asked you a question, boy."

The man's hand lashed out. Frank felt pain, then a spear of icy cold. He looked down in astonishment at the hunting knife buried in his gut. Frank stepped back. The knife withdrew, blood pouring from the wound. His knees buckled and he sank to the ground.

Chaos erupted. It wasn't the first robbery of the Coffey Valley Savings Association, and the manager had stashed several double-barreled shotguns around the bank for just such an occasion. He dove behind his desk and grabbed one. Gunfire roared. Chunks of wood sprayed the customers, who cowered against the wall. Kirby drew a pistol and shot the manager, who made it out the door before collapsing in the street.

The reverend strode into the middle of the fray. Bullets whizzed past his head.

"Watch out, preacher!" someone shouted.

He held out a hand. Royal's shotgun flew across the room and slapped into his palm.

He pointed it straight at Kirby's forehead. Kirby froze.

"Mr. Loving," he said. "Mr. Knox. Settle down, now. We got business to conduct."

"Who the hell are you?" Royal demanded.

"I'm the Messiah. And you just witnessed a miracle!"

Frank Whipple stretched out a hand. "Water," he croaked.

The preacher stared down at him. "You ain't on the list," he muttered.

"What list?"

"God's chosen." He turned his back on Frank. "Don't you worry, folks. I won't hurt you."

The customers huddled together, unsure of this new turn of events.

"I thank you kindly, sir," Mrs. Hoadley finally said. "'Twas lucky we had a linguist among us."

The Reverend Josephiah Jolly stared at her for a long minute. "What did you say?" he asked, very softly.

She swallowed. "I mean, with the shotgun. Wasn't that a phantom?"

"I don't traffic with devils," Jolly said in a cold tone. "Where's your faith?"

"I go to church every Sunday," she replied indignantly. "But I'm no fool. We all saw what you did."

"Lost little lamb," the reverend muttered. "Mr. Cage?"

Cage picked up the valise and carried it over. Jolly unlatched it, reached inside and pulled out a five-foot rattlesnake. Everyone shrank back.

"If you have the Holy Spirit in you," he said, tossing the shotgun to Mr. Cage, "the snake won't bite."

Cage caught the gun and pointed it at Mrs. Hoadley.

"Go on," the reverend urged, holding out the snake. "Take it."

Mrs. Hoadley shook her head, gaze locked on the writhing form.

"Don't you trust God to protect you?"

"Please, I—"

He thrust the snake into her hands. She gave a little squeak and dropped it. The snake coiled, rearing to strike. Jolly snatched it up, stared into its shiny black eyes for a long minute, then put it back in the case.

Mrs. Hoadley's eyes rolled back. She fainted and was caught by the ashen teller, Amos Mitchell.

The robbery had taken such a peculiar turn, Kirby and Royal just stood there, unsure of what to do.

Jolly remarked, "When Jesus went to Galilee, He said, 'Unless you see signs and wonders, you will not believe.'" The reverend studied the terrified customers. "Do you believe now?"

There was a chorus of hearty amens.

"I'm glad to hear it. Because, children, it is the Last Hour. The Antichrist is coming. Revelation tells us the Beast was given a mouth to utter haughty and blasphemous words, and who gave him that mouth?"

He waited. The customers looked at each other uncertainly.

"The almighty Carnarvon family!" Jolly roared. "But it's not too late to repent. Let's have some verses."

He cracked a Bible and started to read. "And these signs shall follow them that believe. In my name shall they cast out devils; they shall speak with new tongues. They shall take up serpents; and if they drink any deadly thing, it shall not hurt them; they shall lay hands on the sick, and they shall recover . . . ."

It was cold in the bank. By the time he wound down, people were shivering and shuffling their feet to keep warm. Frank Whipple lay forgotten on the floor, eyes glazed in death.

"Found the telegraph operator!"

Orville Royal Loving and Kirby Knox had fallen into a waking doze. They blinked and looked over at the door, to the rat-faced man with tobacco-stained teeth and a large, bulbous nose. A skinny old fellow stood at his side, looking petrified.

"That you, Winnie?" Royal asked with surprise.

Cheever nodded at the pair. "Hey, Royal. Kirby."

"I see you already know each other," the reverend said happily, closing the Bible.

"Just do as he says," Cheever told them in a low voice.

Royal nodded so hard, his neck cracked.

They herded the customers outside. By this point Mrs. Hoadley had come to, though she kept her eyes locked on the ground. Jolly made them kneel in the snow for a baptism. A few faces peered out the windows along Main Street, but with the sheriff gone, no one seemed eager to investigate.

"You're reborn now," he declared. "The scales have been lifted from your eyes."

All told, his mission was on track. They'd found a doctor who sewed Mr. Cage up proper and put some mercurochrome in the wound. The doctor didn't survive the treatment, since it stung like Hades, but his son was stronger now. Ready to play his part in the great scheme of things.

Jesus taught forgiveness, if you came to him on your knees. There was nothing wrong with a little mercy.

Still, examples had to be made.

"String him up," he told Winnie, glaring at the telegraph operator.

"What have I done?" the man protested in bewilderment.

"You're a linguist, ain't you?"

"Well, yes, but—"

"Then you cain't be redeemed."

Mrs. Hoadley began to quietly weep as Cheever hauled the man away.

"Go on home," the reverend said sternly. "Tell your families and neighbors to ready themselves for the final conflict. The Kingdom of Heaven awaits for true believers, but only a tenth of a tenth shall be saved. Remember that."

The bank customers scurried off into the night.

They retired to Brown's saloon. The reverend was not a drinking man, nor was Mr. Cage, but he had no objection to spirits when consumed in moderation.

"Why, Solomon, the wisest man on earth, said, 'Go then, eat your bread in happiness and drink your wine with a cheerful heart, for God has already approved your works.'" Jolly beamed at the brothers. "We've done good today, boys."

"What is it you want, Reverend?" Royal asked cautiously.

"I understand you make a brisk livelihood robbing stage-coaches in the summer months and banks in the winter. According to my sources, you hit the Elk County First National Bank, North Fork Savings and Loan, and the T.C. Logan Bank in Easterly."

"Sounds about right."

"Well, I offer a higher calling, and fat rewards to be reaped. Your job is to put a little fear into people. Then I come along with Mr. Cage and show 'em the light." Jolly put the flour sack on the table. Royal blinked. He'd thought it was back in the bank. "Here's an advance."

The brothers eyed it. "All due respect, that money's ours," Royal said.

"No, it's God's." He glanced down at the valise. "'Less you want to test His judgment?"

They looked at each other. "That's all right," Royal said quickly.

He started counting the haul, eyes lit in anticipation of more to come. He wondered if Cheever would demand a third. He didn't have any right to it. He wasn't even inside the bank. But Royal knew Winnie's temper, like a bear with a sore tooth. Maybe he'd settle for twenty percent, plus the loose change—

"Now, there's a little lady over in Wonder who'd be perfect for our outfit," Jolly continued. "We'll head there directly. But first we got to finish our work here."

Royal looked up. Lanterns were gathering outside the saloon. Angry voices drifted inside.

Jolly sighed.

"I'm afraid this town ain't seeing the light after all," he said regretfully.

2

TINY FLAKES of snow sifted down from a leaden sky as I walked along the path to the schoolhouse.

It sat on a bluff above the creek next to a huge spreading oak. On summer days, when the heat made us sleepy, Miss Chen would teach lessons outside in the shade of the tree. I'd listen with half an ear, dreaming about going for a swim when she finally set us free.

But there was an edge of winter in the air now. Dry stalks of waist-high grass scraped in the wind that raced across the prairie. I dropped a hand to the gun at my hip.

The schoolhouse was one room and I knew every inch of it as well as my own house. The warped floorboard just under the row of pegs where we hung our coats. The big Carnarvon Lines map of the Northern Territory, with little rainclouds floating above Lucky Boy and a ghost town symbol for Three Bars. The desk in the third row where Charlie Bowdre had carved my initials with a penknife as revenge for telling on him when he stole a mince pie from Mr. Grady's windowsill.

Charlie aimed to get me in trouble, but he ended up taking the whipping from his dad because everyone knew I'd lost my own knife down by the creek the summer before. Charlie had a hot temper, but he never managed to hold a grudge. Within a month, we were fishing together again at our secret spot where the fattest, wiliest trout lurked under the shadowed ledges.

The schoolhouse had a wood-burning stove in the center of the room, with proper desks on the left for the bigger kids and benches on the right for the little ones. There was only six of us left by the time I got to eighth grade. Me and Charlie were the oldest so it was our job to carry the wood in to keep the stove running through those cold, dark days.

There was no smoke drifting out of the chimney now.

No young voices reciting the multiplication tables or the classes of phantoms.

A gust of wind stuck icy fingers down the neck of my leather jacket.

"Doc?" I whispered.

He didn't answer.

The schoolhouse had been red once, but wind and rain faded it over the years to a pinkish-gray. Checked curtains covered the windows. Miss Chen hung them up when she took over for Mrs. Fields, who retired at the age of seventy-four and moved away to live with her grown son in Carnarvon City. Miss Chen said the place needed brightening up and if we couldn't get a fresh coat of paint, at least we could have curtains. She was young and pretty and less strict than Mrs. Fields. At Christmas, she always handed out sugar candies shaped like a maple leaf. I knew Charlie had a crush on her because despite his tendency to laziness, he always hopped to it when she asked him to do something and made a show of carrying the biggest pieces of firewood for the stove.

The snow thickened, settling on my hair and eyelashes. Dread curdled my stomach. I stamped my feet and exhaled a plume of white.

"Darn you, Doc," I whispered.

My eyes blurred. The door in front of me wavered. For a

moment, I saw a long, low building. Instead of blue and white check, the curtains were paisley. Last time, I'd kicked the door in. But that felt wrong. This was the schoolhouse in Lucky Boy. The safest place in the world. They were probably in there doing worksheets and I didn't want to scare the children.

I opened the door and reflexively threw an arm up even though there was no smell. They were all frozen stiff, eyes open and rimmed with frost. Miss Chen curled on her side in front of the map. Mr. Grady lay face down, but I knew him from the bald spot shaped like a heart. Charlie slumped at his old desk in the back. His yellow hair curled around his ears in the shape of the cowboy hat he wore all the time.

I stepped into the schoolroom, blood pounding in my ears. It was even colder inside than out. Then I saw some feet poking out from behind the teacher's desk. I drifted over, weightless as a haint. A familiar careworn face stared up at me. He was wearing his favorite work shirt, green flannel with two sharpened pencils in the breast pocket. Words covered the blackboard, written in a childish hand.

Do you want to play, Ruth?

My mouth opened but no sound came out.

I turned to run and my dead father reached up and grabbed my leg. His hair was still black, but the frost made him look like an old man. His hollow cheeks stretched in a grin.

"Too late," he said. "You came too late."

I tried to yank free but he held fast. Behind me, I heard the creak of that warped floorboard. The others were stirring. They'd been waiting patiently. Waiting through the long, dark days for me to come home—

My eyes flew open. Someone was shaking me. I scooted back in the seat, a scream trapped in my throat.

"You were moaning in your sleep," Lee Merriweather said, his brow furrowed. "Thought I'd better wake you."

The hum of the zeppelin's propeller sounded like a swarm

of maddened blowflies. I wrapped my arms around myself and sat up with a shiver.

"Nightmare," I muttered. "Bad one."

"Want to talk about it?"

Merriweather was tall and lanky with sandy brown hair he usually wore with a sharp part, slicked back. Having no pomade, it was now sticking out every which way. Both eyes were blackened and the rest of his face looked like the postcard of a tropical sunrise Charlie kept tacked above his bed. Hardin had worked him over good. Would have killed him, if I hadn't intervened.

I shook my head. "Not yet. Just give me a minute, I'll be all right."

But I wasn't. There were monsters in the world, real ones. What if the Reverend Jolly hadn't gone to the N.T. at all? What if he'd gone straight to Lucky Boy?

A sheen of sweat slicked me under my clothes even though it was chilly in the airship. For the first time in my life, I wished I had a shot of Miss White's Thistledew whiskey to steady my nerves. Just thinking of her cheered me some. Miss White carried a big Colt Peacemaker everywhere she went and I couldn't imagine her suffering any intruders.

"Want some breakfast?" Ned Carver came over with a can in his hands. "Bacon and eggs are best for nightmares, but cold beans are a close second."

I forced a smile. For the last two days, we'd been living on canned beans taken from the train. Ned did his best to make them appealing, but you can only do so much with beans. We couldn't make a fire in the zeppelin, so the fresher food was sitting in storage.

"Sure," I said, though I had no appetite. It was Ned's way of offering comfort and I didn't want to refuse. "I'll use my imagination."

"We're passing the Tower of Babel," Lee said dryly. "Thought you might want a look."

I peered out the window. Far off in the distance, the rising sun struck a glass building that rose above the city. Carnarvon Tower. I wondered if Ava and Freddy were back from Aguadulce by now. Sebastian Hardin, too. I wondered what he was doing at that exact moment. It seemed a lifetime ago we'd stood on the roof as Lee Merriweather slipped through our fingers, flying off with his teacher Mr. Beach in this very same zeppelin.

Now I was wanted along with Lee, Calindra Carnarvon was dead by her granddaughter's hand, and Hardin thought I was a madwoman. The last part hurt the worst. We'd all been outfoxed by a Class X phantom, so I was trying not to blame him too much. He'd figure it out eventually when Roger dropped the pretense, but for now, my only purpose was to stop his deranged puppet, the Reverend Josephiah Jolly, and Jolly's adopted son Mr. Cage. Truth be told, I wasn't sure which of them was worse.

"We still setting down outside Charter Oak?" Ned asked.

"That's the plan," I said.

"I don't like it," Doc muttered.

I stood up and carried the beans over to Ned's shaving mirror, where the face of a young man gazed back at me. He had a dusting of freckles across a sharp nose, a springy mop of curls, and wide, sly mouth.

"Me neither," I admitted. "But we're chasing two very dangerous men, probably more at this point. It's winter up there and I'm not about to charge in unprepared. Roger told me he sent them up to the N.T. to do God's work. He talked about pulling together the dregs of the Northern Territory. Which means we're outnumbered and outgunned."

I regarded Lee Merriweather. "His ankles are sticking out of those pants. None of us have a decent winter coat. A couple of shotguns ain't gonna do the trick. Seems bad policy to expect we can get everything we need up in Lovelock. Ned says it's got one general store."

"I'm not disputing the obvious," Doc said tartly. "But Charter Oak is practically a suburb of Carnarvon City. They'll be looking for you."

I tilted my head. "You got a better plan? It's the last place of any account before a thousand miles of prairie."

"There's always Lucky Boy—"

"No! I won't bring more trouble down on them. Besides which, it's the first place Hardin'll look. It's probably crawling with marshals." The thought cheered me further. Of course it was. He knew my dad lived there. First place to start tracking a fugitive is always with family. They'll take you in, no matter what you've done.

"I suppose you're right," Doc sighed.

He turned away and covered a discreet cough. I squinted at his reflection. "Did you just agree with me?"

"That's generally what the phrase 'you're right' connotes, Ruth."

I looked over at Lee, who shrugged, a half smile on his lips.

"Well, that's a first," I said to Doc. "You feverish or something?"

He gave me a long look. "Perfectly well, thank you."

"Because you look a little peaked," I said.

And he did. His skin was sallow and the hollows of his eyes had a purplish cast.

"You do recall that *this*," Doc twirled a slender finger to indicate his appearance, "is merely an illusion?"

"I recall."

"You cannot begin to perceive my true form, Ruth. For the sake of convenience, and to prevent you from running in abject terror, I've adopted the guise of a young male human. A mind projection, if you will. Could such a thing appear peaked?"

"I'm just telling you what you look like." I crossed my

arms. "If we were back home, Miss Johanssen would pour a tonic down your throat and send you off to bed."

He scoffed. "I'd like to see that woman try."

I glanced back at the tower. "I don't see any other airships in the sky. You think they're having the same problem as Aguadulce?"

We'd left a city in chaos. All of Pedro Braga's phantoms had either fled or gone crazy and attacked the guests at his casino complex. I wondered how far Roger's meddling had spread.

"Could be," Lee said slowly. "But it's good for us." He saw my face and threw his hands up defensively. "I'm just saying, we're too far off to be spotted from the ground. Be glad we don't have to worry about patrols."

I stirred the beans and took a half-hearted bite to keep my strength up. Boy, was I sick of beans.

"And I've been thinking, Ruth. About Charter Oak, I still have my pay, but why waste the money? I'll get some phantoms to take what we need," Lee said.

Merriweather was a savant, fluent in all the phantom languages. I still didn't fully understand his talent, but Lee could use his voice to persuade and command—not just haints, but people, too. I didn't like the idea of stealing, though I knew that wouldn't sway him. Lee was more decent than I'd given him credit for, but he had loose morals when it came to other people's property.

"We can't trust any old haint you call out of the ether," I pointed out. "We already talked about this. They could be working for Roger."

Lee scowled. His pride still stung from being hoodwinked by Henry Chance, who turned out to be one of Roger's many disguises.

"I know not every phantom in Aguadulce turned bad, but telling the difference won't be easy and if Roger finds us, I doubt I'll manage to get the drop on him again." I turned to the shaving mirror. "Back me up, Doc."

Another dry rattling cough. "As much as it pains me, I must concede you're right. There, that's twice in one day, Ruth. You must be feeling pleased with yourself."

"See?" I crowed. "Even this stuck-up grim sees the sense in it."

"Grim? There's no need to use offensive epithets—"

"I'll get the supplies," Ned interrupted in a quiet voice. "Been to Charter Oak plenty of times. Folks know me there."

Ned was the most travelled of all of us. I'd hardly been out of Lucky Boy and Lee had spent his life confined to the Distinguished Academy of Phantom Linguistics and Related Disciplines in Carnarvon City before he ran away to the Northern Territory. Compared to me and Lee, Ned was a man of the world. I'd gotten to know him better these last two days and counted him a true friend now. He wore a brown felt derby hat tipped back on his head, and had a handsome, open face with a dimple in his chin. Combined with his easy sense of humor, Ned was the sort you couldn't help but like, and I bet he was well-regarded in Charter Oak. I was about to accept the offer, when Lee cut me off at the pass.

"That's awful kind of you," Lee said quickly. "But we don't want to get you in any deeper than you already are. Ruth and I can handle it."

I shut my mouth. He was right. Poor Ned just happened to be sleeping on the train when I jacked it back in Aguadulce. He'd been a cook for Carnarvon Lines. Now that Ava was in charge, he was scared to go home. Ned knew too much—including the fact that Ava had bonked Calindra over the head to save herself from being disinherited.

"Just sit tight," Lee said with a grin. "We'll be in and out in a jiffy."

It was exactly what Hardin told me when we stopped in

New Jerusalem, and that had turned into a nightmare. But I held my tongue.

"If you're sure," Ned said doubtfully.

"I'm sure," Lee said.

"Then I made a little list," Ned said.

I read it over Lee's shoulder. Hardtack, jerky, cornmeal and sundry other items.

"It's not the menu I'd plan if I had a proper kitchen," Ned said apologetically. "But it'll do until we get to Lovelock."

I folded the list and put it in my pocket. "What about winter things?"

"I wouldn't mind a coat," Ned said. "Some gloves if you come across any." He looked at me seriously. "It's bad luck to wear a dead man's boots, Ruth. Get yourself a new pair."

I looked down at my feet. The boots had belonged to Marshal Hodges, God rest his soul.

"I don't think he'd mind," I said. "But I'll take it under advisement."

The zeppelin was a CL7, a fast little model designed by Richard Carnarvon, the eldest grandson. Within a few minutes, Carnarvon City was lost behind us and I spotted the outskirts of Charter Oak. We'd been following the train tracks, which was the only landmark from above. I stuffed my hair up under Ned's hat and put my sunglasses on. Lee had a wispy beard coming in, but he was so beat to heck, I'm not sure I would have recognized him regardless.

I eyed the flintlock. "You coming with us, Doc?"

The phantom lived in there—was trapped, actually. I didn't expect I'd need the gun, but it was polite to ask. Doc could be touchy about such things.

"Of course I am," he snapped. "You might need me."

I buckled on Hardin's holster, which had his initials burned into the leather. I'd found it on the train and figured he owed me that much. Maybe I'd return it to him someday, if we were ever on better terms.

"True enough," I said. "You can see through the buildings and tell us if there's trouble." Doc's reflection scowled. "Besides which, I'd miss your pleasant company," I added quickly.

He chuckled and started to hum *Little White Lies*.

Doc set the ship down far enough up the line that we wouldn't be noticed. It was a relief to get out and stretch our legs in the fresh air. Ned brought out a frying pan and he set about gathering wood for a fire.

"I'll have some dinner ready when you get back," he said, running a hand through his kinky hair. "Darn, I feel naked without a hat."

"I'll get my own in town," I promised.

Lee and I set off, following the tracks like I'd done the last time when I was chasing him. I couldn't shake the feeling of walking in my own footsteps, except that instead of being the law, I was the criminal.

"No shenanigans," I told him. "We get what we need and we get out."

"Naturally," he said smoothly. "I'm not a fool."

I refrained from pointing out the many occasions on which Merriweather had been just that. At least he was trying.

"I wonder if they fixed the telegraph," I said.

He shot me a look. "That was necessary. I didn't hurt anyone."

"I know, it wasn't an accusation." I shot him a placating look. "I hope they haven't. Then they won't know our descriptions yet."

"Right." He tried unsuccessfully to slick down his cowlick. "Wish I could stop at the barber."

"You look fine," I lied. "You know, Charter Oak is where Pedro Braga and Calindra Carnarvon signed their pact to divvy up the north and south." I gave a mirthless chuckle. "Here they thought they were so smart, figuring out how to make the haints do what they wanted, and it turns out we were just playthings all along."

"Actually," Doc piped up, "humans are the least interesting part of this world."

I glanced down at the shadow trailing along the dirt. "Thanks."

"I'm merely stating a fact. It's the machinery that drew us here in the first place."

"The noise it makes?" Lee asked.

"That's right. We're very sensitive to rhythmic sounds. Clocks are lovely. Pistons and cylinders. The ticks and tocks. The thumps and whumps!"

"What about music?" I asked.

"That, too, but only if it has consonance."

"What's that?"

"Harmony, Ruth. *Not* like your caterwauling in the tub."

We were all quiet for a minute, listening to the wind in the grass. It was big, wide open country. Rolling hills turning the soft brown and gold of autumn, with stands of ash and poplar. A red-tailed hawk drifted in lazy circles high overhead. Except for our footsteps crunching on the gravel between the rail ties, the silence was absolute. It was a balm to my soul, though I imagined a city boy like Lee might find it unnerving.

"Why does Roger hate us so much?" he asked Doc.

The phantom didn't speak for a long minute. "Maybe it's time I told you about him. We go to school together."

I shared a quick look with Lee. Neither of said anything for fear Doc would fall back into his usual deflections, but there was a grave note in the phantom's voice I hadn't heard before.

"It's not a regular school," Doc continued. "It's where they send kids with . . . problems."

"I'm sorry," I said.

"Well, it's not your fault. I was a thief." A heavy sigh. "Just little things, trinkets and doo-dads, gimcracks and gewgaws, but I got caught. Roger was worse. He bullied the younger children. His therapist says he has emotional issues."

"I gathered that, Doc. What kind, exactly? It might help to figure him out."

"Roger likes the picture shows. *Your* picture shows. At first, he thought it was funny that you tell stories in two dimensions. He found it ironic. But then he got . . . a mite obsessive."

"Which picture shows?" Lee wondered.

"Cowboys and outlaws. The ones about our kind, too, of course. Sometimes I suspect he can't tell the difference between what's real and what's made up."

"You think he's reenacting the picture shows?" I said with a frown.

"He always wanted to direct," Doc said.

I remembered the way Roger spread his hands like he was framing a marquee. "Lord help us."

"What did he tell you?" The phantom coughed, a wet rattle. "About Three Bars, I mean?"

I stopped walking. "What's wrong with you, Doc?"

"Nothing!" His shadow lengthened to a menacing black ribbon. "Did he say we had a bet?"

My chest tightened. I hadn't confronted Doc about what Roger told me yet, though it had been eating away at me for the last two days. I told myself there was no point digging up his checkered past, but part of me was afraid to know the truth.

"Yeah, he did," I said softly.

Lee looked between us, confused. "What bet?"

"There used to be a town next door to Lucky Boy. It was called Three Bars." I stared off across the prairie. "It's gone now. Razed to the last splinter." I turned back to Doc's shadow. "Roger told me he and Doc had a wager that Roger couldn't level a town with a tornado and leave the one next door untouched. Doc lost and that's how come he's bound to the gun."

Lee stared at me in shock.

"He's a dirty liar," Doc growled. "There was no bet. I found out what Roger did and I tattled on him to the headmaster. That's why he locked me in the hypercube and stuffed it in the flintlock! He said it was a fitting punishment to get buried until someone found me."

Sometimes it's the glad news that gets to you. I hadn't cried about anything except a little bit on the roof of the train after I walked out on Hardin, but now my eyes got watery. "That really true, Doc?"

"Of course it's true!" There was genuine outrage in his voice. "I'm a thief, not a murderer!" The shadow flitted in agitation. "Roger got a good whipping, I can tell you. He was hot as a whorehouse on nickel night about it."

"Language," I said sternly, though I was smiling.

"Then he started spreading that rumor around school. By God, he's a scoundrel, telling you such falsehoods. When I get out of here, he's as dead as a can of corned beef—"

I let the phantom rant as I dabbed at my eyes, embarrassed to be weepy in front of Merriweather. But I loved Doc despite his rough edges, and maybe because of them. Knowing he was a good egg after all meant there was a little less darkness in the world.

"I never really believed it," I said. "I'm glad he got a whipping."

"He'll get worse one day," Doc said darkly. "Well, now you know my sorry tale. I'm a martyr, Ruth. A true martyr. But I'd do it again. I'm just sorry I wasn't able to stop him in the first place."

"What's the name of your school?" Lee asked.

"Hmmmm." Doc drew the syllable out like warm molasses. "The closest translation would be the Academy for the Moral Rehabilitation of Incorrigible Boys and Wayward Girls. I use those terms loosely because we have six genders, as I believe I mentioned before. The three little brats who assisted Roger in his act are also students at our beloved institution."

"Did they teach you English there?"

"Oh *yes*," Doc replied with relish. "And Spanish and Tagalog and Creole and lots of other languages, too. Dozens and dozens, plus the various sub-dialects. I mastered them all with ease, naturally." Only Doc could make a shadow preen. "So you see, young Merriweather, we're not so different. In fact, one might say we're mirror images of each other." He gave a dry laugh that turned into a hacking cough.

"So you're both savants," I said. "That's what a Class X means."

"Precisely! The studies were part of our rehabilitation. Intended to promote empathy with lesser species, although I fear that laudable goal was lost on Roger. It just made him more dangerous."

I let the "lesser species" remark pass. If I called Doc out on every offensive comment, we'd never get through a conversation.

"They told us more or less the same thing at the Academy," Lee said thoughtfully. "That it was a privilege to communicate with the savage phantoms."

"How delightfully droll," Doc said. "Oh looky, I think we're here."

And with that, he zipped back into the Collier flintlock at my hip.

3

The last time I was in Charter Oak, the neat brick buildings along Main Street had seemed so grand. They were the first ones I ever saw that were more than three stories tall. But after Carnarvon Tower and the ritzy high-rise casinos of Aguadulce, the town seemed small, even though it had to be twenty times bigger than Lucky Boy.

Lee looked longingly at the saloons, but I tugged his sleeve and he kept walking. It was late afternoon and the streets bustled with people and horses. The women wore long dresses and colorful bonnets, while the men stuck with dark coats and trousers. We more or less fit in with the crowd, though I noticed a few people do a double-take at Lee's face.

Charter Oak was a prosperous town, just a few hours from Carnarvon City and well-supplied—not like the frontier. It would get rougher the further north we went, so I figured this was our last chance to get everything we needed. Especially the special item that was key to my plan.

"We'd better split up," I said. "It'll go faster and if they're looking, they'd expect us to be together." We were standing in front of the post office. "Meet back here in an hour?"

"Sound good to me, Ruth." Lee took out an envelope

stuffed with cash and discreetly peeled off some bills. Pedro Braga had paid him well. He admitted that he'd tried to give the money to Mr. Beach for his retirement, but Abel had refused it. I didn't know him well, but he seemed like an upright sort, even if he did fraternize with the likes of Lee.

I didn't see any marshals in the crowd, but I was edgy nonetheless. I watched Merriweather amble down the street, the cowlick like a bull's eye on the back of his head. Then I went to the mercantile two blocks down. A little bell rang over the door as I stepped inside. It smelled like wool and tobacco. The place sold everything from sewing notions to buggy whips, crammed into floor-to-ceiling shelves that stretched to the back of the store.

"May I help you, sir?" asked the proprietor, a blade-thin fellow with a dapper suit and curled mustache.

I lowered my voice to a gruff register. "I'm looking for some cold-weather attire."

"Right over there." He pointed the way to the rear of the shop. "Need some help deciding?"

"I'll just browse a bit," I said quickly.

"Suit yourself." Two more customers came inside and he hurried to greet them.

The moment his back turned, Doc's shadow stretched out long across the plank floor.

"What do you know about John Henry Holliday?" he asked me softly.

I frowned. "Why?"

"Since I'm his namesake, I'd like to hear more about him."

I fingered the lapel of a stout wool coat. "He was a gunfighter and a gambler. Had a talent for remembering which cards were played in a game. Some people claim he was the most dangerous man in the N.T."

"How'd he die?"

"Consumption."

Doc thought about that. "Maybe that's why he was so dangerous."

"How do you mean?"

"He knew he was dying anyway so he was quick to draw his gun and didn't care if he took a bullet. It's a cleaner death."

There was a wistful note in his voice.

"Could be." I tried on the coat. It fit well. "He was a dentist, too. That's why they called him Doc."

"A dentist," the phantom echoed. "Why, I think I'd enjoy drilling teeth."

"I bet you would."

"You need a hat, too, Ruth. What about that one?"

Doc flitted over to a fancy white cowboy hat. I looked at the price-tag. "Too much. I'll just get one of those felt ones the cowpunchers wear."

"You really ought to live a little, Ruth."

"That hat's too flashy."

"And what's wrong with a bit of flash?"

"Now you sound like Merriweather."

Doc heaved a dramatic sigh. "He's a sharp dresser, which I respect in a man. I think you'd wear a flour sack if you could get away with it."

I glanced at the proprietor. He was eyeing me funny, like he'd heard us talking. Or maybe he just thought I was crazy.

"Come on, help me pick out some gloves," I whispered, turning my back. "What size do think Mr. Carver wears?"

We left the shop half an hour later laden with parcels. Next stop was the gunsmith.

I'd thought long and hard about the Reverend and Mr. Cage during the trip from Aguadulce. I'd been a sheriff's deputy in my former life, but we didn't have much trouble in Lucky Boy so I was still pretty wet behind the ears when it came to tracking hard cases. I'd considered what Hardin would do in my place, how he'd go about it. Shotguns were too close. Same for my flintlock. The reverend was a linguist. He could call down phantoms on us. And if Cage was still alive after I stabbed him in the gut, the man was near to indestructible.

I needed a clean shot before they saw me coming.

Even knowing their crimes, something in me still felt uneasy, but they were both mass murderers beyond any shadow of a doubt and there was no other way. If I wanted to get the job done, I'd have to be judge, jury and executioner rolled up in one.

So this is how I figured it: Lee would lure them into the open and I'd pick them off with a rifle from afar. It was more dangerous for Lee being the bait, but he hadn't objected when I laid out my plan. The kid had courage. Or maybe nothing left to lose.

"I need a long-range rifle," I told the gunsmith. "Your best one."

He looked me over skeptically. "It's not cheap."

I pulled out the wad of cash. There was still a fair amount left. "I got money."

The sight of Calindra Carnarvon's face on those bills got him moving. He unlocked a glass case and handed me a long rifle.

"You won't find this 'cept in a few top-notch stores," he said matter-of-factly. "It's a limited run. Got a four-power telescopic sight designed by Colonel Davidson."

The scope was attached to the left side of the gun. I shouldered the rifle and peered through the scope. Everything up close looked blurry, but when I aimed it at the plate glass front window, the street jumped into focus.

"Accurate to a thousand yards. Just watch yourself," he added. "The Whitworth has a fairly substantial recoil. It's got a reputation for leaving sharpshooters with a black eye."

"I'll take it," I said. "What about ammo?"

"If you're a fast reloader, you can get off two or three rounds a minute."

That was less than I hoped, but if I could take the reverend with a head shot first, I figured we'd find a way to deal with Cage.

He gave me a box of bullets. "Forty-five caliber. Smaller than the Enfield, but they're more stable in flight."

I shook one out. It had five sides and twisted at a strange angle. The shell reminded me of Doc's world. Five planes. I hoped it was a good omen.

"You got a shoulder strap?"

"Sorry, we don't carry those."

I paid for my purchases and stopped at the dry goods store to grab the items on Ned's list. By the time I finished, the hour was up. I'd wanted to get new boots, but it was already time to meet Lee.

I hurried back to the post office, keeping my head down and hat pulled low, so I didn't spot Merriweather until I looked up and found him lounging against the hitching post.

"Oh, my Lord," I said.

He wore a suede jacket with a fringe, snakeskin boots, and a diamond pin through his string tie. A pair of pearl-handled six-shooters hung at his hips.

"How do I look?" he asked.

"Like a country jake playing dress-up," I replied honestly. "Do you even know how to shoot?"

He gave me his trademark cocky grin. Hardin had knocked out his right canine tooth and he looked like an overgrown ten-year-old. "You can teach me, Annie Oakley."

I sighed. "You buy anything practical?"

"Some mittens and a fur hat." Lee put it on, adjusting the hat to a rakish tilt. It had a ringed tail dangling down the back.

"We're gonna get beat up the first saloon we walk into," I said glumly.

"What's that supposed to mean?"

"You look like you're wearing a cat," Doc chimed in. "A diseased one."

Lee's eyes narrowed. "Deceased?"

"No, dis-eased. Mange, to be precise. There's a bald spot just over your left ear."

Lee shook his head, unmoved. "It's raccoon. That's what they all wear up in the N.T." He spread his arms to better display the fringe of his jacket. "This get-up didn't come cheap, I can tell you."

"How much did you spend?" I demanded.

The offhand number made my jaw clench. "You may not know the value of a dollar, Lee, but we have to live on this money until who knows when. Everything costs more up north. At least return the diamond pin."

"It accents the whole outfit," he said with a hint of outrage. "The jeweler agreed with me."

"I bet he did," I muttered. "I'm surprised he didn't sell you a gold watch, too."

"Now that you mention it . . . ." Lee produced an ornate timepiece engraved with his initials.

"You do realize he'll remember you," I said, exasperated.

"We'll be long gone by then. I need to look the part, Ruth! Besides, I earned this money fair and square. I deserve a little extravagance."

"You look the part of . . . *something*," Doc murmured. "I'm just not sure what."

"And I did buy some food. Look!" Lee thrust out a parcel. I untied the twine and peeked inside the brown paper.

"Pickled oysters," I said, wrinkling my nose. "And what's the other thing?"

"Jellied eels. You might not appreciate the finer things, but Ned will."

"Well, I'm sure that little jar'll hold us for a month or so," I said. "How much was it?"

He rewrapped the parcel. "I'm not telling you."

I leaned in. "You're returning that tie pin."

"Am not."

"Are so." I balled a fist and he stepped back.

"No need for violence—" Lee began.

"Pipe down, you two," Doc interrupted in a taut voice. "The law's coming."

Our heads swiveled up the street. My heart sank. Two marshals were headed our way. They wore navy uniforms with the insignia of the railroad, C&L, embroidered on their shoulders. Both wore Colt revolvers holstered at the belt.

"Start walking," I hissed at Lee. "But don't run. Just be casual."

We crossed the street and pretended to study the window of an apothecary shop.

"Hey!"

I stiffened at the shout from behind. Everyone in the street turned to look, then scattered as the marshals jogged toward us. "Do something, Doc," I whispered urgently.

A black shadow spilled from the flintlock and puddled at my feet, then flitted off. A pair of bays pulling a cart near the marshals reared up, spilling sacks of onions that burst open and rolled every which way. The marshals had to leap aside to avoid getting trampled. Lee and I took off, clutching our shopping bundles. A bullet whizzed over our heads.

"We'll be long gone?" I growled.

Lee didn't hear me. He was already pulling ahead, that ridiculous raccoon hat flying behind him like the tail of a kite.

4

We tore down the street, dodging townsfolk who had stopped to stare. I had the bundles I bought under one arm and the rifle cradled in the other, which made fleeing a mite awkward. But we needed it all and I was determined not to drop anything.

"Damnit!" Lee shouted. "Can't you run faster?"

Lee had legs like a heron, long and skinny, and he knew how to hustle. I juggled the rifle over one shoulder and almost dropped the hardtack.

"I'm trying!" I protested, as he pulled even farther ahead.

Another bullet whizzed past. There's nothing like getting shot at to inspire a body to run. I picked up the pace, but my lungs were burning and I knew I couldn't keep it up much longer. Then we rounded a corner and I saw a buckboard wagon in front of the railroad depot. A man in farmer's clothes stood not far off chatting with the station master, who sported a shiny cap and dark suit with brass buttons.

"Providence!" I gasped.

The back was empty. Lee vaulted over the side. I threw my parcels after him, jumped into the driver's seat and shook the reins. The farmer came running over as we clattered down the street.

"Don't shoot my horses!" he hollered at the marshals, who were close behind with their guns out.

We jounced down the main road. Lee climbed up to the bench next to me and drew one of his shiny new guns. I reached out and grabbed the barrel.

"Are you crazy?" I demanded. "They're marshals!"

"They're shooting at us," he said with a level stare.

"'Cause they're the law and we're wanted. Doesn't mean we're gonna fire back."

He muttered something under his breath.

I think that cart hit every pothole on the way out of town. The springs under the driver's bench creaked as we bumped along next to the railroad tracks. There was no road and the uneven ground nearly cracked my teeth, but I shook the reins harder, urging the horses to a gallop. Lee's cheeks were flushed, his eyes bright. He looked to be enjoying himself, which didn't surprise me.

"Doc?" I cried. "You there?"

He coughed weakly. "Right here, Ruth."

I glanced over my shoulder and saw a dust cloud rising behind. The marshals must have found some horses, too. The sun was starting to set and it shone straight into my eyes. Fortunately, it was blinding the marshals, too, because they stopped shooting at us. Open prairie sped past. Then I spotted the zeppelin up ahead.

Ned Carver was outside in the field, frying eggs in a pan over a little fire. Bacon, too. It was the first hot food I'd smelled in days. My stomach gave a regretful rumble. He stood up when he saw us coming, shading his forehead with one hand. The cart had barely stopped before I was flying out of the driver's seat. The prop started to spin just as the marshals galloped over a rise. They'd been joined by a posse of four other riders, local deputies by the looks of them.

I knew they'd start shooting at the air sack, which made a pretty big target.

"Can you do something, Doc?"

A whirlwind rose up, bending the grass and whipping dust from the dry ground. In a moment, we were enveloped by a brown cloud. Ned helped grab the bundles from the cart and we scrambled up the ladder. The nose of the zeppelin lifted into the sky. I couldn't see a thing until we finally broke through the clouds and bright sun streamed through the windows.

"Lord, that was close," Lee panted.

I collapsed into a seat and drank some water from a canteen. "Well, they know where we are now," I said.

"Don't be mad, Ruth." Lee plopped down next to me.

"I ain't mad." I stared out the window.

"Yes, you are."

I didn't answer.

"I bought you a present."

I sighed and turned to him. "What?"

He handed me a dime novel. "It's not the same one you lost in the twister, but it's something to keep your mind off things. I figure you can donate it to the library at Lucky Boy when you get home."

He looked so earnest, my irritation faded. I studied the cover. It had a drawing of two desperadoes firing their guns into the air. I'd already read *The Notorious Maxwell Brothers Take Tip Top!*, but I didn't tell him that.

"You remembered?" I said.

"It was my fault you lost that book." He shrugged awkwardly. "I just wanted to make it up to you."

"Well, that was thoughtful," I conceded. "Thank you, Lee."

He gave me a gap-toothed grin. "Sure. Want to try a jellied eel?"

"Not right now. But you go ahead."

I left him and Ned to delve into the delicacies. Then I loaded the rifle and gave it a close examination. "What do you think, Doc? Up to snuff?"

His voice was faint. "They won't know what hit 'em, Ruth."

"You were a hero back there."

"I know."

I laughed, but it was half-hearted. "It cost you, didn't it?"

He stayed silent.

"What's happening to you, Doc?"

Another long silence. Then— "I don't know."

I lowered my voice. "I won't tell anyone, I promise. But you aren't well, are you?"

"I think Roger did something to me. Back in Aguadulce."

He sounded a little scared, which shook me because Doc never sounded scared.

That was another thing we hadn't talked about. The time he spent in Roger's clutches. But I'd heard him scream. The sound of it left a scar on my soul.

"I want to have a look at you." I got the shaving mirror and propped on the table in front of me. His reflection wasn't as sharp as it used to be, but it seemed to me that the shadows under his eyes had deepened.

"Do you remember?" I asked softly.

"Not well. It's all hazy until you came down to the theater."

"Well, don't you worry. Once I've dealt with the Reverend and Mr. Cage, I'm getting you out of there."

"If anyone can, I believe it's you, Ruth."

"Stop being so nice." I turned away and quickly wiped my eye. "I don't like it."

He laughed and it turned into a gravelly cough. "I could insult your taste in hats, but it wouldn't do any good. You're as stubborn as a razorback hog in a wallow."

I frowned at him. "What happened to the union suit?"

The last time I'd seen him, he had red pajamas. Now he wore a somber dark suit and little bowtie.

"What do you mean?"

"You're different."

"That don't seem right. You sure?"

"*Doesn't* seem right." I'd never had the opportunity to correct his grammar before. I should have been crowing in delight. Instead I felt uneasy. "And I'm sure."

"Do I look sporting?"

"I 'spose."

"Then I don't mind," he said cheerfully, but there was a false note.

It all troubled me. Things were happening that I didn't understand, though I knew who was behind it. Which picture show were we all starring in now? I'd never seen one myself, we didn't have such things at home. But I knew that I couldn't go north without setting my mind at ease.

"Listen, can you take us over Lucky Boy? I just want to have a look."

"I planned to," Doc said, sounding oddly gentle. "It's on the way anyhow."

The next hour was an agony. I nibbled at some hardtack and opened the dime novel, though I kept reading the same sentence over and over without absorbing the meaning. Lee and Ned polished off the oysters and Ned tried out his new gloves.

It was almost dark when I saw the first buildings far below.

The Bowdre farm came first. Lanterns glowed in the windows. Then the town proper, with the general store, library, church and meeting hall. And my own house on Line Street, with a speck for the chicken coop. Smoke trailed from the chimney and I knew my dad was at home, sitting by the stove, probably doing sums in his journal. Or maybe he was writing me a letter I'd never get.

I'd been so afraid to find the place burned or leveled by a

twister like Three Bars. But it was still there, just as I'd left it. I knew it was only a matter of time before Roger got around to Lucky Boy. He was playing a game I still could only see the outlines of. But he hadn't bothered my people yet so there was still a chance.

"That your town?" Ned asked softly behind me.

I turned from the window and smiled. "Not much, I know. But it's home." I pointed to a house on the northern outskirts, all by itself. "That's Miss White's place. She's got to be close to ninety, but she runs it all by herself. I hope I'm like her when I get old."

He returned my smile. "Must be quiet on the prairie."

"Ghastly quiet," Doc said. "Only a hayseed like our Ruth could live there without going stark raving, but fortunately she doesn't know any different."

"Pay the haint no mind," I said. "He's all mouth and no manners."

Doc hooted. "That's rich coming from a woman who chews her toenails and only bathes on Sundays."

Ned was used to our banter and just grinned wider.

"Tell me about your cousins up north," I said.

"Big family on my dad's side. I haven't been to visit since I was a kid, but they'll be glad to have me. They run a restaurant in town. It's popular, a better class than most up there."

The plan was for Ned to go stay with his folks in Lovelock while Lee and I put out feelers regarding the reverend. Considering that Jolly had already burned Hazardville half to the ground, I didn't think he'd be hard to find. The man left a trail of death and destruction behind him.

Ned and Lee, who'd finally recovered from overindulging on eels, cracked open the jar of pickled oysters and started feasting. They offered me some, but the smell of the vinegar made my stomach turn. I drew my new coat closer around my shoulders and put on a pair of leather gloves. The CL7 airship was a zippy model, made for quick jaunts, not long journeys.

It had no heat so we were forced to huddle in all our new clothes.

"How long to Lovelock?" I asked Doc.

"Well, we're going about eighty miles per hour, and the distance is approximately nine hundred and forty-two miles. Why don't you practice your mathematics, Ruth?"

"Why don't you just tell me?" I muttered.

"If you round it to a thousand miles, the calculation is simple," he said in a patronizing voice.

"I'm too cold to do sums."

"What does cold have to do with it?"

"You wouldn't know, would you?" I snapped. "You're hardly here at all."

His eyes narrowed. Doc broke into a coughing fit.

"I'm sorry," I said, feeling bad. "I didn't mean it."

"Yes, you did," he said sulkily.

"Maybe it's a cold. But you're just a mind projection. Said so yourself. So how could you have caught a cold?"

"I have no idea," he sputtered. "I'm taking a nap."

And with that, Doc zipped into the gun.

"How you both faring?" I asked Lee and Ned through chattering teeth.

"F-fine," Ned replied.

"Twelve hours," Lee said dolefully.

"Huh?"

"That's how long before we get to Lovelock."

"Shoot." I hugged my knees and closed my eyes. "Wake me up when we get there."

But I didn't sleep. It was too cold and I was too wound up. After a few hours, the snow started. Just flurries at first, but then it got thicker and thicker. I could see my breath in the air. When I went to drink some water, I had to break a rime of ice on the canteen.

We'd been following the train tracks because, despite his know-it-all attitude, Doc was no navigator and none of the rest of us was either. In the chill darkness, my thoughts turned to Sebastian Hardin. I'd fallen hard for the man, even though a little voice kept warning me that his loyalty was to the Carnarvon family, above everything else. It was understandable. Calindra had been the only one to see his potential. To give him a chance to be someone in the world. I guess I'd hoped that he'd gotten to know me well enough to trust me, but that was all water under the bridge. Hardin would never forgive me for helping Lee get away. If I saw him again, I had no doubt he'd try to put me in handcuffs.

Lee came over and stuck the raccoon hat on my head. I gave him a weak smile.

"You'll be vindicated in the end," he said. "Once we get the reverend."

"I hope so." I frowned. "How'd you know what I was thinking?"

"You get this faraway look when you're brooding on Hardin."

"I wasn't brooding."

He glanced over at Ned, who was dozing with his hat pulled low in another seat. "You can talk about it if you want."

I sighed. "Not much to say, really."

"I'm sorry."

"For what? You tried to stop Ava from killing her grandmother. It's not your fault Hardin walked in at just the wrong moment." I shook my head, lips tightening. "What kind of person does that? Kills her own kin for money?"

Lee looked at me for a long minute. "Lots of people, Ruth."

"Not in my town," I said.

"I'd like to visit Lucky Boy some day. Not just from the air or blindfolded on a train." He smiled. "It's a special place, isn't it?"

My throat closed up. "Yeah."

"Maybe I could meet your dad. He used to teach at the Academy, right?"

I pulled myself together. "He sure did. I never knew. He didn't tell me. Guess he wanted to leave the past behind. But he figured out the phantoms before anybody else did. What they really were. That's why Calindra exiled him to Lucky Boy."

Lee thought about that. "If she hadn't, you would have been born in the city and you wouldn't be you, if you get my drift. So maybe that was a good thing."

I'd never thought about it like that. "I think he's happy there. It's a quiet life, but my dad's a quiet man. It suits him."

"And your mother?"

We looked alike, but Rose Cortez had all the glamor I sorely lacked. She liked bright lights and bustle. I used to blame her for leaving, but we'd reconciled after a fashion—also, I realized, thanks to Lee Merriweather. I never would have gone to Carnarvon City and seen her, if not for him.

"She's a whole different type," I said. "It wasn't for her."

The wind picked up, howling against the glass panes. It buffeted the airship this way and that. Doc appeared in the shaving mirror, his thin face taut with worry.

"I don't know where we are," he said. "But this weather's pushing us too fast. If we keep going, we could blow into the mountains." He paused. "That'd be the end of us."

The Northern Range was shown on the schoolhouse map as a series of fearsome jagged peaks that scraped the sky. I shuddered at the thought of being stranded there.

"Can't you see?" I asked.

He coughed. "I'm not a cat, Ruth. It's dark out."

"So what do we d-do?" Lee wondered.

"How long has it been?"

He consulted his new gold watch. "We should be close to Lovelock, unless we're even f-farther off course than I think."

"Then try to set us down, Doc," I said, buckling on the Collier.

I clutched my seat as the zeppelin gave a sickening lurch. It felt like riding a paper boat down the creek when the spring floods came. Judging by Ned Carver's expression, he was regretting his decision to tag along, but it was too late for second thoughts now. I clasped my hands and whispered a quick prayer.

Dear Lord, I know I've made some bad mistakes, but I always tried to do right. There's a man committing evil in your name, though you probably know that already. I swear I'll do my best to stop him if you keep Lee Merriweather and Ned Carver safe. I glanced at the pinched face in the shaving mirror. *And my mean old haint, too. Amen.*

With that plea, the frame of the airship gave a mighty groan. We dropped like a stone. Something slammed into the bottom of the gondola with a terrible scraping noise. Suddenly there was a giant hole in the wall. The floor tilted and we all went tumbling into the snowy void.

5

I FELL THROUGH THE AIR, branches whacking my arms and legs, and landed in a big snowbank. It knocked the breath out of me. All around, I heard cracking sounds as the airship settled. Then, silence.

As soon as I had my lungs back, I called out their names.

"That you, Ruth?"

"No, it's a ghost."

"Quit fooling and come help me."

I pulled myself out of the snow. "Where are you?"

"Over here!"

The lanky form of Lee Merriweather appeared a ways off. We'd torn through a stand of pines and settled in a clearing. I cupped my hands around my mouth to carry over the wind. "Ned!"

I thought I heard a faint cry. I hurried over and started digging. Lee came to help. In a minute, we'd unearthed Ned Carver. He spat out snow and sat up, eyes wide in the dark. We huddled together in the lee of the ship, which had come to rest at an angle. No one was seriously hurt, but the zeppelin was wrecked. It had a huge hole in the side, where silk flapped wildly against the bent aluminum airframe.

“Can’t you fix it, Doc?” I asked.

He chortled. “I’m flattered that you think I’m some kind of miracle worker, but that thing is beyond repair.”

I looked at the others. “Any clue where we are?”

Ned shrugged helplessly. Lee shook his head.

The gondola itself was torn wide open and already filling with drifting snow.

“Then we’d better gather our things and start walking before we freeze to death. Maybe we’re close to town.”

At least we were already wearing most of our clothes. I found my new rifle and the cracked shaving mirror. The dime novel was stowed securely in a pocket. I filled the other with hardtack. We set out into the pine woods. The snow was deep and we took turns going first to blaze a trail.

“Maybe we’ll come across an old lumber camp,” I said hopefully.

Lee glanced over his shoulder. “I thought this was mining country.”

“A little of both.”

We trudged onward. The wind had piled the snow in deep drifts against the trees. In some places, it was only ankle-deep, but one false step and you’d sink up to the knees. After an hour or so, the wind stopped and the stars came out. It was bitter cold, the kind that sinks its teeth into your bones. Moonlight came through the trees and reflected off the fresh snow so it was almost bright out.

“See anything, Doc?” I asked.

He didn’t answer.

“Doc?” I asked again. “You there?”

A long minute passed. Then his voice came, faint and hollow like he was at the bottom of a well.

“I’m sorry, I’m not feeling myself. But there’s something ahead. I can’t quite . . . .” He coughed and trailed off. “Just let me rest a little, Ruth,” he said weakly.

“‘Course,” I said, feeling worried. “It’s all right.”

We kept going. The storm picked up again. Finally, Lee fell down and refused to get up again. I knew he should have bought a decent coat instead of that suede fringe. I crouched down and hugged my arms around him. He clung to me like a child.

"We have to find shelter," Ned said through clenched teeth. His lashes were rimmed with frost. "Stay with him. I'll range ahead."

"Don't go far," I warned. "Don't want to lose you."

He nodded and vanished into the trees. I wondered if we should have just stayed at the gondola.

"Don't you freeze on me, Merriweather," I muttered, chafing his hands. "I'll have to cuff you and drag you back to Ava, see how you enjoy her tender company."

"Never been this c-c-cold," he said.

"I have," I said. "It's no fun, but you'll live."

The woods were so quiet in the falling snow. Almost peaceful. I found myself getting drowsy and tried to fight it. I thought Lee had fallen asleep, but then he spoke.

"Do you love him?" Lee asked.

"Don't be an ass."

"You do. I'd like to fall in love someday."

"Quit talking like that. 'Course you will."

I chafed his hands some more. "Wiggle your toes," I said. "Can you feel 'em?"

"A little bit."

"That's good then."

He was silent for a spell. "Do you think Ned likes me?"

I suppressed a smile. So that's how it was. "They say the way to a man's heart is jellied eels."

Lee laughed. "Hey, I just remembered I have a flint. We can make a fire if you get some wood."

"There's nothing to burn," I said. "You ever made a fire in your life?"

Lee glared at me with some of his old spirit. "Maybe not, but at least I thought to buy a flint."

"Does no good without fuel."

"Tell me some more about Lucky Boy, then."

So I did. I told him about Charlie Bowdre, my best friend and worst enemy. I told him about Miss White and her Thistledew whiskey, and the time I got lost when I was little and my mom finally found me at her house playing with a box of bullets, happy as a clam. I told him about my fierce old cat, Jimmy Jack, and his various adventures, and the potluck suppers we'd have in the summertime, when Mrs. Hernandez would make her famous pecan pie.

I'd nearly given up hope that Ned would come back when he suddenly appeared like a specter in the dark.

"I found a cave," he said. "Not too far."

We hoisted Lee to his feet. Ned slung an arm under his shoulders and we started walking again. The land rose off to the left, then dropped sharply. It was just a crack in the rock, maybe two feet wide. We had to crawl to get inside. But it was warmer in there and out of the wind.

"You're a g-g-genius," Lee stammered.

Ned sounded bashful. "Just lucky."

I passed around the hardtack. The food warmed us all some.

"I still wish we had a fire," Lee said.

"You need dry wood," I explained patiently. "And kindling to get it going."

"I know what kindling is. Little sticks."

"You see any around here?"

"I can't see anything, Ruth. It's pitch dark."

"There you go."

"When we get to your cousins' restaurant, I'm going to order a big stack of flapjacks," Lee declared. "With maple syrup. Bacon, too."

"My Aunt Maisie makes some mean grits," Ned said wistfully. "With fresh churned butter—"

He cut off as a sound came from the depths of the cave. I couldn't tell how far back the crevice went. Maybe a lot farther than we thought.

"You hear that?" Ned whispered.

I gave a tight nod.

"What was it?"

I touched his arm to be quiet. We all listened. I was just thinking it was the wind when it came again. A long, deep rumbling snore.

We all scrambled outside. The blizzard had really picked up. I was instantly chilled to the bone again.

"Well," I shouted over the howl of the storm. "That's not a cave. It's a den."

The boys were holding onto each other for dear life. Lee didn't seem to mind too much, but the way I saw it, we had two choices.

"We gotta sleep with that bear," I said.

"Are you crazy?" Lee demanded.

"It's that or freeze," I said simply. "Just don't make noise."

"Is it hibernating?" Lee wondered. "Or just napping?"

"The former, I imagine," came Doc's dry voice. He was back and sounding almost like his old self.

"But you don't know for sure?" Lee persisted.

"Based on the length of the snore, the creature appears to be breathing once or twice a minute," Doc said. "That qualifies as hibernation."

"So it won't wake up?"

"Not if you quit yammering about flapjacks and grits."

"I can't believe we're even considering this," Lee said.

I turned my back and headed to the den. "I'm not dying out here."

I went in as far as I dared and sat with my back against the wall. It was quiet, and then the sound came again. It was like a person, rumbling and grating, just louder. A minute later, Lee and Ned swallowed their pride and crawled inside.

We listened to that bear snore until dawn. I don't think any of us got a lick of sleep, but at least we were alive the next day—stiff and cold, but alive.

The snow had stopped and in the bright morning sun, the woods were transformed. Mounds of white, fluffy powder bent the branches of the spruce trees. Squirrels scolded from the trunks and I spotted a bright red cardinal singing to his mate. *Too-weee, too-weee, too-weee!*

"Tell us more about the restaurant," Lee begged, as we started walking again.

The temperature rose above freezing and icicles dripped from the needles. Every now and then, a big avalanche would slide off the trees with a wet plop.

"Best maple syrup you ever tasted. Hot coffee with a dollop of sweet cream. Cornbread and jam and fried okra…." For the next hour, Ned regaled us with descriptions of the big breakfast waiting for us in Lovelock. It was torment, but it kept us going.

At last I caught a faint whiff of woodsmoke. "We must be near," I said in excitement.

The prospect of wood stoves and people spurred our steps. Then we topped a rise and halted in our tracks.

There was smoke alright, but that's because the town had burned to the ground and parts were still smoldering. We stared in silent shock. Ned started running pell-mell down the hill, sliding through the deep drifts.

"Wait!" I called after him.

Ned didn't turn, or even acknowledge my shout. I shared a grim look with Lee and we took off after him.

All the storefronts were charred husks. Ned stopped in front of one. He took his hat off, twisting it in his hands. His jaw was set and he stared straight ahead. The only things still standing were a big brick oven in the back and the cast iron stove. The rest was ash.

"Maisie's," he whispered hoarsely.

Lee came up and stood behind him. He half reached for Ned's sleeve but seemed to think better of it, and let his hand fall. "I'm so sorry," he said in a gentle voice. "Come on, let's search. Don't think the worst yet."

Ned turned to him with red, desolate eyes. "I s'pose this wasn't an accident," he said.

"No," I said, anger heating my blood. "The Reverend burned Hazardville, too, though they managed to put out the blaze before the whole town went up."

"Maybe my cousins got out," Ned said with a note of hope.

I thought about New Jerusalem and decided I couldn't tell him all of what the Reverend and Cage had done. Not now.

"Maybe they did," I said. "Lee made a sensible suggestion for once. Let's search."

We sifted through the rubble of his aunt's restaurant and then the other buildings. To our vast relief, there were no human remains except at the bank. It was made of brick so it hadn't burned like the others. Just outside we found a middle-aged man face-down in the snow. He'd been shot in the back. There was another body inside, this one younger and stabbed in the stomach. The vault sat wide open and I saw signs of a gunfight.

"Looks like they tried to rob the place," I said with a frown. "That doesn't exactly fit with the reverend's usual style."

"How do you mean?" Lee asked.

"Well, he's violent and crazy, but he still thinks he's a man of God. It's all twisted up, but he believes he's here to save us. Now, Mr. Cage is another matter. He does it for the kicks. The reverend had him on a leash, but you can't tame a wolf. It'll turn and bite you eventually." I shook my head. "Wish I knew exactly what happened here."

"You said Roger gave him a task, right?" Lee said. "Maybe he's recruiting."

We looked at each other. The thought was not a pleasant one.

"We'll find the men who did this, I promise you," I said to Ned.

He scrubbed a hand across his face. "I just don't understand why. These people never did anything."

None of us had an answer for that. And we had more immediate problems.

Ned stamped his feet and blew on his hands. "Next town is Jackpot, but it's at least two hundred miles down the line."

The skies were already darkening with the promise of fresh snow. The only other building that hadn't been burned was the church up on the hill. I stepped out of earshot, pretending I had to go do my business behind a tree.

"Doc," I said in a low voice.

"I'm here, Ruth." His voice was subdued.

"You see bodies up there? I don't have the stomach to look and it won't do Ned any good to see that."

"No bodies," he said after a moment.

I let out a breath. "Thank the Good Lord. I wonder why they spared it."

"Maybe you'd better go see. There might be a clue where they've gone."

I returned to Lee and Ned. "I'm checking out the church."

"We'll come with you," Ned said.

It was like any other frontier church, one room with rows of wooden pews. Light streamed through the windows, but the pulpit was cast in shadow. My unease deepened as I walked to the rear of the church. A Bible lay open to Joel, Chapter Two. A passage had been underlined in pencil, the lines wavering like it had been done with an unsteady hand.

"And I will show wonders in the heavens and on the earth," I whispered. "Blood and fire and columns of smoke."

I closed the Bible and wiped my hands on my coat. I felt soiled just standing where he'd stood, like he'd left an evil residue behind.

"It was the reverend, all right," I said. "I think we just missed him. That fire can't be more than a day old."

"Does he know we're here?" Lee asked anxiously. "Is it meant for us?"

His bravado had vanished now that reality was setting in. Lee had never spent time with the reverend, nor had he been in New Jerusalem. I'd told him what Hardin and I had found there, but that's not the same as seeing it with your own eyes.

Their paths had crossed briefly back in Carnarvon City when Lee came with Doc to rescue me and Mr. Beach from an underground bunker where we were being held hostage. But again, he hadn't been forced to listen to Jolly's endless sermons or watch Mr. Cage sharpen his big hunting knife. Lee didn't know them like I did, but he was starting to get the picture and he was scared.

I was, too.

We all turned as a distant train whistle cut the air. It sounded like salvation.

Or damnation, if our enemies were aboard.

The whistle came again, one long blast.

"That means the train's not stopping," Ned said. "It's a warning to get off the tracks."

"Run to catch it?" I asked.

It was a decision we needed to make together. Lee and Ned hesitated for a moment, then they both nodded.

We took off for the depot like our lives depended on it, which they almost certainly did. I could see the smoke from the boiler. The train wasn't slowing. As usual, Lee pulled ahead, arms and legs pumping, raccoon tail flying out, a determined look on his face.

We reached the one-room station just as the train chugged by. It had a big plow mounted on the front to shovel the snow out of the way. Lee leapt up to the bottom step of the caboose and gripped the rail, offering a hand to Ned, who nimbly hopped up. I was last. I handed up the rifle and climbed aboard just as it picked up speed.

"Stay in the gun," I panted to Doc as we opened the door to the caboose. "Unless it's the reverend. Then do whatever you can to help me kill him."

6

THE CABOOSE WAS FILLED with stacked wooden crates and a few steamer trunks. Ned cautiously cracked the door to the next car. I peered over his shoulder.

It was a regular passenger car. All the seats were empty.

"I don't like this," Lee muttered.

"What do you see ahead, Doc?"

He gave a hacking cough. "Not sure."

"What do you mean, not sure?"

"I mean everything's blurry. Wait, someone's coming this way."

At that moment, the door at the end of the car opened. A man walked through. He wore the cap and uniform of Carnarvon Lines. He had a full white mustache and big red-veined nose. When he saw us, he stopped dead.

"How'd you all get aboard?" he demanded.

"Climbed up the caboose," I said. "We were yelling but you didn't see us."

We must have looked like desperadoes because he raised his hands. "Just don't shoot me."

I realized I had a hand on the butt of my flintlock and let it go. "No one's shooting anyone, sir," I said.

"What were you doing in Lovelock?" His eyes narrowed. "There's no one left."

Ned opened his mouth and I saw Lee throw a discreet elbow. "Got a tip there might be a claim up in the hills," Lee said in a perfect frontier drawl. "Didn't pan out. When we got back to town, we found the place gone."

The conductor looked us over. "You got lucky then. Train only runs a couple times a week this time of year."

"Did everyone get out?" Ned asked with a note of desperation.

"All kinds of crazy rumors about what happened. Some say it was phantoms, but I don't believe it. More likely a spilled lantern. Plenty of folks escaped though, scattered down the line."

Ned brightened to hear that.

"What about the marshals?" I asked. "Ain't they investigating the source of the fire?"

The conductor lowered his voice. "Telegrams have been sent down to the city, but we aren't getting much of a response. You heard the rumors of some bad business down in Aguadulce?"

Lee shook his head. "Not a thing. We were deep in the bush. What are they saying?"

"That Pedro Braga's phantoms went crazy and killed everybody. Hard to fathom." He rubbed his jaw, gaze moving to the front of the train where the engine was. "Our phantoms haven't given any trouble at all. But what with the fires around here, who knows? Either way, the good people of Lovelock will have to wait for spring to rebuild. It's the worst winter in memory and it's barely even started." He looked us over. "Where you headed?"

"Jackpot," I said.

"You got tickets?"

"Afraid not." Lee started to reach into his pocket. I stepped on his foot.

"We're pretty low on funds, sir," I said. "Any chance you could see clear to giving us a discount since you didn't even have to stop the train?"

The conductor gave me a hard stare. Then he glanced at Lee's banged-up face and sighed. "Tell you what. Just pay for one third-class ticket. Call it my good deed for the day."

Lee peeled off a bill and the conductor punched our tickets.

"You all look half frozen. Why don't you take one of the compartments in the next car and warm up? It's for second-class passengers, but the train's almost empty anyway."

"That's mighty kind of you," Ned said. "We sure do appreciate it."

"How far to Jackpot?" I asked.

"'Bout seven hours with the snow."

There were no sleepers, but the compartment was clean and private. We settled in, me on one side and Ned and Lee facing. I propped the rifle against the seat.

"Nicely done, Ruth," Lee said. "You ought to do the talking from now on."

"I guess your powers of persuasion rubbed off on me a bit."

"Bah," Doc muttered, his reflection appearing in the glass. "You look like half-starved orphans who just escaped the workhouse. He probably figured you'd start eating the seats if he didn't show pity."

"You got no faith in people," I said.

"*Don't have* any faith. And that's not true. I'm just a realist. Wyatt used to say the only honest men were the dead ones."

It was a strange comment. I was about to reply when the reflection vanished.

"Maybe your cousins will be in Jackpot," Lee said, using his hat as a pillow.

Ned stared out the window at the snowy woods. Night was

already falling. The days had grown short. "If we don't find the same thing there."

No one spoke for a minute. I pulled out the last of the hard tack and divvied it up.

"You were too quick to pay for those tickets," I said to Lee. "We need to conserve the money we have left. You spent way too much in Charter Oak." I stood up.

"Where are you going?"

"He said the train was *almost* empty. I'd like to know who we're riding with."

"Be careful," Lee said.

I nodded and stepped through the sliding door.

The next car had a sleeping family, ma and pa and two kids, plus a few solitary strays who looked me over without much interest. A bunch of rowdy miners were in the next one, drinking and playing cards. Beyond that was the boiler. I pushed through, ignoring their calls to join the game, and peeked through the crack in the door.

If you've never seen a haint in the flesh, the sight can be unnerving. They look like naked human kids with buggy insect eyes. There were three, shoveling coal into the boiler with mechanical speed. None of them paid me any mind. I quietly retreated.

By the time I returned, Lee and Ned were asleep.

"Doc?" I whispered. "Can you go talk to the haints running the train?"

"I'm tired, Ruth."

"They might have heard something. I wouldn't ask if it wasn't important."

His shadow oozed from the gun and drifted slowly up the aisle. Normally, Doc would flit around like a hummingbird. Part of me had hoped he might be faking, either for sympathy or to have an excuse to ignore me, but now I knew for certain something was off.

He came back a few minutes later.

"Thank you," I said.

Doc slid into the barrel of the flintlock. I imagined him curling up like a cat before a toasty hearth.

"I didn't find out much, Ruth. There are three phantoms running the engine. They heard there might be some trouble on the other side of the dollhouse, a few bad kids, but they like playing with the train and they won't go home until suppertime."

Hearing my world referred to as a dollhouse was annoying, but I didn't correct him.

"So they don't know where Roger is?"

"I just said so, didn't I?" He made a scoffing noise. "They're little kids. He wouldn't bother with them unless he wanted to use them."

"Then I won't worry about Roger right now. We got enough on our plate with the reverend. He must be ahead of us, so we got to be ready for anything in Jackpot." I paused. "What about the phantom girl with the white stripe in her hair? Have you tried calling her?"

"I have. She doesn't answer."

"Poor thing. I hope Roger didn't hurt her."

"You don't know her," Doc said dryly. "She's a tough cookie."

"Aha! I imagine you do then."

"Yes," he conceded. "We're schoolmates."

"At the reformatory? What'd she do?"

"Likes to set fires. I call her Zippo."

I felt cold. "You don't think it was her, do you?"

"No, she hates Roger. And she never burned anything here, only at home. I'm tired, Ruth. I need to sleep now."

He left me alone with my thoughts. *Zippo*. She'd saved my life when the bandits attacked the train. And Lee said she'd tried to warn him about Roger. If she was around, I wished she'd show herself. We could use another ally, even if it was a juvenile arsonist.

The estimate of seven hours was more like nine and we pulled into Jackpot late the next morning. The platform was crowded with people. Some were looking for relatives, others seemed to be refugees from Lovelock. Ned spent a few minutes searching for his cousins but saw no sign of them. About half the people got on our train, which ended at Winchester Junction. The rest were waiting for the westbound train to Ruby Creek.

As the train pulled away, the conductor gave us a friendly wave. "Stay safe!"

I raised my hand in farewell and he winked at me. The hair rose up on the back of my neck.

Roger used to do that. I knew he could take any form he wanted . . . .

"Doc," I whispered, watching as it puffed away in a cloud of steam. "You sure that conductor was a real person?"

"Well, I think so." He sounded a bit defensive.

"You think so? Can't you see right through him to what's inside?"

Phantoms were made of pink blobby stuff with purple strings. Since they lived on five planes, I imagined their innards looked quite a bit different from ours.

Doc coughed. "Truth be told, my eyes aren't what they used to be. Sometimes I can, sometimes I can't."

"Darn it!" I thought back. Did the conductor have a slight limp? He might have. I'd been too cold and tired to pay much attention, but such a lapse could have gotten us killed. Last time I saw Roger, I'd jammed my knife into his foot—or more accurately, the bit of him that was here in our world, on three planes. Surely he hadn't healed from it yet. That might be a way to tell who was who, if I couldn't count on Doc.

I resolved to be like Sebastian Hardin, on high alert every waking minute.

The depot sat at the end of Front Street. It was the first time I'd seen a true northern frontier town. The snow had been churned to brown slush, and with the temperature above freezing, it felt almost balmy. The air filled with the dry, sweet smell of lumber and woodsmoke. Occasional hints of perfume drifted from the saloons, along with aromas of coffee and baking that set my mouth watering.

Even to my inexperienced eye, I could see there were way more people than normal. We passed a row of rooming houses with ”no vacancy” signs. Some folks must have braved the weather to come from Lovelock by coach, because there were wagons filled with heaps of furniture and other personal belongings. Litter lay all over the street. I stepped over a crushed tin cup and fragments of broken glass. Just beneath the good smells came the stench of out-houses, manure piles, and chicken and pig pens.

I kept a sharp eye out for Carnarvon marshals, but didn't see a single one. It struck me as strange, but with Calindra dead and Ava in charge, the priorities had clearly shifted.

"I'm hungry enough to eat a saddle blanket," Lee declared, putting on his thick northern twang. "Where's the grub around here?"

Ned asked a man smoking in front of the livery stable where to get breakfast and he sent us to the Lady Gay Saloon two blocks down on Arrow Street.

The front room had a bar and tables, all jammed with people. Through a half-parted curtain, I saw a back room with a green cloth poker table. It was surrounded by prospectors, miners, cowboys, and assorted roughnecks looking for a chance to tempt fortune and fate.

We finally got a vacant table and ordered coffee, eggs and fatback, which is all they were serving. The prices for everything seemed sky high, but I imagine the town was hard-pressed to feed everyone. We ate double-helpings, wolfing down the food without speaking. Then we sat and nursed more coffee, eavesdropping on the conversations around us.

Not surprisingly, what happened in Lovelock was the topic of the day.

"Lost everything, I did," one man grumbled, shaking his head. "How could that be God's will?"

"It weren't," his companion said patiently. "You're misremembering, George."

The first man shot him a hard look. "Don't tell me what I saw," he declared. "There was a minister."

A cold feeling came over me. I leaned over. "Pardon, but what did he look like?"

"Black beard. Long coat." The man's voice dropped. "He had snakes."

I shared a puzzled look with Lee and Ned. "Snakes?"

He nodded vigorously. "He baptized everyone and said we was saved, though he hung Mr. Lawson, he was our linguist, just before he burned the town."

The man to the left of him cast an incredulous look. "Don't listen to a word, miss. The fire started in the telegraph office at the depot. A faulty electrical line."

"Weren't the telegraph," a third man put in from the next table. "I was in the bank when Winnie Cheever robbed it."

"Cheever? He was hung over in Ruby Creek last week!"

"Well then, it was his ghost, because I saw him clear as day, along with those brothers. They stole my daddy's watch."

Shouts and arguments erupted until two brawny fellows came over and told them to pipe down or get thrown out. The men fell into sullen silence.

"It's like Aguadulce," Lee says quietly. "Roger's messing with their memories."

"If he can make people believe anything he wants, how do we trust what we see?" Ned wondered.

"Maybe they're all right," I said thoughtfully. "But if he skipped Jackpot, where is he now?"

Something was nagging at the back of my mind. Something the reverend had said, though I couldn't quite put my finger on it. Trying to force it wouldn't work. So I let it simmer, trusting that it would come to me eventually.

Ned asked the men about his cousins, moving quietly among the tables. They knew the Carvers, but weren't sure what had happened to them. It was chaos once the town started burning.

"If you don't mind, I think I'll walk around a bit," he said. "See if I can get some news."

"Want me to come?" Lee offered.

Ned shook his head. "Naw, it's okay. Think I want to be alone for a while."

Lee seemed to understand. "We'll be here. Good luck."

I inquired about a room, but the price made me choke on my coffee. After paying for breakfast, we had barely anything left.

"Let me try to call some phantoms," Lee said in a low voice. "Morals are a fine thing, Ruth, but I'd rather sleep in a warm bed tonight."

His folksy accent was starting to annoy me. "We're not stealing from these poor people. Besides, it'd be lighting a signal fire for the reverend that you're here."

"Well, we need money." His gaze strayed to the back room. "How about I earn some the old-fashioned way?"

"Gambling?"

"I don't see another solution."

"Fine. But you're no card shark. You'll probably lose the little we have left."

He lowered his voice further. "Not if Doc gives me some advice."

I sighed. Cheating wasn't right, either, but I had to keep my eye on the bigger mission. We needed to keep moving down the line and there wouldn't be another train for a few days.

"Will you do it, Doc?" I asked.

We used to play Old Maid on the train. He always won

because he could see through the cards. I figured he'd object since it meant I'd have to let Lee wear the Collier, but Doc sounded eager.

"Why, I told you I'm a gambling man, Ruth. A spot of cards would cheer me right up."

I unbuckled Hardin's holster and handed it over, swapping the flintlock for Lee's pearl-handled six-shooters.

"Just be careful." I gave him a hard look. "You get caught, they'll string you up."

Lee handed me his hat, adjusted his diamond tie pin, and strode into the back room. Heads swiveled. They looked him over like a pack of wolves who just had a little lost calf wander into their midst.

"Evenin', gentlemen!" Lee declared. "Can I get in on the action?"

He took a seat and threw some money into the pot. It looked like everything we had.

I couldn't justify occupying the table any longer so I moved to the bar and ordered a beer, keeping a sharp eye on the door.

The Lady Gay appeared to be one of the more respectable saloons in town, serving food and drink, but nothing more licentious. People came and went. No one tried to talk to me. They respected privacy on the frontier. I was just worrying over where the reverend had gone next, and what he'd get up to if I didn't find him soon, when a man came in all bundled up from the cold.

A scarf covered the lower part of his face and he hunched under a derby hat, eyes flicking left and right. He got to the middle of the saloon when his gaze passed over the parted curtain. He did a double-take, staring hard at Lee. Then he turned and hurried out the door again.

I jumped up, heart racing. I didn't recognize him, but he must be working for someone. Either the Carnarvons or the reverend. I pushed through to the street. He was just vanishing around a corner.

For a second, I hesitated. I'd fallen into the reverend's clutches in just such a fashion at the Academy, chasing Cage. Maybe he was luring me into a trap.

But I couldn't just let him go, either. The look in his eyes when he saw Merriweather was more like fear. He knew something and I aimed to find out what it was.

I dove into the crowds and gave chase down the street. He glanced over his shoulder and saw me, then ducked into a narrow alley between two buildings. I regretted leaving Doc with Lee, but there was no time to get the Collier back now. I ran to the mouth of the alley.

It was full of trash—wagon wheels, old elixir bottles, shattered dishes and scrap metal. I dodged rotten wooden crates and falling-apart barrels. My steps slowed as I reached the rear. It was fairly wide open behind Front Street. There was nowhere to hide.

Nowhere except an outhouse with a crescent moon to vent the stench.

My nose wrinkled as I approached the privy and drew one of the pearl-handled revolvers.

"Come on out," I said sternly. "I got a gun."

Silence. Then a violent sneeze.

I cocked it and eased the door open with the toe of my boot.

The man cowered inside, hands up. "Don't shoot me!" he squeaked.

"Then come on out," I repeated firmly.

He stood up and stepped into the yard. I backed up, gesturing with the gun.

"Get that scarf down." His hand started to move. "Real slow," I added.

He moved like treacle, unwrapping it from his face. I gaped in surprise.

"What on earth are *you* doing here?"

7

He just stared at me, eyes jerking around in their sockets.

I lowered the revolver. "You working for the Reverend Jolly now?"

"What? No!"

"Then you better start talking, and I better believe you."

It was Dean Alexander Rodriguez from the Distinguished Academy of Phantom Linguistics and Related Disciplines in Carnarvon City. His hand shot up and I raised my gun again, but it was only to cover another explosive sneeze.

"I'm sorry," he said, wiping his nose with the muffler. "The weather up here has not been beneficial to my constitution, Miss Cortez."

He'd had a nasty cold last time I saw him with Ava Carnarvon. He was also thick as thieves with her. I didn't trust him a whit.

"Turn out your pockets," I said.

He opened his coat and let me pat him down. When I felt sure he wasn't armed, I holstered the revolver and stepped back. The dean looked different than the dapper man in a bowtie and tweed suit I remembered. He dress shoes were wet with slush. His nose was red, his eyes bloodshot. He still had a little mustache, but it was untrimmed and he needed a shave.

"Can we talk someplace warmer?" he asked in a pleading tone.

The snow had started again and I had no objection to that proposal. "Back at the saloon where my friends are," I said.

His shoulders slumped. "I saw Lee and got frightened." His eyes flickered again. "I'm sure they're looking for me."

"They?"

His voice dropped. "The Carnarvons."

"Well, you're the last person I expected to run into," I said.

It struck me that this man might know quite a bit about Ava and the dark dealings she had going with the reverend. I resolved not to let him out of my sight.

We returned to the Lady Gay and pushed up to the end of the bar. I signaled to Lee to cash out. He emerged from the back room looking well pleased with himself until he saw Dean Rodriguez, and then it was Lee's turn to do a double-take. He stood up straighter, and smoothed his hair down.

"Sir," he said, the northern twang vanishing. "I … It's good to see you, sir."

I could practically see him in his school uniform, books under one arm.

"Mr. Merriweather," Dean Rodriguez said primly. "I'm very pleased to find you well."

Lee flushed. "I suppose I am," he said slowly. "A lot has happened."

"I know." The dean looked guilty. "And I'm afraid some of it is my fault. I hope you can forgive me."

"Forgive *you*?" Lee seemed astonished. "I'm the one who—"

I cut him off before people started listening. "Never mind that. The dean was about to tell us why he's in Lovelock," I said.

The barman walked up, a rag over his shoulder. "What are you folks drinking?"

"May I have a hot toddy?" Dean Rodriguez asked.

"A what?" The barkeep gave him a hard stare.

"Three whiskeys," I said quickly.

He nodded and moved off to pour the drinks. I didn't touch mine, but Lee downed his in one gulp. The dean took a sip, made a face, then sighed wetly and took another.

"It tastes like turpentine," he said.

"'Cause it probably is," I said, looking around. A couple of cowboys stood next to us, but they were deep in conversation about the best way to approach an irate bull. "Now, why are the Carnarvons looking for you?"

He took out a sad-looking handkerchief and blew his nose. "It all started when Lee ran away. Miss Carnarvon was furious. She said he'd betrayed the family and she wanted her own savant, one who would toe the line and do as they were told. She wanted me to find a budding replacement and let her groom them personally." He twisted the handkerchief in his hands. "Of course, Mr. Merriweather was unique among our students. Savants don't grow on trees. When I failed to produce a suitable candidate, I thought she'd fire me. But she just smiled and said she'd found another way to solve the problem."

"Why didn't you go to Calindra?" I asked.

He downed the rest of the bourbon before answering. "Well, now, that's complicated, Miss Cortez."

"I guess Ava had dirt on you, huh?" I guessed.

Lee shot me a look of disapproval, but the dean flinched and I knew I'd hit the mark.

"I am fond of a game of cards," he admitted. "But I'm a poor gambler. I lost quite a lot and I couldn't pay it, not right away, so I was forced to borrow some funds from the Academy." He shot us a sheepish look. "I was going to return the money, of course. But Ava found out somehow. She held it over me. If Mrs. Carnarvon knew, I would have been ruined."

Lee appeared shocked that his headmaster wasn't the upright man he'd always believed. His brows knit in a disapproving frown. It almost made me laugh.

"Did you know she'd hired Jolly to find Lee?" I asked.

The dean bristled. "Of course not! But I figured it out when I heard her talking on the telephone that day you came, Miss Cortez. She ordered them to kidnap Professor Beach. She said it would lure Lee into coming back. I was standing just outside the door and tried to slip away, but she saw me. The look on her face . . . ." He swallowed. "Well, it scared me. She just said, 'I'm sorry you had to hear that, Alex,' with this cold little smile. Ava could be very cold." He shivered at the memory. "I almost went to Calindra then, but I was too afraid of what Ava might do. By the time I'd mustered my courage, they'd left for Aguadulce."

"Mrs. Carnarvon is dead," I said flatly. "Ava killed her."

The blood drained from his face. "What?"

"I saw her do it," Lee put in quietly.

"Oh, my God." He pressed a trembling hand to his forehead. "It's all my fault."

I felt sorry for him. "How long have you been here?" I asked.

He seemed to gird himself. "I haven't told you all of it. I'd vowed to speak up, whatever the cost, when *things* started happening."

"What things, sir?" Lee asked.

"Just little pranks, at first. Objects being moved from where I'd left them a moment before. Shadows stalking me when I walked the grounds at dusk. Of course, we're used to phantoms at the Academy, but these felt . . . malicious. Do you know what I mean?"

Lee nodded. "I do."

"It escalated. Pinches and cuts." He rolled up his sleeve to show us a nasty bruise. "Mocking laughter. I wondered if I wasn't losing my mind. Phantoms don't behave that way. But then I knew. Ava had set them on me, like some awful *game*, and they'd eventually kill me if I didn't do something. So I panicked and ran. I caught the first northbound train."

"That's awful," I said, patting his hand. "So you landed in Lovelock."

His eyes took on a haunted look. "No, Ruby Creek. That's where I saw the Reverend Jolly for the first time." He looked longingly at the empty glass, then met my eyes again. "And the other one."

"Mr. Cage," I said.

Dean Rodriguez nodded. No further elaboration was needed. By all rights, Cage should have been a handsome man. He had regular features and clear green eyes. It was a soul he lacked.

"The town was jam-packed when I got there. Apparently, they were hanging some fellow by the name of Winnie Cheever. A famous outlaw, from all the talk. I took a room at a boarding house and holed up there, trying to figure out where I'd go next." He sneezed into his sleeve. "I was already thinking I should have gone south instead. At least it's warm. But the N.T. is supposed to be where you go to lose your troubles and start over. I suppose I didn't realize how rough it was. I didn't fit in at all." He shook his head. "Not at all."

I imagined the poor dean all alone, in fear of his life, and with a cold to boot.

"Well, now we've found you," I said soothingly. "Go on."

"I wasn't planning to attend the hanging, it's barbaric entertainment, but in the end morbid curiosity got the better of me. I was in the crowd when Jolly climbed up to the gallows to give Cheever last rites. I don't think he saw me, or that he'd know me if he did, but I went icy all over when I saw the man's face. That long black coat. Somehow I knew it was him Ava had spoken to. She'd called him reverend."

Lee and I fell silent, rapt in the tale.

"There were reporters and at least two hundred onlookers. Carnarvon marshals, too, which made me nervous. I kept to the rear, but it was dead quiet when the moment came so I heard everything quite clearly. Cheever spoke his last words, something about how phantoms made him commit his crimes but now he'd seen the light. Then the hangman yanked the lever, but Mr. Cheever didn't fall through. He just stood there, on thin air."

I pushed my full glass of bourbon toward the dean. He nodded thanks and took a tiny sip.

"People started murmuring in confusion," he continued. "Then I heard the marshals yell. They started shooting."

"Each other?" I asked, horrified.

He frowned. "No, at their feet. More people began screaming. Jumping and up and down. There were *scorpions*, Miss Cortez. The ground was crawling with them. In the *snow*." He shook his head in disbelief. "I ran, along with everyone else. It was a stampede. A wagon passed at the edge of town and I begged them to take me. We came straight to Jackpot."

"Good Lord," I said.

"It's the last time I saw the reverend and the other one." He didn't seem to want to speak Cage's name. "Hopefully, the last time *ever*."

"Well," I said. "There might be a little problem with that, sir, since I'm afraid you'll be coming along with us."

"What?" he squeaked.

"You'll be safer," I lied. "Ava killed her own grandmother. What do you think she'll do to you when she finds you?"

"I appreciate the offer," he said quickly. "Truly, I do. But I think I'm better off here."

"With all due respect," I said, "that's not gonna cut it.

When this is done, you can testify against Ava in court. You're the only one who can."

He looked terrified, but I plowed ahead. "You're respectable, not like Lee." Merriweather frowned, but he could hardly contradict me. "They'd believe your word."

Sebastian Hardin would believe you, I added to myself, though I didn't say it.

"If you don't find your courage, you'll be letting Ava inherit her grandmother's empire. How do you think she'll run it, based on her previous record? And do you really think she'll let you go? Once Ava gets around to you, there won't be a mineshaft deep enough to hide in." I hated to twist the knife, but it had to be done. "Or maybe she'll send Jolly and Cage."

He shuddered. "I see your point."

I felt excited. There was a chance to set things right now.

"Where are you staying?" I asked.

"A rooming house down the street."

At that moment, Ned Carver came in the door. He looked around, then strolled up to the bar and tipped his hat back. It was dusted with a fine layer of snow. He looked at Lee, then at me and Dean Rodriguez, and lifted an eyebrow.

"Anything happen while I was gone?" he asked.

Lee Merriweather was still struggling with the sudden appearance of his old dean as he and Ned walked Alexander Rodriguez back to the rooming house on Front Street. He wasn't sure how to behave with the man now. They were no longer headmaster and star pupil, but old habits died hard and he couldn't seem to stop calling him sir.

They'd quickly filled Ned in on what Rodriguez had told them. Lee didn't like the story about the scorpions. Not one bit. It sounded a little too Biblical. Could Roger really bring about the End Times? He suppressed a shudder.

"Where's Professor Beach?" the dean asked as they trudged through the snow. "I expected he'd be with you."

"Staying with family down south," Lee said vaguely. "I thought it better we part ways."

"Understandable," the dean said with a weak smile.

Lee scanned the crowds of people. Every bushy beard made him stiffen. "Are you sure you haven't seen the reverend in Jackpot?" he asked.

That earned a level look. "Do you honestly think I'd still be here if I had?"

"I asked around, too," Ned said quietly. "About a middle-aged frontier preacher with a younger yellow-haired man. It's a fairly specific description. No one's seen them."

"Did you say frontier preacher?" Ruth put in. She'd been quiet for a while, dark brows creased in thought.

Ned looked at her. "That's what you told me a while back. That he had a northern twang."

She stopped dead. "Go on without me. We'll meet back at the Lady Gay."

"What is it?" Lee asked. He knew that look. Like a hound on a scent.

"I need to find a map. Maybe they've got one at the station. Then I can ask about the next train."

Ruth took off without waiting for an answer.

Lee watched her go, irritation mingling with fondness. At least he wasn't the quarry this time.

"It's right here," Dean Rodriguez said, pausing in front of a dingy clapboard building that had been beaten by the climate to a uniform gray. "Do you want to come in?"

He cracked the front door to a sad little sitting room. Scents of boiled cabbage mingled with unwashed body odor and something even worse. Cat pee?

Lee knew he was supposed to keep the dean in sight at all times, but where could the man go? They were in the middle of nowhere. His eye fell on a sign creaking in the wind across the street. *The Gypsy Arcade. Ace-High Amusements for All Ages!*

"Thank you, sir," he said. "But why don't you go rest? We might be traveling soon and you don't look so well."

The dean honked into his handkerchief. "I could do with a nap, now that you mention it. I'm not used to drinking spirits in the middle of the day." He waved at an elderly woman knitting in a rocking chair by the wood stove. "The proprietress collects stray cats." He gave an unhappy laugh. "I suppose I'm not far from being one myself. She's been very kind to me. Gave me a tonic for my cold."

"Hot toddy?" Lee guessed.

He smiled. "A drop of whiskey with hot water, sugar and lemon. I have no idea where she finds the lemons, but the woman is resourceful."

They watched through the window as Dean Rodriguez settled into a chair by the fire. Lee tugged Ned's sleeve. "Let's go to the arcade. I won a load at poker."

Ned hesitated.

"Come on, when's the next time we'll get a chance for some fun?" Lee wheedled.

He didn't use his Voice. That would be unforgivable. Then he remembered that Ned's family was missing. He flushed. "I'm sorry. It was a dumb suggestion."

Ned grinned for the first time since Lovelock. It lit up his whole face. "Sure, why not?"

Lee grinned back. They crossed the street, dodging riders and wagons, and stood beneath the swaying sign. The Gypsy Arcade was sandwiched between a doctor's office and a saddler's. The windows were grimy with dust, giving the place a forlorn appearance.

"You sure it's open?" Ned wondered.

"Let's find out." Lee pushed on the door. It opened with the tinkle of a bell.

Kids were running loose all over the streets, but there was

only one inside, about twelve, sitting on a stool under a mounted elk's head with glazed eyes. His nose was buried in a dime novel.

"Welcome to Jackpot's pride and joy," he said with bored disdain. "Two tickets? That's ten cents."

"Here's a quarter," Lee said, handing him the coin. "You can keep the change."

The kid pocketed it without looking up from the book. "Through the curtain," he said, turning the page.

They walked to a red velvet curtain, also thick with dust, and pushed it aside. A long windowless room stretched back into the gloom. Wooden stereoscopes lined the walls, along with a few slot machines and other mechanical apparatus. The constellations had been painted on the ceiling in gold with an artistic hand, though that too had faded. Threadbare carpet whispered beneath their feet.

"It's bigger than it looks from the outside," Ned said.

The front part of the arcade was devoted to wooden boxes with hand cranks and penny slots. Lee rummaged though his pockets for more change and divvied it up. Each stereoscope played a short film. Some were burlesque, others as simple as a child picking flowers in a garden.

"This one's got a naked lady with a feather fan," Ned remarked. "Want to look?"

"Not especially," Lee said.

Their eyes met and held for a moment. Ned cleared his throat. "Yeah, I'm not big on that sort of thing, either," he said. "Let's see what else they got."

They bypassed the slot machines—it reminded Lee too much of Aguadulce—and ventured deeper into the arcade. Stereoscopes were familiar, but not the other amusements.

Marvelous Automaton Palm Reader! Press down hard with palm and fingers, and the Machine Reveals the Secrets!

Beyond that was a device that told your future based on the shape of your eyes, another on the color of your hair.

There was a game shaped like a grandfather clock with a punching bag to test your strength. Ned surprised him by sitting down at the bench of a coin piano and banging out a jaunty tune.

"Where'd you learn?" Lee asked with admiration.

"My dad's restaurant in Carnarvon City has one," he said. "I taught myself a few songs." He played a scale, strong fingers running over the keys. "This one's in desperate need of tuning. You're from the city too, right?"

"Yes, but I spent most of my time at the Academy."

"Did you like it there?"

"Sometimes."

"You must miss your friends."

"Didn't really have any," Lee admitted.

"Why not?"

Lee wandered over to the palm reader and dropped a coin in the slot. A swarm of tiny Class A phantoms made the bulbs light up. "Well, it's hard to get to know people when you keep skipping grades."

"I guess you're some kind of genius, huh?"

Lee tensed, but Ned's tone was easy. Not awestruck or, worse, afraid. Everything about Ned Carver was easy. He took the world as he found it, without fuss. It was the first time Lee had been treated as a normal person instead of some freakish oddity.

"I don't know about genius," he said. "They say it's a talent you're born with. I'm not good at anything else, just languages." He pressed his palm flat on the glass. The machine lit up with a mechanical groan. A few Class A's fluttered around his hand. Then it spit out a piece of paper.

"What's it say?" Ned asked.

He squinted at the paper. "Follow your muse."

"That's good advice."

"What about you?" Lee asked. "Must be exciting to ride the trains everywhere."

"I do enjoy travel," Ned admitted. "Itchy feet."

"Well, we have that in common," Lee said. "I'm never going back. I want to see the whole world when this is over."

"Maybe you could work on the trains," Ned ventured. "The pay isn't great, but you ride for free."

Lee smiled. "I think I'd like that. Maybe I could be a conductor."

"It's a plan then." Ned stood up from the bench. "We better get back and check on the dean."

"In a minute." Lee strode to the rear of the arcade. "There's one more. Looks like the grand finale."

The Gypsy Fortuneteller was the largest machine of all. It sat alone, framed by more red velvet curtains tied back with gold tassels. The others had painted facades, but this was a full glass case with a life-sized dummy inside. She had black hair and a jeweled turban. Two speaking hoses ran from her mouth to the sides of the case. She wore an elaborate yellow and green embroidered tunic with puffy sleeves. Stiff wooden hands framed a scattering of cards on a shelf at her waist.

"Two nickels left," Lee said. "One for you, one for me."

He pressed the coin into Ned's warm palm. The touch lingered on his skin. They stood quite close, but Ned didn't step away.

"Who goes first?" Ned asked. In the soft light of the bulbs, his teeth gleamed against the dark of his skin. Lee had an urge to touch the little cleft in his chin.

"You," he said.

One side was the fortune for men, the other for women. Ned dropped the coin in the left slot.

The lights flickered. The dummy's black eyes animated, ratcheting to and fro. Papier-mâché teeth clicked menacingly behind the frozen smile.

"Jesus," Ned said, taking a step back.

Her head turned, seeming to gaze directly at him. A

mechanical voice echoed from the depths of the speaking tube.

"*You have a secret admirer.*"

The lights flickered and went out. Lee thought he might die on the spot. They were both quiet for a minute.

"Well, lucky me," Ned said, with a quick glance.

Lee felt his face heat. He quickly fumbled his own nickel into the slot.

More whirring sounds. The teeth clicked and clacked. The Gypsy's eyes moved, landing squarely on Lee.

"*A closed mouth gathers no feet*," she intoned.

Ned took his hat off and slapped it on his knee. "By God, Lee, she read you like a book!"

Lee couldn't help but laugh, too. "I'll take that one to heart," he said lightly.

"Guess we better go," Ned said, with a touch of regret.

But neither of them moved. The moment stretched out. Lee found himself leaning forward on his toes, eyes slipping shut—

"There you two are! I been looking everywhere!"

Ruth Cortez barged in, rifle over one shoulder. Dark eyes flashed. "Think I got something," she said tensely.

Lee sighed. "What?"

"Well, what Ned said got me thinking. The reverend has a special hatred for Hardin. He knows he's from a town called Hatchet. I can't imagine he'd give it a miss. So if we just—"

The Gypsy Fortuneteller sprang to life.

Lee jumped, and so did Ned.

"You put a coin in there?" Ruth asked.

Lee shook his head.

The eyes rolled from side to side. *Searching*. The wooden jaw opened and closed. Her hands started to move, pushing aimlessly at the cards.

"What the devil—" Ned muttered.

Ruth stood stock still, staring at the machine, transfixed.

The Gypsy stared back. Her hollow voice echoed down the speaking tubes.

"*Do you want to play, Ruth? Do you want to play, Ruth? Do you want to*—"

Glass shattered as Ruth shot her straight between the eyes. The Gypsy fell silent, smoke trailing from the bullet hole.

"Hey!" came a shout from the front.

The kid appeared at the end of the arcade. "No gunplay!" He thrust a finger out. "Can't you read the sign?"

"Roger knows we're here," Ruth snapped. "Let's collect the dean and get out."

"Well done," Doc muttered, with a painful-sounding wheeze.

Ned looked shaken as they hurried to the front of the arcade and pushed past the curtain. Lee knew how he felt. He threw a handful of bills at the irate kid as they passed.

"For the damage!" he called over his shoulder.

"Dang," the kid exclaimed. "Just 'cause you don't like your fortune don't mean you gotta shoot the place up."

Dean Rodriguez waited on the steps of the rooming house across the street, a suitcase in tow. "Where are we going?" he asked with a worried expression, as Ruth charged off down the street.

"Lady Gay," she muttered. "There's no train today, but there might be a mail coach. I'm gonna ask the barkeep."

The saloon was fairly busy. Ruth made her way to the bar and signaled for his attention.

"I'm glad she shot that thing," Ned said grimly. "Was it haints inside that made it talk?"

"Had to be," Lee replied. He looked at Ned seriously. "You should stay here. Keep looking for your cousins. Someone's bound to know them."

"What about you?"

"I guess we're following the trail where it leads."

Ned let out a long breath. "I'll admit, I'm not eager to

tangle with the reverend and his gang. But they burned out my family. Lots of other folks, too. Doesn't seem like anyone else is doing anything about it." He looked around the saloon. "I wouldn't feel right sitting here while you were off risking your lives to save the world."

Save the world.

"Is that what we're doing?" Lee asked softly.

"I don't know," Ned said. "But it might be. And I'm going with you."

They shared a wordless look. Lee nodded. Something loosened in his chest. It sickened him to put Ned in danger, but the man had every right to make his own choice. And he liked him rather desperately. More than anyone he'd ever met. At first it was the good looks, a simple crush, but he sensed hidden reserves in Ned Carver. Loyalty and courage Lee wished he possessed himself.

"I'm glad to have you then," he said warmly. "Ruth said you're a decent shot."

"I'm no gunslinger," Ned said with small grin. "But I can point and fire."

"*There he is.*"

Lee turned as five men poured out of the back room in a cloud of cigar smoke. He realized with a sinking feeling that it was the same ones he'd been playing cards with earlier.

"Howdy, gentlemen," he said.

"Been waiting for you. Come on, we'll deal you in." Their leader was a prospector with a glass eye and beard waxed to a devilish point. He smiled coldly. The others, a mix of cowpunchers in leather coats and black-nailed miners, hovered behind him with flat expressions.

"Sorry, fellas," Lee said regretfully. "I have a pressing engagement."

"Well, the way I see it, you cleaned us out," the prospector retorted. "It's only sporting to give us a chance to win some back."

Lee smiled. "Tell you what. I'll be back tonight. Maybe you'll have better luck at faro."

"I'd rather play now," the man said. His friends nodded.

Ned moved to Lee's side. He was shorter but stocky. "No offense, boys, but he cashed out. Sometimes you just have to cut your losses."

"Well, I think he cheated," the man said loudly.

Conversation ceased. Heads turned throughout the saloon. Ruth shot Lee a worried look from the bar.

"That's a low accusation," Lee said calmly, though his palms started to sweat.

He'd thrown some persuasion into the words and a few people started nodding in agreement, but then the man's eye caught on his pearl-handed revolvers.

"Where's the flintlock you were wearing?"

Lee looked down at his six-shooters. He'd switched back with Ruth after the game.

"None of your business."

The man stared at him in mounting rage. "Bet you got that licking from the last men you swindled."

A dozen cutting retorts sprang to mind, but Lee had learned some hard lessons. If he poured oil on the fire, Ruth would murder him herself and rightfully so. He shouldn't have won so much, but the last hand ended up double or nothing. He was about to use his Voice to defuse the situation when the deck of cards flew out of the man's hands and rained down like confetti. His eyes bulged.

"I knew you had a haint! Why you lowdown—" Lee reeled as the man punched him square in the nose.

In a flash, Ned was swinging back. He landed a roundhouse that sent the man staggering into his friends. Lee cupped his face, blood dripping through his fingers, and dodged a whiskey bottle. It smashed into the mirror behind the bar. Chairs scraped as the patrons fled outside. The Lady

Gay's two enforcers tried to break it up and were swept into the brawl.

Ruth waded through the fray. She grabbed Lee's arm.

"Time to go," she said grimly.

Ned ducked a punch from one of the miners and laid him out with an uppercut. Then they were dashing for the street, a sneezing Dean Rodriguez in tow.

Someone shouted for a rope as they reached the door.

"You all can go to Hell," Lee shouted over his shoulder with a wink. "I'm going to Hatchet!"

8

Angry yells chased us down Front Street. Glass shattered as the fight spilled outside. When I glanced back, I saw the one with a pointy beard who'd punched Lee in hot pursuit.

"Did you do that with the cards, Doc?" I demanded as we ran for our lives yet again.

"Of course not," he sputtered.

I leapt over a broken barrel. "Must have been one of Roger's then!"

The shouts grew louder. People drifted from the other saloons and rooming houses to watch the commotion. Dean Rodriguez was huffing and puffing, but his dress shoes weren't made for running in slush. He went down with a painful thump. Lee hauled him to his feet. Ned grabbed his suitcase.

"I can't," the dean gasped. "Just leave me."

"Not a chance," I said, prodding him into motion. "They'll string you up!"

He moaned but started running again.

"Stop them!" the prospector hollered. "They're thieves and cheaters!"

Jackpot tolerated all manner of vice, but those seemed to be magic words for in short order a mob was forming behind us. Luckily, most were drunk or we would have been done for. But they had an ugly look, not to mention an excess of firearms. A few wild shots went off as we sprinted past the Gypsy Arcade.

"It's just like Tombstone," Doc muttered. "If only Wyatt was here, he'd set 'em straight."

Merriweather started growling in a phantom tongue. A stream of what looked like fireflies flew out of the arcade. We called them Class A haints, the kind that infested clockwork. They danced around Lee for a moment, than zipped off.

"That'll keep 'em busy for a while," he panted.

I glanced back. The mob was swatting the air and hopping around.

"Where are we off to now?" Dean Rodriguez panted, still struggling to keep up.

"Just keep running!" I urged.

We made it to the end of Front Street and the train depot. I'd already asked the station master and there was nothing coming through until the next day. The prospect of hiding in the woods didn't hold much appeal, but we had no choice. Those little grims wouldn't stick around making mischief forever.

Then I spotted a dark mass ahead, down past the end of the platform where the tracks divided. An engine sat on the siding, with three open cars filled with slag and coal. One of the mine trains.

"You up to running a boiler?" I asked Doc.

He coughed. "No, but I'll try."

We ran to the siding. Back on Front Street, the mob had re-formed. I climbed the ladder into the narrow gap between the coal car and the cab. The others squeezed in behind me.

"If you can't, there's likely to be a hanging today," I said. "Four of 'em."

A shadow poured from the barrel of the flintlock, almost

too pale to make out. For a split-second, I thought I saw flailing tentacles. Then they disappeared.

"Doc?"

The hubbub of voices grew louder. I stuck my head out the window. It looked like half the town was marching on the depot. The first ones spotted us and broke into a jog. From the shouts, I gathered that they'd decided Lee was the one who burned down Lovelock and he was here with his phantoms to do the same to Jackpot.

I started loading the rifle, though I didn't want to have to shoot anyone.

"Darnit, Doc. Come on!"

Suddenly, the boiler fired up. The pistons started to crank. We sped away just as the snow started falling again. A few of the men chased us up the tracks, firing shots that drew sparks from the iron carriage.

"Thank the Good Lord," I breathed, as the town dwindled behind.

"I didn't do it," Doc gasped. "Didn't . . . have it in me."

"Then who did?" Ned wondered.

The only other phantoms around were Roger's minions. I had the unpleasant sensation of being a doll in truth, with a mean kid moving me around in his grubby fist.

"Maybe we better jump off," said Lee.

But the train was going too fast now. I peeked into the boiler. Shadows moved to stoke it. Woods flashed past. The embankment on either side fell away to steep ravines.

A girl walked straight through the side of the train. Pure white streaked her long black hair. Like other haints, she was naked, though her body was smooth and sexless.

She did not look friendly. But then, I'd never seen a grim who did.

"Say something," I hissed at Lee.

His nose was still bleeding. Lee wiped it with a sleeve, snuffling. He made a cooing sound. Her head tilted.

"Tell her we know her name's Zippo," I said. "Tell her thanks."

Lee repeated my message.

To my surprise, the girl answered in English. "Hear you call for help," she said to Lee in a raspy voice. "Have to go now."

"Wait!" Lee cried.

Syllables rolled like foreign music from his tongue. Merriweather could be a chameleon and I sometimes wondered who the real one was. At school, he'd been a straight-laced prodigy until he snapped under Calindra's relentless pressure and ran off. Once he was on the lam, Merriweather played the part of an arrogant outlaw who took nothing seriously. But now his whole face changed. He looked gentle and kind. Older somehow.

I think we all fell under his spell. The girl answered. I listened to them talk, not understanding any of it but feeling warm and safe for the first time since I left home. Dean Rodriguez watched with an expression of pride. Ned seemed fascinated. His brown eyes never left Lee.

Finally, Lee turned to us. "She's scared. Roger hurt her back in Aguadulce. He told her if she said anything, he'd burn the school down and make it seem like she did it. She took a big risk coming here."

"Why did she?"

He shrugged, cheeks coloring. "She likes me."

"What else did she say?"

"Not much. She knows Roger's three cronies have been causing trouble. She said they're gone now. But she doesn't know where Roger is."

All this time, Doc had been hiding in the ether, not saying a word. I wondered why.

"Maybe she can do us one last favor," I said. "All our problems would be solved if we just got Doc out of the hypercube. He'd deal with Roger. Doc told me there's a key, but he doesn't know where it is. If she could help us find it—"

"He ain't nice," Zippo croaked.

"Roger? We know that—"

"No," she said, pointing at the gun. "*Him.*"

"Come on out, Doc," I said sternly, digging out the shaving mirror. His reflection appeared, looking askew because of the crack down the middle. Still, there was a sheepish cast to his features.

"Were you mean to her?" I demanded.

"Another inquisition?" he said dryly. "I suppose you'll take out the hot pincers next—"

"Quit stalling and say you're sorry."

He was silent.

"It's swallow your pride or stay in there forever," I added.

Zippo crossed her skinny arms.

"Well, I am sorry," Doc finally said in a more subdued tone. "I suppose I could be a bully, too. But I've mended my ways. If she could see her way clear to letting bygones be bygones—"

"Tell her yourself," I said. "Proper. That means admitting all you've done wrong and asking forgiveness."

He gave a little eye roll, but then he spoke in the same tongue as Lee. It sounded like a flowery speech. At the end, Zippo gave a satisfied nod and spat out some sounds.

"She says she'll try, but she has to be careful," Lee told us. "Roger's scary."

The phantom girl vanished, but she left her friends to keep the train running.

"So what's your big plan?" Lee asked.

Him and Ned gazed at me expectantly. I felt flattered at their confidence, though I wasn't sure I'd earned it.

"We skip Easterly and Wonder and go straight to Hatchet," I said. "Maybe we have a chance to get ahead of the reverend for once."

"Makes sense," Lee said. "You sure he'll go there?"

"I'm sure of nothing in this life, Merriweather, except that it'll eventually come to an end," I replied wryly. "But I figure we need to think like Roger if we hope to outwit him, and he's the one calling the shots. So let's say it was a dime novel."

"I thought he liked picture shows," Ned said.

"True, but I ain't never seen one, so we gotta improvise."

Doc heaved a deep sigh. I'd thrown in the *ain't never* for his benefit. After being corrected a thousand times, I knew how to speak right, but it gave the haint something to moan about.

"In a dime novel, a good one, the big finale has to happen someplace significant. Usually, there's some old grudge involved. Now, it could be the reverend's own hometown, but I don't know where that is. And Roger knows I don't." I rubbed my hands, feeling a sudden chill. "He wants us to find Jolly and Cage, don't you see? That's the third act."

"You're making sense, Ruth," Doc remarked. "That's why you're a good manhunter."

"Well, it's fairly obvious," I said, warming at the compliment. "Everything's been pushing us west. You really think it was luck that train passed through Lovelock just when we needed it? They only run but twice a week."

That put a damper on things. No one liked hearing they'd been robbed of free will, but after the haints in Jackpot, they couldn't deny it, either.

"But if Jolly knows where we're going, what's the point?" Ned wondered.

"Well, maybe he does and maybe he doesn't. It wouldn't be any fun if we showed up and got killed right off the bat. That's too easy. There needs to be an element of unpredictability to hold Roger's interest." I leaned forward. "If Jolly's in Hatchet, we'll have to adapt to circumstances. If he isn't, we'll wait for him. Take turns watching the train depot. He's gotta to be riding the rails, there's too much ground to cover on horseback. Once we get a fix on him, Lee will present himself. Maybe even arrange a meeting. I'll find a nice snug place to set up with the rifle."

"My life will be in your hands, Ruth," Lee said.

I met his earnest hazel eyes. "I know."

"Oh, she won't miss," Doc said fondly. "You should have seen her shoot at the Dunk-a-Haint in Carnarvon City. She won a mystery prize!"

I had to laugh.

"What was it?" Ned asked, grinning.

"Don't know," I said. "I never had a chance to collect it."

The boys found a corner to curl up in. I gathered that Ned Carver had already decided to stick with us to the end and felt both surprised and grateful. Not many men would in his place. He was a sunny, stalwart presence that knitted us together in some way, like a motley quilt. Lee was a bit careless, and I suppose I could be severe at times. Mr. Carver struck a balance between the two extremes. He had a good head, and I'd seen him shoot a man, so I knew he was capable. But he also kept our spirits up with his easy banter and it just felt right to have him along.

Dean Rodriguez was the one I pitied the most. He'd barely made a sound except to sneeze since the mob chased us out of town.

Night fell. The gentle rocking of the train lulled me into a sort of half doze. When I woke some time later, I saw Doc's reflection in the dark glass. He looked pensive.

"Well," I said, softly so as not to wake the others. "You're still alive."

"Pardon me?"

"It didn't kill you to apologize."

He chuckled. "I must confess, I feel better. It was nothing terrible. Just pranks. But I suppose they *were* mean. Roger was a bad influence on me."

"He's a savant, too. I guess he can be persuasive."

"Well, I can't put it all on him. I made poor choices." He coughed. "I'm glad you found me, Ruth."

"Me, too." I paused. "You keep mentioning Wyatt. Do you mean the famous lawman?"

"I don't know, I . . ." Doc sounded vague. "I think we were friends."

"He's dead, you know. Long time ago."

Wyatt Earp was a name still well-known on the frontier. Some held him in the highest regard. Many claimed he was just a cold-blooded killer. Regardless of his status as hero or villain, all agreed he possessed great physical courage and cared little for the opinions of others. It wasn't considered policy to draw a gun on Wyatt, unless you got the drop and meant to burn powder without any preliminary talk.

He'd made a reputation for himself taming some of the roughest towns in the Northern Territory. I knew he'd been tight with John Henry Holliday until they had some sort of falling out.

"I insulted him." Doc coughed again, harder this time. "Shouldn't have said it. I'll always regret . . . ."

Doc trailed off. He didn't speak again.

9

THE NINTH WEDDING of Elmira Poole took place on Sunday afternoon in a small chapel crowded with the groom's family and closest acquaintances.

The gifts included a horse, two goats, a parlor stove, six fruit sets, two salt castors, a toothpick holder, a ceramic butter dish of sky blue that matched her eyes, and three silver spoons. Bowls of steaming meat broth had been laid out to curb the guests' appetites until the wedding feast. The men stood in the doorway, smoking and stamping their feet, while the women arranged the presents and tended to the bride.

Elmira had found her latest betrothed in the usual way. She took an advert in the matrimonial column of the local newspaper.

Personal—Comely widow who owns a large farm in one of the finest districts desires to make the acquaintance of a gentleman equally well provided, with view of joining fortunes. Triflers need not apply.

It worked like a charm. Within a fortnight, she had several proposals. August Butler, himself a widower, seemed the most promising. He owned sixty head of cattle and had a fine house with real wallpaper. The young children from his previous marriage would have to be disposed of, but illness was common enough in the north.

Having poisoned her last eight husbands, for which she now enjoyed notoriety in four of the N.T.'s six sprawling counties, Elmira used a different name each time. On this occasion, she was Lily Dunn.

"You look lovely, Lily," her future sister-in-law gushed, arranging the train of her white gown. It was trimmed with lace and had tiny pearls sewn into the bodice.

Elmira regarded herself in the oval standing mirror. She was twenty-five, but with her wide-spaced eyes and creamy milkmaid complexion looked more like a girl of sixteen. She pinched her cheeks to give them color.

"Thank you, Anne. I'm feeling a mite nervous." Her eyes brimmed. "I just wish my own dear parents could be here."

"Now, now," Anne said, offering her a handkerchief. "They're watching from Heaven."

Elmira dabbed at her eyes. "That's what my papa said on his deathbed. That I should look up to the sky and know he'd be there on a cloud, playing his harp and looking out for his little angel."

Anne teared up in sympathy. "Ain't that the sweetest thing."

Elmira turned to the window. "The snow makes everything so pretty and clean. Is the preacher here yet?"

The town was too piddling to have its own church, so she'd insisted that Augie build a little chapel on his property for the occasion. He was so smitten, he'd agreed immediately. But they'd still had to find a circuit preacher to do the honors, one of those fellows who rode from town to town doing baptisms and weddings. It had held things up longer than Elmira would have liked. Luckily, one had finally turned up and they could get rolling.

The advert was true, in a way. Elmira was rich as Croesus from the various life insurance policies she'd cashed and joint bank accounts she'd emptied. She owned property across the N.T., all under fake names, so it was a simple matter to move from place to place when the mood struck her.

There'd been an unfortunate brush with the law after her last husband, an elderly doctor named Gee McMeans, bit the dust four weeks after the wedding. He'd posted a letter to his brother accusing her of slowly poisoning him with arsenic. She'd been a fool to marry a doctor. They were too savvy about symptoms. In the end, Elmira had been forced to flee just ahead of a posse of marshals.

But that was the beauty of the N.T. It was too darn big and rowdy to keep a handle on. She was a needle in a haystack. Elmira decided to give Augie a good two or three months of marital bliss before dropping the proverbial hatchet. It was only prudent, and he deserved it for building the chapel.

"I'm glad to see you smiling," Anne said warmly.

Elmira adjusted her veil, snugging it into her soft blond curls. "I always wanted to be a mother," she said absently.

"I'm sure you'll love my nieces as your own," Anne said. "Poor little creatures. They're in such desperate need of a woman's tender care."

Through the window, Elmira saw a man ride up. He wore a long black coat, dusted with snow.

"Preacher's here," she said brightly. "You sure I look presentable?"

They were in Augie's second-floor guest room. His house was nicely appointed, for which Elmira thanked his dead wife. The woman had good taste. Well, they'd be reunited in the afterlife soon enough.

"More than presentable," Anne said. "I thought my brother'd never wed again. And to find a bride who's young and pretty to boot! He's over the moon." She laughed. "You could be wearing mourning black and he'd never notice the difference, he's so cow-eyed."

Elmira shot her a sharp look. “Don’t say that. It’s bad luck.”

“I was only playing,” Anne protested. “Now, give me a twirl.”

Elmira complied. She loved the way the white gown hugged her bosom and billowed around her slender ankles. Weddings were such fun. Almost the best part. Everyone fussed over her, and the gifts! She had a barn full of them, neatly packed in straw crates.

Anne escorted her down the stairs and outside to the chapel. It still smelled of green lumber. Maybe she could use it for the funeral when the time came. That’d be nice. The gift table would be perfect for flowers and notes of condolence.

August Butler waited at the altar, crushing his hat in big, work-roughened hands. He looked at her with a googley-eyed, half-stunned expression that pleased Elmira. Augie was old enough to be her father, but he wasn’t bad-looking for a farmer. She’d married uglier men. Prettier ones, too. It didn’t make a difference to Elmira. All she really saw was a big dollar sign.

She blushed and cast her eyes down. In her experience, all men wanted a meek virgin to conquer, even if they knew better. A complimentary murmur ran through the chapel as she took her place at his side.

The saddlebag preacher beamed at them both. He was a scruffy sort, with an unkempt beard and wild black hair, but that was typical of his ilk. She’d been married by one or two before. Half the time they were drunk, but at least this one seemed sober. She didn’t smell any whiskey on his breath, though he could do with a bath.

“Dearly beloved,” he began a rich, mellow voice that struck Elmira as being at odds with the rest of him. “We’re gathered on this joyous occasion to join together these two souls in the loving bonds of matrimony. Mr. Butler, do you have the ring?”

Augie cleared his throat. "Sure do," he muttered, fishing in his suit pocket.

The preacher's eyes gleamed as he looked at Elmira. She felt a twinge of unease.

"Such a beautiful bride." He frowned. "Why, you almost seem familiar. Have we met before?"

Augie cast her a puzzled glance.

"I don't believe so," Elmira said impatiently. "I'm sure I'd remember."

"Well," he said after a long moment. "Let's proceed."

He led them through the vows. To honor, cherish, obey, et cetera, et cetera. Elmira found herself stumbling over the words, though she knew them well enough by now. For once, she just wanted to get it over with. All the joy of her wedding day had collapsed like a bad soufflé. She disliked this preacher. They'd stuff him full of cornbread and send him on his way.

Finally, he pronounced them man and wife. Augie stuck the ring on her finger. She heaved an inward sigh of relief.

"In sickness and in health." The preacher chuckled. "'Til death do you part." It turned into a belly laugh that rang in Elmira's ears.

"What's so darned funny?" Augie demanded.

He wiped his eyes. "Well, my good fellow, that last bit'll be arriving a lot sooner than you think."

Behind Elmira, the guests started murmuring.

"What do you mean by that?" Augie asked.

Elmira stiffened.

"You just married the Black Widow of Cobb County," the preacher declared merrily. "Not to mention Atchison County, Monroe County and Kinder County." He gazed at Elmira. "I leave any out?"

The blood drained straight to her toes. She swayed on her feet and Augie caught her in the crook of one arm.

"You're crazy, mister," he cried. "This here is Lily Dunn!"

"Is it?" He unfurled a large poster and held it up for all to see. The sheriff of Cobb County had used her last wedding portrait and the likeness was dead accurate.

Elmira Poole, Alias Belle Starr, Alias Charlotte Burrows, Alias Louise Mayfield, Alias . . .

WANTED FOR FRAUD AND MURDER
$500 Reward

A collective gasp rolled through the pews. Augie dropped her like a hot stone. Elmira landed on her rump. She stomped a foot in rage. Her new husband glared down at her with narrowed eyes.

"Augie?" she pleaded in a trembling voice. "Buttercup?"

"Don't call me that," he spat. "You're a cold-blooded murderess!"

Elmira got to her feet and brushed off her skirts. Her gaze raked the crowd, then settled on Augie. "Maybe I am," she whispered in honeyed tones. "Better go check on your little brats. One of 'em was complaining of a stomach ache after I made her my special tonic!"

The reverend guffawed. "That's the spirit!" he exclaimed.

Anne gave a high-pitched shriek as the doors to the chapel burst open. Three men stood on the threshold, pistols out.

"Hands up!" one barked.

The terrified guests raised their hands.

"Don't fret," the preacher said. "We're not here to rob you. Just to take this sweet lass."

"Take me where?" Elmira demanded. She'd be damned if she'd let herself be kidnapped by outlaws on her wedding day!

"To a brighter future, Miss Poole," he replied in soothing voice. "Among company that appreciates your talents."

Elmira stared at him. "Go diddle a sheep."

"It's that or wait for the law." He glanced around. "If they don't lose patience and string you up themselves first."

Elmira regarded the sea of hostile faces. He had a point there.

"Well, I'm not leaving empty-handed," she said.

She strode up to the gift table and grabbed the silver spoons. "The horse is mine, too," she said. "Lead on, boys."

Elmira departed the chapel with a straight back. The outlaws had their own mounts waiting outside. A yellow-haired man stood in the snow, holding the bridles. When Elmira met his green eyes, she sensed a kindred spirit, even though he looked at her without interest.

"What's your name?" she asked briskly.

He didn't reply. She turned to the others. "Doesn't he talk?"

"Not often," said the skinny fellow with stained teeth and a red, bulbous nose. He took his hat off. "I'm Winslow Cheever, ma'am. This here is Kirby Knox and his brother, Royal Loving."

The pair gave her a nod. Royal had long dirty hair and a mustache that covered half his face, which was a mercy judging by the rest of it. Kirby was built like a lumberjack and looked about as smart as a pile of logs. Elmira decided she'd have no trouble managing them.

"What's he doing in there?" she asked, glancing back at the chapel.

"Spreading the Word, ma'am."

"So he's a real preacher?"

"His name's the Reverend Jolly. We're his Apostles."

Religious nuts, then. Elmira knew there were some strange cults up in the hills.

"How'd you find me?"

"Jolly said the angel told him."

She shivered and Cheever started to take his coat off. Elmira eyed it with distaste.

"Thank you, sir, but I'll fetch one from the house."

She started walking. The yellow-haired man followed at a

distance. She felt his gaze on her back, but didn't break stride. There was a row of pegs inside the door. She took one of Augie's coats and wrapped it around herself. The girls were sleeping upstairs. She hadn't done a thing to them except for some poppy milk. Children were awful nuisances, loud and sticky, and she hadn't wanted them to disrupt the ceremony. But let those fools think otherwise.

When she came out, the preacher still hadn't appeared.

Elmira peered through the open doors to the chapel. He was holding something over his head. Something alive.

"Is that a snake?" she asked in disbelief.

Cheever looked uneasy. "He uses 'em to separate the wheat from the chaff. It's God's will."

"How long does the process generally take?"

"Depends."

"On what?"

"How quick they repent."

A sudden gust slammed the doors shut. She heard . . . sounds . . . from inside.

Elmira knew a bit about venom, but it was too hard to come by. She preferred simple poisons like arsenic and strychnine, which they sold at every mercantile to kill rats. The man must be a lunatic. He had some hold over his followers and the chance might not come again.

She looked around, rather desperately. "Well, I can't wait. If you gentlemen will excuse me—"

The preacher strode from the chapel, a leather valise in his hand. "My work is done here," he declared. "Best get a move on."

"Sir," Elmira said firmly. "I'm a God-fearing woman, but I don't see what use I'll be to you. If it's money you need, I'm glad to oblige."

"Those who trust in their riches will fall, but the righteous will thrive like a green leaf." His smile didn't touch his eyes. "I don't want your ill-gotten gains. I want your service. Even the worst of us can be redeemed in the war against the phantoms."

"War?"

"That's right. You have a higher calling now, Miss Poole."

He leaned in and Elmira recoiled, but then he was gripping her wrist and whispering in her ear with that rich voice. Her wide eyes went blank. She saw things. A city with a great glass tower and her standing at the very top, looking out over her domain. Furs and finery. Caviar and champagne on ice. Multitudes of people crying out her name.

The pictures faded and her face felt cold. Elmira wiped away frozen tears.

"Tell me what to do," she managed.

Jolly patted her head like a faithful dog. "Why, Miss Poole, we're hunting the antichrist."

"Lee Merriweather." The name came to her on a fanfare of heavenly trumpets.

"That's right."

Elmira shook herself. "But we're not complete yet."

He took out a piece of paper and studied it. "Not yet. But soon, Miss Poole. Soon."

Kirby led her wedding gift from the stable, a fine chestnut mare. Elmira hitched up her gown and took the reins. "Is Augie still alive?" she asked.

"'Fraid not," Jolly said gravely.

She admired the three silver spoons, then tucked them into her coat pocket. Another strong gust tore the veil from her hair, sweeping it into the darkening afternoon.

"Good," Elmira said with a faint smile. "I'd hate to tarnish my reputation."

10

Sebastian Hardin was one of the six pallbearers who carried Calindra Carnarvon's coffin from the phantom-powered carriage to the cemetery where her children were buried.

It was a small plot on the grounds of the Academy. She'd built her empire on the railway, but the phantom school where talented youngsters trained to be linguists was her greatest pride. At least she would be at peace there.

He stood with head bowed as her oldest grandson, Richard, gave a eulogy to the woman who'd founded Carnarvon City and the Northern Territory. Ava leaned heavily on Sebastian's arm, weeping. She was clad head to toe in dull black crêpe and wore large tinted glasses. Her twin, Freddy, stared straight ahead during the service. Hardin noticed that he didn't look at his sister once, nor offer her a word of comfort.

Since arriving back in the city, Sebastian had performed his duties in a fog of misery and self-doubt. He'd devoted his entire adult life to the family, Calindra in particular, and her death was a hard blow. But the events surrounding it were even more disturbing. He could barely think of Ruth Cortez without a weight pressing down on his chest.

Adding to the mystery, the long-time dean of the Academy had tendered a resignation letter and vanished without a trace. Ava had appointed herself interim director, overriding several (in Sebastian's mind) far more suitable candidates. A seed of suspicion was growing in him, but he had no evidence.

None except for Ruth's word.

A woman with more integrity than anyone he'd ever known.

But it couldn't be. It just couldn't.

He pulled himself back to the present. The least he could do was pay his proper respects.

"She refused to believe those who claimed the phantoms couldn't be tamed," Richard was saying to a small crowd of professors and administrators. "She transformed them from a thorn in our side to an integral aspect of society. Why? Because she had vision. Determination. Because she knew that a thousand failures only brought her that much closer to success. And in the end, she changed the world."

Richard's wheelchair sat next to the above-ground crypt. A bout of childhood polio had damaged his legs and face, but he possessed a brilliant mind, inventing an array of clockwork and haint-powered conveyances, including Carnarvon Tower itself, which rotated on hidden gears.

"It's a lesson I took to heart as a young man who'd suffered setbacks of my own. My grandmother believed in me when no one else did. I won't pretend she was a gentle woman." A few people smiled. "She wouldn't want me to. When I made mistakes, she'd tell me exactly where I went wrong in no uncertain terms." Freddie gave a mirthless chuckle. "But the one thing she never advised me was to quit trying. Truthfully, sometimes it was the desperate desire to please her that kept me—"

Richard paused as the lid of the casket gave a thump.

"What the devil?" Sebastian muttered.

It was a gleaming rosewood coffin, hand-carved with the

Carnarvon Lines logo and elaborate gold rails. Calindra would have found it frivolous, but Ava insisted.

The coffin, which sat atop a temporary bier, gave another hard thump.

As if someone were banging to get out.

Sebastian pulled free of Ava's clinging hand and took a step forward just as the lid flew open.

To the horror of the assembled mourners, Calindra's body rose up out of the coffin and started performing a macabre jig. She wore a high-necked dark blue taffeta gown and shoes with silver buckles that flew off as her arms and legs jerked in a merry pantomime. Strands of white hair broke loose from her upswept bun. Her skin held the grey cast of death, the patrician face set in stern lines. The smell that rose from the coffin clogged Sebastian's throat.

He froze, knowing he ought to do something but at a complete loss as to what.

Ava stared in mute horror. Richard rolled his chair backwards, mouth working. To everyone's surprise, it was Freddy who found the stomach to intervene. He leapt over the coffin and seized the body. For a long moment, he wrestled with an invisible force. Then the corpse went limp in his arms. The corners of his mouth pulled down in revulsion as he eased her back into the casket. Freddy slammed the lid shut and sat down on it.

As if a spell had been broken, all the linguists present erupted in a cacophony of phantom tongues, trying to banish—or at least soothe—the haints who were obviously behind the prank.

"Get her out of here," Sebastian said tersely, trying to hand Ava to her brother. "Both of you, go back to the tower. I'll meet you there."

Ava bristled. "I'm not a child," she said tartly, taking off the dark glasses. Her green eyes—one of them bearing a spectacular bruise—skipped over to the coffin, then away again. "This is an outrage and I won't have it!"

She rounded on a small woman with spectacles and a wool jacket bearing the Academy insignia. "Professor Kaminsky! I thought you had the phantoms at this institution under strict control."

"We do!" the professor said anxiously, wringing her hands. "It couldn't have been any of ours."

"I find that difficult to believe," Ava said coldly. "This is a clear case of negligence and I'll discover the culprit—"

"You seem to be forgetting something," Freddy interrupted from his perch on the coffin.

"Oh?"

"As the interim dean, dear sister, *you're* the responsible party."

"Do be quiet, Freddy," she said in a fretful tone. "You're not helping."

"How can you be so blind?" Richard demanded, wheeling over. "After what happened in Aguadulce? It's time we face some hard truths. Grandmother didn't tame the phantoms as well as she thought! Something is happening and we need to prepare for the worst."

"Don't you dare speak to me about Aguadulce," Ava retorted. "You weren't even there. I was. Merriweather riled them up! This is nothing like—" She cut off, sputtering, as a clod of dirt nicked her ear.

The peaceful glade beneath the elms came alive with darting shadows. One resolved into a red-haired phantom with a fox-like face. Dirt and debris pelted the mourners. The linguists scattered, some sheltering behind the crypt, others running for the red-brick Academy buildings. Richard's wheelchair tipped to the side. Sebastian ran to help him just as a mighty crack resounded over their heads. He dragged Richard out of the way moments before the thick branch of an elm descended with a crash.

"My God, are you all right?" Freddy asked, leaping from the casket to his brother's side.

"Fine," Richard murmured. His sallow face grew even paler as he regarded his mangled wheelchair.

Sebastian looked around, wary. Dead leaves skittered in the wind, but the attack had ceased. For now.

"Does everyone agree it might be prudent to continue this conversation at the tower?" he asked.

Richard and Ava nodded. Freddy shrugged, though he looked shaken. "Is it any safer?"

"We've got to keep this quiet," Ava said. "It'd cause a panic. You'll see to that, won't you, Sebastian?"

He met her cool green eyes. How like Calindra she was. "I'll bring the car around," he said.

"What about grandmother?" Ava wondered.

They all looked at the casket.

"She'd want me to protect the living over the dead," he replied.

And how, Sebastian wondered, as he hurried to Ava's stylish clockwork automobile, was he going to do that?

Back at his office in Special Services on the fifteenth floor, with the Carnarvons ensconced in their various suites, Hardin paced the carpet, tugging at his short dark hair.

He didn't like where his thoughts led him.

Ava had been whacked with a clod of dirt. Freddy was untouched. Only Richard had been in mortal peril.

Richard, who stood to inherit a third of his grandmother's fortune.

Back in Aguadulce, he'd seen phantoms yank people into the ether. If they'd truly wanted to kill everyone, Richard included, they could have done it with ease. Did Merriweather send the haints today, as Ava had suggested?

Was it just another taunt?

He longed to give chase, but Ava wouldn't have it. He'd made a solemn promise to Calindra not to abandon the family when she was gone. Unlike his father, Sebastian was a man of his word—even when it nearly killed him.

He looked up as Marshal Ford burst into the office. One arm still hung in a sling, but he'd done a good job running Special Services in Hardin's absence.

"We got a firm sighting," Ford said. "In Charter Oak. Cortez and Merriweather. They bought supplies and took off in a zeppelin."

Sebastian gripped the edge of his desk. "You sure?"

"Positive identification." He held up one of the wanted posters Sebastian had ordered and sent north on the first mail train two days before.

"What kind of supplies?"

"Cold weather gear. Seems clear they're headed north. And that's not all. There's rumors of trouble up in the N.T. Lovelock's been burned."

"Dammit. Get some more men up there. Find out what's what."

Ford gave him a level look. "Thought you might be going yourself."

"I'm working on that," Sebastian snapped. "What about Lucky Boy?"

"I telegraphed right away. The two men we posted there haven't seen Cortez."

"Tell 'em to stay put. She could still show up." His face hardened. "And they're not to touch a hair on that woman's head, understood? Not even if it means letting her go."

"Understood, sir." Ford sighed. "I liked Cortez. She splinted my arm. Did a fair job of it, too. What about Merriweather?"

Sebastian hesitated. "I want him alive, too. Though they've got latitude on keeping his mouth shut."

Hardin felt an odd twinge of guilt when he considered the beating he'd given Lee. He'd been out of his mind at the time. But if there was any chance at all the kid was innocent . . . .

He shook his head. "With everything that's happened, surely Miss Carnarvon will see the need for me to go north. It seems to be the source of the troubles. I'll go speak to her."

Ford cleared his throat. Hardin trusted him to handle just about any situation that arose. The story they told in Special Services about Ford was that Hardin had once dispatched him to quell a riot of drunken miners in Tip Top. When the train pulled up and Ford stepped off, the anxious mayor looked around and said, "They only sent one marshal?" To which Ford replied, "Well, you only got one riot, don't you?" He then proceeded to calm things down and get back on the train.

Hardin's deputy was rock solid, but now he looked worried. "I was thinking. Could what happened down south be, I don't know, *contagious*?"

Hardin met his eyes. "If it is, we're in serious trouble. That's between you and me."

Ford nodded. "I'll find you if I get any news."

"Day or night," Hardin agreed. He slept on the couch in his office, so he wouldn't be hard to track down.

He took the elevator up to the seventeenth floor and raised a hand to knock on Ava's suite when Freddy came down the corridor. He blanched when he saw Sebastian.

"That was bad today," Hardin said quietly. "How are you holding up?"

Freddy looked a good deal like his sister—they were twins, after all—but he lacked her fierce will. If Sebastian had to choose one word to describe Freddy, it would be aimless. He didn't have Ava's ambition, or Richard's ingenuity. He seemed content to play the black sheep, drinking heavily and skulking around in his grandmother's long shadow. Now that Calindra was gone he had no one to rebel against—except his sister, but

Hardin had never seen Freddy stand up to Ava, despite the little barbs he shot her way. They seemed to truly understand each other, though he sensed a new chill between them.

"Oh, I'm fine," Freddy said carelessly. "What brings you to our lofty heights?"

"News from the N.T."

"Not good, I presume?"

"No."

"That doesn't surprise me. We should have just let them secede, but grandmother wanted the mines and timber. More trouble than it's worth, you ask me."

"Towns are burning up there," Hardin said through gritted teeth.

Freddy dropped the cavalier tone. "Jesus." He closed his eyes. "It's all falling apart, isn't it?"

"Doesn't have to," Hardin said. "Not if you let me go—"

The door opened. Ava stood there in a dressing gown, hair falling over her shoulders in auburn waves. "Go where?"

"Can we speak inside?"

She stepped back. The sitting room stretched the length of one wall, with floor-to-ceiling windows that looked out over the city. Lights shone far below in the gathering darkness. She switched on a table lamp.

"I tried to sleep, but I kept seeing grandmother . . . ." Ava trailed off with a shudder.

Freddy slouched into an overstuffed armchair and lit a cigarette. Ava shot him a look of disapproval but held her tongue for once. Sebastian remained standing.

"Can I pour you a drink?"

He shook his head.

"God, yes," Freddy said with feeling.

Ava poured two brandies and handed one to her brother. "That's all you get. Don't ask for a refill."

"Miser," he said with a trace of his old cheer.

Sebastian chose his words carefully. "I understand that you

want me to stay until the will is settled, but there's been developments. I'm getting dire reports from up north. You know about Ruby Creek, but now Lovelock's been torched. Right down to the ground."

Ava stared at him without expression. "That's awful," she murmured. "But it's rather primitive up there, isn't it? Lanterns are dangerous."

"Not just Lovelock. There's strange rumors from Ruby Creek, as well. My marshals there have disappeared. Some of the witnesses mentioned a preacher. It's all confused, but there's no doubt something's up."

"You can't seriously consider leaving, after what happened today," Ava said.

"I'm no linguist," Sebastian replied. "I'd take a bullet for either of you, but I can't do a thing about phantoms. I'm no use here. If Merriweather's behind it, I'll track him down. But if it's the Reverend Jolly, it'd be a sore dereliction of duty to leave those poor people at his mercy. I saw what he did in New Jerusalem. That's blood on all our hands if it happens again."

"Send someone else." She set her glass on the table.

"I already have. But they're not as good as me." He didn't speak the words with arrogance. They were just fact.

"What evidence do you have that it's Jolly?" Freddy wondered.

"Besides the description? Just a gut feeling. But do you really think we've seen the last of that man?"

"I need to think about it," Ava declared. "It's been a very trying day."

"With all due respect, ma'am, don't think too long."

"Don't *ma'am* me, Sebastian. I understand what's at stake. And of course I feel a responsibility for the people of the Northern Territory. But I also feel a responsibility for this city. The Academy." She waved a hand. "All the rest of it. I'm sensitive to the fact that the north is your birthplace, but we need to keep our heads. Maybe that's exactly what Jolly wants, to have you running off after him while we're left here defenseless."

"There's at least thirty marshals in this building," Hardin said dryly. "You're not exactly defenseless."

"You know what I mean."

Sebastian turned to Freddy. "What about you?"

Freddy seemed startled to be asked his opinion. "I'll need to discuss it with my sister. And Richard, of course."

"This isn't a democracy," Ava said dismissively.

There was a moment's silence. The twins locked eyes. Freddy was usually the one to blink in these contests, but this time he held his ground.

"On the contrary," he said with a smirk. "I think it is." Freddy drained his glass and stood up. "I'll talk to Richard. He's the clever one, isn't he?"

"Oh, for God's sake," Ava muttered. "Go ahead. I suppose he ought to know."

Freddy strode to the door. Hardin followed.

"Sure you won't stay for a drink, Sebastian?" Ava asked innocently. "We've hardly spoken in days. I miss your company."

Once, he'd counted Ava as a friend. But the thought of being alone with her made his skin crawl. How could never have seen who she really was? The hostility towards Richard was more open since Calindra died, but it had always been there. And except for the performance at the funeral, Ava's eyes had been dry since they left Aguadulce. She only mentioned her grandmother when she was trying to manipulate him into doing her bidding.

"I wish I could," he said with a regretful smile. "But I'm still catching up on work."

She frowned.

"And I need to go down to the Academy and have a talk with the staff," he added. "If you expect to keep a lid on what happened today."

That did the trick. "Of course." She pressed a hand to her forehead. "I'm tired anyway. Perhaps I'll see you at breakfast tomorrow."

They walked to the elevator bank together. "Richard must be in his laboratory," Freddy said. "He practically lives in there."

Sebastian glanced down the hall. Ava's door was securely shut. "You saw Deputy Cortez after she . . . left me," he said in a low voice. "Did she say anything to you?"

Freddy flicked his lighter open and shut, open and shut. "Just that she was, and I quote, *jacking this train*. I asked if she was fooling and she pointed a gun at me. It was very uncivilized of her."

The tone was light, but Sebastian sensed a strain beneath his words.

"Did she say anything else?"

Freddy's gaze strayed to his sister's door. "Not a thing."

"Hmmm."

"What?" Freddy asked sharply.

Sebastian smiled. "Nothing."

The elevator arrived. They stood in awkward silence as it descended. Freddy practically lunged out the door when it stopped at the twelfth floor where Richard's workshop was. Hardin popped a piece of mint gum in his mouth and hit the button for the sub-basement level.

"Liar," he said softly.

Hardin found Professor Abel Beach sitting in his cell reading a book. Lee's former mentor from the Academy looked up and closed it as Hardin approached.

"Thank you for permitting me to have some of my things, marshal," he said. "Helps pass the time."

Abel Beach was in his fifties, with long graying deadlocks and a round, pleasant face.

Sebastian nodded. "They treating you okay?"

"I can't complain."

"I'm sorry how this all worked out," Hardin said. "But I couldn't just let you go."

"I imagine not." Beach gave him a shrewd look. "So why are you here?"

"Just wanted to talk."

The professor sighed. "I already told you, Lee Merriweather is not capable of murder. I've known the kid all his life. It's utterly ridiculous to think he hurt all those people, including Calindra."

"I'm not here about Lee." Sebastian paused. What did he have to lose? "I'm here about Dean Rodriguez. He's missing."

Abel frowned. "Missing?"

"Well, he left a letter. Said he felt responsible for Merriweather's escape and was unfit to run the Academy anymore."

"I see." Beach looked troubled.

"You must know him well."

"For twenty years," he agreed.

"That sound like something he'd do?"

"No," the professor responded immediately. "Alex could be fussy. He was more of an administrator than an academic. But that job was his entire life. No one blamed him for Lee, not even Calindra. He ran a school, not a jail."

"That's what I figured, too. Only a single suitcase was taken." Sebastian curled a hand around the bars. "He has no family outside the city. It's one thing to quit, another to vanish. You ask me, it sounds like he was running from something."

"Or someone," Beach pointed out.

"Yep."

"May I see the letter? I know his handwriting well. It's like the man, cramped and precise. And he does a fancy swirl with the Z at the end of his signature. At least I could vouch for the authenticity."

Sebastian nodded. "I'll see what I can do."

"Has the family appointed a successor?"

"Ava's the interim dean."

Beach held his gaze. "Interim? Or permanent?"

"I guess it's her call."

"She had Alex under her thumb," Beach said. "I heard her tearing into him on more than one occasion."

"You think he might have known something?"

"Like what?"

"I don't know. There's a lot that doesn't add up."

The professor gave him a level look. "I always liked you, marshal. I think you're an honest man. Get me that letter. It might be a start."

Sebastian felt weary. Was he an honest man? He didn't know anymore. It all felt so complicated. Ruth saw the world in simpler terms. There was right and there was wrong. What would she do in his place?

"I'll get it," he said. "Thank you for your help, professor."

Abel nodded. "Be careful." He returned to the book.

Be careful.

That from a man waiting to be arraigned as an accessory to grand larceny, aiding and abetting a fugitive, and a host of other charges.

Sebastian's thoughts spun as he went in search of Marshal Tanaka. Along with Ford, she was the only one he fully trusted.

He couldn't share his suspicions with Richard, not without a shred of evidence.

But before he did anything else, he intended to post a guard over the eldest Carnarvon.

11

We abandoned the mining train on a siding just outside Hatchet and walked into town later the following day, Lee and Ned taking turns carrying Dean Rodriguez's suitcase, and me with the Whitworth rifle propped over one shoulder. A quick stop at the depot confirmed that no trains were due for two days. The station master jotted down the schedule on a scrap of paper that I tucked into my pocket. I figured we'd discreetly watch the passengers disembark. If Jolly were on any of them, we'd have advance warning.

The morning was fair enough that Lee took off his raccoon hat, but we still stuck out like a sore thumb. So it was with a good deal of caution that I approached Hatchet, which sat almost at the western terminus of the railroad, one stop from the Winchester spur line.

Hardin had described his hometown as "lively" and "a bit lawless," but this laconic description did not do justice to the reality of the place.

"Why, Hatchet's a regular seething cauldron of vice and depravity," Doc observed cheerfully as we walked down the Main Street, past boisterous saloons and gambling hells and dance halls.

Hard, uncurried men with jangling spurs prowled the streets, eager for a fight or a drink, or both at the same time. I dodged a pair of riders who would have run me down, whooping it up like a pair of moon-sick wolves. Dean Rodriguez hunched deeper into his coat. He looked like he'd rather be any place else in the world. I couldn't blame him.

"Money and whiskey flowing like water downhill, and youth and beauty and womanhood and manhood wrecked on the shores of the far fringes of civilization," Doc exclaimed. "I must say, Ruth, your tastes have sunk low if your chosen sweetheart hails from such a valley of perdition!"

He was in a mood to wax poetic. "Ain't my sweetheart anymore," I muttered.

"Isn't."

"Oh, go hang!"

Maybe apologizing to Zippo had relieved his conscience, but Doc was feeling his oats again. His shadow stretched out beside me, pale on the churned snow. "I imagine Hardin's a sore spot," he conceded. "I don't see any marshals, though. They've probably given up on it."

"Let's find a hotel," I said. "Stow our things and refine the plan."

"How about that one?" Dean Rodriguez said, a bit pathetically. "If there's a bed, I'm in it."

The Hotel Yorba looked fairly grand by the standards of Hatchet. Three stories of whitewashed wood with freshly painted black lettering and a busy saloon below. The tinkling strains of a piano spilled into the street.

"It looks expensive," I said.

"And respectable," Lee pointed out. He knew my tastes.

"Oh, I s'pose. Okay with you, Ned?"

Ned Carver sniffed the air. "Food smells fresh. That's a good sign."

My stomach rumbled. "Then it's settled."

We went inside. To one side was a long paneled oak bar,

polished to a splendid shine. Encircling the base was a gleaming brass foot rail with a row of spittoons spaced along the floor. Every spot was taken.

The other side had a desk with a pigtailed girl behind it. Lee moved to speak with her about rooms while I took a better look around. It wasn't as rough as most of the other places we'd passed. The laughter was quieter and I didn't see any gambling, which seemed a good sign.

Then my eye lit on the man playing the piano. He had thick silver hair, parted sharp on the left and slicked down. I moved around to catch a glimpse of his profile.

Thin, hawkish nose. Bright blue eyes. The resemblance was uncanny.

"You coming, Ruth?" Lee asked. He dangled room keys from one hand.

"In a minute," I said. "Here, take the rifle."

"Suit yourself," he said. "Come on, Ned."

They followed the girl to a staircase in the rear. I inched closer to the piano player, unsure what I had in mind but burning with curiosity.

"Got a request?" He noticed me and winked.

"Sure," I said. "How about Sweet Molly from Hatchet?"

He laughed. "Everyone likes that one." He launched into it with gusto, fingers flying over the keys.

"*Did you ever hear tell of Sweet Molly from Hatchet,*
Who misplaced her virtue and hoped she might catch it,
Across the wide mountains with her old yeller dog,
Two yoke of cattle and six Shanghai hogs …"

He had a nice baritone, a bit roughened from drink, but I found my toe tapping a rhythm.

"What's your name?" I asked when the last verse had faded.

"You can call me H.J., lass."

Horatio James Hardin.

He launched into another song. It sounded like Strawberry

Roan, though the words were different than the ones I'd been taught.

I listened to the music for a minute, contemplating the turn of fate that had led me to this particular hotel, out of every other one in town.

Hardin claimed he bore his father no ill will for shooting him, since it was a drunken accident. I'd seen the pellet scars on Sebastian's back. At the time, I'd thought it was mighty forgiving of him, but Hardin's dad did have a certain roguish charm.

"And your name, lass?" he asked me.

"Lucy," I replied without thinking.

My sweet little songbird, the reverend had called her.

"Well," another wink, "if I was thirty years younger, I'd be twirling you around the dance floor, Lucy," he said. "But my knees ain't what they used to be."

I smiled. "If you was thirty years younger, I might say yes."

He studied me. "You look like a nice girl. I won't ask what brought you here, but my advice is not to stay long. Hatchet has a man for breakfast every morning, and a woman for supper." His gaze lit past my shoulder and H.J. quickly turned back to the piano. "Boss is here," he whispered. "He don't like it when I fraternize on the job."

I moved away, watching the man who'd just entered the hotel.

He was small and bug-eyed like a toad, with heavy jowls and a tiny waxed mustache. His coat had ermine trim and he leaned on a silver-headed walking stick. He looked around, checking that all was in order, then went though a door behind the front desk.

I was about to go look for Lee and Ned when one of the serving girls gave a little shriek.

"No pinching," she said, rubbing her rear with an aggrieved expression.

The man who'd done it grinned up at her. "That's what you're here for, darlin', ain't it?"

She set his beer down on the table and hurried off.

I imagined this kind of abuse was common enough in Hatchet, but it irked me. The man tipped his chair back, watching her go with a smug look. He wore a fancy loop holster rigged for a quick cross-draw, with the grips facing forward instead of back. No more than thirty or so, but his blond hair was already thinning. He wore a spotless white shirt with a stiff collar and a stick pin on his lapel. A diamond ring glittered on one finger.

"Hey, H.J.," he called out.

Hardin's father turned and nodded.

"Play somethin' more high-spirited. Sounds like a wake in here."

"You got it, Chalkey," he said, quickly switching from Little Old Church in the Valley to a bawdy ballad about a miner's daughter.

"Who wants to play some cards?" Chalkey called out.

He looked around, but none of the other patrons would meet his eye.

"Used to be a man could find a spot of action at the Yorba," he complained.

"Try Clay Allison's place," H.J. suggested, without missing a note.

Chalkey laughed. "Clay banned me after I shot some disrespectful cowpunchers. Said I had a bad reputation. But they drew first. I just returned the compliment." He jammed a silver toothpick between his teeth. "You oughta know, H.J, it's immoral to let a sucker keep his money." He beckoned to the serving girl. She came over with tight face. "Get me another beer."

"But you haven't even drunk the first one," she said.

Chalkey knocked his glass to the floor. "Now I have," he said. "Clean it up and get me another."

No one said a thing.

The girl fetched a rag and started to mop up the mess.

"By God, this town's gotten boring," Chalkey declared. He grabbed the girl's arm. "Come on, sit in my lap and I'll tell you a bedtime story."

"There's plenty of other establishments for that sort of thing," she said wearily. "Please, Chalkey, you know I'm a married woman. Let me fetch your beer."

"Not much of a husband if he lets his wife work outside the home."

H.J. turned from the piano bench. "Leave her be," he said mildly.

Chalkey stared at H.J., his face expressionless. H.J. held his ground. The tension grew thick. Then he laughed. "I'm just fooling around."

The place had gone dead quiet. Those nearest the door rose from their seats and slipped outside. Chalkey hadn't noticed me yet. I knew I ought to leave, too, but my blood was starting to simmer. I disliked bullies.

"Tell you what," he said to the girl. "I'll pay you five dollars to give my boots a shine. The snow's wreaking havoc with the leather." Light eyes—blue or gray—gleamed with amusement as he propped a foot on the table. I knew then he wouldn't stop. Not until he got a fight.

The girl stood, color high in her cheeks. "I don't shine boots. Not yours or any man's."

I admired her greatly at that moment. She looked barely sixteen, but she had her pride, if little else.

He leapt to his feet without a word. So quick, it was like a spring uncoiling. He backhanded her. The girl staggered into another table. I dimly sensed H.J. rising to my left, shouting something, but I was already crossing the space. My fist caught Chalkey on the jaw. He spun away. I saw him reach for his guns, but I had the drop on him and we both knew it. The flintlock was already in my own hand, cocked and pointed at his forehead.

"Don't," I said.

He looked shocked that a woman had drawn on him. For a second, I thought he'd test me. But I didn't waver and he seemed to think better of it.

"Just leave," I said.

"Do as the lass says," H.J. said, coming to my side.

I didn't like how close his hands were to the loop holsters. My gut told me this was a very dangerous man. He wasn't drunk. I hadn't seen him touch the beer. And clearly others thought so, too, because the saloon was quietly emptying out.

"Fancy yourself a gunslinger, eh?" Chalkey said softly. "How many men you killed? 'Cause I got twenty-seven notches on my gun. Last one was for snoring, which I cannot abide. Shot him right through the wall of the Silver Dollar Hotel."

"Just one," I replied. "But I'm willing to increase the tally."

We stood there, stalemated, for a long minute. Then I heard a commotion outside. I didn't dare take my eyes off Chalkey, though he turned to look.

"Dammit," he muttered.

Two Carnarvon marshals walked in the door.

"He started it," H.J. said, nodding at Chalkey.

"We'll settle this," the first one said calmly. He stepped up to Chalkey and relieved him of his guns. A strong hand pushed Chalkey to his knees. The dandified killer looked annoyed to find himself in custody, but didn't resist.

I glanced at their insignia. Special Services. My heart was already racing from the expectation of sudden death. I wasn't sure if I should be relieved or worried.

"You can lower the gun, ma'am," the second one said firmly.

Like most marshals, they were big and clean-shaven, with

smart navy blue uniforms and brimmed hats. I realized I was still pointing the flintlock at Chalkey's head and did as he said.

"Mr. White got up to his usual hijinks," H.J. explained. "No one stepped in 'cept for her. You ought to thank the lass."

They exchanged a look. "Let's see that firearm," one said.

I reluctantly handed over the Collier, praying Doc wouldn't make a hash of things. But he stayed silent and meek as a church mouse.

"Funny thing," one of the marshals said. "We just came in on the mail train to deliver some wanted posters for Mr. Hardin." They shoved me down to my knees next to Chalkey, who arched a brow and smirked. "Looks like we just got lucky."

I WAS HALF-SURPRISED Hatchet even had a jail, considering the liberties granted to its inhabitants, but the calaboose turned out to be fairly large, with six cells to accommodate prisoners. They put me in one, with Lee on the left and Chalkey on the right. Ned and Dean Rodriguez were just past Lee, who they'd gagged so he couldn't call any haints.

It was miserable cold in there.

The marshals locked us up and left. I could hear them talking down at the end, though I couldn't make out the words. I supposed I'd made a mess of things, but I didn't regret punching Chalkey. I wished I could do it again, since he wouldn't shut up.

"See, that's what you get for playing the hero," he declared. "No good deed goes unpunished around here. You should take that lesson to heart." He laughed. "Lord, they're the sickest-looking bunch of marshals I ever seen. Got nothin' under those hats but hair."

I stood up and paced to keep warm. Would Hardin come north himself? Knowing the man, it'd be hard to stop him. I brightened a little. When he talked to the dean, he'd come around. And he'd help us catch the reverend. Hardin would be worth ten men in a fight.

In truth, I longed to see him. When Sebastian Hardin entered a room, you knew it. He had a fierce energy that lit the place up. But he could be kind and gentle, too. Not to mention handsome as sin. I'd tried not to dwell on him, but he kept my heart in his pocket.

Most of my brain had tuned out Chalkey's incessant chatter, but now my ears perked up.

"When my friends get here, we'll have a little shindig. You like to play, don't you, Ruth?"

I froze.

"What'd you say?"

"You heard me." There was a sly edge to his voice. "I'm the catnip and you're the little kitty. Just couldn't resist, could you?"

"Darnit," I muttered. Then, "Doc? Please, if you can hear me, give me a sign."

The marshals had the Collier, though I still had Hardin's empty holster. Just the fact that Doc hadn't intervened told me something was very wrong. He'd sounded better when we first got to Hatchet, but I knew he was sick and getting worse. Usually, he could go a little ways from the gun before the trap Roger set pulled him back. I'd whispered his name a dozen times since they locked us up.

But Doc didn't answer.

I banged on the bars and hollered until one of the marshals came over.

"Quit that racket," he said sternly.

"Listen," I said, desperate. "Just please listen to me. Chalkey told me there's some men coming to break him out. They're real bad, marshal. You better get reinforcements."

He weighed what I said. I knew Chalkey was wrong.

These men weren't dumb. They wouldn't be alive otherwise. If I was lying, no harm done. But if I wasn't . . . .

"Sheriff of Cedar County's coming any minute with his deputy," he said finally. "Just sit tight."

"That was a real pioneer try," Chalkey remarked when he'd left. "Won't do you any good though."

I ignored him. The minutes dragged past. I called out to Ned and he called back, which gave me strength. But I'd be lying if I said I wasn't more scared than I'd ever been in my life, like a beast waiting for slaughter. It grew dark. Outside, the blizzard howled like a live thing.

Then I heard a door bang open. My heart stopped.

"What do we got, boys?"

It wasn't Jolly. I'd know that voice anywhere. Must be …

"It's Bose Cahill!"

The dry whisper in my ear made me start.

"About time," I hissed. "Who?"

Doc sounded agitated. "The old sheriff of Three Bars. He's so crooked, he could swallow nails and spit out corkscrews!"

"Three Bars?" I repeated in astonishment.

As you might recall, that was the town next door to Lucky Boy that Roger had destroyed twenty-odd years before.

"Bose was my previous owner, Ruth. I imagine he survived the twister and went north. The man has the devil's own luck!"

"Hush, here he comes!"

A man in his late sixties appeared. He had a ruddy face and triple chin that bulged from his collar. A big ten-gallon hat tipped back on his head. A lanky deputy with a long, dour face walked at his side. Bose held a lantern high, glancing into each of the cells. "This the one?" he asked the marshals, who followed behind.

"Yep," the one I'd spoken to replied. "That's Ruth Cortez.

Deputy out of Lucky Boy. We got a warrant for her and the others. You can have Chalkey White."

Sheriff Cahill squinted at me. "What's she wanted for?"

"Aiding and abetting a fugitive. Assault. Train robbery."

He whistled. "It's a shame when a woman turns bad. Deputy, too."

The lantern shone straight in my face. I shielded my eyes. Then he moved on and took a look at Chalkey. "Now, this one's been a thorn in my side for far too long. We'll get him before a judge in the morning and on the gallows by noon."

"Miss Cortez seems to think there might be some trouble," the marshal said, God bless him. "Can you round up more deputies? We'll head over to the telegraph office. Mr. Hardin will want word we found her and Merriweather."

"Right away," the sheriff agreed amiably.

The marshals turned to go. Cahill drew and shot the first one in the back of the head. His partner reached for his gun, but he was a second too slow. The sheriff's deputy shot him twice in the chest. It happened so fast. All the air left my lungs. I backed against the wall of the cell, eyes locked on the dying marshal and the spreading pool of blood. He gave a last gasp and went still.

"Ruth!" Ned cried out.

"I'm still alive," I called, my voice shaking.

Cahill holstered his gun. "Let him out," he said.

The deputy unlocked the cell next to me. Chalkey came out and stretched. He winked at me. "Told you my friends were coming."

The sheriff took out a big black book. At first I thought it was a Bible, but then he held it up with a chuckle. The Revised Statutes of the N.T. I knew them all by heart, since they governed Lucky Boy, too. He tore a page out, lit it with a match, and produced a cigar. In a minute, he was puffing away.

"You yellow-bellied snake," Doc growled. A weak man-shaped shadow darkened the lamplight.

"Why, looky here!" the sheriff exclaimed. "It's the mouthy haint! Thought I left you buried in the dirt."

"You're so greedy, you'd steal a fly from a blind spider, Bose. That tornado was almost a mercy! I'm just sorry it spared you."

Bose laughed and blew out a cloud of foul smoke. "Three Bars was a cesspool. My justice might have been rough, but it was all they had south of Hazardville."

"Justice?" Doc gave a dry cackle that turned into a horrible coughing fit.

"Well now, we never did hang the wrong one but once or twice," he replied thoughtfully, "and them fellers needed to be hung anyhow jes' on general principles. What time is it, Jim?"

The deputy checked a pocket watch. "Ten-thirty."

"They should be arriving any minute now," Bose muttered.

I thought my heart couldn't sink any further.

The sheriff smiled nastily. "You make any trouble, Misty, she gets a bullet in the head."

Misty?

"My old name," Doc hissed. "He thought it was funny."

I stared at the cell lock as the evil sheriff and his deputy retreated to warmer climes at the front of the jail. "Guess that door'd be open if you could manage it."

"The gun's too far," Doc replied. "I'm so sorry, Ruth. It hurts me awfully just to be here."

"Then don't," I said. "Go back inside."

"No! I *ain't* leaving you."

I gave a shaky smile.

"What happened, Ruth?" Ned called out softly. He was down at the end, past Chalkey's cell, and hadn't seen it.

"They shot the marshals," I called back. "I think the reverend's coming."

He digested this. "They gonna kill us, too?"

"I don't know. But I won't go down without a fight."

"Me neither."

Lee made some muffled sounds, I guess to let us know he agreed.

There wasn't much more to say. We waited in the cold and dark.

I wondered if Roger was watching from the ether. Maybe eating some popcorn.

The thought made me mad and I clung to the anger like a lifeline. Otherwise I might go mad with fear. It helped that Doc stayed with me. He didn't speak, but I could sense his presence.

At last the door opened again. A frigid gust swept the jail. I braced myself.

Slow footsteps echoed along the cells. A figure resolved from the gloom.

"Well, here she is," the Reverend Jolly said. "Judas Iscariot."

I hadn't seen him in the flesh since the underground bunker. He wore his customary long black coat and looked even wilder and dirtier than he had before, which is saying something. He carried a leather valise.

"Jolly," I said in acknowledgement.

I refused to call him reverend anymore. If he was ever a man of God, that time lay in the distant past.

My eyes went over his shoulder to the tall, yellow-haired man who leaned on a cane just at the edge of the light. For the last three weeks, he'd haunted my nightmares. We stared at each for a long minute and a funny thing happened. My terror melted away. Cage was just a man. A pure psychopath, yes, but he still needed a cane to walk.

I think he expected me to wet myself, but I gave him a cold smile instead.

A tiny flicker of life shone in his eyes. Surprise.

I vowed to myself that one way or another, I'd kill him before I died.

"Legion said I'd find you here," Jolly said. "All wrapped up like a Christmas present."

"You gonna shoot me, get it over with."

He smiled. "In due time."

Chalkey sauntered up with Sheriff Cahill and four other men. I didn't recognize three of them, but one was the buggy-eyed owner of the Hotel Yorba.

"You got my money?" Bose demanded, eying the dead marshals. "I'll have to clean up this mess before any more show up."

Jolly regarded him with disdain. "Pay the man, Mr. LeBlanc," he said.

The hotel owner handed Bose a wad of bills. He licked a finger and counted it with avid eyes. "Train's waiting at the depot."

"Let's get 'em hogtied," Jolly said. "Watch the girl. She's a spitfire."

"Where are we going?" I demanded.

He ignored me. I studied the men. So this was his infamous outfit. Other than LeBlanc, who was clearly rich, they didn't look much different than the rest of the riff-raff in Hatchet. I heard the clank of a cell door opening and they brought out Ned and Dean Rodriguez. Then Lee, who glared defiance from behind his gag.

Dean Rodriguez's watery eyes darted around. His nose twitched.

I sensed Cage still staring at me as I raised my hands. One of Jolly's accomplices drew a gun, while Bose unlocked my cell.

"Turn around," he growled.

Out of the corner of my eye, I saw them shove Ned against the bars and start tying his hands. Then Dean Rodriguez gave a mighty sneeze. They all turned. Ned wheeled and kicked out at the man behind him. They hadn't secured his hands yet. He swung a fist as I lunged at the fat sheriff and grabbed his gun from the holster.

"Drop it or I blow his head off," Chalkey said calmly from a few feet away.

He had his pistol pressed to Dean Rodriguez's temple. The poor dean looked like he might faint. I lowered the gun and tossed it down. Chalkey laughed and patted the dean on the shoulder. "Good boy," he said.

"I'm so sorry, Ruth," Dean Rodriguez moaned, wringing his hands. "But it's better to go quietly."

I stared at him, uncomprehending.

"They made me. I'm so sorry." He couldn't look me in the eye.

"Betrayal stings, don't it?" Jolly said in a ruminative tone. "I'd read some verses for the occasion, but they'd be wasted on you, Ruth. We'll make time for a chat later on."

In a trice, we were all tied hand and foot except for the dean, who trudged outside with his face tucked into the muffler. A cart waited outside to carry us to the depot. Despair nearly took me at how neatly we'd been herded into the trap, but at least we were all alive.

And we'd found our quarry, though not exactly according to plan.

Where, oh where, was my dear phantom? He hadn't uttered a peep since Jolly arrived.

"I've been freezing out here," a churlish voice declared. "What took so long?"

I twisted my head. Through the slats of the cart I saw a young woman with thick blond hair pinned up into a bun and a pretty, wholesome face. She wore a man's coat but I could have sworn I saw the trail of a white wedding dress underneath.

"So that's the antichrist?" she asked, peering down at Lee. "He's just a kid."

"Appearances can be deceiving, Miss Poole," Jolly replied. "But the Beast is captured now. No longer will he spread blasphemy and chaos."

"Well, that's the pot calling the kettle black," I muttered under my breath.

She must have had sharp ears because she turned to look at me. I felt a moment of hope that there was a woman among their number, but her eyes held no trace of sympathy.

"Won't you help me into the cart, Mr. White?" she said.

Chalkey leapt to obey. The other men watched her, too, with mingled fear and admiration.

And then we went rattling off, towards whatever Jolly and his apostles had in store.

12

THERE WAS no train due for two days and the depot was empty.

I don't know where Jolly got the train, but it looked like one of the fancy private ones, just four cars long. The snow fell thick and fast as his gang hauled us from the cart. I could hear distant sounds of merriment from Main Street, punctuated by the occasional wild shot, but the depot was at the far end of town.

"Pleasure doing business with you," Bose called from the driver's seat of the cart.

"Same here," Chalkey replied, pulling his gun.

The sheriff gaped in surprise. "Now, look—"

The bullet took him right between the eyes. It startled the horses, which took off in a gallop for Hatchet. I watched his body slowly tilt to the left. He still had the reins in his hands.

I'd be a liar if I said I was sorry Bose was dead, though I wasn't sure how much more I could stomach in one night.

"Burn it," Jolly said.

The hotelier rubbed his hands together. "It's been a while since I've set a real blaze."

He picked up a rock and broke one of the depot windows.

Chalkey kicked the door in. I'd smelled the kerosene in the cart. Six gallons of it. They threw one inside, then poured the rest around the edges. LeBlanc tossed a lit match. In an instant, the station was ablaze.

We were pushed up the train stairs and into an opulent carriage. The boiler fired and the train pulled away, flames dancing beyond the windows.

Carpet covered the floor, and various sitting areas with tables and little shaded lamps. We sat lined up on one of the sofas, hands and feet securely tied. I twisted at my wrists, hoping there might be some give, but they'd done a good job of it.

"I think introductions are in order," Jolly said. He seemed in high spirits to have his plan go off without a hitch. "These are my Apostles, sent by Legion to spread the Word. Our number is not yet complete, but it will be soon." He nodded at a man with a red-veined nose and small, mean eyes. "Mr. Winslow Cheever. Lately of Ruby Creek and wanted for too many outrages to list here."

"Sounds about right," Cheever said.

"Kirby Knox and his half-brother, Orville—"

"Royal," the man snarled. "I *told* you!"

"Royal Loving," Jolly continued serenely. "Bank and coach robbers extraordinaire."

The pair was as scruffy as Cheever. Knox had all the brawn, with heavy shoulders and shaggy hair, while his brother looked older and marginally wiser.

"Mr. White you've already met."

Chalkey grinned at me. "I'm a gambling man." He smoothed his thinning blond hair back, diamond pinky ring winking in the lamplight. "Just mind my temper. I can be a bit fussy."

With a name like Chalkey White, I imagined he'd grown up with a sizeable chip on his shoulder. Not to mention his ears, which stuck out like barn doors.

"Mr. Moritz LeBlanc. Never owned a hotel he didn't eventually burn down for the insurance money."

"Why, that's hearsay," LeBlanc said, beady eyes widening. "My record's clean."

I'd just watched him torch the station depot, so I took that denial with a grain of salt.

"And last but not least, Miss Elmira Poole, the charming Black Widow of the N.T." Jolly gave her a gentle smile. "Was Augie number seven or eight?"

"Nine," she replied primly, taking off her coat.

The woman was still wearing a wedding dress. I shuddered to think of what had happened to poor Augie.

"We're only missing the Ghost and Billy Easter," Jolly said. "But that gap in our number will soon be remedied."

I'd never heard of the Ghost, but the second name was familiar. Billy was known as the best horse thief on the prairie. Used to work rodeos as a stunt rider. I'm not sure why Billy went bad, but he was a true cowboy. Legend had it that he once sold a sheriff his own recently stolen horse.

Yet he wasn't known for violence. I'd heard Billy was soft-spoken, just a darned good thief. He didn't seem to fit with the rest of them.

Chalkey stood up. "Let's have some fun," he said, light eyes resting on Lee. "Maybe carve the Mark of the Beast on his forehead so no one can miss it."

I tensed. Next to me, Lee watched him with scared eyes.

"Leave him alone," Ned said with quiet heat.

"Shut your bazoo," Kirby snapped. He looked at his brother. "We oughta gag him, too."

At the end of the car, Mr. Cage watched with his usual wooden expression. I'd avoided his gaze, but I could sense his hatred. Of all of us, but me in particular. After my display of bravery back in the cell, the fear was creeping back.

"Now, you promised you wouldn't hurt him, reverend," Dean Rodriguez squeaked.

He'd been standing in the corner of the carriage, nervously toying with his muffler. Jolly slowly turned his head. The dean shrank back under the force of his gaze.

"Did I?"

"You said if I cooperated, you'd hand him over to the Carnarvons. Collect the bounty and be done with it."

"Those devils? They made him what he is! You must have misheard me."

"But, I—"

"You calling him a liar?" Chalkey demanded.

Dean Rodriguez fell silent.

"Merriweather has a part yet to play," Jolly said after a long, awful minute. "I'd like him intact for now."

Chalkey's mouth twisted, but he sat back down. My heart raced with relief.

"Let's get a game going," he said, pulling out a deck of cards. "Come on, you boys in?"

Kirby looked to Royal, who nodded. "That okay with you, reverend? Or is gambling a sin?"

"Well, it may be, but I'll make an exception," Jolly said magnanimously. "Go on."

I studied his face. He'd probably used his linguist powers to talk them into following him, but I wondered if his control was really as solid as it looked. These were not men accustomed to taking orders. With a little encouragement, they might chafe at the bit. I think Jolly knew it, too.

"How about you, Moritz?" Chalkey asked.

"Oh, deal me in," the hotelier said with a sigh. "I suppose it'll pass the time."

"Miss Poole?" Royal took his hat off. She preened under the attention.

"I'll just watch," she said. "It isn't proper for a lady to play cards."

Chalkey offered her his arm, earning an irate glance from

Royal. They regrouped around a table at the other end. Jolly sat down where Chalkey had been, just across from us.

"It's been a while," he said. "I hoped Beach might be with you."

So he didn't know everything. I felt a spark of hope.

"Abel Beach is dead," I said. "Back in Aguadulce."

If he thought so, Jolly would leave him be.

"Wish I could have seen it." He smiled and opened the valise at his feet. "The first sign of the coming Apocalypse. Soon it'll flow north in a great tide and the rivers shall run red."

We all pressed back against the couch. He held a rattler in his dirty hands. A big one.

"It's time for that little chat," Jolly said, blue eyes twinkling. The snake coiled around his arm. A tongue darted out to taste the air.

How I wished for Doc at that moment. He was my best friend and confidante—and, of course, my savior on more than one occasion. Even if he couldn't do anything, just a whisper in my ear would have cheered me. I wasn't even sure they'd taken the Collier. It could be back at the jail in Hatchet.

"Let's have some verses. Something suitable for the mood."

I'd been on the receiving end of Jolly's sermons before, but never with a loose snake. Ned and I shared a glance of mutual trepidation. Then a second rattler emerged from the valise. It slithered up the arm of the sofa and across our laps. When I tell you that no one twitched a muscle, I mean we sat there like boards, staring straight ahead. Sweat gathered in my palms as Jolly launched into Revelation, 22:12.

"Look, I am coming soon! My reward is with me, and I will give to each person according to what they have done. I am the Alpha and the Omega, the First and the Last, the Beginning and the End . . . ."

I WON'T BORE you with the rest of that ride to Hell.

None of us got bit, though even Jolly's droning voice failed to lull anyone to sleep.

At length, he returned the snakes to their valise.

The card game at the other end of the carriage grew rowdy. Mr. Cage loomed over them, which put a damper on things. Then we pulled into Winchester Junction and switched tracks for the northern spur to Tip Top.

Eventually, even the Apostles grew tired, departing one by one for what I assumed to be a sleeper car. Dean Rodriguez, that rotten turncoat, must have already retired, for I didn't see him. It left Jolly and Mr. Cage to watch over us. Hours of tugging at my bonds achieved nothing but sore wrists. I'd have to wait for my chance when we got wherever we were going.

My eyes flew open, blurry with grit, when the train jolted to a stop. The light of dawn was breaking through the curtains.

"End of the line!" Jolly called out.

I peeked outside. There was no station. We seemed to be in the middle of nowhere. Snow piled thick on the pines, glistening beneath crystals of ice. The land rose up into steep hills and valleys—the start of the Northern Range.

The gang assembled, Elmira in her rumpled wedding dress, Kirby and Royal looking worse for drink, and Moritz now lacking his silver walking stick, which Chalkey had apparently won from him in a game of Brag. Our feet were untied, though Chalkey and Royal kept a sharp watch with guns out. They herded us off the train.

Another cart waited, driven by a small, dark man with baggy trousers tucked into high boots.

"Mr. Morales," Jolly said. "Right on time."

We set off up a steep winding road. It was hard going through the snow and I was numb with cold by the time we reached a hole in the hillside, braced with old timbers. Boards had once been nailed across the entrance to the mine, for a heap of weathered planks sat nearby.

"How long are we staying here?" Elmira asked dubiously.

"Not too long, my dear," Jolly said. "And you'll find it more comfortable inside."

This turned out to be a bit of an overstatement. We passed through a long, low tunnel reeking of damp earth and emerged into a rough-hewn chamber. A campsite had been set up, with bed rolls and other supplies.

"You told me I'd be wearing silks and enjoying the view from the top of Carnarvon Tower," Elmira said, looking around. "I was a woman of means before you found me, reverend. I'm used to the finer things in life. And this ain't fine!"

Elmira put on airs, but I doubted she'd been to school past the sixth grade.

"You shall have all those things," Jolly said soothingly. "As soon as I find Mr. Easter, we'll depart this place. Two days at most."

She sniffed, but gave a grudging nod. "I'll need my own quarters. And just 'cause I'm a woman, don't expect me to cook for you!"

From the looks on their faces, I don't think any of them had considered this alarming possibility.

"He can cook," I said, jerking my chin at Ned.

In truth, I was worried about Mr. Carver. He didn't fit into the reverend's plans, which made him disposable. Unless Ned had some value, I feared they'd kill him.

"His daddy owns a restaurant," I added. "Mr. Carver's a gourmet chef."

"That true?" Chalkey asked appraisingly.

Ned was quick-witted. He'd probably been thinking the same thing. "That's right," he said. "Trained in the kitchen my whole life."

I'd thought it best not to mention he'd worked for the devil Carnarvons, and was glad Ned didn't mention it, either.

"That means untying his hands," Kirby said slowly, and I could practically hear the rusty cogs in his brain struggling to turn. "I don't trust him."

"We'll keep the others separate," Royal explained. "If he acts up, they take the punishment." He glanced at Morales, then quickly looked away, and I wondered exactly what the little man had done. None of the Apostles seemed easy around him, except for Elmira, who didn't look scared of anybody, not even Cage.

"I could use a hot meal," Jolly agreed. "Getting tired of camp grub."

The small victory lifted my spirits, but I was careful not to show it.

They untied Ned. He quickly did an inventory and got a small fire going, his movements deft and efficient. I smelled sausages frying, but the "hot meal" apparently didn't extend to me and Lee, because, as promised, they led us off down the main tunnel. It had rough rock walls with thick support beams every few feet along the sides and roof. A peal of Elmira's girlish laughter chased us down the shaft. Sound carried in the mine and I could hear every word.

"What's your secret, Mr. White?"

"Shoot first and never miss!"

We reached a junction. Cheever pushed Lee one way, while Kirby steered me down a side tunnel, Jolly and his brother just behind. It delved deep into the mountain, with the black mouths of crossing tunnels occasionally making the flame of the lantern flicker and sway. At last we reached an alcove full of discarded junk. They retied my feet and pushed me to the ground. The air was stale and moist and bitter cold.

"Go have some supper," Jolly said, crouching down to look me in the eye. He set the lantern on the earthen floor.

The men left. He regarded me for a long moment, eyes glittering.

"Young Ruth," he said softly. "Do you remember our conversations?"

"I do."

"There's one thing I been wondering. You never told me who you killed."

I'd given up all hope of reaching the man, he was too far gone. Maybe it was the prospect of being left alone in the dark when he left, but I decided to tell him the story of how I earned my deputy star at the age of sixteen.

"It was the Dalton Brothers. Bill, Clancy and Emmett. They came through Lucky Boy and stole some horses from Flor Hernandez. She's my neighbor. Nice lady, going on seventy. No one wanted to give chase so I decided to do it myself."

"You shot 'em?"

"Not dead. Bill I hit in the rear." I smiled in the dark. "I did blow Clancy's hat right off his head. They thought a whole posse was shooting at them and turned tail, but Bill couldn't ride and that's how I caught him."

The reverend frowned. "Thought you was a murderer."

"No, I didn't kill him. But they hung him at Charter Oak after I brought him in, so I figure it's on my hands."

"Do you regret it?"

"I was enforcing the law. Bill Dalton knew the consequences."

He considered this. Then he reached for the lantern.

"Why do you hate the phantoms so much?" I asked. It was a question I'd mulled over before.

"They're devils," he muttered.

"I bet you got a personal reason though." The longer I kept him talking, the longer he'd stay away from Lee. I might be Judas Iscariot, but the antichrist would be worse in his eyes.

Jolly's hand rested on the wooden handle of the lamp, but

he didn't pick it up. A blankness entered his face. I'd seen that before, too. It scared me. He sat like that for a while, then looked over like it hadn't been ten minutes since I asked the question.

"I'm from a town called Refuge. Ever heard of it?"

"Just on the map," I said cautiously. "Thought it was a ghost town."

"It is now. Wasn't always."

He drifted off again.

"You were talking about Refuge," I prompted.

Even in the cold, I could smell him, a greasy stench like spoiled meat.

"I wasn't always a preacher," Jolly said, staring into the lantern. "In fact, I got off to a bit of a bad start in life. Fighting and drinking. I know that probably shocks you, but it's God's own truth."

"Heavens," I said. "Who'd imagine it?"

He shot me a sharp look. "When I was fifteen, I got into a brawl. Beat the man so bad he lost an eye. They locked me up in the calaboose. It was a hard winter and the flu came with some miners. I heard the sheriff talking. They kept on wiring Carnarvon City for medicine, but it never came."

I shifted a little to move off a rock digging into my back.

"One by one, my jailers perished. I begged 'em to let me out, but they wouldn't. Then the last one succumbed to fever. I hollered through the bars for three days. No one came and I realized flu had wiped the place out. All except for me."

It was a fairly horrible story. Had it been anyone else, I might have felt pity.

"Wasn't the hunger that maddened me, though it felt like rats gnawing at my innards. T'was the thirst. Then, on the fourth day, a phantom came. I pleaded with it to open the door. It laughed at me!"

He shook his head like he could still hear the sound. "I'd never gone to church once, but I started to pray then. Down on my knees. I swore I'd mend my ways if only the Lord saw fit to show me salvation. The next day, rescuers came from Winchester Junction. They set me free and burned the place on account of the plague."

I thought of his fascination with fire. "Did you have a family?"

"What's it matter now?" he replied angrily. "They're gone. That Carnarvon witch killed 'em."

I assumed he meant Calindra.

"From that day forth, I've been a humble servant of the Lord," Jolly declared in his familiar booming cadence. "Never imagined I'd be the chosen messiah, but I won't shirk my duty." He stood. "Now, you be a good girl until I come back, Ruth."

"You heading off somewhere?" I felt a spurt of hope.

He picked up the lantern. "Don't worry, Mr. Cage will keep a close eye while I'm gone."

A shadow filled the doorway.

"Hold up!" I cried, but Jolly had vanished.

13

Elmira Poole was not pleased by the turn of events.

She sat in a camp chair by the fire, which did little to dispel the terrible chill of the mine, trying to work out how exactly she'd ended up with a bunch of desperadoes all the way out by Tip Top. She recalled the aborted wedding but not what came after, except in vague terms. The Reverend Jolly had promised her riches and renown. There was something about an angel, and a task that had seemed very important at the time, though over the last day or so the urgency had faded, leaving her confused and irritated.

Elmira didn't think of herself as a criminal. Merely an entrepreneur, not much different from the prospectors. She'd find a profitable seam and work it until it ran dry. But she certainly wasn't some gunslinger—or killer for hire, like the Ghost. Listening to the men's whispers, she gathered that Juan Garcia Morales had murdered upwards of fifty people, from judges to errant spouses. If you wanted to get rid of somebody, he was the one you called on. An unassuming little man who wouldn't earn a second glance, he never left witnesses, which is why they called him the Ghost.

Even Chalkey seemed cautious when Morales was around,

though Elmira knew a consummate professional when she saw one and doubted the Ghost would trouble anyone if he wasn't being paid to do it.

She sighed, wiggling her toes in the white shoes. It was a puzzle what Jolly wanted with her. He seemed immune to her charms, which Elmira found suspect. The others, though . . . . Well, she had them wrapped around her little finger.

"Won't you fetch me a blanket, Mr. Loving?" she asked with a shiver.

"Certainly, Miss Poole!"

"You're a true gentleman," she declared.

He snatched his hat off and offered her a blanket that smelled of horse. "That's kind of you to say."

"I loved all my husbands dearly, you know." She settled the blanket on her knees and stared pensively into the flames. "If they hadn't been so rough with me . . . . Well, a court might not see it that way, but I call it self-defense. I always honored and obeyed, but some men just don't know how to treat the weaker sex—"

"Where's the grub?" Jolly demanded, striding into the chamber.

The fellow they had cooking slid some grits onto a plate. He added a few sausages and silently handed it over, avoiding the reverend's gaze.

"Ain't burned for once," Jolly said approvingly. "I do value Mr. Cage's talents, but cooking don't figure among 'em. Might be we'll keep you alive for a while more."

Elmira turned away as he started to shovel grits into his mouth. No wonder he was so smelly and unkempt. Half ended up in his beard!

"So what's the plan?" Royal asked.

"I'm heading out to Ace-in-the-Hole," Jolly said. "Moritz, you'll come along."

"Why me?" the hotelier asked in a plaintive tone. "My feet just thawed out."

"Because you're the worst shot. Won't be much use here. And I hear you know Billy Easter."

"We've crossed paths," LeBlanc muttered. "But he won't be alone, reverend. Billy's got a whole gang."

"All for the better," Jolly said with a slow smile.

"What's Ace-in-the-Hole?" Elmira wondered. "A saloon?"

"Only the most infamous hideout in the N.T.," Royal drawled. "Between Crouse Creek and the Dirty Devil River lies a wild stretch of land, crisscrossed with steep valleys and hidden draws." He glanced at his brother. "We've laid up there a time or two."

Kirby nodded. "In summer. T'was cold even then."

"I imagine you think you'll find Easter?" Royal said.

"Oh, he's there," Jolly replied, wiping his mouth with one ragged sleeve. "Once I bring him back, we can spread the Word south." His gaze turned inward. "To Sodom and Gomorrah. Bet you never burned a whole city, Mr. LeBlanc."

An eager light flickered in Moritz's flat eyes.

Elmira cast them a dubious glance. "I thought we was going to take it over, not burn it."

She didn't give a damn about the Carnarvons either way. She'd lived her whole life in the Northern Territory. In her mind, Carnarvon City must be like Hazardville, except ten times bigger. She'd heard tell of the glass tower that pierced the clouds—and seen it in that hazy vision outside the church—but clearly Jolly didn't mean to keep his promises.

Elmira felt the sting of betrayal. She decided it was time to leave, but she needed at least one of the men to shoot anyone who gave chase. Royal was the obvious choice. Or maybe Chalkey. He was hot-tempered, but at least he dressed nice. She hadn't made up her mind yet, though it must be Providence that the crazy preacher was leaving.

"Winnie's watching over the Beast," Jolly said. "Kirby, why don't you go relieve him for a spell so he can eat some supper?"

"What about the girl?" Royal asked.

"Mr. Cage is in charge of her." He glanced over at the middle-aged man huddled in one corner, knees pulled tight to his chest. "I've half a mind to drag you behind my horse, but I can't afford the delay." To the chamber at large: "If he so much as sneezes again, put a bullet in him."

The man had his muffler pulled up. His watery eyes looked bleak. Elmira didn't know who he was, but they all bullied him. He was no hard case; more like a fish hopelessly out of water. Since he was neither threatening nor useful, she didn't pay him any mind.

"You riding?" Elmira asked the reverend.

"Yep. Mr. Morales, would you saddle two mounts?"

The Ghost slipped silently from the chamber. Elmira smiled. He was leaving the cart, then. She watched Jolly and LeBlanc gather a few things and head for the main shaft. Kirby Knox dutifully shambled off to relieve Cheever.

"So, boys," Elmira said brightly. "What shall we do to pass the time?"

They stared at her dumbly.

"I know! Let's play truth or hogwash. I'll go first." She laid a finger to her lips. "Mr. White, have you ever been married?"

He grinned. "Not so far."

"I think he's telling the truth. What do you think, Mr. Loving?"

"Truth," Royal muttered.

"Yer both right," Chalkey said. "I've been chased, but no woman's caught me yet."

"My turn," Royal said. "How old are you, Miss Poole?"

She cast him a cool look. "Twenty."

"And you been married nine times?" He scratched his long, stringy hair. "Must have started awful young. I'm going to call hogwash."

Spots of color burned in her cheeks. "You saying I look

old, Mr. Loving?" Elmira made up her mind right then. Royal was just plain rude. "Mr. White?"

His light eyes met hers. "I think you just insulted the lady," Chalkey said in a low voice.

"We're playing a game," Royal replied reasonably. "By God, she ain't twenty. At least twenty-three, I'd reckon."

Elmira gave a small gasp. "Are you gonna let him impugn my honor?"

Royal's small eyes narrowed. "Let him? Ain't no man tells me what I can and can't say—"

Chalkey was on his feet in a flash. "Save part of your breath for breathin' or you won't be doin' it long."

They glared at each other. Elmira didn't want them both dead.

"Now listen, boys—" she began in a calmer tone.

Royal's hand twitched. She didn't see Chalkey draw, it was that fast. Two shots rang out, deafening in the small chamber. Royal sank to his knees.

"He's got a knife!" Elmira screeched.

The instant Chalkey had fired, the cook leapt over the campfire and grabbed a paring knife. He took off like a streak of lightning. Not for the exit, but deeper into the mine.

"We got to go!" Elmira exclaimed, jumping up to grab Chalkey's sleeve. He turned to her, then spun away as a bullet took him in the throat. Kirby Knox loomed in the tunnel.

"You shot my brother!" he howled.

Elmira backed away, then tripped and stumbled over something. The smell made her eyes water. Small teeth bared. She screamed again as it bit her on the arm.

"Help!" she cried.

Kirby ignored her pleas. He ran to his brother, cradling him in his big arms. Elmira scooted over to Chalkey, who was gurgling blood. She shoved him aside and picked up his gun, but the damned skunk had already vanished. The bite throbbed.

"You plumb fool!" she spat at Chalkey.

In the ether, a phantom burst into laughter. Merry tears ran down his face.

"And . . . that's a cut!" he whispered.

I LICKED my dry lips as Mr. Cage limped closer.

"You're not supposed to hurt me," I said, twisting against the ropes. "Jolly'll be mad."

Mr. Cage paused. He wore a dark coat buttoned up to the neck. His hands were empty save for a lantern, but this did not reassure me.

"Legion'll be mad, too," I added desperately.

Headless dolls couldn't play his game. But maybe we were past that point.

"Say something!" I exclaimed. "I know you can talk."

He set the lantern down. "I've been dreaming about you, Ruth. I always knew we'd be together again. My daddy said so." A cold finger brushed my cheek. "Don't worry, I won't rush things. Been waiting too long for that."

I jerked my face away. The rock dug into my back.

"Ain't you afraid of Hell?" I asked to gain time. "For what you've done."

"There is no Hell," Cage said softly. "Well, none except for the present moment."

But a shadow of pain had crossed his face when he bent to set the lantern down. I'd hurt him and he hadn't yet recovered from it. I readied to lash out with my feet when he stepped back out of reach.

"I think I'll just watch you for a while, Ruth. Wait for daddy to be well gone."

He leaned against the wall, empty green eyes fixed on me.

I would have preferred a dozen Jollys over one Mr. Cage,

but I knew he wanted me to quake in fear. That was part of his game. Prolong the agony of anticipation.

"If you don't believe any of it, why do you do what he tells you?"

"Because he gives me what I need. Feeds my hunger." The eerily calm tone was worse than anything.

I flexed numb fingers and discovered something interesting. The object digging into my back wasn't a rock at all. It was a piece of metal. Moving very slowly so he wouldn't notice, I leaned my weight back and sawed the rope against it.

"You stabbed me," Cage said at length. "With my own knife."

"Gave me no choice."

"I want to show you what it feels like. When I'm done, you'll be in little pieces, Ruth. Little bite-sized pieces." Cage opened his coat and drew out a hunting knife.

I could feel the ropes starting to give, but it would be minutes more before I was free. Whatever it was, the edge was dull. Terror bloomed in my chest.

"Help!" I yelled, knowing it would do no good.

My own voice echoed back. Cage limped over, unholy glee in his eyes.

Then two shots rang out from a distant part of the mine. The sound set off trickles of rock dust from the ceiling. It felt like the whole mine was shifting, settling, and I thought of those rotten age-black timbers hiding up the mountain. Cage paused and I feared he'd keep coming, but a third shot made his face tighten in disappointment. He seized the lantern and loped away.

The instant he was gone, I set hard to work on the rope. Chill sweat slicked my face as I threw every ounce of energy into getting loose. The minutes ticked past. I felt the last fibers giving way when a light burst into the alcove, blinding me.

"Hurry, hurry," Dean Rodriguez panted. "He's coming!"

"What happened?" I tore my wrists free and reached around for my salvation. It was the edge of a rusty, smashed-in tin lunchbox. Sawing would take too long, so I picked at the knots around my ankles. The dean helped, casting quick terrified glances at the tunnel.

"Chalkey shot Royal, and then Kirby shot Chalkey," he explained. "Ned got away."

"We have to find Lee!" I staggered to my feet.

"I'm so terribly sorry, Ruth. They found me when I fled Ruby Creek. Said they'd kill me—"

"Never mind that," I snapped. "You can atone later, after we all get out of here. You got a weapon?"

He shook his head. I swept my gaze across the junk in the alcove. Nails and screws, a broken handcart, bits of chain . . . my eye lit on an old pick handle. The head was gone, but it was better than nothing.

We dashed into the tunnel just as Cage came around the bend.

"Run, Ruth!" Dean Rodriguez cried. He shoved me in the opposite direction. I tried to grab his sleeve, but then Cage was on us. The dean's eyes went wide as the hunting knife flashed. It plunged deep into his chest. Cage tore it out and I swung the pick handle. He saw it coming and dodged. It caught him on the shoulder. He winced and I took off down the tunnel.

Into the pitch dark.

The echo of boots pursued me deeper into the mine. I took turnings at random, just running headlong and praying I wouldn't hit a dead end. Loose stone scattered under my feet. I tripped over an old rail for the handcarts, skinning my knuckles on the rock wall.

Cage had long legs. And a lantern. I knew I couldn't outrun him for long.

The light behind me came in brief, dizzying flashes. Then

I saw a square of pure darkness ahead. A tight horizontal shaft. I threw the pick handle ahead and dove in after it. The rock tore my pants, scraping both knees. I could sense that my feet were still sticking out and used my elbows to wiggle deeper, tasting the cold tang of rock and my own fear.

Boots pounded past in the tunnel behind. They slowed and returned to my hiding spot. Something brushed the soles of my boots and I frantically inched deeper.

"Come on out," Cage said.

I didn't answer.

"You can't hide from me, Ruth. Maybe a bullet will get you moving."

Cage must have been too big to fit, or his injury forbade wiggling into shafts, because I heard him leave. I guessed he planned to get a gun and shoot me.

I waited for a minute to make sure he was really gone, then tried to reverse course. I had a moment of pure panic when I couldn't budge. There was only one way out—forward. I slithered through that hole, inch by inch, breath too loud in my ears. It gradually widened so I could crawl. A single prayer ran through my mind. *Don't let this seam peter out. Don't let this seam peter out.*

Then a draft hit my face. I crawled faster and dropped out into another tunnel. I was careful not to stand too quick, I'd already bumped my head enough, but the ceiling was just high enough to walk crouched over.

I listened intently for a minute. The only sound was dripping water.

I had no idea where I was. Grit crunched between my teeth and I followed the sound until I found a trickle coming through the slick, mildewy rock. It tasted funny, but I was so thirsty I didn't care. I cupped my hands and drank. There had to be a way out, I told myself firmly, though the panic wasn't far away. It waited patiently in the dark.

Who knew how far into the mountain these tunnels went?

I kept thinking about Dean Rodriguez. He found his courage at the end and I hoped God would see fit to forgive him the rest.

I'm not sure how long I walked, back aching. Each time the tunnel joined others, I choose the one that smelled the freshest. When your sense of sight is taken away, the others hone to a keen edge. I heard every tiny creak of the timbers, felt every little whisper of air on my bloodied skin. The roof of the tunnel finally sloped so I could stand upright. I picked up the pace, trailing a hand along the wall, though I couldn't be sure I wasn't wandering deeper into the maze.

And that's how Cage caught me.

He'd hooded the lantern so it gave off only a glimmer. I came around a corner and threw an arm up as light suddenly flooded the tunnel. He pounced, grabbing me with strong hands and trying to twist the pick handle away. Without thinking, I brought a knee up and crashed it straight into the place where I'd stabbed him. He growled in pain, but he had the knife. I swung for his head with all my might. Cage ducked and the blow struck the support timber.

It must have been hanging by a thread. With a roar, the ceiling came down. Dust and rock choked the tunnel. Cage gave a single, startled cry and then he was buried. I staggered back, debris raining down on my own head, but the angels must have been watching over me because by some miracle the next timber groaned but held. The lantern had rolled to its side and I leapt to right it before the wavering flame went out.

I imagine I looked like a ghost, covered in rock powder from head to toe. The monster of my nightmares was finally dead, but there was no real victory in it. I just wished I'd stopped him sooner. I coughed and started off before my luck ran out when I heard a weak whisper.

"Help me."

Every muscle trembled with exhaustion as I looked back at the rock pile. It jammed the tunnel, edge to edge, save for a tiny crevice. The weight must have been excruciating. Deep in the recesses, I saw the gleam of a single emerald eye.

"You're beyond help," I said, turning my back and limping away.

14

I WANDERED through that mine for an endless stretch, heart racing every time the old timbers creaked and groaned. But now I had a lantern, and I realized that the miners had marked the passages with crude scratches on the walls. It was a number system that meant nothing to me, but I reasoned that the lower numbers might be closer to the entrance. This slim thread supported all my hopes.

I was wary of resting for fear the lantern would go out, but at last exhaustion overcame me. I dreamt of falling rock, only this time it was Doc begging for aid. I tore at the rubble, but his voice just kept getting farther and farther away. The loss was like a splinter lodged in my heart. I'd just begun stirring again when a hiss came from the darkness. My first thought was Jolly's snakes. I jumped up and raised the pick handle.

"That really you, Ruth?"

I dropped the weapon and threw myself into Ned Carver's arms, hugging him tight. It's impossible to describe how I felt encountering a dear friend under those circumstances, except to say that tears welled in my eyes, and in Ned's, too.

"I've been searching for you," he said when we finally parted. "I was so afraid . . . ."

He trailed off and I knew what he meant. "Cage is dead," I said. "What about the others?"

"Jolly took LeBlanc and the Ghost with him. Elmira, Cheever and Knox have Lee," he said grimly. "Up at the front."

"Well," I reflected, "that's an improvement over all of them."

We sat down and I hooded the lantern. Ned produced some stale biscuits from his coat pocket, relating the ill-fated game of truth or hogwash as we wolfed the food down. It was gone too soon. I licked the last crumbs from my fingers.

"Was the shots that saved me," I said. "They distracted Cage long enough for me to get free." Ned's face clouded as I told him what happened to Dean Rodriguez, and then my flight through the tunnels.

"Where are we?" I asked.

"Not too far from the exit," Ned said.

He'd spent the last day—and yes, it had been a whole day since the reverend left—lurking in the mine, waiting for a chance to free Lee and hoping I might turn up. He showed me the paring knife he'd stolen, but the men had guns. So far, he hadn't seen a way to get close.

"We need to make our move before Jolly comes back," I said. "How are they getting on with each other?"

"Elmira got bit by an animal. Skunk, I think. She never stops complaining about it. Knox . . . well, he beat Chalkey's corpse to a pulp. They dragged the bodies outside. Mostly he just sits there, drinking and staring into space. Cheever's the one to watch out for. The man's a weasel, but he's not stupid. I made some noise and tried to lure him into one of the tunnels, but he wasn't having it."

I thought that was fairly brave of Ned, considering Cheever's reputation.

"Let's go see," I said.

We crept through the passage until we reached a juncture. I saw the glow of a fire ahead. "Stay with the lantern," I said.

"Don't try anything without me, Ruth," he warned.

I raised a hand. "Scout's honor. I just want a peek."

I crawled up until I could see the three of them sitting around the campfire. Lee lay blindfolded and gagged against the wall. He was so still I feared the worst, but then he gave a faint snore.

"When are they coming back?" Elmira asked plaintively. "I need a doctor!"

"Can't be long now," Cheever answered.

"I don't feel right. Think I'm getting feverish."

"Wash it out with water."

"I already did that. There's ill humors in this place." She shivered. "Can't we just leave? Wait at the train?"

"Not until Jolly comes back," Cheever said flatly.

"But—"

"Hobble yer lip," Kirby Knox growled.

Elmira cast him a venomous look. "That's no way to talk to a lady!"

"Don't see any ladies here," Knox replied. "Just a jumped-up filly who don't know her place."

Elmira stamped a foot and pouted. Kirby ignored her. Cheever heaved a windy sigh. He had his gun out, propped over one knee. Given enough time, they might do each other in, but we couldn't wait. I crept back to the juncture, hatching a wild scheme involving the handcarts. Maybe we could send one hurtling down the tracks and pelt them with rocks—

The hooded lantern sat where I'd left it. But Ned was gone. Barely a minute or two had passed since I left him.

"Ned?" I said softly.

There was no answer.

The hair on my neck lifted as a phantom stepped through the rock wall.

It had red hair and narrow, mean features. Multifaceted

black insect eyes caught the dim light, reflecting it back. A tittering sound came from between thin lips.

I retreated as two more phantoms came out of the solid rock, their bodies naked and slug-pale. The darkness stirred in the passage behind them and I saw the Ghost. He had Ned.

Guess he hadn't gone with Jolly, after all.

I raised my hands high. Morales made a tiny gesture with his chin and I walked back to the campsite, the phantoms drifting along a foot above the ground to either side of me.

Elmira's eyes went comically wide. Her rosebud mouth opened like a beached fish.

Cheever jumped to his feet with a slow grin. "All the lost dogies accounted for then," he said with satisfaction.

At that moment, Jolly returned with Moritz LeBlanc and a dozen rough-looking men.

"Who killed Chalkey and Royal?" he demanded. "Practically tripped over the damn bodies coming in."

"They done each other in," Cheever replied matter-of-factly. "Over that one."

He pointed to Elmira. She looked ready to launch into an indignant rebuttal, but Jolly cut her off with a slash of his hand.

"Where's my boy?" he demanded, eyes searching the chamber.

Everyone looked at me.

"Mr. Morales," Jolly said.

The Ghost pressed his pistol to Ned's head. He wore an expression of indifference that made my skin crawl. The man didn't care whether he pulled the trigger or not.

"Let's try again," Jolly said, voice low. "Where's my son?"

"Dead in a rockfall," I said quickly. "He was chasing me and one of the tunnels came down on his head."

A slow flush crept up Jolly's cheeks. "Liar! Legion would never let that happen. He promised us vengeance."

But I saw the doubt in his eyes. He'd left me alone with

Cage on purpose. It was supposed to be his boy's big moment. If Cage was missing, it meant one thing. There'd been payback, all right—just not Mr. Cage's.

"Ask your haints if you don't believe me," I said.

He glared at me, then growled at the phantoms in their own tongue. Insect eyes shone as they answered in a series of barks and hisses. Jolly's face darkened further. A muscle twitched on one eyelid. I knew then that he'd kill me no matter what. Might as well tell the truth.

I snorted. "You're dumber than a box of rocks. There's no angel. Legion's name is Roger. He's been duping you this whole time. Just a Class X phantom using you for his own amusement."

Jolly stared at me. "Who told you that?"

"Doc. They know each other—"

In an instant, he had me by the hair and was dragging me back down the tunnel. A few of his new recruits followed with torches. I thought he'd make me show him Cage's tomb, but he stopped at a lightless shaft, about a foot square. This one was vertical, like a well. He shoved me to the ground and reached into his coat, drawing out the flintlock. I leapt at him, but strong hands pinned my arms.

"Ruth?" A hoarse, broken whisper.

"Doc!" I shouted. "I'm here! Don't worry—"

Jolly dropped the Collier into the hole.

It fell for an eternity. At last, I heard a tiny splash.

"I oughta throw you in after him, but dying in a fall's too good for you," Jolly panted. "So's a bullet. You buried my son, so I'll bury you with him."

They hauled me back to the campsite, cursing and struggling, and threw me to the ground next to Ned.

"Move out!" Jolly roared. "Tie 'em up first."

We were trussed and left to watch while they packed up anything worth taking. Jolly squatted down next to me. "Here's something to think about, Judas," he spat. "Lucky

Boy'll burn, along with every soul in that Godforsaken town. We'll head there directly."

"Why are you following him?" I shouted at the men. "Can't you see he's crazy?"

No one paid me any mind. None except for one of the cowboys, a slim black man with the bowed legs of a trail rider. Billy Easter. He cast me a bleak look. I think he would have stepped in if all the rest weren't under Jolly's spell, but he glanced at the three haints and I guess he wasn't willing to die for us, because he turned his back and walked out.

Jolly picked up his valise. Winnie Cheever grabbed Lee and shoved him toward the exit. I expected they'd board it up again, but the thin daylight coming down the tunnel remained.

"Why'd they leave us alive?" Ned wondered. He seemed astonished.

The answer came an instant later. A *whumph* and several loud *bangs*, followed by a deep, sustained rumbling like a freight train bearing down. The square of light dimmed, then vanished.

"What the hell was that?" Ned exclaimed. "Thunder?"

"Hush!" I hissed. "Not so loud. Let's try to get free."

We wiggled so we were back to back, and set to work untying the knots. It took a while, but they'd done a fairly sloppy job. We hurried down the main passage. It was blocked with snow.

"The haints set off an avalanche," I whispered. "We need to be real quiet."

Ned took my hand. "Lantern," he said softly.

We crept back until we found the one I'd left with him. I opened the hood and we had light.

"Doc," I said, drawing Ned further down the tunnel.

We found the shaft. I leaned over it and called his name a dozen times, straining to hear. My voice echoed back at me. There was no answer.

"Ruth—" Ned said.

"We'll find a rope." My hands were shaking. "You can lower me down."

"Even if there was one long enough, I'm not dropping you into that shaft," Ned said firmly. "It's too deep. You might get stuck."

"I can't just leave him down there!"

A strong arm folded around my shoulders. "We'll find your haint," Ned said in that calm, steady way he had. "But we have to dig our way out first."

I broke down and wept. For Doc, for Lee, for poor pathetic Dean Rodriguez. I needed to let it all out or I might go crazy. Ned seemed to understand, for he just sat with me until I calmed down a little.

"It's just that Doc and I have been together since I was a kid." I wiped my face. "He's family."

"I know."

"And he's sick. What are we gonna do, Ned?"

"Only thing we can," he replied, pulling me to my feet.

They hadn't left us any food or water, but Ned found a couple of rusty picks and we started digging at the snow.

"I can't stop thinking about Lee," he confessed in a heavy voice. "Why's Jolly so fixated on him? He's just a regular fellow."

Despite everything, that made me smile. Lee had finally found a real friend—and maybe something more. Ned was protective of him, and though I didn't regard Lee as *regular* in any way, I wasn't about to argue the point.

"It's not Jolly. It's the Class X phantom he works for. Who knows? Maybe he's jealous because Lee's a savant, too."

"You could be right," Ned said thoughtfully. "The only others were Calindra Carnarvon and Pedro Braga. Calindra's dead and Braga's empire is in ruins. Makes me pretty worried about Lee."

"Roger's got some plan for him or he'd already be dead," I said. "But Lee's smart. If he gets a single chance, he'll take it."

"I should have done something sooner."

"Like what? They had guns. You had a paring knife."

"I dunno. Something."

"It's not over yet," I said, swinging the pick. "Not as long as we're still breathing."

"There might be a hundred feet of snow on top of us," Ned said glumly. "And even if we do get out, we're in the middle of nowhere. I expect Jolly took the train."

"I can't let him get to Lucky Boy," I said, gritting my teeth. "I just can't."

We dug in silence for a bit. My mind kept chewing over the horrible dream I'd had about the schoolhouse. The dead waiting patiently in the cold and dark. I felt a chill come over me. It was palpable, like icy fingers on my neck.

I paused. "Ned, where'd you find the picks?"

"Over in that tunnel." He gestured to the main passage.

The unsettled feeling grew stronger. I felt sure they hadn't been there before.

And then it came to me. We were being watched.

"Maybe we could try calling to that phantom girl," I suggested. "The one who helped us get out of Jackpot."

Ned brightened. "Hey, that's a good idea!"

"I don't speak any tongues, but she knows some English." I took a deep breath. "Zippo?" I hissed. "You there?"

Silence.

"Please, if you can hear me, we're desperate. Show yourself."

A few minutes passed. I had the glimmer of an idea, but I couldn't tell Ned. Whoever was watching was also listening. I'd just have to hope he played along when the time came.

"She ain't coming," Ned said at last. He patted my shoulder. "Well, it was worth a try."

He hefted his pick to swing it at the wall of snow. Then I

heard footsteps coming down the tunnel. My heart started to race. Ned frowned in confusion.

"That's not a haint," he said slowly. "That's—"

"Howdy, pardners!" He mimed shooting us with his index fingers. "Quite a pickle you're in."

Roger wore the body of Henry Chance, a young man with green eyes and a pleasant face, but instead of the suit I remembered from Aguadulce, he was dressed like a cowboy with a big white hat and jingling spurs on his boots.

"Sorry about Doc," he said, mouth turning down. "That's a derned shame."

I lunged and he vanished, reappearing an instant later across the chamber. Ned's jaw dropped. He'd never seen a phantom in the flesh that didn't look like a creepy naked kid.

"Now, Ruth," Roger said, clucking his tongue. "I know you're mad enough to swallow a horn-toad backwards, but I'm not here to play games." The Northern drawl was even more perfect than Lee's.

"Sure you are," I retorted. "And you could bring him back."

"I *could*," he said slowly. "But he can't help you, Ruth. See, I thought it'd be fitting for Doc to share the fate of his namesake, Mr. Holliday. Consumption ain't pretty at the end. Better you don't witness it."

I'd suspected for a while, but none of it made sense.

"So that's the trick you pulled? Consumption?"

Roger looked pleased with himself.

"But he's not even human!"

"You have no idea what I can do, Ruth. Not the slightest inkling."

"Where's Zippo?"

"Indisposed." Roger yawned. "Well, it's been dandy seeing you again, but I got work to do. The Apocalypse ain't gonna run itself. Jolly's made a start, but the main attraction's in

Carnarvon City." He winked. "Castles made of sand and all that." He tipped his hat. "Happy trails!"

"Wait!" I cried.

Roger arched a thin brow.

"I have one question."

"Do you now?" He winked. "Make it quick, Ruth. Clock's a ticking."

"I'll admit, it's been fun," I said. "But this whole storyline is feeling a tad weak to me."

Roger frowned. "How so?"

"Well, I got my big duel with Mr. Cage," I said slowly. "That wrapped up nicely. But he's just a side character. The way I see it, this picture is still lacking a proper emotional climax."

He tilted his head.

I hated talking about my hometown this way, but it was the only thing that might reach him. I held my hands wide, framing a marquee.

"Here's what I'm thinking. Showdown at Lucky Boy! What you need is someone to rally the townsfolk before the bad guys get there. Otherwise it's just . . . ." I seized on a phrase Doc had taught me. "A foregone conclusion. No audience wants to watch *that*."

"Showdown at Lucky Boy," Roger repeated softly, staring into space.

"You could leave us to die, but that's awful predictable. A plot twist might be in order, is all I'm saying."

"Like *Fastest Guns in the North*," Ned added, and I wanted to kiss him. "When they take on the corrupt sheriff who's been working for the gang of greedy prospectors. By God, I was gripping my seat when Burnt Valley made its last stand!"

Roger studied me for a long moment. "That's an interesting proposal. It might be the ticket." I didn't care for his smile. "But the good reverend has a head start. There's only one way to get you there in time."

I swallowed. "Through the ether?"

"Naw." He chuckled. "You wouldn't survive. But I could make an interdimensional doorway. Like a little fold in space. "His eyes glittered. "They're unstable, though."

Ned and I exchanged a look.

"How unstable?" Ned asked.

Roger shrugged. "Never made one before, but it's theoretically possible. Let's say fifty-fifty odds you come out with your insides on the inside and your outsides on the outside." He burst into hilarious laughter. Ned's eyes narrowed. His hand tightened around the pick handle.

"Can I talk to Doc?" I asked. "One last time?"

Roger hesitated.

"You know, the goodbye scene?" I ventured. "Like in . . . ." I cast a desperate look at Ned.

"*Prairie Rose*," he said quickly, coming to my rescue.

Roger was silent. He reached up and wiped a tear from his eye. "Oh boy," he said hoarsely. "I remember that one. When they rode right over the cliff rather than get captured."

In truth, I think he only agreed to rub salt in the wounds. He tossed something into my lap. It was the cracked shaving mirror.

"You got five minutes," he said, drawing a silver pistol and spinning it around one finger.

I moved away, not that it provided any privacy. A thin, deathly white face appeared in the mirror. He had bruised circles under his eyes.

"Don't get all sentimental," Doc warned. "I can't abide it."

I couldn't speak for a minute, my throat was too tight.

"Are you hurting?" I finally asked.

"No, I enjoy sitting at the bottom of a mineshaft in this frozen hellscape—" He broke into a wracking cough.

"Four minutes!" Roger called over merrily.

I pulled myself together. "Is what he's saying even possible?" I whispered.

Doc wiped his mouth. The blood on his sleeve cut me to the quick. "It might be. What choice do you have?"

"I don't want to leave you," I said miserably.

He gave another wet rattle. "I'm dying anyway."

"How can that be?" I exclaimed. "You're a whole different species, ain't you?"

"Just go, Ruth." His voice was low and urgent. "Kill those scoundrels."

"I'm coming back for you when it's over, I swear it."

"I know you will." A sad smile touched his lips. "We're friends, aren't we?"

"Yeah." I touched the mirror. "We're friends, Doc."

"Egads, don't start blubbering. Remember what I told you on the way to Charter Oak. And don't trust—"

He vanished. I hugged the mirror to my chest.

"Time's up!" Roger said. "Here's something to sweeten the deal. If you can beat the reverend and his apostles, I'll spare the town. Give you a happy ending. I think that's more than fair."

I slowly turned to him. It was impossible to conceal the hatred I felt at that moment.

"But once I open the doorway, this whole mine'll collapse on itself. Warped geometry ain't for the faint of heart, Ruth." He eyed the ceiling. "It's about to go anyway. In another hour or so, the weight of the snow will crack the supports."

As if on cue, I heard a terrifying groan deep in the bowels of the mine.

"You left the picks," I said.

He shrugged. The gun spun faster and faster around his finger until it was a blur. "It's only sporting to give you a chance. Dig fast enough and you might make it out." Roger grinned. "But you won't save your town."

I turned to Ned. "It's your choice. I won't abandon you here if you don't like Roger's odds. They're pretty poor."

Relief flooded me when he gave a tight nod. "I saw what Jolly did in Lovelock," he said quietly. "Ain't gonna stand by while he does the same to Lucky Boy."

"Well said, Mr. Carver!" Roger exclaimed. "Let's get this rodeo started."

"Only if you call off those three phantoms," I said, pressing our advantage. "We got zero chance if they're around."

"My trusty assistants?" He winked. "Suppose I could do that. They're more use in the city anyway. Got a surprise in store."

Dread lodged in my gut. "Like Aguadulce, you mean?"

He made a little-boy sorry face. "I know what you're thinking. That prank was over the top." He held his fingers an inch apart. "Just a wee bit. But don't worry, Ruth, I would never repeat myself. Got something else in mind." He chuckled. "Can't wait to see Ava's face when it all comes crashing down."

"What are you planning?" I demanded.

"Come on, I already told you it was a surprise. So, what's it gonna be, Ruth?"

I stared down the tunnel. I'd dig Doc out if it took me the rest of my life, but I couldn't leave my dad and everyone else at Jolly's mercy. And we'd be no use dead—assuming Roger wasn't about to tear our flimsy bodies apart in his interdimensional doorway.

"Do it," I snarled.

Roger holstered his gun. "I might be the director, but you're the star, Ruth." The corners of his mouth turned up in a smile, but his eyes were flat and cold. "I expect the performance of a lifetime."

"Oh, you'll get it," I vowed through gritted teeth. "Just wait."

Roger strode to the rock wall. He reached through and pulled it apart like taffy. The lines of his face grew strained. The form of Henry Chance flickered. I saw flashes of something else. Something with a hundred flailing tentacles. Fear rooted my feet to the spot as daylight poured through the widening crack.

"Quick!" Roger snapped. His voice sounded thick and strange. "I can't hold it long!"

We joined hands and ran forward. I pushed Ned through first, afraid it might collapse. Then I uttered a wordless prayer and stepped into the rift.

For a moment that seemed to last an eternity, I saw the mine from a dozen different angles at the same time. Or maybe I was just seeing *through* it. I saw that mountain come down, imploding in a landslide that seemed to cover the whole world. A sharp pain shot through my eyes. I squeezed them shut and fell to my knees, retching.

My palms closed around tufts of dead grass. A cool wind lifted my hair. I was trembling all over. Might have been drooling, too.

"Ned?" I whispered.

A metallic CHUH-CHUNK broke the silence. I lifted my head and opened one eye.

And found myself staring straight down the double barrels of a Remington shotgun.

15

"Ruth Cortez? That you?"

A white-haired lady with more wrinkles than Methuselah squinted down at me.

"Miss White!" I gasped.

Gnarled brown hands lowered the shotgun. "Where on earth did you come from?" she demanded. "I was feeding the pigs when I heard a bang and you fell out of the damn sky!"

"Never mind that." I climbed shakily to my feet. "I was with a friend. You seen him?"

Miss White slowly shook her head. "Been strange goings-on around here since you left, Ruth," she muttered.

I spun in a circle, shading my eyes against the setting sun. Miss White's place was about five miles outside of town. She kept to herself except for every third Saturday, when she walked into the general store and bought a gallon of whiskey. People were always amazed that an old woman survived out here on her own, but they didn't know Miss White—mainly because she never let them. My mother and I were the only folks she tolerated on her property. I felt a twinge of guilt. After my mom left, I'd stopped coming out regular to visit.

There was an apple orchard off to my left and a vegetable garden to my right. Between sat a two-story clapboard house with a front porch and a single rocker. The paint was peeling, but it was all neat as a pin.

"Where you goin'?" she demanded, as I took off running.

"To find Ned!" I hollered over my shoulder.

I made a circle of the house. Except for a couple of cows grazing, there wasn't a living soul. I checked the barn and the pigsty, but Ned wasn't anywhere.

"Settle down and come on inside," Miss White said sternly. "I won't have you trampling all over my yard."

I felt sick. "It's my fault," I muttered. "I pushed him through first."

She didn't ask me anything more until I was perched on a stool in her kitchen. Stacks of yellowing newspaper bound with twine sat against one wall, not a single one with a date inside the last twenty years. Miss White went to a cupboard and took out a bottle of Thistledew. She wore a man's plaid shirt rolled up to the elbows and her arms had the wiry strength of a person who works outdoors in all kinds of weather.

"Thank you, but I don't drink spirits," I said.

Miss White poured some and pushed the glass at me. I sighed and took a sip, then coughed. It tasted awful, but it did calm my nerves some. She studied me over the rim of her glass for a long moment.

"Pushed him through *what*?" she said.

"Interdimensional portal," I muttered, swirling the Thistledew so I didn't have to meet her penetrating gaze.

"Ah."

I wasn't sure what to make of that *ah*. She must think I'd gone crazy.

Miss White sucked the stubs of her teeth. "So the invasion's started," she declared. "By God, I knew it!"

"Invasion?"

She lowered her voice to a whisper. "The *alien* invasion."

"Who told you that?"

"No one. I always knew the haints weren't ghosts. That's superstitious nonsense. " Her black eyes gleamed. "Your dad didn't deny it."

"You talked to my dad?"

"He came out here a few days ago." She scowled. "He's been worried sick about you."

"I told Marshal Hardin to send a telegram," I mumbled.

Miss White snorted. "Gael showed it to me. It said next to nothing." She looked me over. "Where's Doc?"

"Had to leave him behind."

My face crumpled and she patted my hand. "Don't worry, I know Doc's one of the good ones. Gael will sort it all out."

"Can you take me home? We'll get a search party looking for Ned."

She eyed me speculatively. "He your sweetheart?"

I shook my head. "Just a friend. But a dear one." I knitted my hands together. "We got no time, Miss White. No time at all."

She gave a brief nod. "You're a steady woman, Ruth. One of the few around here with a lick of sense. I believe you." She rose and took a broad-brimmed straw hat from a peg, settling it over her two long silver braids. "Gael said there'd be trouble. Tried to get me to come stay with him, but I've slept in my own bed every night for the last fifty-three years and I ain't stopping now."

"Well, you might want to reconsider," I said. "There's some bad men coming after me."

She paused with one hand on the doorknob. "How bad?"

I held her steady gaze. "Real bad, Miss White."

"Hmmph. Better get going then."

In short order, we'd put the cows in the barn and

harnessed one of the horses to a buckboard wagon. Miss White clambered up to the driver's seat and and we set off down the track for Lucky Boy, her big Colt Peacemaker on the bench between us. Night fell over the prairie. The moon was just a pale sliver in that great dark expanse, for which I felt grateful. I didn't want anyone to see me just yet.

"Where you been for the last three weeks, Ruth?" she asked, the reins loose in her hands.

Where hadn't I been? It was hard to believe that less than a month had passed since the day Hardin rolled into town with Merriweather trussed up in the caboose.

"It's a story, Miss White," I said wearily. "Can you wait until I get home so I don't have to tell it twice? And it would be better if no one knows I'm here just yet."

She grunted. "I'll take the long way around. Folks in this town are too nosy by half."

My pulse quickened when I saw my house. Smoke drifted from the chimney. I leapt from the wagon before it stopped and ran up to the front door. I heard voices inside. My dad and—

"Ned!" I cried, rushing inside.

He jumped to his feet, hat in his hands. I hurtled into him, squeezing him tight, then embraced my father. He smelled like soap and coffee and him. I got a good poke from the sharpened pencil he always carried in his shirt pocket, but it was a long time before I managed to let go.

"Mijita," he murmured, cupping my cheek with a calloused hand. Tears stood in his brown eyes. "We thought we'd lost you."

It seems Ned had fallen out of the rift inside the chicken coop. I smiled at the little pile of feathers on the carpet. One or two were still stuck in his curly hair.

"You need to change that coat," I said, wrinkling my nose.

He grinned. "We made it, Ruth. Both of us."

Miss White came inside, rubbing her hands briskly. "Found your friend, I see," she said.

"Miss White, this is Mr. Ned Carver," I said.

"Nice to meet you, ma'am." He gave a little bob of his head that seemed to please her.

"I like a boy with manners," she said. "You're a dying breed."

We settled around the wood stove in the parlor. My dad brewed more coffee and brought out a tin of Mrs. Hernandez's sugar cookies. I watched him moving around the kitchen with a new tenderness. His black hair needed a trim and he hadn't shaved in a few days. We used to give each other haircuts in the yard once a month. He'd haul out a kitchen chair and we'd take turns sitting under a sheet. My dad never swept up the cuttings because he said the birds could use it to line their nests.

I stretched my feet to the fire. My big tomcat wandered in and gave my leg a rub of greeting, then curled up in his favorite spot on the rag rug. I leaned down to scratch his cheek. He purred in contentment, rolling over to tempt me with his belly, but I knew that cat's tricks. Jimmy Jack liked to be petted, but he had what my dad called the *right* side and the *bite* side. You'd better know which was which if you wanted to keep all your digits.

"This is a nice house, Ruth," Ned said. "Real cozy. Did you paint that?"

He was looking at a watercolor of the creek with the schoolhouse in the foreground. I'd always loved that picture. It was because of the sky. Half was dark and half was light, so you couldn't tell if the storm was coming or going.

"No," I said. "My mom did."

I looked around our little parlor, hardly believing I was home. It felt like a dream, and I was half-scared I'd wake up in that cold mine again. I sipped the hot coffee, trying to untangle my muddled thoughts. I'd barely eaten or slept in days. Throw in travel through a space fold and I wasn't at my finest. But the story had to be told tonight.

Clock's a ticking, as Roger said.

"I'm not sure where to start," I said, when my dad returned and settled into a chair.

He smiled gently. "How about at the beginning?"

Not even Ned knew all of it. He listened as I told them about the twister that derailed us on the prairie, how I tracked Lee to Charter Oak and met him on the train. The Class X that came and shook the trestle, how Lee jumped into the river and I made my way to Carnarvon Tower, where Doc went crazy when they tried to take my gun away. When I got to the part about finding Rose at the circus, my dad's eyes widened in surprise.

"You saw her?"

I nodded. "She's doing good. She misses you."

My mom had left Lucky Boy three years before. She just wasn't cut out for it. But I think she still loved him, even though she hadn't said it outright.

He cleared his throat. "Miss her, too."

I smiled. "She sold Doc to some gypsies, but he got away." I took a sip of coffee. "Doc saved my life when the Reverend Jolly kidnapped me and Mr. Beach."

"Professor Abel Beach?" my father exclaimed. And then: "*Kidnapped*?"

I'd gotten ahead of myself. "He was Lee's favorite teacher. I thought Lee might go see him before he left town. And I was right."

I told them the rest. How Ava Carnarvon betrayed us to Jolly and Cage. My escape from the underground bunker, with Lee as my prisoner. His dashing rescue from the top of Carnarvon Tower by Mr. Beach in the zeppelin.

"You never told me you taught at the Academy," I said evenly. "How come?"

My dad stared into the fire. "I always meant to, but somehow I never got around to it."

It was a pretty weak excuse. I felt a spark of anger. "You knew what the phantoms really were. All this time!"

He shot me a quick, embarrassed look. "Calindra thought I was crazy when I told her my theory about higher dimensions. So did my colleagues. They treated me like a joke. I suppose I was afraid you wouldn't believe me, either."

"I would have," I said stoutly. "You're the smartest person I know."

He looked ready to cry. "I'm sorry, Ruth. Sorry for all of it."

"Wasn't your fault. They should have listened to you when they had the chance."

"Can't see it would have made much of a difference," Miss White remarked. She'd commandeered the best armchair and sat with her ankles crossed and the Peacemaker in her lap. If Miss White believed in anything, it was being prepared. "Whatever the damn creatures are, they're near unstoppable. Finish the tale, Ruth."

I launched into our ill-fated pursuit of Lee to Aguadulce and all that happened in that city. My throat was hoarse by the time I got to the Northern Territory, so Ned took over, telling the rest while I added bits and pieces. He'd already explained some of it after my dad found him in the chicken coop.

"So Jolly's on his way here with a gang of bloodthirsty outlaws," Ned finished. "Aims to burn the town, just like he did in Lovelock and Hazardville. You folks need to leave right away."

"Leave?" Miss White echoed, her eyes narrowing. "I ain't goin' nowhere."

Ned lifted a finger to his lips. He pointed to the window. *Saw something*, he mouthed at me.

I mimed for them to keep talking and crept down the hall

to the back screen door. I eased it open, stopping at the creaky part, and stepped into the yard. The crickets were going full force, but the night was otherwise silent. I tiptoed around the side of the house, steering clear of the dried leaves. A dark figure hunched just below the sill. I pounced, hand clamping around a worn flannel collar.

"Charlie Bowdre!" I hissed. "What are you doing eavesdropping?"

He jumped a mile. "Wasn't—"

"Don't you dare deny it," I muttered, hauling him to the front door and giving him a little push inside. Charlie yanked his hat off. "Mr. Cortez," he said with a weak smile. "Miss White. I was riding past when I spotted your cart out back. Just making sure everything's okay."

"Poking your nose into other people's business is more like it," she said tartly. "Sit down, Charlie Bowdre. You're a part of it now, God help us."

He glanced at me. The corner of his mouth twitched. "Glad you're back, Ruth."

I couldn't help but smile. Charlie had big shoulders and bright yellow hair like Mr. Cage, but any resemblance ended there. His face was lively and open, with crinkles at the edges of his blue eyes that hinted at mischief.

"Me, too," I said. "You big sneaking lug."

Charlie dragged a chair in from the kitchen. Our house wasn't big to begin with and it felt awful small with the five of us crowded around the stove, but I was happier than I'd been in a long time.

"How much did you hear?" I asked.

He studied his boots. "Uh, all of it?"

"Why didn't you just come in?" I asked in exasperation.

"Too busy listenin'." He looked at me with grudging admiration. "Did you really do all that?"

"More like it happened to me," I grumbled. "The main thing is what we do now."

"How soon will these ruffians get here?" Miss White asked.

"I don't know. They're on a train."

"Well, let's work it out," my dad said. "Ruth, would you fetch me a scrap of paper?"

I went to his desk and found what he asked, eying the leather-bound journals and notepads with mathematical equations in a tiny, precise hand. The answers had been sitting right here all my life and I'd never thought to read them. Though in fairness, I doubt I could make sense of most of it.

"How long were you at the mine before Roger came?" Gael asked.

I looked at Ned. "Couple of hours," he said. I nodded. That sounded right.

"I wish we had a railway timetable," my dad said.

"Don't need one," Ned said. "I know all the lines by heart."

He sketched out a quick map, including the scale of miles.

"Excellent, Mr. Carver!" Gael studied the drawing. "So if we assume the portal was instantaneous and the train is traveling at sixty miles an hour, that would put him somewhere near Hatchet by now."

"It'll be going slower," Ned said. "There's snow on the tracks. They'll have to plow it off as they go. More like thirty."

My father jotted down some swift calculations. The sound of his pencil scratching away, accompanied by the occasional pop of a pine knot in the stove, brought me back to all the quiet evenings we'd spent together, each immersed in our own activity but together at the same time. Sometimes I'd read, and sometimes I'd clean and oil my gun because Doc was a terrible fuss about maintaining the flintlock in good condition. The thought of him down in that dark shaft, coughing blood, made me feel like a beast for sitting here all comfy and warm.

"The southern junction intersects at Ruby Creek." My dad ran a finger along Ned's map. "That's more than a thousand miles. Say another eight hundred to Lucky Boy. I think we have at least one full day before he arrives. Maybe two if we're lucky."

"Better say one," I put in. "Which ain't much time at all."

"We gotta tell my dad," Charlie said. He shot me a sidelong glance. "There's a warrant for you, Ruth."

Miss White sniffed. "If Sam Bowdre thinks he's taking her into custody, he can come through me and my Colt."

"I'll go talk to him," Gael said, rising to his feet. "Charlie, you come along." He turned to me and Ned. "You two get some sleep."

"Sleep?" I protested, though I could hardly hold my eyes open at this point.

"Yes, sleep," my dad said sternly. "You're burned down to the wick, both of you. Jolly's not coming tonight. And you need to be fresh tomorrow if we have any hope of stopping this."

"But—"

"No buts, mijita. Ned, I'll show you to the spare room." He grinned. "And get you some clean clothes."

"I'll keep watch," Miss White declared. "What do you say, Jimmy Jack?" The cat eyed her with disdain. Miss White cackled. "He reminds me of my third husband. Fat and lazy, but warm company on a cold winter's night."

With very little encouragement, I stumbled up to my bedroom on the second floor. Everything was as I'd left it. A shelf of dime novels. Mama's old hairbrush on my chipped blue and white dresser. A soft flannel nightie folded under the pillow that I was too tired to put on, though I managed to unbuckle Hardin's holster. When I toppled into bed, I felt something poking my chest. The cracked shaving mirror. I must have shoved it into an inside pocket. I stared at it for a minute, tears blurring my eyes.

"Hang tight, Doc," I whispered, pulling the covers up.

I suppose I should have been scared, knowing all I did, but

I could hear Miss White humming to herself downstairs and the soft voices of Ned and my dad as he got settled in the room next door. There was more good in the world than bad. Not even Roger could kill it all.

"This picture," I murmured as my eyes shut, "is gonna have a happy ending."

And I knew it to be true.

16

THE ROOSTER WOKE me at dawn. Ned was still sleeping, but my dad was up, drinking coffee in the kitchen. He'd already hauled water from the well and heated it for a bath. I was too dirty to stand myself another minute so I went straight to the washtub and scrubbed off days' worth of grime. My knees and elbows were banged up from crawling around the mine, but the scrapes were already healing over. I dressed in a clean shirt and dungarees, combed my hair and brushed my teeth.

Whatever the day brought, at least I felt human again.

"Where's Miss White?" I asked, helping myself to scrambled eggs.

"Went home. Said she had to tend to her cows." Gael sighed. "I guess we all need to evacuate. It won't be easy to talk her into it. Or the rest of them, either. Folks in this town are stubborn."

"We'll talk them around." I poured some coffee and met his gaze. "But I'm staying, dad."

"What?"

"I have to. I promised Roger a showdown. If he doesn't get it, he'll hunt us down."

His jaw tightened. "How many men are with this reverend?"

"At least a dozen."

"Plus phantoms? And you don't have Doc? This is crazy, Ruth."

"I'm not denying it." I blew on the coffee. "But Roger made the rules. And I'm not letting Lucky Boy burn."

"If you stay, I'm staying with you."

I knew I wouldn't talk him out of it. "That's three of us, then. Ned'll stay, too. Now, tell me what's been going on. Any marshals in town?"

"There were two," my dad said slowly. "They left yesterday morning. Got a telegram calling them back to the city."

"They say why?"

He shook his head. "They hardly spoke to me except to search the house. Mr. Berry put them up on pallets in the spare room over the feed store. They paid him for room and board, but I think they were glad to go. There's no stove in that place."

"Darn," I muttered. Then it hit me. "So the telegraph is working?"

My dad nodded. "It was yesterday."

I pushed my plate back. "I'm sending a message."

He arched a brow. "To whom?"

"Sebastian Hardin. We need all the help we can get."

"Won't he arrest you?"

I gave a mirthless laugh. "That's the least of our problems. We need him, dad. Whatever he thinks of me, he won't let Jolly hurt anyone."

We turned at a knock on the door. My dad was standing at the sink. He inched the curtain aside and looked through the window.

"It's Bowdre. He wanted to take you into custody last

night," Gael said heavily. "I talked him out of it. Promised you wouldn't leave town."

"Leave town?" I snorted. "All I've wanted to do since the day I left is get home."

"I'll tell him to come back later," my dad said, looking grim.

"No. Better we settle this now." I rose and opened the door, coffee in hand.

The sheriff and Charlie stood outside. Sam Bowdre had his uniform on, never a good sign. The town had elected him sheriff years ago, mainly because no one else wanted the job, but his livelihood was a dairy ranch and he only donned his badge when there was trouble.

"Ruth," he said stiffly.

I used to insist on my proper title, but I wasn't a deputy anymore. The weight of that hung between us.

"Come on in, sheriff," I said, standing back.

He entered the kitchen and took his hat off. "Gael," he said.

My dad nodded warily. Charlie shot me a look of commiseration.

"Listen, Ruth," Sam Bowdre said. "You've put me in a darned awkward position here—"

"I got a proposition," I said. "We send a telegram to Mr. Hardin. Tell him I'll surrender if he comes right away with some marshals."

The sheriff looked surprised.

"But I want you to call a meeting at the town hall. First thing this morning. Let me have my say."

His weathered, deeply tanned face gave little away. But I knew Sam Bowdre was a fair man. He'd known me all my life.

"If I'm lying, you got nothing to lose. But if I'm right, people deserve a chance to make up their own minds."

He hesitated and Charlie stepped in. "Come on, dad," he said in a low voice. "It's Ruth."

Sam Bowdre finally nodded. "Let's go see Fran."

I grabbed my coat and we headed out. It was a fine, crisp morning. The leaves had turned on the red oaks, flaming against the bright blue sky. Down along the creek, the cottonwoods made a counterpoint of vivid yellow. And in all directions, the waist-high prairie grass shone a mellow gold.

"I'll admit, I didn't believe it when they told me the charges," the sheriff said, casting me a sidelong glance. "Seemed impossible."

"I only took the train after I saw Ava Carnarvon kill her own grandmother," I said.

The sheriff shook his head. "They told us about Calindra, but they said it was Merriweather who did it."

"Lee was framed," I said firmly as we approached the Main Street. Folks rose early in Lucky Boy and it wouldn't be quiet for long. "Does everyone know I'm wanted?"

"'Fraid so. The marshals stuck those posters up all over town."

I winced. "Yeah, I saw one. Right before Chalkey White shot Sheriff Cahill."

Bowdre stopped walking. "Bose Cahill? He's been dead for twenty-three years!"

"Guess he wanted you to think so. But I saw him up in Hatchet."

The sheriff tipped his hat back with a dubious squint. "What'd he look like?"

I thought for a minute. "Fat, red-faced, and crooked as a dog's hind legs."

Sam Bowdre laughed uneasily. "That does sound like Bose."

"He called his deputy Jim."

"That'd be Jim Shirley," he said slowly. Bowdre's grey eyes fixed on me with new alertness. "Might be I'm starting to believe you, Ruth."

"She don't lie," Charlie said with a crooked smile. "Though it'd do her good to give it a try sometime."

I swatted at him and he nimbly dodged away. "Guess your ankle healed," I said.

Charlie had sprained it when the train derailed. His grin widened. "I was just faking so you'd have to walk to Charter Oak."

I shook my head. I'd seen the swelling. "You would have liked Aguadulce, Charlie."

His blue eyes lit up. "Did they have follies?"

"Yep." I thought of the theater where I'd met Roger and suppressed a shiver. "Though it was a shambles by the time I left."

"When I heard what happened down there, I knew it was all starting to unravel," my dad said. "I'm just surprised this didn't happen sooner."

"They're not all bad," I protested. "Roger's the ringleader."

"So this Roger is a Class X phantom?" Sam Bowdre asked, brows knitting together.

In the light of day, it sounded outlandish. Everyone knew I read dime novels. I didn't have a shred of proof to back any of it up.

"Yep. Doc knows him."

"Hmph." He shared a look with Charlie. "We got a letter from Amy. She said there was a botched hanging up in Ruby Creek. That some marshals died, and the Prince of Hangmen, too."

Amy was Charlie's older sister. She'd married a prospector and moved up to Ruby Creek a few years before.

"That was Jolly," I said. "He used haints to free Winnie Cheever. I'm just glad to hear she's okay."

"Seems crazy," Sam muttered. "Didn't you say the man hates phantoms?"

I gave the sheriff a level look. "Jolly's worldview don't

exactly make sense. But Hardin'll back me up on all of it. He saw the bodies in New Jerusalem. He knows the kind of monster we're dealing with and he won't let that stand in his jurisdiction."

The library wasn't open yet, but we found the stooped form of Fran Gomez shelving dogeared paperbacks from a cart. She peered at me through thick spectacles with a tentative smile.

"It's all right, Fran," Sam Bowdre said. "Ruth's free on her own recognizance."

The look he gave me added, *for the moment.*

"Well, of course she is!" Miss Gomez snapped. "I never believed a word of that nonsense they're saying." She dug through the cart and held up a dime novel called *The Haunted Trapper*. "I ordered that book you've been nagging me for."

I reached for it and Miss Gomez snatched it back. "Now, Ruth, your last one is overdue."

I stared at my boots. "Afraid it's lost."

"Twister took it, Miss Gomez," Charlie put in. "Wasn't Ruth's fault."

I suddenly remembered Lee's gift. I rummaged through my coat and found it was still in my inside pocket. *The Notorious Maxwell Brothers Take Tip Top!*

"How about a replacement?" I said, offering her the book.

She eyed it. "We already have that one. I suppose you can work off the fine. The roof's been leaking. Ruined some of the children's picture books. Maybe you could fix it?"

"Yes, ma'am."

"I'll just check the list price in the catalogue—"

"Can we do that later?" Sam Bowdre said firmly. "We need to send a cable to Carnarvon City."

"Well, why didn't you just say so?" She sniffed. "I'll fetch my hat."

We walked down to the depot, which was only about a quarter mile distant. Lucky Boy didn't have a proper station, just a little wooden building with the telegraph and storage for goods that came in on the railway. The machine sat on a table in one corner. It looked a bit like a typewriter but with cables running from a box. Miss Gomez gave me a blank form to fill out. I stared at it for a minute.

"Where's it going?" she asked.

I remembered what Hardin had told me when I was about to set off for Charter Oak.

If you were sending it to me personally at Special Services, you'd write Handcuffs, Carnarvon City. It's telegraph shorthand.

I carefully printed the information, along with my name and the date. Then I considered the message itself.

I'm in Lucky Boy. Come get me, you rascal!

I swallowed a smile. Maybe a bit of Lee had rubbed off on me. But Sam Bowdre was hovering at my shoulder and I doubted he'd approve.

Bad trouble in Lucky Boy. Jolly's coming. Please help us.

I paused. Then I wrote, *I'm sorry*.

"That acceptable?" I asked the sheriff.

He grunted. I handed the page to Miss Gomez. She adjusted her spectacles and counted the words.

"That'll be six dollars and forty cents," she said.

I looked at Sheriff Bowdre. He sighed and fished in his pocket for the money. The bills had Calindra's portrait and I felt like the woman was scowling at me from beyond the grave as he handed it over and counted out the change.

Miss Gomez put the money in a box and said some words in a grim tongue. A little haint, the kind that looks like a lumpy toad, popped out of the machine. She cooed at it. The telegraph whirred to life. She pecked at the keys, translating the message into code. Then she printed a receipt and handed it to me. I exhaled a sigh of relief.

"Who's this Mr. Jolly?" she said, lowering her spectacles.

Sheriff Bowdre cleared his throat. "We'll be meeting about that, Fran. Town Hall at nine o'clock this morning."

"Don't like the sound of that cable, Sam," she said.

He opened his mouth and closed it again. I could see he was still on the fence about whether I'd gone crazy or not. "Just wait here to see if we get an answer from Carnarvon City," he said gruffly. "Then come on over to the meeting."

He sent Charlie to make the rounds and tell everyone. My dad insisted on going, too. I figured he'd be putting in a good word for me.

"You got an hour, Ruth," Sam Bowdre said. "I'll wait for you there."

I headed back to my house. Ned was awake and bustling around the kitchen in my dad's apron. I made more coffee and caught him up on the telegram while he fried bacon and eggs. The day was warming, so we sat out on the porch. I figured I was entitled to a second breakfast since it might be the last meal I ever ate.

Our house was on a little rise so I could see out over the town. Jimmy Jack dozed in a patch of sun while the chickens scratched for worms in the dirt. Everything looked so peaceful.

"How's this gonna play out, Ruth?" Ned asked, balancing a plate on his knee..

"I don't know. But I'm gonna save this place, whatever it costs." I forked some perfectly scrambled eggs into my mouth. "Darn, these are good. How'd you get 'em so light?"

"You just add a little warm water and whip it for four minutes. What about Roger?"

I sighed. "One thing at a time."

Ned shook some salt on his eggs. "How many people live in Lucky Boy?"

"Seventy-three. Including the kids."

"That's a fair number."

"Well, everyone's pretty old. They're farmers, Ned. Got no business taking on outlaws."

"You think Hardin'll come?"

"I do. Whether he'll come in time is another matter."

He nodded, gaze following the railway north. "Lee's still alive. I can feel it."

The food turned to ashes in my mouth. I set my fork down. "I should never have asked him to come. He'd be lounging on a beach right now if I'd just let him go."

"No, I think he needed to," Ned said. "Can't run forever."

"But I handed him right to them! Roger was leading us by the nose every step of the way."

"You beat Cage."

"Got lucky. I almost died myself." My voice sounded sullen and childish, but I was deep in the well of self-pity.

Ned shook his head. "You're looking at this wrong, Ruth."

"What do you mean?"

He tipped his chair back, eyes bright. "You got us here, didn't you? You did it by playing the game. There *are* rules, and if we can figure them out, we stand a chance. I mean, none of it makes sense when you think about it as real. But it does if you make a story out of it. See what I mean?"

I thought of the sheer number of outlandish events I'd been involved in over the last few weeks. The crashes—zeppelin and train—multiple abductions, fistfights, gunfights, coincidental encounters, twists of fate and near misses.

It wasn't like a dime novel.

It was like every dime novel I'd ever read rolled into one.

"I think maybe I do," I said.

But another idea struck me then. A dark one.

"Ned," I said casually. "What's your aunt's name again?"

He stared at me. "Maisie."

"Oh, that's right. I guess you told us about her when we holed up in that coyote den."

"It was a bear," he said flatly. "I ain't Roger."

"Didn't say you were."

He held his arm out. "You want to cut me? See if I bleed red?"

"Oh Lord, no." I eyed him, abashed. "It's just that the very last words Doc said to me were *don't trust*. And then he got cut off. He surely didn't mean Roger, since we don't trust him to begin with."

"You think Roger might already be in this town," Ned said slowly.

I nodded. "He might. I'm sure it's not my dad because he smelled right. I don't think Roger can fake that. But I don't know about the rest of them. And I hate it!"

Ned thought about that for a minute. "Well, I don't see how we can tell. Just keep a close eye on everyone."

I sighed. "You're right. Won't do any good to be suspicious of everyone. We'll just stay on our guard." I took a sip of coffee. "So tell me what you're thinking."

"We have to think outside the lines, like you did on the train to Hatchet."

"But that was a disaster!" I pointed out.

"Look, it don't matter how crazy our plan is. In fact, the crazier the better." Ned's dimples flashed. "Crazy's the only thing we can count on. Now, we'll need to distract them somehow. Long enough to free Lee, so they can't use him as a hostage. Then it's a straight fight and we'll make sure we have the high ground."

I took out *The Notorious Maxwell Brothers Take Tip Top!* "You know, this is the first brand-new book I've ever owned," I said softly.

Ned chewed a piece of bacon. "What's it about?"

I grinned. "Funny you ask."

I told him my idea. Ned liked it. He made a few suggestions of his own. The beginnings of a plan started to take shape.

"Doc said something else back at the mine," I said. "He said, *Remember what I told you on the way to Charter Oak*. I've been chewing it over. There might be a way to deal with those three phantoms, even without Lee. Roger promised he'd keep them out of it, but we know Roger's a liar. If things go bad, we need to be ready."

"I'm all for that," Ned agreed. "Wish we had some haints of our own."

"Me, too. They can't all be on his side."

We set our plates down as my dad approached. "You ready?" he asked. "It's about time."

"As I'll ever be," I said with a sigh. "Any word from Hardin?"

He shook his head. "Not yet. But Fran's waiting down at the depot. She'll let us know."

We walked over to the Town Hall, following a path that ran parallel to the creek. Everyone was there except for Miss White, who never attended these gatherings, not for love or money. A sea of lined faces and gray beards filled the benches. Half of them had canes resting across their knees. Very few still owned all their teeth. Three kids crawled around on the floor under the watchful eye of Miss Chen, who bounced a fat, apple-cheeked baby in her lap.

The back of the hall was partitioned off from the benches by a low wooden rail, with a couple of chairs and a table we referred to as "the dock." The frail, silver-haired minister Mr. Weeks was talking with Sam Bowdre there. The sheriff beckoned me over. Ned and Gael found seats next to Charlie.

We met here to make decisions, air disputes, and, very occasionally, to lay criminal charges against a prisoner, though the nearest courthouse was in Charter Oak. Lucky Boy had no mayor, so as sheriff and justice of the peace, Sam generally ran the proceedings.

"I'm not sure the kids should be here," I said quietly, stepping into the dock. "Don't want to scare 'em."

The sheriff beckoned to Charlie. "Take the children out to the square," he said. "Keep an eye."

"Why do I have to be their nursemaid?" Charlie objected.

"Because you already know what Ruth has to say," his father replied patiently. "Just do as I tell you."

Charlie muttered, but a second later he was crouching down with a grin. "Who wants to play some tag?"

Edgar Folliard looked at him with awe. Half the time he followed Bowdre around like a duckling with its mama, though Charlie rarely gave him the time of day. "Really?"

"You're it!" Charlie poked his ribs.

Edgar squealed and took off running, followed by the others. Charlie sauntered after, growling like a bear.

Sam raised his hands for quiet.

"You all have heard what they're accusing Ruth of," he said gravely. "I promised her she'd have her say, so I ask that you listen and then we'll decide what to do."

I faced the crowd and took a breath. "There's some dangerous men on their way here, but before I talk about that, I need to explain about the phantoms. What they really are."

Everyone looked at me expectantly.

"They're not magic and they're not spirits of the dead." *Here goes.* "They're from a higher plane that's invisible to our eyes."

Someone snorted. I plowed ahead. "Most of 'em are just youngsters. They come here to play. They don't really want to do harm. But some of the older ones aren't so nice. We call them Class X's."

People looked at each other dubiously.

"See, the X's are savants, just like Calindra Carnarvon and Pedro Braga. They speak our languages and their voices have power."

"How do you know all this, Ruth?" a gruff voice demanded from the front row. It was Mr. Grady, tall and whip-thin with a nose like a bird of prey and bushy gray eyebrows.

"Doc told me most of it. He's a Class X."

There was a collective gasp.

"Where's the haint now?" That was the Widow Hernandez. She sat next to Mr. Grady. The two of them pretended to hate each other, but I had a feeling it was all a front.

"Back in Tip Top. But Doc's our friend—"

"You just said he's an X!"

Muttering started and I raised my voice. "Point is, the Carnarvons got no control over the phantoms anymore. Nobody does. And one of the X's is sending a crazy reverend and his minions to Lucky Boy because he thinks it's a funny prank to kill us all. You folks need to pack and get out, right away."

"And go where?" asked Mrs. Johanssen. She was a big, strapping woman with a voice to match. "I got thirty head of cattle!"

"Now, wait," I began. "I have an idea about that—"

"Winter's coming!"

"My rheumatism—"

"What about the flock—"

"You got no business—"

Outraged murmurs rippled through the crowd. Sam shot me an "I told you so" look. Mr. Weeks made a feeble attempt to restore order, but they ignored him. Then Mrs. Johanssen shot to her feet, hands on hips. "She's plum crazy, just like her father!"

My dad paled. Everyone knew about his quirks. He wouldn't touch food with his left hand. He counted things and got anxious if the number was off. Sometimes he did chores more than once just so it added up right. But he wasn't crazy.

Everyone stopped talking. They studiously avoided looking at my father. Mr. Grady rose with a glower. "How many times has she chopped wood for you, Eleanor? Mended a fence or fixed a wagon?"

Mrs. Johannsen flushed. "I'm just saying, they haven't been here as long as the rest of us . . . ."

"Twenty years ain't enough for you?" he muttered.

Annie Chen handed the baby to her husband and stood up. "Gael brought a casserole when the baby got sick and stayed until the fever broke. And it's because of Ruth we got a new crib from Mrs. Carnarvon."

I'd forgotten all about that list I made in Hardin's office. So Calindra had kept her promise.

"I meant to thank you, Ruth," Sam Bowdre said, clearing his throat. "For the thresher."

"Ruth dug my well," Mr. Grady said. "Didn't ask for a thing. And that rolling chair Miss Christie got. That was Ruth Cortez!"

Miss Christie waved at me from the back of the hall, beaming.

The Widow Hernandez brandished her cane in the air. "Ain't a soul in this town Ruth hasn't helped out at one time or another. Gael, too. Let's hear the woman out! We owe her that much."

One by one, people got to their feet, nodding in agreement. I turned away, swallowing the lump in my throat. Folks could be mulish and prickly, but they had good hearts. Mrs. Johanssen cast me an abashed look and nodded briskly.

"Oh Gael, I didn't mean it," she said to my dad in a kinder tone. She gave a brittle laugh. "Lord knows, we have our share of eccentrics. You surely aren't worse than Miss White—"

"What's that, Eleanor?"

Everybody spun as Miss White strode into the hall wearing her big straw hat. Mrs. Johanssen blinked in surprise.

"Why, nothing at all," she replied, a bit flustered. "Glad you could make it."

She sat back down so fast, I heard the thump of her rear end hitting the bench.

"Looks like I got here right on time," Miss White said dryly. "Came to say I saw Ruth drop out of a hole in the sky into my yard yesterday. So if you fools got any doubts she's telling the truth about the aliens, let me put 'em to rest." She walked down the aisle and joined me in the dock. "Now, I plan to stay and fight. Ain't got much, but it's mine and it'll stay that way."

Minister Weeks stared at her in wonderment, and perhaps a touch of fear. I don't think he'd seen Miss White for at least a decade. The last time he'd gone out to her place, my mom said she'd chased him off with a broom.

"What are you aiming to do, Ruth?" Mr. Grady asked.

"I'm staying," I said. "This is our town." I glanced at Sam Bowdre. He nodded. So did Charlie.

"Then I am, too," Mr. Grady said.

"And me!" cried the Widow Hernandez.

"Now, just hold on," I began, but they drowned me out—even the ones who always complained about the place. We'd never had a town meeting that was so lively. I'd wondered if Lucky Boy had any fire left, but there was a cinder smoldering in the ashes that only needed a little fanning to roar to life.

"Quiet down!" Sam Bowdre shouted. "Now, you all have the right to choose for yourself. But the children can't stay."

"They can come out to my place," Miss White offered. "Annie?"

Miss Chen came over. "I'll take charge of them."

"I'll help you out, Annie," my dad said. "We can use my wagon."

She gave him a warm smile. Merry shrieks came from outside. "Sounds like Charlie's running them ragged. Maybe we'll luck out and get them down for a nap."

They left to gather up the kids. I turned back to the waiting crowd.

"Here's what I'm thinking," I said.

I laid out the plan. There was plenty of arguing, mainly from Miss Johanssen, but in the end they agreed that while it was "plumb crazy," no one had a better idea. Sheriff Bowdre signaled to me and we stepped into the dock, leaving them to sort out the details.

"Tell me one thing," he said softly. "Do we even stand a chance?"

I felt the weight of responsibility for the seventy-three souls in Lucky Boy settle squarely on my shoulders. But I couldn't stop it now. Their minds were made up—and that's why I loved them. We'd live or die together this day.

"Yeah," I said. "I have to believe that, Sam."

He nodded. "Then let's put these wolves down."

I stared at him for a moment. "That's an odd thing to say, sheriff."

He squinted at me. "What?"

I shook it off. "Never mind. Now, how many of you got guns?" I called out.

A few hands went up. Not nearly enough. If you read a lot of dime novels, you might think everyone on the frontier is armed to the teeth, but it isn't true. The ranchers keep rifles to drive off predators, but the folks who farm a patch of land barely break even after buying fertilizer and whatnot. Until I found Doc in that field, we never had a gun in the house. My dad always said that's what the sheriff was for.

"Got six shotguns and crates of ammo over at the jail," Sam said.

"That's a start," I said. "Who else?"

All heads turned to Miss White. "Well, I own some firearms," she said grudgingly. "Suppose you could borrow 'em."

"Then let's get moving," I said. "We're running out of time."

The hall emptied as everyone hurried off to their assigned tasks. I stepped out the back door, looking over the prairie. It was a perfect autumn day. A flock of geese winged north, honking down in derision at us poor land-bound creatures. I watched them dwindle into the blue, envying their freedom.

"Can you feel it, Ruth?"

I jumped at the husky voice behind me. Miss White rubbed her skinny arms. "Reminds me of the day the twister took Three Bars. Came out of nowhere. But in the hours before, the air changed. Like an invisible storm brewing. Know what I mean?"

I nodded.

"Tried to warn that dumb sheriff, but he wouldn't listen." She cocked her head, dark eyes solemn beneath the brim of her hat. "It ain't here yet, but it will be soon."

We stood together in silence. Not a puff of cloud marred the sky, but I could feel that storm, too, as sure as if heavy black thunderheads raced towards us from the northern horizon.

I finally turned to Miss White. "Let's go get those guns," I said.

17

Sebastian pressed his ear to the door of Ava's suite.

She was meeting with the family lawyers in the Carnarvon Lines offices on six, along with Richard and Freddy, but he wanted to be sure there wasn't a maid inside. Ava insisted they clean twice a day, once in the morning when they brought her coffee and again in the late afternoon. It was just after one, so he should be safe.

Silence.

He slipped the lock picks into place and found the tumblers within seconds. Sebastian eased the door open a crack, listened for another moment, then slipped inside and quietly closed it.

He could smell a hint of Ava's floral perfume on the ermine coat carelessly draped across the sofa. Other than that, the sitting room was spotless.

He'd spent the last day at the Academy, talking to the staff. They all concurred with Abel Beach that it was entirely out of character for Dean Rodriguez to tender his resignation and disappear. He also searched the dean's office. Ava had been preoccupied with the will and the place seemed largely unchanged from its previous occupant. But he hadn't found the letter.

When he asked her about it directly, she paused for a moment and said she thought she'd kept it. Ava promised to look. But her gaze had been cool and he knew she wouldn't.

Her rooms were the last logical place to search.

He swiftly crossed to an elegant rosewood escritoire and rifled through the tiny drawers. They held writing materials and old correspondence bound in pink ribbons, none of which was the letter he sought. He moved to the bathroom, which held a sunken marble tub, bidet, and mirrored dressing table with a gold-plated telephone. Ava had enough cosmetics and perfumes for ten women, but he came up empty-handed.

He searched a small library, shaking all the books in case she had slipped it between the pages, and moved into the bedroom, running his hands under the mattress of the enormous canopied bed. He was just turning for the wardrobe when he heard voices outside the door.

Sebastian swore under his breath. He darted into the hall and folded himself into a closet just as the door swing wide.

"Those girls are too careless," Ava said fretfully. "They know they're supposed to lock the door behind them! I'd better do an inventory of my jewelry. I wouldn't put it past them to be pilfering and blame it on a thief."

"Oh, shut up," Freddy said. "Your diamonds are the least of our troubles."

The door slammed. The voices grew louder as the pair entered the sitting room.

Sebastian's heart thudded as heavy footsteps approached. The closet held a few long evening coats, but there was nowhere to hide. Then they veered away towards the sidebar where Ava kept her glass decanters.

"Go ahead," she spat in an acid tone. "Have another drink, Freddy."

"You might as well join me."

"It's barely past noon!"

"I have a high tolerance." Glass clinked. "This is my afternoon tea."

"Oh, Freddy."

The ritual was a familiar one. Sebastian found he was holding his breath and forced himself to relax.

"That meeting was interminable," Freddy grumbled. "Who knew C&L had so damned many holdings? You could choke an elephant with the heap of papers they made us review."

"Trusts are complex. You'd do well to pay attention."

"Well, my hand is still cramped from signing." A lighter clicked. "What are you going to do about Chance?" Freddy asked in a subdued tone.

"Nothing. What can I do? He *promised* me."

"He's an X. A bloody Class X, Ava! What the hell were you thinking?"

"I was trying to save the family." Her voice sounded brittle, as if Ava struggled to convince herself. "We still can. Everything is fine—"

"Fine?" Freddy demanded, his voice rising to a high pitch. "I watched my dead grandmother dance a jig yesterday! How is that *fine*?"

Sebastian felt as though he stood on a hill of sand that was slowly giving way beneath his feet. The reference to Chance could only be Henry Chance. Pedro Braga's security chief, presumed dead in Aguadulce.

But Chance wasn't a man at all.

Chance was . . . .

Sebastian suppressed a groan.

Chance was the phantom known as Roger.

The one Jolly called Legion.

And the heirs he'd sworn to protect were dancing on his strings.

Like a long line of dominoes, it all fell into place. Ruth's "hallucinations" had been staged to make her seem unstable. As for Lee—

"At least we almost have the will settled," Ava said soothingly. "Everything will be divided between the three of us."

Freddy was silent for a long moment. "About that. Was it really Merriweather, Ava?"

"What exactly are you implying?"

"Chance did the rest. You can't deny that."

"I'm not denying anything!" Her voice receded toward the windows. "But you can't blame the theater on me. I had no idea he intended to harm anyone—"

"Oh, my God." It was muffled, as if Freddy had covered his face. "I can't even think about it."

"Pull yourself together. We'll get through it like we always do. Together."

"Tell me the truth, Ava. Did you . . . ?"

"Did I what?"

"You know."

"How can you even suggest such a thing!"

"Ruth said you did." He sounded like a little boy.

"Ruth Cortez is unhinged and a liar. I don't know why she hates me, Lord knows I've only ever been kind to her, but you can't possibly believe her, Freddy?" Her voice trembled. "Tell me you don't. Why would I harm grandmother?"

Because she found you out somehow, Hardin thought, cold with rage.

He knew Calindra. She'd show no mercy. Not even to her own kin.

"Why would Lee Merriweather?" Freddy retorted.

"Ask him yourself! I won't discuss this anymore. It's ridiculous. Here, I'll pour you another drink." Her voice brightened with false cheer. "I'll even join you."

More glass clinking.

Hardin considered stepping out of the closet. He wondered what Ava would do.

Deny everything, of course. And Freddy would back her up, the coward.

Then he heard his own name spoken.

"Sebastian has been nosing around at the Academy," Ava said. "Dubbs said he went to see Abel Beach."

Jack Dubbs was one of the marshals in Special Services. Hardin had never liked him. He once beat a handcuffed prisoner so badly the man nearly died. Now Hardin realized he must be Ava's spy.

"Why?" Freddy asked.

"I don't know. But it's worrisome."

"Will you dispose of *him* now, too?"

"Of course not! I value Sebastian. But he hasn't been himself lately. Everyone knows he suffers from headaches. Perhaps we should put him on a medical leave."

"Sebastian saved my life," Freddy said angrily. "I won't throw him away."

When Freddy was a child, he'd been kidnapped by bandits during a visit to the N.T. Hardin was still a teenager, but he'd stumbled across the hideout and killed the men holding Freddy hostage. It was the start of a lifelong bond with the family that ended with him running Special Services. And Freddy hadn't forgotten the debt.

"No one's throwing anyone away. But until the will is settled, we must be very careful. We don't need last-minute complications."

"Do you think he knows about Chance?" His voice lowered until Hardin could barely hear it. "Or Jolly?"

"No," Ava said decisively. "He couldn't. But Abel Beach might. Oh, I wish I knew what they talked about!"

"Ask him."

"Don't be stupid, Freddy, I can't. Don't worry, I'll speak to Dubbs. We'll handle it."

Hardin knew exactly what that meant. Beach would be found hanging in his cell. Maybe tomorrow. Maybe today.

"How could you have hired that crazy preacher to find Lee?" Freddy demanded. "You didn't know the first thing about him! The man's a maniac."

"There's no point regretting it now," she said in a cool tone. "I told you, I'll take care of it."

A long pause.

"I'm done, Ava," Freddy said dully.

"What does that mean?"

He stayed silent. Hardin silently cheered him on. Stand up to her, Freddy. Tell her you're going straight to Richard—

"I'm going to my club," Freddy said. "I can't breathe here."

"Well, don't lose your whole allowance this time."

"What will you do about Sebastian? Tell me the truth, Ava, or I swear. . . ." He trailed off.

"Exactly what I said. A temporary medical leave. It'll do him good. He works too hard. Dubbs can handle things until his return."

Freddy muttered something unintelligible. The door opened, then slammed shut.

Perfect silence descended. Sebastian could picture her standing there, staring after Freddy, or maybe out the windows at the vast empire she was about to inherit, achingly beautiful and as cold as a marble statue. Then her light footsteps passed his hiding place. He heard her humming as she started to draw a bath.

How long did he have before his authority was revoked?

Not very long at all, if he knew Ava.

Sebastian had never known their parents. The twins' mother died in childbirth. Their father had drunk himself to death within a year. The double tragedy—and Calindra's lack of warmth, if he were being honest—left them inseparable. But the dynamic between the siblings had taken a darker turn of late. When had she become such a bully? And Freddy so spineless?

Sebastian waited until she was ensconced in the tub, then slipped from the closet and crept like a cat to the door.

He'd find Ruth. Beg forgiveness on his knees, if that's what she wanted.

But he couldn't leave without Abel Beach. That would be tantamount to murder.

Hardin's leg jiggled impatiently as he pressed the button for the elevator.

"Come on," he whispered. "For the love of God, hurry it up!"

18

AVA CARNARVON WAS APPLYING coral lipstick at her vanity when the phone rang. It was Jack Dubbs.

"Got something you'll be interested in," he said.

"Go ahead, Jack." She studied her jewelry tray, trying to decide between a ruby choker and an amethyst pendant.

"Telegram just arrived from Lucky Boy. Claims to be from Ruth Cortez. Says the reverend's headed her way. She's asking for aid."

Ava's hand froze. "Has Sebastian seen it?"

"Not yet. I did as you asked."

She'd instructed Dubbs to intercept all telegrams coming into Special Services, and particularly Sebastian's private line. "Good. I was just about to call you. Mr. Hardin is temporarily relieved of his duties. You're in charge."

"Yes, ma'am."

Jack Dubbs wasn't near as intelligent as Sebastian, she thought bitterly, but at least the man was loyal. He didn't even ask why.

"I'd prefer to tell him myself. Have you seen him?"

"No, ma'am."

"Find him. Send him to me. And don't mention anything about Lucky Boy."

"No, ma'am." He paused. "What about Beach?"

"I think it's time," Ava replied, selecting the ruby choker. In the light of the sconces, it gleamed a deep bloody red. "Make sure it looks like an accident. What about the marshals who were in Lucky Boy?"

"I already pulled them out."

"That's good, Jack." Ava blotted the lipstick and examined her reflection with a critical eye. "Make yourself available later this afternoon. I need your opinion on each and every marshal. Mr. Hardin was popular. If there's grumbling about my decision, we need to nip it in the bud. Promote your allies."

"I agree a hundred percent, ma'am." He paused. "Hodges and Tanaka might be a problem."

"Then we'd better anticipate them, Jack, before they turn into one," she said coldly.

"Yes, ma'am. I'm on it." A heavy breath. She could picture him sitting at his desk, uniform bulging over a substantial beer belly. It probably had lunch stains on it. "What about the telegram?"

"What do you think?"

"I don't—"

"Destroy it!" she snapped. "Inform me when you're finished with Beach. *Discreetly*."

Ava set the receiver in the cradle. Had she given the order to Sebastian, there would be no need to add that final directive. But then, Hardin would almost certainly refuse to carry it out. How much simpler things would be if they'd just left Abel Beach in Aguadulce.

"Would you have done it for grandmother?" she whispered to the mirror.

He might have, she thought sourly. But it seemed his devotion to Calindra didn't extend to her heirs. Not anymore.

Once, Ava thought she loved Sebastian, but he'd turned out to be as fickle as the others. If not for Ruth Cortez . . . . Ava's lips tightened. She was the one who'd planted suspicion in Sebastian's mind. She'd helped Lee Merriweather get away and now she had the temerity to beg for help!

Well, if the reverend wanted to erase that pathetic flyspeck town, Godspeed to him. Jolly would have to be dealt with eventually, he was a rabid dog, but with Jack Dubbs and the Carnarvon marshals at her command, that shouldn't present much difficulty. Let him have his fun. As long as their interests coincided, she didn't particularly care what he did.

Beach would be the first test of Dubbs's obedience. Once he murdered the professor, he'd be at her mercy completely, although he was too stupid to see that. Then she could consider the problem of Richard. He was too clever by half. And she feared his influence over Freddy. She'd need to bide her time—another accident too soon would look suspicious—but there were numerous ways Jack Dubbs could get rid of her half-brother. A malfunction with the elevators, perhaps. Or something to do with Richard's laboratory. He had all sorts of dangerous equipment in there.

She smoothed her black velvet dress. Luckily, mourning clothes flattered her red hair and pale complexion. She supposed she'd have to wear black for at least another week or so. People would expect it. More troubling was the incident at the funeral. The X had promised to keep the lower classes of phantoms in line. Now, a vague unease stirred. Ava wondered if it had lied, and what she could do about it if it had.

She snapped the clasp on the ruby choker as the telephone rang again. Ava picked it up. "Yes?"

"Miss Carnarvon?"

"Speaking. Who's this?"

"Professor Walsh. We have, uh, a bit of a situation over at the Academy."

Ava frowned. "What's going on?"

"The phantoms have left." A pause. "All of them."

She rose to her feet. "That's not possible."

"I'm afraid it is." The voice was dry. Professor Louise Walsh, she recalled, headed the department of Phantom Assignment and Location Monitoring.

"Well, call them back!"

"We've been trying. No one answers, not in any dialect. It's the oddest thing."

"Where did they go?"

"Haven't the foggiest. They just disappeared into the ether, oh, about twenty minutes ago."

"Has this ever happened before?"

"Not to my knowledge, and I've been at the Academy for thirty-six years."

Ava bit her lip. "Damn, hang on." She leaned toward the mirror, using a finger to scrub the lipstick from her teeth. "I'm coming down there right away."

"You might want to find out what's happening at the factories. Transport, as well."

The condescending tone irked Ava. "Obviously," she retorted. "You do your job and I'll do—Christ!"

Ava spun at the sudden reflection behind her. A leering face pressed against the glass window above the bathtub, insectile eyes gleaming. It gibbered and vanished.

"What happened?" The tinny voice came from the receiver dangling from Ava's limp hand. "Miss Carnarvon?"

Phantoms flitted beyond the window. A host of them. They blotted out the view of the city below. Ava slowly raised the phone, eyes locked on the swirling darkness. "Professor Walsh? Hello?"

She tapped the button with a trembling hand.

The line was dead.

~

Hardin stopped in his office and unlocked a gun cabinet, slipping two boxes of bullets for the Colt Walker into his coat pocket.

For eight years, he'd called the tower home. Now he took a last look around, still a bit stunned at the thought he might never return.

Plaques and citations covered the walls, but he didn't care about those. Nor his few belongings. Sebastian's entire adult life had revolved around Special Services and he owned very little save for a rack with extra uniforms and a shaving kit, though he preferred going to the barber. It was the one luxury he allowed himself. Sebastian still remembered watching his dad get a shave at Easy Jackson's. The soft scrape of the razor over his beard and the good clean smell of soap. Afterward, if his dad had won some money the night before, he'd toss Sebastian a nickel for chewing gum and a soda pop.

Never trust a young doctor or an old barber, H.J. used to say.

He strode to his desk and took a small cameo of his mother from the top drawer. The climate of the Northern Territory hadn't been gentle on her fair features, but warmth and laughter shone in her eyes. He'd been meaning to look in on her, and his brothers and sisters, too. Maybe after he found Ruth—

"Sir?"

Ford stood in the door. Sebastian's head jerked up.

"Go ahead," he said evenly. Was the axe falling already?

"We're getting reports from across the river. It's a bit muddled, but the clocktowers have failed. The haints are just . . . gone. All the omnibuses and trams are dead. In the middle of evening rush hour! It's a mess out there."

Sebastian tucked the cameo in his pocket. His fingers brushed Ruth's copper star. He'd been carrying it around since Aguadulce like a talisman. As long as he had the badge, it meant he'd see her again. Someday.

"Anyone hurt?" he asked, frowning.

"Not that we've heard." Ford shook his head. "But it ain't looking good."

"Send a message to Richard."

"But . . . what should we *do*, sir?"

Sebastian thought hard. Things were falling apart. Might as well use his last few minutes of authority to do some good. God knows, he couldn't trust Ava and Freddy to make the right decision.

"Initiate a city-wide evacuation to the underground bunker. You know the protocol. Get the linguists together. See if they can find any haints to talk to. And send a pair of marshals out to the circus. I want Rose Cortez escorted to the bunker immediately. You'll find her in one of the wagons. Goes by the stage name Madame Esmeralda."

"She under arrest?"

"Lord, no. But she's a . . . friend." He grabbed his coat.

"Where you going?" Ford asked with a frown.

"I got something to do."

"Well, make it quick." Ford shot him a look. "We need you."

Sebastian felt a stab of guilt, but there was nothing more he could accomplish here. Richard was more than capable of taking the situation in hand. He rode the elevator down to SL-3, deep beneath the tower where the holding cells were located. The marshal on duty was talking on the phone when he stepped off the lift. She stared at Hardin and started to say something, but Sebastian ignored her, striding into the corridor beyond. A few prisoners eyed him sullenly as he passed their cells. When he reached the end, he stopped. His pulse ticked up a notch. Beach's cell was empty.

He ran back to the front desk, unbuttoning his coat so he could get to the shoulder rig. "Where's Abel Beach?" he demanded.

The marshal set the phone down. "That's what I was trying to tell you, sir. Jack Dubbs just took him up to see you."

"How long ago?"

"Two minutes."

Sebastian's gaze flicked to the bank of two elevators. One was descended to SL-4. The other had stopped at the roof.

"What's going on, sir?" the marshal asked. She was a petite blonde named Blake, fairly new to Special Services. "I just got a call that we're evacuating."

"Do it," Hardin growled, slamming a hand on the call button. "Code X. Ford's in charge for now."

Blake jumped to her feet and ran for the coffee room to gather reinforcements. Sebastian's heart hammered as he waited for the elevator to arrive. The one on the floor below him wasn't moving at all. The other descended at a glacial pace. He watched each floor number light up, praying it wouldn't stop on the way down.

"Son of a bitch, come *on*," he muttered, as the phone started ringing.

Sebastian picked up the receiver and slammed it down again.

He dashed inside the car before the doors had fully opened, key in hand. Access to the top floors was limited to a select few individuals. By all rights, Jack Dubbs should never have had the key. He jammed his own key into the slot, then hit the button for 20, the level just under the zeppelin landing pad.

On the way up, Sebastian took his gun out and checked that it was fully loaded. He shook a few bullets from one of the boxes and kept them loose in his pocket.

If he hadn't stopped in his damned office—

The door opened into the family's luxurious private meeting area. Elegant couches surrounded a horseshoe bar, with floor to ceiling windows that looked over the city. The room was dark and empty. He slid the door open to the terrace and took a set of winding metal stairs up to the zeppelin waiting area. Faint voices drifted from the roof.

"Go on," Dubbs said with a chuckle. "Let's see if you can fly, professor."

"Why don't you just shoot me," Abel Beach said fiercely.

A gun went off and Hardin's heart stopped, but when he peered through the glass windows and saw the two men standing on the landing pad, he realized that Dubbs had deliberately shot over Beach's head. A small zeppelin was tethered to the mooring mast.

"Next one won't miss. Now get over there!" Dubbs gestured with the gun.

Hardin stood behind Dubbs, who was facing away from the tower. He touched a finger to his lips. Beach gave no sign he saw. He raised his hands, which were cuffed in front. "Okay, okay, I'm going."

Beach took a shuffling step backwards. It was windy up there, and a strong gust nearly sent him over the edge. His eyes went tight and Dubbs gave another dry chuckle.

"We'll call it the Merriweather backflip," he said. "Except this time there won't be an airship to catch you."

Hardin crept forward on the balls of his feet. He'd hunted game in the northern woods since the tender age of six, when it became clear that while H.J. could charm the skin off a snake, he wasn't much of a provider.

"You don't have to do this," Abel Beach said. The icy wind whipped his long dreadlocks around and tore at his coat. "I don't know anything!"

"Now, Miss Carnarvon thinks different. And this ain't a negotiation." Dubbs' voice hardened. "You jump or I'll take you apart, piece by piece—"

He stiffened at the cock of Hardin's Colt behind his left ear.

"Drop the gun," Sebastian snapped. "Do it!"

Dubbs laughed, though he stood stock still. "You got no authority here. Go on before I arrest you."

"I ain't letting you murder an innocent man. On your knees, Jack, or I blow your head off. Won't be much of a loss."

Dubbs moved faster than Hardin expected. He slammed an elbow back into Hardin's ribs, sweeping his own gun up. Beach leapt forward and kicked it from his hand. Sebastian brought the Colt around, cracking Dubbs savagely across the face with the barrel. The marshal fell on his rump, clutching the ruin of his nose.

"We got that little bitch in custody," he spat. "She'll be hung by tomorrow."

Abel grabbed Dubbs's gun from the ground and aimed at his chest.

"What?" Sebastian seized a handful of the marshal's thinning blonde hair and yanked his head back. "Where?"

Dubbs grinned through bloody teeth. "Yer own hometown, Hardin. She's up in Hatchet. You'll never see her again."

Sebastian shook him until Dubbs howled in pain. "Liar!"

"Am I? She's with Merriweather and that Negro cook."

Hardin had kept it quiet that Ned Carver was on the train. He didn't want to get the kid in trouble. Sebastian stood and kicked Dubbs in the kneecap. He grunted.

"That's for being an ignorant piece of trash. Now *where exactly is Ruth Cortez?*"

Dubbs hesitated and Hardin delivered another vicious kick, this one to the groin. When Dubbs managed to breathe again, he coughed out an answer. "Jailhouse, you son of a whore."

Hardin rummaged through his pockets and found the keys to Beach's handcuffs. He freed the professor and gave him back Dubbs's gun.

"You can fly that thing, right?" he asked, eyeing the zeppelin.

Abel smiled. "Sure can."

Jack Dubbs started to wheeze with laughter.

"What's so damn funny?" Sebastian demanded.

"You . . . ain't going nowhere."

Hardin followed his gaze. The skies over the city were thick with haints. All headed towards the tower.

"Sweet Mother Mary," he whispered.

Every class, from the tiny fireflies through the misshapen toads and, worse, the children, flew like witches through the night, jaws wide, tiny teeth shining. There had to be at least three hundred. They circled the tower in a vortex of squeals, grunts, and slobbering shrieks that lifted every hair on his body.

"Look out!"

Hardin tensed as Dubbs lunged for the Colt in his hand, then fell back with a bullet hole between the eyes. Abel Beach stared transfixed at Dubbs' body, the gun still pointing down at his head. He looked horrified, but his hand was steady.

"Move!" Hardin shouted, tugging the stunned professor by the sleeve.

They ran inside the waiting area just as the phantoms reached the airship. Walls wouldn't keep them out, but even a thin layer of glass felt better than nothing at all.

To Hardin's surprise, the haints didn't give chase. They alit on the zeppelin, clustering on the frame like a colony of over-large bats until the Carnarvon Colors, red and gold, were barely visible. More roosted on Dubbs's corpse. It was a singularly gruesome sight.

"Think you can talk to them?" Hardin asked shakily.

Abel Beach gave him a level look. "I *could*, but it might just piss them off. Got any other ideas?"

Hardin thought, his frustration boiling. Transport was grounded, but there were stables at the edge of the city. Ava liked to go riding sometimes. He didn't care for horses, but he'd do whatever it took to reach the suburbs. Maybe trains were still running there. It was a slim hope, but it was all he had.

She'll be hung by tomorrow.

Panic almost dragged him under, but Hardin ruthlessly shoved it into a box, drawing on the reserves of calm under pressure that had carried him through the ranks of Special Services. *I'll find a way. There's always a way.*

"We'll leave through the tunnels," he said decisively. "Take it from there."

Sirens wailed in the city below as they jogged to the elevator. The car was still waiting and the door slid open when Sebastian pressed the button. He just prayed Ford didn't lock down the lifts in the next two minutes. The tower had multiple banks of elevators, most of them used by support staff. Evacuation was supposed to be completed in fifteen minutes, and they'd rehearsed it, but never in an actual emergency.

Sebastian felt a pang of regret at abandoning Richard, but Marshal Tanaka would watch out for him.

As best she could under the circumstances.

"Ruth was right," he said grimly to Abel as the doors closed. "Ava killed her grandmother, I'm sure of it. She made some deal with the X, but it's falling apart."

"How'd you know to look for me?"

By the time Sebastian had recounted the conversation between Ava and Freddy, they were at the fourth sub-level where the tracks ran through. Abel turned to him with a serious look as the car touched down.

"You saved my bacon, marshal. I owe you."

Hardin cleared his throat. "Way I see it, I owe you all. Especially Merriweather."

"If Ruth is with Lee and they're in danger, I'm going north," Beach said, his jaw set. "That boy's like a son to me."

Hardin nodded as they strode from the car and passed through the private waiting area. "How'd you know?"

"About what?"

"The Carnarvons." His mouth twisted. "That it was all . . . rotten."

"Well, I didn't know all of it. But it seemed to me that the reverend couldn't have found out about that bunker unless someone told him."

Hardin had wondered the same thing. He should have listened to his instincts.

They stepped out to the platform. Sebastian expected it to be empty, but a train sat there, the boiler still ticking and steam trailing from the furnace. It must have arrived only minutes before. When he saw the number on the side of the engine, he stopped dead.

"The hell?" he muttered.

"What is it?" Beach asked.

"That's the train I took south to Aguadulce." Hardin drew his Colt. "The same one Ruth stole."

A phantom with spiky green hair materialized on the platform. Both men took a step back.

It tilted its head and made a series of clicking vocalizations. Abel's face lit up. "I know that dialect," he said. The professor responded in the same phantom tongue. Two more haints drifted from the engine car, these with hair of a shocking orange and pink. Sebastian waited, simmering with impatience.

"What are they saying?"

Beach turned to him. "Last they saw Ruth and Lee was just north of Aguadulce when they switched to a zeppelin. Ned was with them. The phantoms were told to bring the train back to Carnarvon City, so that's what they did."

"Ask them what on God's green earth is happening in the city," Hardin exclaimed.

Abel communicated the question. The phantoms chittered for a minute or two.

"They say the *big boy* is stirring things up. I'm thinking they mean the X."

"That's plain to see," Hardin replied in exasperation. "Why are they surrounding the tower?"

"The others are waiting on his orders."

Well, that sounded ominous.

"What orders?" Sebastian asked, remembering Aguadulce with a chill.

More clicks and screeches. "No one knows," Beach said. "From what I gather, the X has some kind of power over them. They do what he says. But these three phantoms don't like the big boy at all. They say they kept their promise of returning the train to Carnarvon City and now they're going home."

"Wait! Ask them if they can take us north. Tell them it's important. Do whatever you have to, but if we don't get there quick, Ruth and Lee are dead. Ned, too."

Beach addressed the haints. They seemed reluctant, though with those gaunt, wooden faces, it was hard to tell. He spoke more emphatically, an edge of desperation running through the foreign sounds that even Hardin could recognize.

Please, he thought. *Just . . . please.*

Never had Sebastian felt so useless. This wasn't a problem that could be solved with his fists, or with his wits. The woman he loved was more than a thousand miles across the frontier, and if the haints decided they'd rather zip off into the ether than save her from the noose, there wasn't a damned thing he could do about it.

Finally, the trio vanished. His breath caught.

"They'll run the train," Beach said with a relieved grin.

Hardin felt the air rush back into his lungs.

"Long as they don't have to stay here," the professor added. "They're scared of the X. It was him who carried out the slaughter at the theater, not Lee."

"I gathered as much," Hardin said, resisting the urge to seize Abel Beach in a bear hug. "You did good. Heck, let's go! Tell 'em to push it as hard as they can."

The boiler fired up, and they hopped aboard the dining car as the pistons started cranking. The train steamed out through the tunnels, gradually gaining speed. When it emerged aboveground, Hardin walked back to the caboose. He stepped out to the railed balcony.

Carnarvon City glittered in the morning sun, the tower a dark silhouette against the sky. Even from a distance, he could make out the swarms of phantoms. Circling, circling, like vultures around a carcass. Sirens wailed full blast from every direction.

"I feel like a traitor," he muttered. "Leaving all those people behind."

"You're not the traitor, marshal," Abel Beach said at his shoulder. "If you stayed, you'd be in the cell next to me. Most likely we'd both end up dead."

"I know," Sebastian said heavily. "Don't make it better." He turned away from the sight. "How fast can this train go?"

Abel lifted a brow. "How fast do you want it?"

"Can we make ninety?"

The professor licked his lips. "Without derailing? I'll see what I can do."

He hurried up front. Sebastian slid a hand into his pocket, gripping Ruth's star. His head was starting to pound.

They crossed the river and the tower shrank to a nub on the horizon, but he couldn't shake the image of all those phantoms, gibbering in excitement.

What were they waiting for?

19

Atop the tower, at the heart of the vortex, Jack Dubbs stirred.

The phantoms perched on his body squealed and took flight.

He sat up with a wince.

"Dammit, that stung," he muttered, touching the bullet hole between his eyes.

Pink goo clung to his finger. He shook it off.

"What are you little brats goggling at?" he snarled.

The kids on the airship eyed him fearfully, which pleased him.

"So the hero's on his way to Hatchet, rushing off to save the girl," he mused, features rearranging themselves into the likeness of a cowboy in a big ten-gallon hat. "I'll have to think up a good end. Mayhaps daddy'll shoot him again." He took aim at one of the kids with his index finger. "Pow, you're dead!"

It toppled over, then bounded up, sniggering. Roger slapped it on the side of the head.

"Get on with you," he said. "Impudent little turd."

It skittered away to a chorus of jeers and giggles. He stood and looked out over the city. *His* city, now. The cowboy hat on his head didn't stir though the wind howled like a banshee.

"It's starting," he said softly. "Everything's in apple pie order!"

A smaller kid started to creep away and Roger pounced, grabbing it by the scruff and shaking it like a terrier with a rat. "You'll do as I say, or I'll eat you up!" he growled, growing taller and larger with each word. "Drink your blood and grind your bones for my bread!"

That line never failed. The kid squeaked in terror. He gave it a last shake and tossed it aside. The rest cowered, their mind-forms barely holding. A few tiny tentacles waved in distress.

"All you extras wait here," he commanded, using the Voice to ensure compliance. "I got a scene to shoot in Lucky Boy."

Three hundred bug eyes watched as his features changed yet again, this time to a face that Ruth knew well.

"Lots of cameos in this picture," he said with a wink. "Some of you might even get a bigger role if you play your cards right. So sit tight until I say action, you hear?"

Three hundred heads nodded fervently.

There was a faint pop, a rush of air, and Roger vanished.

20

I RODE one of Sam's horses, a black mare with one white eye called Domino, alongside my dad, who drove a wagon with the children and Miss Chen, rocking the baby on her lap. Miss White sat astride her own elderly stallion in the rear. The sun was past midday, but I figured we still had a few hours to settle the kids and ready ourselves.

"I'm hungry," whined Little Edgar Folliard.

Everyone thought of him as Little Edgar, since Big Edgar was his grandpa. All three of the kids had been left here by too-young parents who went off to work in the city. I hoped some of the little ones might stay when they grew up, but it rarely happened. Charlie was the last one under forty besides me, and I knew he was dying to leave the first chance he got.

"We'll have some dinner as soon as we get to Miss White's house," Miss Chen said.

"Why we goin' there?"

"I told you, Edgar," she replied patiently. "We're taking a field trip today."

"What's in the field?"

"A field trip. It means like an adventure."

Edgar threw his head back. "Wanna go home," he howled at the sky.

"You can go home tomorrow, I promise."

"But I forgot Horsie! I need my Horseeee!"

His freckled face went red. The kid was gearing up for a full-blown tantrum. His friends looked on with interest, especially the baby.

"You like digging for treasure?" Miss White asked, riding forward.

Edgar quit wailing. They all eyed her, a bit scared. Miss White had that effect on people, even five-year-olds.

"Pirates live on islands," Edgar muttered suspiciously.

"This ain't pirate treasure. It's haunted treasure." She cackled. "Or hainted treasure, more like."

"What's that?" piped up Daisy Berry, who was the boldest of the gang.

"Well, once there was a prospector who lost his arm in a terrible accident. So he replaced it with an arm of pure gold."

"What kind of terrible accident?" Edgar wondered, curiosity piquing.

Miss Chen shot her a look, but Miss White ignored it. "Run over by a mining car." She made a slashing motion. "Sliced it clean off!"

"Now, I really don't think—" Miss Chen began, but the kids were leaning forward, eyes shining.

"Damn!" Daisy exclaimed.

"Language, Daisy Berry!"

The girl mumbled an apology.

"Tell us about the arm!" Edgar urged, Horsie forgotten.

"Well, it was made of solid gold. The finest work you ever saw, with real mechanical fingers that moved." Miss White hooked her hand into a claw. "He got a haint to live in there and made it do his bidding. They say he could eat with chopsticks and thread a needle with that golden hand. Play the piano, too."

"He never did," whispered black-haired Pedro Hernandez, chubby fists gripping the edge of the wagon.

"The other prospectors grew jealous of his arm. It was worth a fortune. A hundred fortunes! So one dark night, they crept up on him while he slept and bonked him on the head with a cast-iron cookpot!"

Miss Chen wearily shook her head. "How many murders occur in this tale, Miss White?"

She smiled. "Almost there. They stole his arm, but then they got to squabbling among themselves over who got to sell it. Now, the haint who lived in there was still loyal to his former master. So it set to whispering and turning them against each other."

"Bible says you can't steal," Daisy declared, shooting a look at Miss Chen clearly intended to curry favor. "Guess those nasty men had it comin'."

"That's right. By the time the haint was done, only one of the thieves was still standing."

"How'd they die?" Edgar asked eagerly.

"Oh, all sorts of gruesome ways." Miss White's lips twitched. "I won't get into details, but you can take my word for it."

He scrunched his pug nose in disappointment. "Aw, c'mon—"

"*Tell* us, *tell* us," Daisy chanted, swaying from side to side like a tow-headed metronome. Pedro copied her, laughing.

Miss White held up a hand and they silenced instantly. "The last one was driven half-mad with fear. He decided the only way to keep the arm was to wear it. So he rode his horse down from the Northern Territory, galloping through a blizzard, to the first town he found."

"Lucky Boy!" they all cried.

"You guessed it. He figured he'd gone far enough to escape the curse, but he still had to find a way to wear the arm. He was just too greedy to give it up. So he lay down on the railroad tracks and waited for a train to come along and run it over."

"Makes sense," Daisy said thoughtfully.

"Then what happened?" Pedro asked, bouncing on his knees.

"Fool bled to death." Miss White lowered her voice, forcing them all to lean forward. "But they say that arm is still out here somewhere, guarded by the haint. And whoever finds it will live a live of ease and good fortune."

"But what about the curse?" Miss Chen asked, sucked in despite herself.

"Well, the haint only hated the men who killed his master. So as long as you got a clean conscience, it'll do your bidding." She winked. "I have reason to believe that golden arm is somewhere on my property. So if you kids are good and eat all your dinner, I might let you poke around the orchard later looking for it."

They turned to each other, dumbfounded at this stroke of good luck.

"Bet I'll find it first," Daisy said smugly.

"Will not!" Edgar retorted.

"Will so. I'm older."

"You got two arms anyhow," he muttered. "Can't even wear it."

"I'll do what the bad man did, 'cept I'll do it right. Make a turkey-kit."

"Huh?"

"It's part of a turkey you tie round yer arm to made the blood stop," she explained in a lofty tone. "My grandpa did it when he cut hisself on the fence."

"No one's lying in front of any trains," Miss Chen snapped, shooting daggers at Miss White.

"Here comes one now!" Daisy exclaimed, standing up in the wagon.

We'd just topped a rise. My breath caught, but it came

from the south. I rose up in my stirrups, heart racing. Gael drew the wagon to a halt.

"I knew he'd come!" I said. "See, it's the special private train. They're shorter."

The kids all craned to look. Brawny Daisy lifted up Pedro, who was the smallest.

We were a few miles north of town. Now I wished I'd stayed behind. My spirits rose as it approached Lucky Boy.

"Who's comin'?" Edgar asked.

"Mr. Sebastian Hardin," I said with a grin. "The head of Special Services himself!"

"What's that?"

"Railway police." Miss Chen gave me a quelling look. "They're, uh, coming to talk to Sheriff Bowdre."

"Can we get on the train? See what it's like inside?" Daisy begged hopefully. "Pleeeeease?"

"Maybe later," I said with a frown.

It was moving faster than I'd ever seen. A second later, the train blew straight past the depot without slowing.

"How come it didn't stop?" Edgar wondered, crestfallen.

Our heads moved in unison as the cars blurred by, smoke pouring from the boiler. The faint clatter of the wheels faded away.

"Never mind." I swallowed bitter disappointment. "We'd better keep going. You're hungry, right?" I forced myself to smile and the kids sat down again, already back to their debate over the hainted treasure.

"Well, that was odd," Miss White remarked.

"Very odd," Miss Chen murmured, settling the squirming baby back in her lap.

I shared a troubled glance with my dad. Gael snapped the reins and the wagon lurched forward.

~

Sebastian watched Lucky Boy flash past the window of the observation car. It was there and gone in an instant. Faded wooden buildings that sagged on their foundations like all the other ghost towns littering the prairie since the rise of Aguadulce and Carnarvon City set off a great southward migration.

Lucky Boy was the last to hang on, though from the way Ruth talked, the place was headed for oblivion. Why scrabble out a living on the farm when you could get a real paying job in the city? After Sebastian left Hatchet, he'd never looked back—and his hometown was a lot bigger than Lucky Boy.

Winters on the prairie were almost as bad as the N.T. Then there were the tornadoes that churned through every spring. He'd only seen one twister up close, but that was enough. It was easily the most terrifying experience of his life.

Sebastian flexed his left hand. It still bore the faint scar of Lee Merriweather's teeth.

Ruth Cortez wasn't like any young woman he'd ever met. She didn't mind the isolation, or the capricious weather, or the grinding hardships. He knew she'd never leave, not for good. Her father still lived here, but it wasn't just Gael Cortez that tied her to Lucky Boy, or some stubborn sense of loyalty. She genuinely loved the prairie. He could see it in her eyes when she talked about it.

"I can't afford to waste a single minute," he muttered aloud.

There'd been no sign of trouble in the town—not like what was happening up in the N.T. He'd posted two marshals in Lucky Boy, just in case, but all the rumors were coming from the north. And Dubbs said she was in Hatchet. If he hoped to save Ruth from the gallows, he needed to get up there as fast as possible.

Yet it felt wrong somehow.

Sebastian stared out the window at the endless grasslands

stretching in all directions, a sea of green and gold dotted with the occasional homestead.

They'd already passed the depot. It was miles behind.

But that little voice wouldn't shut up.

"Stop," he said.

Abel Beach dozed on the couch across the car. His eyes blinked open. "What?"

Sebastian lurched to his feet. "Stop the train!"

The urgency in his voice sent Beach hurrying up to the boiler room. Hardin grabbed his coat and buttoned it up as the brakes hissed and screeched. The train started to slow.

"What's going on?" Abel asked, stepping back through from the engine car. "You see something?"

Hardin shook his head, feeling a bit foolish.

"So why are we stopped in the middle of nowhere?" Abel inquired mildly.

"Just give me half an hour."

"For what?"

"We just passed Ruth's hometown. It means more to her than anything in the world." Sebastian cleared his throat. "I can't blow past without checking in. Make sure they're okay. She'd want me to."

Abel drew a deep breath. He looked skeptical. "Your call, marshal."

"Guess the haints can't back it up?"

The professor shook his head. "We'd need a siding to turn around."

Hardin squinted through the window. "Too far to walk back to town. But I see a house out there. I'll just go ask. If the folks are home and tell me everything's fine, we'll keep on going."

"Want me to come?"

"No, better one of us stays with the train. Don't let those haints wander off."

"I'll do my best." Abel stretched out on the couch again, lacing his hands behind his head. "But don't take too long."

Hardin strode lightly down the stairs, the cool breeze ruffling his dark hair. At least the headache had passed. Not a migraine, thank Christ, just a run-of-the-mill thumper.

Everything looked peaceful, like the picture book his mother used to read when Sebastian was a little boy. *Little House on the Frontier*. It made prairie life sound idyllic, though he knew better now.

He hesitated, almost turning back. It was surely a waste of time.

But they were already stopped. It was still afternoon, plenty of time to make Hatchet by midnight at the rate the phantoms were pushing the engine.

"Oh, the hell with it," he murmured, setting off at a brisk pace for the homestead in the distance.

21

ONCE WE RODE down into the hollow, I couldn't see the train anymore. It was just as well. The sight of it vanishing over the horizon would have broken my heart for good.

Maybe the marshals were heading north to protect the N.T. If so, it was overdue. But Jolly wasn't up there anymore. He was on his way here. The two trains would probably pass each other at some point, there was only one north-south line, but that might not ring any alarm bells. The marshals wouldn't have a clue who was on board.

We'll make do ourselves, I thought with resignation. *Just like always.*

When we got to Miss White's house, Gael herded the kids inside to wash up for dinner while Miss Chen changed the baby in Miss White's little sitting room. I was dispatched upstairs to gather extra bedding. I'd never been to the second floor of her house. It was much nicer than I expected, with a real grandfather clock and heavy, well-made furniture. I rummaged through the linen closet in the hall, arms heavy with blankets and sheets, and found my eye drawn to her bedroom. The door was open, and I could see a dresser with photographs in silver frames on top.

I glanced down the stairs, feeling vaguely guilty. I could hear Miss White in the kitchen, supervising the shelling of peas while she told some yarn about a ghostly rocking horse that carried naughty children off to serve the King of Dreamland.

No one knew a thing about Miss White's mysterious past except for my mom, who claimed she'd made a fortune and lost it back in the days when Calindra Carnarvon was just a slip of a girl and bandits roamed the plains. The phantoms were much wilder then, throwing objects around and scaring the bejesus out of folks. But my mom said there were opportunities, too, if you were bold enough to seize them.

I inched into her bedroom. It smelled of lemon oil and whiskey, on account of the empty bottles of Thistle Dew that filled four wooden crates. The woman had quite a collection.

"Just a peek," I muttered, drifting over to the dresser.

The first photo was of Miss White with a mining hat and pick over her shoulder, grinning. She looked pretty much the same, down to the two long braids, except her skin was smoother and her lips fuller. Her gaze was direct and confident, which I always thought was true beauty. Snow-capped mountains rose in the background. A faded handwritten note at the bottom said, *Tip Top, Summer 1847*.

There were other pictures, of a handsome young man in a fur hat and a group photo taken in front of a saloon, but I didn't want to snoop too much. As I turned away, I glanced through the window. From up on the second floor, the tracks were visible in the distance.

So was the train.

It had stopped a little way north of us. Steam trailed from the boiler, but I couldn't see anyone.

I pelted downstairs and dropped the linens on the kitchen table. Gael was in the sitting room with Miss Chen, cooing at the baby.

"What is it, Ruth?" Miss White asked sharply.

I glanced at the children, who sat on the floor around a bowl of peas, and beckoned her into the yard. "I spotted the train," I said in a low voice. "It's out there, not more than a mile off. Just sittin'."

"Huh. What do you make of that?"

"Don't know, but I aim to find out. Can I borrow a shotgun?"

I didn't dare ask for the Peacemaker on her hip.

"Hang on." Miss White strode into the barn and returned a minute later, leading Domino. She handed me a McNaughton double-barrel. "Fully loaded," she said.

I slung it over my shoulder and scrambled up to the saddle.

"You take care, Ruth," Miss White cautioned, shading her eyes with one hand.

I nodded once and kicked the mare to a gallop.

It was reckless of me. The ground was uneven and if she'd stepped in a gopher hole and broke a leg, I would have been sick about it, but Domino didn't hold back. She ran full tilt, mane streaming back, with just the lightest touch of the reins to guide her.

We thundered through the apple orchard, the ground still thick with windfalls, and down past the pond where Miss White grazed her cows. October was an unpredictable month and usually ended with the first snowfall of winter, but summer was still clinging on and the air was mild. I laughed with exhilaration as Domino leapt over a fallen log, though the landing nearly knocked me off. I lurched forward in the saddle, wrapping my arms around her neck, and she shook her head with an annoyed whinny.

"Sorry," I gasped, clinging with my knees for dear life. "Guess Charlie's a better rider."

I managed to right myself as we tore across the open field on the other side. I hadn't been out for a gallop in ages. The exertion brought a flush to my cheeks and I finally stopped fighting the mare, letting her have her head. My dad said horses were too much work to care for, but they were more fun than chickens, that's for sure.

Then we crested a hill and I saw a figure striding through the grass. Even from a distance, I recognized the determined set of those shoulders. The navy uniform, primly buttoned to the top. No hat, neither.

My heart beat wildly as I trotted down the hill. His head jerked up. When he spotted me, Hardin started to run. I reined up. Then I slid from the saddle and threw my gun down, raising my hands. The look on his face scared me.

"Look, marshal—" I began.

He bulled straight into me, lifting me off my feet. We held each other tight for a long minute, his face buried in my hair and mine in his coat. His shoulders were shaking and when he pulled back, I realized he was laughing.

He cupped my cheeks in his warm hands, eyes shining with wonder. "My God, is it really you, Ruth?"

"It's me." I squinted, fearing it was all too good to be true. "But is it *you*?"

He frowned. "What?"

I decided there was only one way to find out. I grabbed his coat and kissed him.

His lips were soft and tasted like mint.

A slow grin spread across his blade-sharp face. "If that's a test, maybe you better try it again. Just to be sure."

Then we were making out like a couple of randy teenagers and I knew for sure it was really Sebastian Hardin because there was a thing he did with his . . . . Well, never mind about that. Let's just say it was him alright.

"By God, I missed you so much," he murmured. "I thought you might never speak to me again."

"Same here." I smiled. "Well, except to read me my rights."

We kissed some more. His hair was silky and the scrape of

his beard made me tingle all over. I couldn't get enough, but the knowledge that another train was drawing closer with each passing minute made me pull back.

"Okay," Sebastian said raggedly, blue eyes a bit glazed. "Guess we'd better settle down before it goes too far."

I nodded. Reluctantly. We both started talking at once, then fell into an awkward silence.

"You go first," he said.

I drew a deep breath. "So you got my telegram."

Hardin frowned. "What telegram?"

"I sent it to Handcuffs early this morning. Said we were in trouble and I was sorry."

The frown became a scowl. "No one gave it to me." It was his turn to draw a deep breath. "And you got nothing to be sorry for. You were right. I was wrong. End of story." A cheeky smile crept in. "Guess I'm forgiven though."

Domino cropped at the short grass, giving him the occasional suspicious glance.

"Then how'd you know to come here?"

He looked toward Lucky Boy. "I thought you were up in Hatchet, but I couldn't pass by without checking on your people."

That was the moment I lost the last little piece of my heart to Sebastian Hardin. I took his hand and laced my fingers with his. "Well, I *was* in Hatchet. Not long, but long enough to meet H.J."

Hardin was a difficult man to surprise, but now he did a double-take. "You're putting me on."

"Nope. Talked to your dad." I grinned. "Liked him, too."

Sebastian barked out a short laugh. "He still playing piano at the Hotel Yorba?"

I nodded. "He sang *Sweet Molly From Hatchet* for me."

The ghost of a smile touched Hardin's lips. "That old rascal okay?"

"He looked well. But the owner, Moritz LeBlanc, is in tight with Jolly."

"The Frog." Hardin's lips thinned. "He's a firebug, though we never managed to prove it."

"Moritz set us all up. Your dad had nothing to do with it." I gave him a sorry look. "They killed two of your marshals."

His eyes went flat. "What else?"

"Oh, there's more," I said dryly. "A lot more. Just tell me one thing first."

He cocked an eyebrow.

"Please tell me that train over there is packed with armed marshals."

Hardin sighed. "Not quite. I got a linguist though. Abel Beach."

"Mr. Beach?" I gasped in astonishment. "I thought he went to stay with family in Braga Territory!"

Hardin glanced away. "I might have arrested him."

I poked him in the chest. "You didn't! That nice professor?"

"Well, I got him out of a jam afterwards, so we're calling it even." He held my gaze, and now he was totally focused. "There's trouble in Carnarvon City, too. What's yours?"

"Jolly's coming with a trainload of hard cases to burn the town. Maybe phantoms, too."

"Dear Lord." His jaw tensed. "We'll see about that. Son of a—" Sebastian trailed off. He knew my views on cussing.

"What happened in the city?" I asked.

"All the haints are besieging the tower. Abel and I got out through the tunnels. I sent some marshals for your mom. She should be in the underground bunker by now."

My gut tightened. "Will it keep them out?"

"I don't know." He squeezed my hand. "I'm so sorry I couldn't get her myself, Ruth. But Jack Dubbs told me you were a prisoner up in Hatchet, about to be hung. I couldn't afford the time."

"Who's Jack Dubbs?"

His face darkened. "Ava's lapdog. She sacked me. Well, she was about to anyhow."

"Who else is with you?" I asked, glancing at the train.

"Just the professor. He'll sure be glad to see Merriweather. Is the kid . . . recovered?"

"From the hiding you gave him?" Sebastian nodded, shame-faced. "More or less. But he ain't here. Jolly's got him."

Hardin paled. "What about Doc?"

A wave of sadness overtook me. "Gone, too."

"Oh, that's bad," he muttered.

"Who's running the train?"

"Three haints. They aren't like the others." He looked amused. "You do realize it's the train you left down south?"

"They all look the same," I admitted. "But you brought us just what we needed! *Good* phantoms. They'll be worth a hundred marshals."

He glanced up the hill. "You staying at that house?"

"It's Miss White's." I thought for a minute. "You think Professor Beach can wait? If we go back to the house, I can send my dad to go get him with another horse. Then he won't have to walk."

"He was nodding off when I left. I imagine he'll be fine if it's not too long."

"Good," I said, slinging the shotgun over my shoulder. "We can ride together."

Hardin bounced behind me, grousing like a city boy the whole way back.

"I can't believe I planned to ride to Charter Oak," he muttered. "These beasts are torture."

Domino didn't seem thrilled about the arrangement either, but no one fell off so I counted it a win. When we trotted into the yard, Gael came rushing out, a dishtowel in his hands. He drew up short when he saw Sebastian. My dad watched warily as we slid down from the horse.

"This is my father," I said.

Hardin extended a hand. "Mr. Cortez," he said with a warm smile. "It's a real pleasure to finally meet you, sir."

Gael's face relaxed. They shook hands. "Same here, Mr. Hardin." He shot me a quick look. "My daughter's spoken highly of you."

Hardin seemed surprised and pleased at that.

"He brought someone with him," I said. "Abel Beach."

My dad gave a startled smile. "Abel? Here?"

"I'm sure Mr. Hardin can explain everything, but we ought to fetch him from the train. Would you mind, dad?"

"Of course." He handed me the towel. "The bottomless holes just finished eating, but we saved you some crumbs. Why don't you go on inside? I'll ride down to the train."

He headed for the barn and I ushered Hardin into the kitchen. Miss Chen was in the sitting room, reading the kids a book aloud. Miss White sat at the table, nursing a glass of whiskey with her legs stretched out long. There was a bowl of peas and cornbread and fried chicken, though not much. The kids had demolished most of it.

"Have a seat, marshal," Miss White said with her crooked little smile.

He gave a respectful nod. "Ma'am."

"You're from up north."

"That's right."

"I can hear it in your voice." She sighed. "You're too young to remember the way it used to be. It's civilized now." Miss White almost sounded regretful about that.

Hardin chuckled. "You think so?"

"Oh, I know so. Go on, get yourselves some plates."

The dishes were half-washed. We found two clean ones and scraped up what was left. Hardin tore into the chicken like a half-starved fox and I wondered when he'd eaten last.

When we finished, he turned to me expectantly. "So, what's the plan, Ruth?"

"You ain't taking charge, marshal?" I asked with a laugh.

"It's your town." He grinned. "I know you got one. You're not the sort to wait around twiddling your thumbs. So let's hear it."

I laid out the basic idea, filling in some of the gaps of what had happened after we got to the N.T. and my views on Roger's character. It sounded insane when I explained it out loud, but to my relief, Hardin didn't scoff.

"It's unorthodox," he said slowly. "But I'll follow your lead. You seem to know this Class X the best."

"It's our last chance to stop him," I said. "If we fail here, I don't think there'll be anywhere left to run."

Miss White knocked back her whiskey. She tilted the bottle at Hardin, who shook his head. "Better not," he said. "Never held my liquor well. How much time we got?"

I glanced out the window. "I reckon not much. Let's get those kids on the train—and anyone else who wants to go."

I felt infinitely better knowing that no matter what happened, the children would be gone. Either way, things were looking up. Just Hardin alone might turn the tide our way. The man was a devil in a fight.

"What about guns?" he asked, reading my mind. "No matter how this plays out, there's men of flesh and blood coming."

I looked at Miss White. She rose, perfectly steady on her feet. "Like I said, I got a few firearms."

She led us out to the barn and directed us to the far corner, where we hauled bales of hay out of the way. There was a hidden cellar underneath.

"That's my safe room," she said matter-of-factly. "Always knew the goddamned aliens would get feisty someday. Go on, open it up."

Hardin shot me an amused look. Rusty hinges protested as he bent down and lifted one of the doors, then the other. Miss White handed him a lantern. A ladder led down, but it was too dark for me to see. Hardin descended into the bunker. There was a long silence.

"Well, damn," I heard him say softly.

I hurried down the ladder. "Sweet heaven above," I whispered.

Water barrels and stacks of canned food crowded one wall. Also more crates of Thistledew and a big four-poster bed that I couldn't fathom how she got down there. But that's not what Hardin was staring at.

Miss White had a full-on arsenal. Shotguns, rifles, pistols, boxes of ammo. I even saw a few sticks of dynamite.

"Think that'll do?" she called down, sounding a little anxious.

Hardin cleared his throat. We shared a look of awe.

"It'll do, ma'am," he said.

22

By the time we finished loading up the wagon, my dad came trotting up with Abel Beach.

"Professor!" I shouted, giving him a wave.

Beach waved back. He looked glad to see me, but I could tell something was wrong.

"The phantoms are gone," he said to Hardin as they reined up. "I went up to the boiler and found it empty. I was calling when Gael came. No answer."

"Darn," I muttered. "Can you keep trying?"

My father must have got him up to speed during the ride, for Abel nodded. "Gael's a linguist, too. He'll help."

Well, of course he was. I felt stupid for not suggesting it myself. But I still thought of my dad as a farmer who happened to like books and mathematics.

"Tell 'em to look for the one called Zippo," I said. "She helped us before. Roger said she was indisposed, so he probably locked her up, too."

I hoped that was the worst he'd done, but I'd never forgotten that little haint he'd devoured when Jolly held us captive in Carnarvon City, and the block of wood they'd pinned it to. The memory made my skin crawl.

"We'd best move the children into the safe room," Miss White said. "It's getting late."

My father dismounted and pulled me into a wordless hug.

"If it goes bad," I whispered, too soft for the others to hear, "you take those kids and ride for Charter Oak."

He nodded and cleared his throat.

"Swear it. Don't come looking for me. Annie'll need you."

"I swear," he said hoarsely. "But it won't go bad."

I climbed up to the wagon seat next to Sebastian. The horses whinnied nervously. Maybe they sensed it, too.

"I'll ride into town when everyone's settled," Miss White said.

"You're not staying?" Gael asked with a frown.

She gave him a level stare. "This is war, son. Just 'cause I think they're a bunch of fools don't mean I won't stand with my neighbors. Besides which, it's been a dog's age since I was in a proper gunfight." Miss White looked thoughtful. "Wonder if I still got it in me."

"I don't doubt that you do, ma'am," Hardin said, earning a gap-toothed smile.

We set off at a brisk trot, the sun low in the sky. It might be hours yet before Jolly arrived, but I knew he was close.

"Nearly forgot," Sebastian said. "This is yours."

He reached into his pocket and handed me my copper star. I stared in surprise. "Thought I left it back in Aguadulce."

The badge was still warm from his hand. Holding it made me feel strange. Was I still a deputy? Sam hadn't exactly clarified that.

"Found it in your hotel room. I hoped I'd get to give it back someday."

I leaned over and kissed his stubbly cheek. "Thank you. I got something for you, too, but it's in my bedroom."

Blue eyes lit up. "Oh, really?"

I swatted him. "Your holster. The one with your initials burned into the leather. I borrowed it from the train."

"Well, I can't wait to get it back," he said with a straight face. "Wish we could go there right now."

"Got some bad men to kill first," I quipped. "But it's definitely on the agenda. You can meet my cat, Jimmy Jack. He's a scrapper."

"Like his mistress."

I smiled. "I think my dad's taken a shine to you, Hardin."

"God, I hope so. Seeing as I mean to stick around."

I shot him a sideways look. "Won't they come looking for you?"

He raised his hands with a laugh. "One war at a time, Ruth."

We bantered all the way to town, though Hardin turned occasionally to keep a sharp eye on the tracks behind, and I did, too. Main Street roiled like a kicked anthill when we reined up at the Town Hall, folks hobbling to and fro, getting everything into place. I ran inside and fetched Sheriff Bowdre. Him and Hardin shook hands, and Sam seemed relieved that I wasn't under arrest. He was less happy to learn the marshal was alone, but Bowdre took it in stride. We dispensed Miss White's arsenal to those who knew how to aim a gun and didn't have palsy, which ruled out Mr. Liddel and Mrs. Berry. They grumbled until Hardin slipped them a rifle to share when the sheriff wasn't looking.

The lady herself arrived shortly thereafter, galloping up in her straw hat.

"They're all tucked away, safe and sound," she announced, hopping nimbly from the saddle.

"Miss White," the sheriff said, tipping his hat. "You might have saved the day. Just want to say we appreciate your generosity."

"Well, thank you, Sam," she replied, a bit awkwardly. "Glad I could be of some use." Her eye lit on the Widow

Hernandez. "Lord, Fran, that's not how you load it. Let me show you."

Miss White strode over and demonstrated the correct way to rack a shell. One by one, the others drifted to join them. She seemed to enjoy the spotlight and I marveled at the sight of old enemies … well, not exactly getting along, but joined in a common cause.

"We all set?" I asked Sam.

He nodded. "Followed your instructions to the letter. Wasn't easy to move that piano."

"But you did it?"

"Yep. I'd better fetch Miss Gomez. She's still waiting on an answer from Carnarvon City—"

He cut off as Charlie burst through the doors, panting and waving his hat.

"Train's coming!" he announced.

I shared a look with Hardin.

"Go raise the alarm," the sheriff said tensely.

Charlie nodded and dashed outside. A moment later, I heard the clanging of the rusty iron bell in the square at the end of Main Street. I'd only heard it rung once before, when Charlie and his pals banged on it for a joke. The sound raised the hair on my arms.

"Okay, everyone," I called out, keeping my voice calm. "Let's do it like we planned. You all ready?"

There was a moment of stunned silence. Suddenly, it seemed like madness. Sweat trickled down my spine. Maybe we should have run when we had the chance—

"Hell, yes!" Miss White declared, brandishing her Peacemaker. "Who's with me?"

The old folks of Lucky Boy let out a battle cry.

~

Down at the telegraph office, Fran Gomez was nodding off when the machine suddenly lit up.

The Gomez family was one of the first to settle in Lucky Boy, going back four generations now. As a little girl, she'd shown a talent for tongues and spent two terms at the Academy in Carnarvon City, but she didn't like the crowds there and chose to come home when it became clear that she'd never master any phantom languages beyond a Class C. This worked out fine because the town needed a telegraph operator.

She liked the wee little haints. They were easy to work with and she'd grown fond of them.

Her brothers and sisters had all moved away years ago. Her parents passed on. But Fran stayed, spending most of her time at the library. It was very rare for Lucky Boy to receive a telegram, and rarer still for anyone to send one. Most of them pertained to railroad business, like the one she'd received from Marshal Hardin several weeks before.

Still, she'd kept faithfully to her post all day, hoping to get a reply to Ruth's telegram.

Now, the machine began to rattle and whir.

She called to the phantoms. No one answered.

"How peculiar," she remarked, settling her spectacles on her nose.

Incoming messages lit up a dial that had all the letters of the alphabet, with lights next to each one. She was practiced at reading the signals and kept a blank form and pencil next to the machine. Fran studied the dial, left hand carefully printing out the message.

It was the same words, over and over.

DO YOU WANT TO PLAY, RUTH?
DO YOU WANT TO PLAY, RUTH?
DO YOU WANT TO PLAY, RUTH?

"Miss Gomez?"

Fran jumped at the voice over her shoulder. It was Sam Bowdre.

"You startled me, sheriff," she said, blinking up at him through her glasses. "What do you make of this?"

He studied the sheet of paper, staring at it in puzzlement.

"There's no sender, Sam. And . . . the haints aren't even here."

He gave the cryptic message a last glance, then crumpled it in his fist. "Never mind, you can't stay here, Fran. They're coming. Let's get you somewhere safe."

They stepped outside the office. A glossy black train was speeding towards the depot. She felt a chill as it began to slow.

"Where's safe, Sam?" she asked.

He gave her a reassuring smile, but she saw the fear in his eyes as they hurried back up the hill to Lucky Boy.

23

SOMETHING WAS wrong with Elmira Poole.

Lee watched her warily from his place on the floor of the train car. He was still gagged, but they'd taken his blindfold off. One side of her face seemed to be frozen. She was sweating profusely and her skin had a grayish tinge.

"I need to go home," she said, picking mechanically at the tattered sleeve of her wedding dress. "Got things to do. Augie's expecting me. Where's all the presents?"

No one paid her any attention. Elmira had been rambling for a while now. Lee thought she might be drunk, but he hadn't seen her touch the whiskey the others were passing around. The men smelled ripe, but it was nothing compared to the reek of kerosene. Even through the gag, Lee could barely stand it. The acrid stench had sunk into his clothes, his skin.

"There's always *presents*," Elmira continued. Her whining tone reminded Lee of a spoiled child at Christmas. "That's the best part of the whole wedding. But I don't see none." Her voice rose. "It stinks in here—"

"For the love of God, shut up!" someone called from the end of the car.

"Don't tell me to shut up!" she hollered, leaping from the couch. "You're just the *guests*. I'm the *bride*!"

"Now, now, settle down."

The door opened and Jolly entered the car, rat-faced Winnie Cheever behind him. Cheever wore the diamond tie pin Lee had bought in Charter Oak, as well as the new snakeskin boots. He'd even stolen Lee's socks.

"What seems to be the problem, Miss Poole?" Jolly asked.

The tone was calm, soothing. Elmira's face gave a spasmodic jerk, but she sank back onto the couch. "Those men are rude," she declared.

"Well, now, my Apostles are a little rough around the edges, but they're God-fearing boys, aren't you?"

A chorus of amens drifted from the gang at the end of the car.

"Not like this piece of filth." The reverend's crazy eyes bored into Lee, who quickly looked away.

He'd learned what any show of defiance brought.

Time with the snakes.

Jolly never went anywhere without the leather valise. He handled the rattlers constantly, and they often struck at him but met an invisible barrier. Lee knew the phantoms had to be protecting him, but Jolly took it as a sign of his own divinity.

How they hadn't bitten Lee yet, he didn't know. When Jolly set them loose, he just tried his best not to provoke them, which was fairly easy since he was tied hand and foot. He sought to escape into happier memories, like the trip to Fanny's Fountain in Carnarvon City, but his thoughts always returned to Ruth and Ned, and the sure knowledge they were dead.

Just as he would be eventually.

"I'm thirsty," Elmira said. A white-coated tongue poked out from her cracked lips.

"There's water up in the dining car," Cheever said.

She gave a strange shudder. "Don't want *water*."

"Drink some whiskey then."

"Don't want that neither."

Jolly finally tired of her complaining. "*Quiet, woman,*" he growled.

Lee knew a Voice when he heard one. Jolly had raw power, though he wasn't a savant. Elmira lapsed into sullen silence.

Jolly set the valise next to Lee's bare feet. "Bet you're thirsty, too," he said. "It'll get worse." His face darkened beneath the thick beard. "There's no worse torment on earth."

They'd given Lee nothing to eat or drink since Tip Top. He didn't know what had happened to Dean Rodriguez, but the whole gang was firmly under Jolly's spell, doing his bidding without question. The only one who seemed immune was Billy Easter. He'd sidled up to Lee an hour or so after they left, glancing over his shoulder to make sure the reverend wasn't looking.

"You really a savant?" Billy had whispered.

Lee nodded, holding Billy's brown eyes, hardly daring to hope.

Billy reached around to untie Lee's gag.

"Easter! What are you doing?" Jolly had stormed over, face contorted in rage.

"Just giving him some water," Billy replied, holding up a tin cup.

"Did I give you permission?" Jolly knocked it from his hand. Water soaked Lee's pants. He nearly screamed in frustration. "Kirby, get over here. No one touches the Beast without my say-so or you shoot 'em, hear?"

"Yes, sir," Kirby Knox replied, knitting his thick brows.

Lee had been under guard with his own pearl-handled six-shooters ever since.

Jolly seemed to move in and out of sanity. Sometimes, he was lucid and decisive. Other times, he ranted like a man possessed. From what Lee gathered, Jolly planned to parade him in a cage around Carnarvon City until he perished from thirst.

Having spent more than a full day in the company of the Apostles, Lee knew them fairly well by now. Moritz LeBlanc was just eager to burn everything down, starting with Lucky Boy. God only knew how much kerosene they'd stashed on the train, but the fumes made his head ache. Winnie Cheever, marginally more intelligent than Kirby Knox, had appointed himself the reverend's righthand man. Billy Easter's bunch stuck together, though Billy himself never came back. Maybe the reverend had banished him to another car.

Juan Garcia Morales, the Ghost, remained the only enigma. Silent and watchful. None of the others openly avoided him, but on his rare appearances, they always found an excuse to move away.

Altogether they numbered about twenty, all of them but Billy Easter with the ice-cold eyes of men who took human life without a second thought. Lee felt sick at what would happen when they arrived in Lucky Boy. If he could only get the gag off, he might counter Jolly's influence—

"Let's have some verses!" the reverend announced. "Our work shall be great this day, brothers, but there's a long road before the Rapture comes and we reap our eternal reward. God's charged us to separate the wheat from the chaff." His voice gained strength, hitting the sing-song stride of a tent evangelist. "Can you *picture* that *bubblin' lake of fire* waiting to fry all the *sinners*?"

"I can!" Moritz piped up, rubbing his hands together.

Elmira's face started to spasm again.

Jolly stared down at Lee, fanatical hatred in his gaze. "I'd say the Book of Revelation is in order." He thumbed through the Bible. "*And the smoke of their torment goes up forever and ever, and they have no rest, day or night, these worshipers of the beast and its image, and whoever receives the mark of its name . . . .*"

The sermon went on and on, punctuated with tirades about smiting the phantoms that Lee felt fairly certain weren't in the official version of the Bible. Kirby Knox started to nod off. Lee wondered if he could throw himself out one of the windows. At least it would be a quicker end. He was judging the thickness of the glass when the brakes hissed.

Jolly picked up the valise, bracing one dirty hand against the wall. "We're here, boys. Get ready to unload."

The Apostles rose in unison. Half walked single file into the next car. The others gathered around the cans of kerosene.

"What about the Beast?" Kirby wondered.

"Bring him along. I want him to watch."

Kirby took out a big knife and sawed through the rope around Lee's ankles. He hoisted Lee to his feet as the train screeched to a halt.

"Try to run and I'll beat you to death," Kirby warned.

He dragged Lee to the door and shoved him down the stairs. Lee hadn't stood for an entire day, let alone walked. He felt light-headed and would have fallen if a hand hadn't reached out to steady him at the bottom.

Billy Easter. Lee tried to catch his eye, but the horse thief slipped away.

The train had stopped at a small depot. Lucky Boy lay perhaps a half-mile distant, just a cluster of buildings with scattered homesteads.

"Maybe them haints ought to scout ahead," Winnie Cheever suggested.

Jolly gave him a hard look.

"I mean the cherubim," Winnie amended quickly.

At some point, Jolly had declared that the three phantoms must be angelic, and not really haints at all.

"They have their own task to perform," Jolly said. "Hark! The first plague cometh."

He pointed to the east, where an unnatural-looking cloud was forming low to the earth.

Winnie shifted nervously. "What is that, Reverend?"

Jolly ignored him, striding up the hill toward the town. The Apostles each carried two cans of kerosene. Elmira lurched along, wedding gown trailing in the dirt. Every few seconds, her head gave a tiny jerk to the left.

"Thirsty," she said. "Where's the champagne? Augie promised me champagne."

"Right up that hill," Jolly replied serenely.

The cold, rocky ground tore at Lee's bare feet, but he feared if he stumbled again, Kirby might deliver on his promise. Knox seemed to hate him almost as much as Jolly. They reached the end of Main Street. It was dead quiet save for the wind, and an odd humming sound came from the cloud. Lee wondered what the hell "the first plague" was.

"Maybe they all ran off," Winnie Cheever said.

"They're here," Elmira said tonelessly. "I can smell 'em."

Jolly raised his voice. "Judgment Day has arrived for this den of iniquity! The birthplace of Judas Iscariot and her devil!"

No one came out to investigate. Lee felt a surge of hope. Maybe they'd been warned somehow.

"Doom has come upon you, upon you who dwell in this land." He spread his arms wide. "The time has come! The hour is nigh! I shall pour out my wrath on you and spend my anger against you! So sayeth the Lord!"

There was no response. His arms fell. Jolly scowled. "Where is everyone?"

"Over here!"

Five of the Apostles stood in front of a nondescript building. The windows had been blocked off with plywood.

"Heard something inside," said one of the boys from Ace-in-the-Hole.

"What if they got guns?" another asked.

"The Lord'll protect us," Jolly said confidently. "Try the doors."

They did. "Locked," the first one called.

"Maybe you should ask the haints," Winnie said. "Uh, I mean cherubim. See what's in there."

"I know what's in there," Jolly roared. "Buncha unbelievers with forked tongues and black hearts. Burn it!"

The men started pouring kerosene around the building. Off to the west, the humming noise grew louder.

"You've fallen short of the glory of God!" Jolly thundered. "Far short! And the wages of sin is death—"

He cut off as the doors suddenly burst open.

I WATCHED from the second story of the general store as Jolly and his men climbed the hill.

"They got Lee," I said. "Right over there!"

Kirby Knox walked behind him, gun out, bushy red beard swinging side to side as he scanned the grassland.

Ned Carver's gaze was riveted on Merriweather. "No shooting," he said tightly. "Not until we've got him back."

"Everyone knows," I said, catching Hardin's eye. "They'll hold fire until the signal."

The gang drew closer. I was afraid they'd stop out of range, but they kept coming. We knelt on the same pallets the marshals had bunked on. I held my head low, peering over the sill.

"Almost there," I whispered.

Jolly started blathering about hellfire and brimstone.

"They're pouring kerosene," Ned whispered. "Dammit . . . ."

"Just wait." A slow smile spread across my face as they kicked the doors to the Town Hall. "Here it comes—"

Mrs. Johanssen's bull galloped out. He was notoriously ill-tempered. As I'd hoped, the men were caught by surprise. They stood there gaping as it snorted and pawed at the ground. I laughed as the bull lowered its head and charged. One fired and missed before the bull bowled them over like ninepins. He caught a screaming bandit in his horns, shaking him like a rag doll.

A second shot from Miss Christie, who was stationed at the back of the hall, got the rest of the cattle moving. All thirty head. Total chaos erupted as the herd stampeded down Main Street. Glass shattered as rifles and shotguns poked out of windows. The gunfire was deafening. Men screamed and ran for cover, firing back.

"You better move!" I exclaimed. "Kirby just dragged Lee into an alley."

I turned to Ned, but he was already rushing for the door. He'd volunteered to rescue Merriweather and I trusted him to get the job done.

"What *is* that?" Hardin asked, pointing to a dense black cloud on the horizon.

I squinted. The cloud drew nearer. I heard a high-pitched buzzing sound.

"Looks like a swarm of locusts," I said in disbelief. "In October."

"Jesus, Mary and Joseph," he muttered. "This really *is* gettin' Biblical."

Then I spotted Jolly. He stood in the middle of the street, long black coat blowing back in the wind, staring up at me with a hellish look in his eyes. I took careful aim with the big-bore Smith & Wesson Model 3 that Miss White used to let me practice with when I was a kid, resting it across my left forearm and squeezing the trigger. The bullet should have hit him in the heart. But it passed right through and bounced off the dirt behind him.

The reverend leered. His body melted into the red-haired phantom.

Just as I expected, Roger was playing dirty.

I signaled to Mrs. Johanssen, who sat pale but straight-backed at the piano Charlie and Sam had hauled up from the church.

She swallowed nervously and poised her fingers over the keys. Mrs. Johanssen was a fine player, even better than H.J. She had perfect pitch and played all the hymns on Sundays. But the music that poured out now was a discordant mess. The phantom in the street below gave a violent grimace. Its face sagged, then twitched again as she hit an especially jarring note.

"Keep going!" I urged. "I think it's working."

The halting, off-key rendition of *Amazing Grace* gained speed.

"I have to find Jolly," I said. "The real one. If he's dead, it might break the spell over his followers."

"Comin' with you," Hardin said, blue eyes sparking.

"We'll hold down the fort," Mr. Grady said, nodding at Miss White. She hunched at the window, squinting down the barrel of her gun.

"Sons of bitches," she whispered. "Think I got one." The roar of the Colt Peacemaker made Miss Johanssen jump. Miss White cackled. "Bull's eye!" she exclaimed, then ducked as the windows blew out.

Miss Johanssen gave a little shriek.

"Keep at it, Eleanor," Miss White snapped. "You're out of the line of fire back there."

Miss Johanssen shot her a dark look, but resumed playing.

Hardin and I crawled to the stairs and went down into the dark store. Gunfire echoed outside.

"Where do you think he is?" Hardin asked quietly.

"Back at the train, maybe."

"There's no cover on the approach to the depot. He could pick us off with a rifle."

"That's why we'll sneak around the back way and come up on the tracks. There's a path—"

I nearly had a coronary as a figure in white darted out from behind the counter and grabbed me. Foul breath hit my face. "Where's my trousseau? I'm late for the wedding!"

Elmira Poole looked bad. *Real bad.* Her skin was pasty, with a sheen of sweat plastering limp hair to her forehead. A muscle in her cheek spasmed. I yanked my arm free and took a big step back. She stared at Hardin with glassy eyes. "Augie? That you, buttercup?"

"By God," Hardin muttered, peering at her in wonderment. "It's the Black Widow of Cobb County!"

Elmira hissed like a feral cat and spun away, running for the back door. Hardin chased after.

"Wait up!" I called.

We spilled into the dirt yard behind the general store. Winnie Cheever stepped out from the narrow alley next to the Town Hall. He took aim and fired. Hardin fell, crashing against the wall. I heard a blood-curdling scream. It was Elmira, her face contorted in rage.

"You shot my husband!" She lunged at Cheever, who fled down the alley.

I dragged Hardin back inside the store, panic rising in my chest. "Where'd he hit you?"

"Arm," he rasped through gritted teeth.

I eased his coat open. A chunk of flesh was gone, but I'd never been so relieved. "Looks like he nicked you," I said. "Let's tie that off."

I knew every shelf like the back of my hand and returned in a jiffy with a bandage and some ribbon for a tourniquet. Hardin had lost some blood and looked pale, but he'd live.

"Go on," he said, raising his Colt with a weak smile. "I'm a lefty anyway."

I gave a terse nod and crept out the door, following the

sounds of a commotion in the alley that ceased abruptly as I approached.

Elmira hunched over the prone body of Winnie Cheever. She must have sensed me, for she looked over her shoulder. Blood smeared her face. She slowly chewed and swallowed.

"Holy [cuss deleted]," I muttered, too shocked to move.

Elmira lurched to her feet. Gore streaked her wedding dress. "Thirsty," she said in a clear, decisive voice. "So thirsty."

She staggered out to the Main Street. I stepped past Winnie. It looked like his throat had been torn out, but I kicked the gun away from his hand just in case. I cautiously reached the mouth of the alley. Charlie and Sam Bowdre were holed up in the one-room jailhouse, shooting it out with Jolly's men who'd taken cover behind some water barrels. Rifles poked out from the windows of the feed store and library. Anyone with hands steady enough to hold a gun was firing away, and it looked like we were winning. Bodies littered the street, none of them folks from Lucky Boy.

Miss Johanssen was still playing that awful, discordant music. The phantoms hung suspended in the air, mesmerized just like at the clocktowers in Carnarvon City, except their faces were constantly flinching and wincing. I almost laughed.

That's when I saw Moritz LeBlanc. He stood outside the Town Hall. The reek of kerosene filled the air. Elmira walked toward him, her movements jerky and uncoordinated. She must have been quite a sight because Moritz did a double-take. He fumbled with a box of matches. I raised my gun and fired just as he struck the sulphur.

Moritz keeled over dead. I watched that match tumble end over end, praying it would go out before it hit the ground. It didn't. A pool of kerosene caught. In an instant, fire leapt to the next one, and the next. Elmira took off running, flames trailing from her wedding dress. It looked like she was heading for the train, but she didn't make it far before she stumbled and went down. Through the choking black smoke, I saw a thin line of fire racing for the depot. One of those cans must have been leaky.

I ran back down the alley and grabbed Hardin, hauling him to his feet and dragging him into the yard. A few seconds later, I heard a series of earth-shaking thumps. Down the hill, I saw the train rock over onto its side, flames shooting from the windows. If Jolly was on board, he'd be done for.

"Sweet Jesus," Hardin breathed. "How much fuel did they have on that train?"

We both looked up at at the cock of a pistol. It was The Ghost, aiming straight for Hardin's forehead.

"Goodbye, Servicios Especiales," he said with a tight smile.

24

"I OUGHT to jest kill you, boy," Kirby Knox grunted.

Thick fingers wrapped around Lee's neck, pinning him to the wall of the building. Sour breath washed across his face.

"You set us up!" he growled. "It's yer fault my brother's dead." Small, mean eyes teared up. "Royal was all I had in this world. And you took him from me!"

Lee might have pointed out that Chalkey White was the one who'd shot Royal, but he was gagged. The fingers tightened. Black spots whirled at the edges of Lee's vision. He kicked out with one bare foot and met a leg like an old tree stump.

"Jolly was right," Knox said. "You got a demon in you."

Lee dimly heard a hammer cock. His temples throbbed from the pressure around his neck.

"Get ready to meet the devil—"

An enormous boom rolled through the alley. With strength born of sheer panic, Lee jerked from Kirby's grasp. The world tilted as he struggled to draw air. He sank to his knees.

Knox looked around, scowling. "What the hell was that?"

He grabbed Lee by the collar and raised his gun.

"Talk, you son of a bitch!" he screamed, seeming to forget that Lee had a filthy rag stuffed into his mouth.

A figure hurtled into him from the side. Lee's heart soared at the sight of Ned Carver. The two men stumbled to the ground, punching and grappling. Lee had just landed a solid kick to Kirby's ribs when he saw one of the outlaws from the train creeping up. Smoke filled the alley. The building was on fire. He yelled a muffled warning to Ned. The man started to draw, then spun and fell. Lee blinked as a little old lady with an enormous gun strode towards him.

"Guess you're Merriweather," she said briskly.

Lee nodded. Behind her, three phantoms drifted along the alley. The piano music that kept them at bay had cut off after the explosions.

"Mmmph!" Lee managed.

She turned and fired off two more shots. They passed harmlessly through the haints.

Ned grunted as Kirby landed a punch to his gut. The pistol lay not far off. Kirby's gaze caught on it. He lunged for the gun.

"Mmmmmmph!" Lee repeated, eyes bulging.

The old lady reached up and yanked his gag down.

"What are you saying, kid?" she demanded.

Lee drew a deep breath, filling his lungs to bursting. Pressure built inside him. Days of abuse and neglect and terror. A lifetime of containing his own Voice, too afraid to release it fully.

But Ned would die if he didn't do something.

"Stop!" Lee bellowed. "JUST STOP!"

THE SHOT ECHOED through the yard. I felt the bullet myself, an agonizing pain in my chest that I knew I'd never, ever recover from.

Then Juan Garcia Morales slowly toppled forward.

Billy Easter stood behind him. He holstered his gun.

"Never liked that man," he said. "You okay?"

Billy had a soft voice, hardly more than a whisper.

I covered my face with my hands, shaking. "Yeah," I muttered.

When I looked up, he was still peering down at me, a question on his face.

"I'm fine," I managed. "Thank you."

Hardin gave a pained chuckle. "Mr. Easter. Didn't 'spect to find you here."

"Didn't want to be here. Man gave me no choice." He looked ashamed. "Sorry I left you back there, miss—"

A wall of sound hit us, ten times louder than the avalanche. A hundred times louder than the depot blowing. I tried to cover my ears but every muscle seized up. It roared through me like a tornado. I swear to God, the sun stopped moving in the sky for a minute.

Next thing I knew, Billy Easter was gently shaking me. I blinked up at him, stunned, but once my eyelids moved, the rest of me followed. Hardin was still staring into space.

Like a big, handsome doll.

It gave me the creeps.

"What *was* that?" I whispered hoarsely.

Billy smiled. "The savant, I expect."

I touched Hardin's neck and felt a strong, steady pulse. He was alive and breathing, just motionless.

"How long's it gonna last?" I wondered. My molars still ached from the vibration.

"Don't know." Billy's face was grim. "But he's at the church. Thought you'd want to know."

I knew he wasn't talking about Merriweather anymore.

"Course he is," I murmured.

I gained my feet and staggered out to the Main Street. The phantoms were gone. The swarm of locusts was gone.

Not a stalk of grass moved on the prairie. Even the flames had doused themselves, though the air smelled of ash and blood. The depot was destroyed. Half the Town Hall was charred, and some of the general store. But it could have been so much worse.

"Ruth!"

I turned. Lee stared at me from the mouth of an alley, his eyes huge.

"I didn't mean to," he stammered. "I just . . . I wanted it all to stop."

"Stay there," I called. "I'll be right back."

Lee braced a hand against the wall. He looked like he might faint at any moment. Merriweather didn't have much meat on his bones to start with. They must have starved him, for the hollows in his cheeks had grown deeper and his shirt sagged on a gaunt frame. He slid down next to Ned, murmuring in soothing tones.

I walked up the hill to the church. My dad and I didn't go every Sunday. There was always work to do and I got a bit restless sitting on that hard pew for an hour. But I tried to stop in enough that God knew I meant well, and I figured He understood.

A small cemetery sat next to the church. I knew all the names on the headstones, though they were barely legible anymore. Grady and Gomez. Hernandez and Bowdre and Liddel and Berry. Someday, I wanted to be buried there, too.

I thought they'd be proud of us today.

When I got to the doors, I took out my deputy badge and pinned it to my shirt. Then I pushed through the doors. It was nearly dark, but the last rays of the sun came through the windows. Jolly stood silhouetted at the pulpit, three groggy-looking snakes coiled around his arms. He swayed and I realized he'd already been bit more than once.

"It's over," I said, stopping halfway down the aisle. "You lost."

The snakes were starting to wake up, which I figured was a good omen for everyone else. One struck at his neck. He barely seemed to notice. "I can't die," he gasped. "I'm the Messiah!" A line of spittle ran from his mouth. "God's chosen messenger!"

Hatred rose in my heart for all he'd done.

"I got a message for you," I said, cocking my gun.

Jolly stared down the barrel, defiant.

"It was never the Lord who protected you from the snakes," I said. "Just some nasty phantoms. And they're gone now."

"Go on, Judas," he sneered. "Do it."

I won't pretend I wasn't tempted. But I couldn't pull the trigger on an unarmed man. Not in church.

"I'm no murderer," I said, lowering the gun. "So I'm leaving you to face God's judgment." I regarded the red streaks running up the veins in his neck. "Looks like He already passed it."

A rattle blurred. The snakes struck again and again.

"Legion!" he cried, flinging them away. "Bring your wrath down on this sinner! Smite her with fire and brimstone!"

I braced myself, but Roger didn't show.

The reverend slid down the pulpit. "Thou hast deserted me," he panted, disbelief on his face. "Thou hast deserted me!"

His heels drummed against the floor as he gasped for air, face darkening. I turned away, feeling no desire to watch his gruesome end. Sebastian Hardin stood framed in the doors. He aimed his Colt Walker down the aisle. "Get down, Ruth!" he yelled.

I dove to the side. Sebastian fired. The bullet took Jolly in the chest. The gun in the reverend's hand spun across the floor. He gave a final twitch and lay still.

"God was a little slow," Sebastian said in an unsteady voice. "Thought I'd better hurry things along."

I ran over and hugged him tight, careful of his right arm.

"Billy told me where you went," he said.

I kissed him, thinking Minister Weeks would have a fit if he saw me now. "Mr. Easter didn't seem to be affected. I wonder why."

Sebastian tucked a strand of hair behind my ear. "He's deaf. Has been since he was thrown from a horse as a kid."

"You know him?"

"Mainly by reputation. Between you and me, I've always secretly admired Billy Easter. He's the greatest horse thief of all time."

"Marshal," I said with mock severity. "Thought you were supposed to be the greatest lawman of all time."

Hardin laughed. "That's a stretch, though I appreciate the compliment. But Easter never harmed a soul except to steal. Not sure how he ended up running with the rest of those boys."

I frowned. "Billy doesn't fit, does he? Nor does Elmira Poole. She was mean and crazy, but I don't see what use she'd be in a fight."

"Well, they all have one thing in common," Sebastian remarked. "Most wanted in the N.T."

It made a stupid kind of sense if you looked at it from Roger's point of view. They were just characters, playing roles in his story.

A hiss not too far off snapped Hardin's head around. We regarded the timber rattlers. They regarded us back. Hardin started to draw his gun, but I laid a hand on his arm.

"They're God's creatures, too. As far I'm concerned, they've done a good deed."

He looked dubious.

"Go on," I said. "Shoo."

The snakes coiled up defensively. The poor things were probably hungry. I doubted Jolly bothered to care for 'em right.

"Let's just leave the doors open," I said. "If they don't vacate the premises, we'll sweep them out with a broom later."

Sebastian laughed. "You're the boss, Cortez. I'm out of my jurisdiction here."

I sighed. "I don't think either of us have jurisdiction over anything but our own boots." I looked down. "And these ain't even mine."

The reminder of his exile put a sad look in Hardin's eye. I wished I hadn't said anything.

"Come on, let's go see what's happening," he said.

Back on Main Street, the townsfolk of Lucky Boy were coming back to life. People emerged from the buildings with the stunned look of animals emerging from their dens after a long winter.

"What was that?" Mr. Grady demanded, grey brows drawing together. "Thought I was having a coronary!"

"Lee Merriweather drove off the phantoms," I said loudly. "He's a hero."

There was a moment of silence. Then a ragged cheer went up.

"Someone help me!"

Ned's panicked voice drew us to the mouth of the alley. He cradled Lee in his arms. I feared the worst, but when I drew closer, I saw Lee was breathing shallowly.

"I looked him over," Ned said in a rush. "He doesn't seem hurt. I must have been knocked out. When I woke, he smiled. Then he just keeled over."

"Let's get him to my house," I said. "I doubt Jolly treated him gently."

I helped Ned carry Lee to the guest room. Sebastian fetched a cup of water and Ned pressed it to Lee's parched lips. Lee's eyes fluttered. He swallowed, then lapsed back into unconsciousness.

"I'll stay with him," Ned said, tucking a quilt around Lee.

I nodded. "I'll be back soon as I can."

Sebastian and I hurried to Main Street. The long day was catching up to me, but I wanted to get Jolly's gruesome body out of the church before Minister Weeks saw it—not to mention the snakes. We needed to do a head count, make sure everyone was accounted for. And send a rider out to Miss White's farm to tell them we'd won. Then there was Mrs. Johannsen's cattle. We had to round 'em up before they wandered too far. So much to do.

Knots of people stood in the street, sharing their war stories. I knew they'd be talking about this day for years to come. Decades, probably.

"Where's Sheriff Bowdre?" I asked, looking around.

They shook their heads.

"Last I saw, him and Charlie was at the jailhouse," I said. "Let's try there first."

I walked with Hardin to the end of the street. Three dead outlaws lay sprawled in the dirt outside. My heart sank when I saw Charlie kneeling over his father, shoulders shaking. I hurried to his side and crouched down. Blood soaked the sheriff's shirt. His eyes were closed.

"He died trying to protect me," Charlie said brokenly. "One of 'em got the draw on me. Dad shoved me aside and took the bullet."

Tears pricked my eyes. "That sounds like him."

"It should have been me."

"They're all dead now," I said. "Jolly, too. Your dad saved the town, Charlie. It's how he would have wanted to go."

People crowded in behind us. The men took their hats off.

"What am I gonna do?" Charlie looked dazed. "I can't run that farm by myself."

"You got all of us," I said firmly. "Ain't that right?"

The good folk of Lucky Boy surrounded him, offering words of condolence and promises to help out. Charlie nodded weakly. I knew he didn't want to be a rancher. He'd always had bigger plans for himself. But with his dad gone, he'd feel an obligation to keep it going.

"We'll sort all that later," I said. "First we ought to take care of him proper."

I carefully unpinned Sam's badge, cleaned the blood off, and pressed it into Charlie's hand. He curled his fingers around the five-pointed tin star, staring at it with a lost expression. We were the same age, eighteen. His mom had died from flu a while back. I know Sam had secretly hoped Charlie would take over as sheriff someday, but neither expected it to be so soon.

"Miss Gomez," I said. "Would you mind fetching a sheet—"

Sheriff Bowdre's eyes fluttered. Everyone gasped.

"My God, he's alive," Miss White exclaimed. "Don't just stand there! We need to move him to a bed."

"You can't move him until we know how bad he's hurt!" Miss Johanssen retorted.

"We need a doctor," Sebastian said, pushing through the crowd. "Everyone get back. Give him some air."

"I'll send for one from Charter Oak," Fran Gomez said briskly. Then her face fell. "Oh darn, the telegraph's gone, isn't it?"

Charlie stared at his father. "He had no pulse. I checked a dozen times. Saw him take his last breath."

"It's a miracle," Minister Weeks declared loudly.

"Probably it was just too faint to notice," Miss White muttered.

Sam Bowdre sat up.

I scooted away, heart pounding. I knew every laugh line and furrow on his kind, hard-worn face, and they looked perfect. But his grey eyes shone with a cruel glee I'd never seen before.

"Bet you thought that was the grand finale," he said with a wink, leaping to his feet. "But we're just getting started!"

25

Abel Beach watched the sleeping children.

They curled up together like kittens on Miss White's feather mattress. The baby dozed in a crate of Thistledew that she'd turned into a makeshift crib. It had been nearly two hours since the train passed. Abel gestured to Annie Chen and Gael Cortez, who nodded. They silently climbed the ladder from the bunker and eased the trap door up.

All was quiet now, though they'd heard the booms coming from the direction of town.

The three left the barn and stood in Miss White's yard, staring at the cloud of black smoke hovering over Lucky Boy. A carpet of dead locusts crunched underfoot.

"Dear Lord," Annie murmured, eyes tight with worry.

Abel knew her husband had stayed to fight.

"Maybe you'd better take the children and run for it," Gael said slowly.

"What about you?" Annie asked.

He didn't answer.

"Charter's Oak's hundreds of miles," Abel pointed out. "It's getting cold, and it'll be worse when night comes."

Annie bit her lip. "The phantoms can see through walls?"

He nodded.

"Then how is this bunker safe?" she demanded.

"Ruth will stop them," Gael said firmly.

"How? They can't be killed! From what you've told me, only a fragment of their bodies even exists in our dimension. It's impossible."

"We have to try calling for help again," Abel said.

Annie wrapped her arms around herself, staring toward town. The struggle on her face was clear. "You already tried. None of those things answered."

"Then we'll try again." Abel cleared his throat. "I know Class A through C. Gael can handle D through G."

Both were linguists, though only Lee knew all the phantom tongues.

Annie's head turned. Abel thought the faint sound was just the wind, but she must have a sixth sense. "Baby's awake," she said, looking exhausted. "Come down when you're done. But if they don't show, we're saddling up those horses and riding out." She gave them a fierce glare. "All of us. I need you both to carry the little ones."

"Fair enough," Abel said, shooting a quelling look at Gael, who reluctantly nodded.

Annie Chen marched off for the barn.

"I believe in Ruth," Gael said. "The smoke doesn't look good, I admit, but we don't know what happened."

"What about . . . that other thing?" Gael said.

Annie had been dozing when the wave of sound washed through. She didn't seem to notice at the time, or remember if she had. But Abel had felt it. So did Gael. A brief paralysis that faded quickly. If it had started in the town, Abel figured the effects would have been much greater. Miss White's farm was a good five miles off.

"Might have been Lee," Abel said. "I always suspected he was holding back on me."

"What if it was Roger?"

"Then we need reinforcements. You ready?"

Gael nodded. They stepped apart and starting calling into the ether.

It wasn't just the pitch and tone you had to get right, it was the emotion behind the words. Abel Beach and Gael Cortez poured their hearts into their voices, telling the story of Lucky Boy's last stand and pleading for aid in their time of dire need. They spoke of their affection for the phantoms, despite everything, and deepest wish for peace between the two species. They repeated the message in sixteen different dialects.

At last, the two men leaned against each other, wrung dry.

The only answer was the low moan of wind through the grass.

~

CHARLIE SUCKED IN A RAGGED BREATH. "You lowdown son-of-a—"

"Hush!" Roger raised a finger to his lips. Charlie instantly fell silent, his face flushed and rigid with tension.

We all backed away as Roger stepped out of the jailhouse into the street. He looked around with a satisfied expression. The body of Sam Bowdre flickered, then became Henry Chance in his big cowboy hat.

"Well, that was mighty entertaining. You were right, Ruth. It went even better than I hoped for." He laughed and slapped his knee. "Who knew that skunk was rabid? Elmira sure went out in a blaze of glory! And Jolly . . . Oh, boy. When he said *Thou hast deserted me*, I nearly busted a gut. Perfect last words. I couldn't have written it better!"

I stepped up to him. "You promised to leave us alone if we beat him."

Roger tilted his head. "I did say that, didn't I? Tell you what. Let's have a last wager. Double or nothin'!" A coin appeared in his hand. He tossed it into the air and caught it in a fist.

"No."

His face fell. "Well, you're no fun."

"Give me Doc back and we'll call it even."

"Dear old Doc!" Roger sang, pressing a hand to his heart. "He used to be a riot, but you ruined him."

"Doc told me all about you. You're just a bully."

Roger's green eyes darkened. He squared his hips, hands hovering over the silver six-shooters. "Them's fightin' words, cowgirl."

I rolled my eyes. "Oh, knock it off. What is it you want? A duel at high noon?"

He smirked. "I told you, Ruth. A simple wager. Heads, I level this hayseed town with a twister. Then I go home and never come back."

"Well, that's an enticing offer," I said. "And if it's tails?"

"I destroy Carnarvon City instead. You all can go back to milking your cows and whatnot." He winked. "But this picture needs to end with a bang. Leave 'em begging for a sequel!"

"You got no army anymore," I pointed out.

"Oh, I don't need Jolly," he scoffed. "All the phantoms in the city are just waiting for me to say *action*."

"Not all."

I spun at the harsh voice. Zippo floated down the street, long black hair hanging on either side of her thin, pale face. Her mouth was set in a line. Murmurs ran through the crowd.

Roger's smile slipped.

"Coward," Zippo croaked, pointing an accusing finger.

"How'd you get out?" he demanded.

"Friends."

Roger clutched his sides, tears of mirth streaming from his eyes. "You have no friends," he gasped. "You're just a pathetic little firebug. Even your own parents hate you! They sent you off to a boarding school for maladjusted delinquents and you don't even go home for holidays!" He took his hat off and slapped his knee. "Friends! Oh, that's a good one."

Zippo gave up speaking English and started telling him off in a phantom tongue, which sounded like someone sharpening a knife on a grinding stone while goats bleated in the background. Roger made a grotesque face and answered in kind.

I startled as a phantom materialized next to me. It had bristly green hair. One of the gang from Hardin's train. It growled at me. I shook my head in frustration.

"Can't you speak English?"

It answered in broken Spanish. The accent was terrible, but I gathered that the haints had heard my dad calling. They were scared, but they finally decided they had to do something.

And there was more. Roger had the key to Doc's prison.

"Where?" I asked urgently.

The phantom pointed at its naked stomach. I frowned and shook my head again.

"Adentro," it croaked.

Ew.

"Darnit," I muttered.

Roger and Zippo were still arguing. I hurled myself at Roger's back. His coat didn't feel like cloth at all. It was cold and a bit slimy. I formed my fingers into a wedge and reached into his gut, rummaging around. It was squishy in there, like a bucket of slops. Roger gave a wordless roar. He tried to pull away, but Zippo and the green-haired haint leapt on him. My fingers closed around something small and hard. I yanked it out. A fragment of metal sat in the palm of my hand, covered in pink goo. I cleaned it on my shirt.

It was a bullet.

Fifty caliber, like the ones for the Collier flintlock.

Roger was still tussling with the two haints. Green-hair made a popping sound and vanished into the ether. Zippo hung on, wrapping herself around his face. He was distracted, but I knew she couldn't hold him off for long.

I had the key, but I didn't have the gun.

What good was it?

I took a hasty step back as their forms merged into a mass of whipping tentacles.

"Whatcha got, Ruth?"

It was Hardin. I showed him the bullet.

"Maybe the flintlock is here," I said. "Hiding in plain sight."

He gave me a quizzical look, but my heart beat faster.

"What's a picture show without an audience?" I muttered. "Roger thinks of us as insects. It would have to be one of his own kind. One he considers an equal."

"You may be right," Sebastian said, glancing over his shoulder. "But I'd reckon we have about thirty seconds to figure this out." He winced at the battle playing out in the middle of the street. "Oh, that's gotta hurt—"

I could see at least two dozen firearms scattered around. It had been a real bang-up fight. And the light was dying.

"Doc!" I cried. "If you're here, give me a sign!"

I started running around like a lunatic, ear cocked to listen over the gibbering shrieks. Then I heard a faint cough. I leapt at the source of the sound.

It was Winnie Cheever's gun.

The one I'd kicked away from his hand, too revolted by the state of his gnawed-on corpse to pay close attention.

I snatched up the Collier and thumbed the cover plate from the brass cylinder as Roger spun around. The illusion of Henry Chance was gone. A ten-foot wall of pulsating pink flesh with whipping tentacles loomed in front of me.

"Well, [cuss deleted] me sideways!" Miss White exclaimed. "So that's what the derned aliens really look like!"

Roger lashed out with one ropy arm, sending her wagon flying. It landed on the roof of the library.

My hands shook as I slipped the bullet into the chamber and rammed it into place with the rod on the underside of the barrel. I cocked the hammer halfway. The powder dropped into the pan.

"Don't you dare!" Roger howled.

I thumbed the hammer to full-cock and fired into the dirt.

The gun dissolved in a shower of sparks. I flexed singed fingers.

"Doc?" I whispered.

Hardin strode to my side. We looked around, waiting, but nothing happened.

The Roger-blob started to laugh. "He's gone, Ruth."

I spun to the phantom, fists clenched. "He wouldn't leave us!"

"Of course he would. You left *him* to rot. Fair's fair."

"We're friends," I shouted.

The Roger-blob quivered with merriment. "You're just a doll to him. Doc's MY friend." Laughter boomed. "That was the real bet, Ruth. To see if he could gain your confidence." Tentacles flapped. "It was all just a game! And you lost. Now it'll be both heads *and* tails!"

He vanished. The clouds on the horizon grew thicker and darker, forming an ominous anvil shape. They slowly started to spin. Mrs. Johanssen's cattle had regrouped down by the creek. I heard them lowing. The bull gave an anxious bellow and the herd took off. Cows tend to laziness, but they can sure move when they need to.

"Find cover," Hardin shouted, but the folks of Lucky Boy were already fleeing to the nearest storm cellars. All the buildings on Main Street had one. Charlie Bowdre lifted Miss Christie from her wheelchair and ran into the feed store. The ones in their sixties helped the ones in their eighties and nineties. Loose shutters started to bang.

"We have to go, Ruth," Sebastian urged, pity in his eyes.

I just stood there, unable to move, my heart a cold thing in my chest.

Miss White gripped her hat, head bowed against the swirling grit. In a minute or two, the three of us were the only ones left on the street.

"He'll come, Ruth!" she cried. "I know that haint loves you! Don't give up—"

The sky blackened. The wind rose to a low, piercing moan. The trees along the edge of the creek bent and swayed, shedding the last of their yellow leaves. I saw not one but seven twisters touch down, the tips dancing along the earth. An instant later, the roof of the schoolhouse peeled off and sailed into the void.

Hardin wrapped his good arm around me as the funnels tore toward Lucky Boy.

26

DUST FILLED THE AIR. The windows on the storefronts started to rattle. I blindly reached out and found Sebastian's hand. We twined our fingers tight.

"If this is the end," he shouted, "I just want you to know—"

"Yeah," I shouted back, squeezing his hand. "Me, too!"

The sky turned an ugly, evil green. Rain pattered down, plastering Sebastian's dark hair to his forehead. Lightning forked. Two of the smaller twisters slammed into each other, joining to form an even bigger one. It skipped over a shed and vaporized the Berrys' silo. The wind gusted in a crazy pulsing ebb and flow that made my ears pop. I watched dumbly as the tree break between the Berry and Yocasta pastures got torn out by the roots.

"Dammit, Ruth, come *on*," Hardin urged, tugging my arm.

Then a figure walked out of the storm.

A young man with a sharp nose and sly, wide mouth. He wore a red union suit. I pulled free and ran forward. As I flung my arms around his neck and hugged him tight, his form felt solid though a bit squishier than a person, like the bones were in the wrong places.

"You came," I cried.

Doc's springy hair lashed around in the wind. "Give me a little more credit, Ruth," he said, gently pushing me behind him as Roger rematerialized and walked up to us.

Okay, he didn't exactly walk. More like oozed. He was a solid wall of pulsating flesh. A hole split open, lined with jagged teeth. I assumed that was for my benefit since the real Roger probably didn't even have teeth.

The twisters tracked closer, tearing a wide swath through Mr. Grady's cornfield.

"Go home," Roger bellowed.

"You go home," Doc replied with his usual sauciness.

"You're *DYING*," Roger growled.

I felt the power in his voice. It was a hundred times worse than Lee. Doc winced. A tentacle lashed out, knocking him to the ground. Fluid like black ink ran from his nose. Another misshapen limb smashed down. Doc rolled away at the last instant.

"You can't stop me," Roger screamed. "You never could. Because you're *WEAK*."

"Get away from him!" I shouted, moving between them.

A whip-like tendril reached for me and two shots went off, splattering the street with pink goo. Hardin and Miss White fired again in unison. Roger howled and swept out an arm, knocking them aside.

"Do you know how vast I am?" he shrieked. The hole opened wider, and wider still. Fangs gnashed, and darnit if they didn't look sharp and real. "I could eat you all up without even whetting my appetite! Drink your blood for my soup and grind your bones for—"

Doc smiled through black-stained teeth. He started to laugh, slapping the ground.

I stared down at him. Had he lost his mind?

"What the hell is so funny?" the Roger-blob demanded in an almost normal voice.

The wind suddenly died. The atmosphere dimmed to an eerie twilight. A shadow descended on the land, covering the earth from horizon to horizon. Doc laughed and laughed. He could hardly catch his breath. I followed his gaze to the west.

That's when I knew we were done for.

A naked woman eighty feet high, eyes glowing like bonfires, came stomping across the prairie. Jets of black hair billowed around her face. One foot smashed down on the train, then kicked it aside. The ground shook beneath her strides, which closed the distance to Lucky Boy in about five seconds.

Roger stood stock still, though a couple of his tentacles twitched.

Doc caught his breath. He dusted himself off.

"Oops," he said. "Looks like your mom's here."

I craned my neck, jaw sagging open, as she halted over the town, one thick leg on Line Street, the other planted squarely in the creek. Her body was smooth and dark blue. Two heavy breasts hung over us like the balloons on a zeppelin.

The Roger-blob went through several rapid transformations, each one more diminished than the last. It ended with Henry Chance in that silly cowboy hat. His shoulders hunched. He made a sort of squeaking sound.

Her mouth opened and an avalanche of fury spilled out. It blew my hair back.

Roger started to blubber.

A huge hand came down. It seized him by the scruff and hauled him aloft.

The illusion dissolved completely at that point. I saw a few kicking pink limbs. Then she turned and stomped off toward the horizon, one foot narrowly missing Eleanor Johanssen's barn. A mile or so away, they vanished into the ether.

The tornadoes faded to shimmering veils of dust.

Miss White hobbled over, shaking off Sebastian's arm. He looked terrified and awestruck at the same time, which summed it up for all of us.

"Now *that,*" she remarked hoarsely, "must have been a Class Z."

I looked at Doc. He smirked back at me.

"I think this picture's a wrap," he said.

"You okay?" I wiped the inky blood from his face with a sleeve.

"Just a scratch. Roger hits like a girl."

I balled a fist and he danced away. "Not you, Ruth. We all know about your left hook."

The skies were clearing, blue streaked with fingers of pale rose. We watched the sun sink below the western horizon. Despite the damage, I'd never seen the prairie so achingly beautiful.

"Sorry, it took me a while to find her," Doc said. "She was at work. I had to take the bus and I didn't have exact change, so I had to buy a candy bar first."

"You're fooling with me," I said, slapping his arm.

"Ow! I am not," he said tartly. "That's what happened. I mean, it wasn't exactly a bus, and it wasn't exactly a candy bar, but that's as close as I can get with your primitive vocabulary."

"How come you're all better?"

He looked embarrassed. "I was never ill, Ruth." He tapped his forehead. "Power of suggestion."

"So Roger hypnotized you?"

"Something like that."

"Wish I knew how to do that. I would have had you scrubbing floors and cleaning out the chicken coop."

He chuckled. "Not likely. But I do owe you one for setting me free." He stretched his arms over his head. "Sure feels good."

"What will happen to Roger?"

"After his mom's done with him? Well, he's definitely grounded. And after she tells the headmaster, I imagine he'll get a two-week detention."

I scowled. "That's all?"

"In your time, it'll be a good forty years, Ruth."

"Still don't like it. What about after?"

"I have an idea about that. I tattled on his three little minions, too. They're in deep, deep—" Doc turned to Sebastian. "Marshal," he said in an oily tone. "So delightful to see you again. I hope you've been taking good care of our Ruth."

I whacked him again. "Mind your beeswax."

Hardin swore as Zippo appeared in our midst, hovering a foot off the ground.

"Damnit, I'll never get used to that," he muttered.

"Stopped at the big machine place," she rasped.

That must be Carnarvon City. "What happened?" Hardin asked tensely.

"Told the kids Roger got in trouble. They're glad. Some go home. Others listen to the good voices again."

"She means the linguists," Doc said with a touch of condescension.

"No damage?" I pressed. "Are the . . . dolls okay?"

She nodded.

"Well, that's a relief. Thank you, Zippo," I said. "For everything."

She stared at Doc. He sighed. "Yes, yes, thank you. It was brave to stand up to him like that."

Zippo's mouth curved upward. It was weirdly mechanical, but the sentiment seemed genuine.

"See you at school," she croaked.

He looked away with studied nonchalance. "If you're around at fourth period lunch, I guess you could sit with me. If you want."

The smile widened. Zippo vanished into the ether.

"So you're really free," I said to Doc, feeling glad but a bit wistful, too.

He tipped his head back, studying the first faint stars. "I am."

"Can you stay a little while longer? Come back to the house for a spell?"

I feared he'd refuse, but Doc nodded. "I'd like that."

By this point, people were emerging from the storm cellars. They looked surprised to see the town still standing.

"It's truly over now!" I informed them, to more than one dubious look. "Go on home. We'll meet up again in the morning. Talk about fixing the damage."

"What about my dad?" Charlie Bowdre asked.

I'd almost forgotten the poor sheriff. "Might be he's alive. We'll search for him, but it's getting dark. Unless . . ." I turned to Doc. "Can you see him anywhere?"

Doc peered around, hazel eyes intent. At last, he shook his head. "He could be farther out, though."

"Wait," Charlie said, goggling at the young man in red pajamas. "You're Ruth's haint?"

Doc made a noise of disgust. "Typical," he muttered. "Am I an individual, with thoughts and feelings of my own? Of course not! I'm *Ruth's haint*. No different from that flea-ridden, mangy cat—"

"In the flesh," I confirmed. "He saved us all."

"Damn," Charlie said.

Mr. Grady cleared his throat. "Let's head out to the farm. Maybe Sam found his way home."

Charlie nodded, still eying Doc askance. "What happened, Ruth? Those twisters were headed right for town. How'd they miss us?"

I looked at Doc. "The X is gone, back to his own world. He's probably getting a whipping from his mama right now."

Charlie laughed uncertainly. "If you say so. Hey, it's your dad."

Two horses trotted up carrying Gael and Mr. Beach.

"The children are fine," Abel said, glancing around. "My word, looks like you had your hands full. Did you find Lee?"

"He's up at the house," I said. "He ain't hurt. Just worn out, I think. He's with Ned."

I could see the professor was dying to check on him.

"Go ahead," I said. "We'll come up in a minute."

Abel rode off. My dad slid from the saddle and lifted me up, jubilant.

"You did it, Ruth!"

"We all did it," I said, laughing and squirming until he put me down. "The haints did come, thanks to you and the professor. They helped us free Doc, and . . . well, he can tell you the rest."

My dad turned to the young man standing behind me, wonder on his face. He'd never seen him as anything but a shadow before.

"It's good to meet you, sir," he said politely, holding out a hand.

Doc took it, looking a bit awkward. "Mr. Cortez."

"There's so many things I want to ask you." Doc looked alarmed and my dad laughed. "But I won't chew your ear off. I'm just grateful for your timely intervention." He shook his head. "Dios mío, when I saw that giant woman, I thought it was all over."

Charlie was walking away. He froze in mid-stride and looked back.

"What giant woman?" he asked.

27

LEE OPENED HIS EYES. He lay on a bed with a quilt pulled to his chin. Ned dozed in a chair, face soft in the light of a single candle burning on the windowsill. A shotgun sat propped against the wall. Dark had fallen. Lee watched him for a minute. He ached all over, but the physical pain didn't compare to the shame in his heart. They probably set a guard on him and he couldn't blame them.

Maybe he could get away before anyone noticed. He hated to steal from whoever lived here, but he needed some shoes. And a horse. Lee had never ridden in his life, but how hard could it be?

He gingerly sat up, swinging his legs over the edge of the bed. The floorboards creaked under his weight. He cringed as Ned sat up.

"You're awake!"

Ned jumped to his feet and came over, grinning. He perched next to Lee on the edge of the bed. It wasn't the greeting Lee expected. He cleared his throat.

"Think I might have some water?"

Ned filled a cup and handed it to him. Lee drank it down and cradled the tin mug in his hands.

"Listen," he began, unable to meet Ned's eye. "I didn't mean to do it. And I never will again, I swear."

"What are you talking about?"

"I hurt people, didn't I?" Lee muttered.

"Naw, everybody's fine. But you missed the best part." Ned chuckled and Lee's spirits lifted. "Roger's mama came and dragged him off. Saw her right through the window. If it wasn't dark, I'd show you the footprint. Just missed the house."

Lee stared at him. "Seriously?"

"Would I make something like that up?"

"So what did she look like?"

"You ever see *Attack of the Fifty-Foot Amazon*?"

Lee shook his head.

"Well, like that. Except bigger. And blue."

"My word." He scrubbed a hand over his cowlick. "Where are we?"

"Ruth's house." Ned squinted at him. "How you feeling?"

"Sicker'n a barber's cat," Lee drawled in his best northern twang. "But you're cheerin' me up." His mirth faded. "What about Jolly?"

"Bit by his own snakes," Ned replied with a grim smile.

"Dead?"

"As a coffin nail."

Lee couldn't repress a shudder. "Thank God."

Ned gave him a serious look. "I remember how it was on the train," he said softly. "Must have been a hundred times worse for you. Sure you're gonna be okay?"

They were sitting awfully close, but Ned didn't seem to mind.

"I'm just glad it's over." He picked at a loose thread on his trousers. "So you're not scared?"

"Of what?"

"Me."

Ned frowned in puzzlement. "Why would I be?"

Lee gave a helpless shrug.

"You got a talent, but you're still *you*." Ned took his hand. Lee's breath caught as he leaned in and kissed his cheek. It was just a quick brush, but it made Lee tingle straight down his toes.

"That's all I get?" he murmured boldly.

Ned laughed. "You're a mess. How about a little food first? Maybe a bath, too."

"I suppose I am fairly ripe," Lee said with a frown.

"Yep." Ned grinned. "But I still like you. Hey, there's supper downstairs if you're up for it."

In truth, Lee was so hungry, he felt nauseous. The smell of cooking got him moving.

"How'd you come up with the cattle thing?" he asked.

"It was the book you gave to Ruth. *The Notorious Maxwell Brothers Take Tip Top*."

Lee pulled on the worn boots Ned tossed over. "Not really?"

"There's a scene at the end where the wounded marshal lures the outlaws to a barn. The Maxwell Brothers think he's hiding in there and aim to finish him off, but they get a surprise."

Lee laughed. "So what are you going to do now?"

"Head back north, I guess. Look for my family."

"I was wondering if you might like company," Lee said tentatively.

"You'd come along?"

"If you'd take me."

Ned smiled. "Sure would."

"I'm still wanted," he reminded Ned.

"Me, too." Ned's handsome face clouded. "Guess neither of us can ever go back to the city."

"Don't worry, I know we'll find your cousins. I'll do whatever I can to help them get set up again. Maybe I can call some phantoms to help rebuild—"

Ned kissed him again, on the mouth this time. Lee couldn't believe his luck.

"Hope I'm not interrupting."

The boys stepped apart. Lee felt a wave of unreality as he recognized the man standing in the doorway. "Professor Beach?"

"Sorry, I should have knocked." White teeth flashed. "But boy, it's good to see you up."

"What are you doing in Lucky Boy?" Lee asked in befuddlement.

"Sebastian Hardin brought me."

"He's here?" Lee glanced at the window. He wondered how far the drop was.

"Yes, but don't get all in a lather. He's not here for you." Abel Beach lowered his voice. "I felt what you did."

Lee tensed.

"You're a hero, son!"

"I am?" Lee asked doubtfully.

"The whole town would have burned down if you hadn't put a stop to it. I don't know how you managed it, but they're about ready to erect a statue in your honor."

"No one's mad?" He paused, thinking of Ruth's temper.

"The opposite. Come on down." A pause. "Sebastian wants to talk with you."

Lee glanced at Ned, who gave an encouraging nod.

When they got to the kitchen, Hardin came straight over. The marshal was coatless, with his right arm hanging in a sling. He studied Lee's face, which was still pretty colorful.

"I owe you an apology," Hardin said. "More than that. If you want to take a whack at me, go on. I deserve it."

He braced himself, clearly expecting Lee to take a swing. Not so long ago, Lee would have been happy to accept the offer. But things were different now. *He* was different.

"I know what it looked like. Can't blame you."

"Why the hell not?" Hardin sounded angry, though it was

directed at himself. "I should have listened to what Ruth was trying to tell me."

"Forget about it, marshal." Lee held out his hand. "We both made mistakes."

Sebastian let out a sigh. He shook it. His palm still bore a half-moon scar from Lee's teeth. "We're in the same doghouse now, Merriweather."

"How do you mean?"

"I started investigating the disappearance of Dean Rodriguez. It just didn't sit right."

"What did happen to him?" Lee asked, turning to Ruth.

"Mr. Cage," she said sadly. "Rodriguez tried to help me at the end."

Lee felt pity for the man. "So who's running the Academy now?"

"Ava," Hardin said, his face grim. "I overheard her talking to Freddy. She admitted that the X had done it all in Aguadulce. And she planned to get rid of Professor Beach. I went to the cells to get him out just as the phantoms surrounded the tower."

"Who wants supper?" A man popped his head out of the kitchen. He had Ruth's coloring and stocky build.

They gathered around the table and made a simple meal of chicken stew and buttered bread. Lee devoured three plates. Ruth introduced him to her father, and Miss White, whom Lee had already met in the alleyway. Doc was there, too, though he didn't eat and had lapsed back into shadow form. No one mentioned what Lee had done or treated him differently, and he found himself relaxing.

After dinner, they crowded around the stove. Miss White passed out the whiskey. Ned sat on the rug next to him, knees touching. That warmed him further.

"Where's Mr. Easter?" Lee asked. "He showed me some kindness on the train. I'd like to thank him." He paused. "You didn't shoot him, did you?"

Ruth and Hardin shared a look. "Billy's gone," Sebastian said.

"And coincidentally, so's my best horse," Miss White added wryly. "But since he saved the marshal's life, I guess he can keep it as payment."

The talk turned to the Carnarvons, and what would happen now that the matriarch was gone. Every single person in the room was solidly on Ava's bad side, with the exception of Miss White.

"I knew Calindra back in the day," she said. "We was born in the same town."

"Bonner Springs?" Hardin said in surprise.

"That's right. She nearly stole my first husband. He was a looker, but too dumb for her." Miss White smiled. "Calindra was whip-smart. I knew she'd make something of her life, though I never imagined she'd end up an empress."

"So you went north to seek your fortune," Ruth prompted, leaning her head on Hardin's shoulder. Lee felt glad for them both. They deserved a little happiness.

"That's right. There was no train in those days. I rode the whole way. Had plenty of adventures on the trip, but I followed the rumors of gold and ended up in the foothills of the Northern Range." She sipped her Thistledew, eyes misty. "If you'd climbed the big hill behind Tip Top and looked down the gulch, you would have witnessed a chaotic sight. Thousands of people digging, pushing, sluicing, cursing and fighting. Most were young men, but there were a few gals, too."

A knot popped in the wood stove. Jimmy Jack lashed his tail, then curled it back over his nose.

"Made my fortune there. Got married and widowed twice more, bought a hotel, lost it all in a fire. But I still had some gold left. I took the train to the first stop south and set up here." She shook her head. "Still seems impossible that Calindra's dead. And at the hand of her own granddaughter." Miss

White clucked her tongue. "Ain't gonna let her get away with it, I hope."

"That depends on Lee," Hardin said. "He's the only one who saw it happen."

Lee felt uneasy. "It's still my word against hers. I'm willing to testify, but I wonder if I'd live to make it to trial."

"You can't ask it of him, marshal," Ned said. "Not if you can't even offer him protection!"

"I wasn't," Hardin said wearily. "Not without knowing who's running Special Services. Dubbs might be dead, but Ava's got other lackeys waiting in the wings."

"What about Richard and Freddy?" I asked. "Can't they do anything?"

"Ava's their sister," he replied. "They don't want to believe it of her. And she's a mighty fine actress. You should have seen her weeping at the funeral."

Doc's shadow lounged against the wall. Now he spoke up.

"So Ava was conspiring with Roger to rule the world," he said.

Hardin nodded.

"But she hasn't a clue what happened here today, has she?"

Sebastian smiled. "I don't see how she would."

Doc gave an evil laugh. "That raises some interesting possibilities, don't you think?"

28

Ava sat in her office at the Academy, drafting a press release that blamed the strange phenomenon on a temporary malfunction of the clocktowers surrounding the city.

After a tense few hours in which the tower was besieged, most of the phantoms had dispersed like nothing ever happened. The X must have finally handled the situation. It was the only explanation, though she felt annoyed that it had taken so long.

She paused, then began typing again.

"New measures will be implemented to ensure such a disruption never occurs again," said Dean Ava Carnarvon. "Please be assured that there's nothing to be concerned about. It was simply the fault of a routine maintenance procedure. The employees involved will face disciplinary proceedings."

She'd already chosen the scapegoats to be fired. Professor Walsh topped the list. The woman was insubordinate and pushy. Ava's lips thinned. Yes, it was time for a major reorganization, both of the Academy and Special Services.

Jack Dubbs had vanished, along with Sebastian Hardin and Abel Beach, which was certainly a setback. But there were others who would do her bidding. Her enemies would be hunted down and quietly dealt with.

She resolved to keep Freddy on a tight leash. It turned out he hadn't gone to his club at all. She'd sent a message for him and learned he'd never appeared. When she went looking, she'd found him with Richard. Ava didn't care for the way the two of them looked at her. She scowled. They'd both better tread carefully. She had powerful friends now.

Ava looked up from her typewriter as Henry Chance stepped through the wall of the office. He smiled, but she still felt a twinge of unease.

"I did all you asked," Ava said plaintively. "What happened? This whole thing is very embarrassing. You promised they'd obey!"

"And you promised me Merriweather." The smile faded. Bright green eyes regarded her coldly.

"It wasn't my fault he got away in Aguadulce. Ruth *hit* me!" She pointed to the black eye. "Besides which, I thought the Reverend Jolly has him."

"Jolly is dead."

Ava wasn't exactly sorry for that. It saved her the trouble. The reverend had outlived his usefulness. "What about Lucky Boy? Did he burn it?"

"He failed." The voice grated. "And I was nearly captured."

"By who?" She hadn't believed such a thing was possible.

"It doesn't matter." He stepped closer. "I'm more concerned about *your* troubles."

"It's nothing I can't manage—"

"Freddy suspects."

Ava stared in silence, her cheeks flushing.

Chance perched on the edge of the desk. He wore a sober dark suit, blond hair combed back. A pleasant-looking fellow, though his nearness set off a tingle along her spine.

"I don't see the point in allying with someone who barely has control over the Carnarvon empire," he said softly.

"What do you mean?"

"Secure your position. Or you can forget about our deal."

"That's not what you promised. You said you'd give me Aguadulce!"

"The terms have changed."

"Freddy doesn't know a thing," she said firmly. "He believes it was Merriweather. I already intend to get rid of Richard, but I can't do it right away! My brother's a naive drunk, but even he will suspect something if we move too quickly. Just give me more time."

"And you'll continue to feed me?" He clicked his even white teeth together.

Ava nodded, mouth pursed in distaste. "I'll ensure you have a steady supply of phantoms." She rose and pressed her palms on the desk, determined not to appear cowed. "But I want Ruth Cortez and Sebastian Hardin dead. Do whatever you want with Merriweather, as long as he keeps his mouth shut."

A rap came at the door. Ava made a shooing motion and Henry Chance vanished.

"Come in!"

Freddy entered the office, a cigarette dangling from his mouth.

"I told you not to smoke in here," Ava snapped, still jarred from the encounter with Chance. "It sets a bad example for the students."

He looked around. "Were you with someone? I thought I heard voices."

"I was just practicing for the press conference," she said quickly, tearing the paper from the typewriter roller. "Do you want to read what I wrote?"

"Oh, I don't know," Freddy said carelessly. "I'm just a naive drunk, aren't I? So it doesn't really matter what I think."

Ava opened her mouth, then closed it again.

"What matters," Freddy continued, "is what *they* think."

She followed his gaze. The telephone was off the cradle. How had that happened?

Freddy picked up the receiver. "Did you get all that?" he asked, blowing out a stream of smoke.

Ava stiffened at a muffled response on the other end.

"Who are you speaking to?" she demanded. "What on earth is going on?"

Freddy smiled as the door opened. The family's two estate lawyers stood there, frowning at her. Spots of heat burned in Ava's cheeks. It couldn't be. They couldn't have.

"What is the meaning of this?" she demanded, squaring her shoulders. "We don't have a meeting scheduled."

Uniformed marshals pushed past into the the study. Tanaka and Ford. Tanaka held a pair of handcuffs. Ava's stomach sank as she saw Richard's wheelchair behind them. He rolled up to Freddy.

"Take her into custody," Richard said. His expression was grim.

Ava stared at them, heart racing wildly. "Mr. Chance!" she cried. "Do something!"

She felt a moment of triumph as the phantom reappeared. It's body swelled, filling the chamber. The applications on her desk blew up into the air and spun in a flapping circle. The lawyers covered their heads with their briefcases. Freddy threw a protective arm over his brother.

"I don't need you," Ava spat. "I don't need any of you!"

Suddenly, Henry Chance popped like a balloon. Ava jumped. A grinning youth stood before her.

"Ooooooh," he said, in a nasty, dry voice. "I bet you thought I was *Roger*."

Freddy started to laugh as the papers slowly settled.

Ava rounded on him, chest heaving.

"This is Doc," Freddy said, chuckling. "He came to me

about an hour ago and offered to have a little chat with you, sister. Since I knew you'd never confess on your own, it seemed like a fine idea."

Her hands curled into claws. "You dirty—" She lunged at Freddy. Tanaka stepped neatly between them and twisted Ava's arm up behind her back. The cuffs snapped around her slender wrists.

"You're under arrest for the murder of Calindra Carnarvon," Ford said. "Not to mention the deaths of sixty-two people in Aguadulce."

"This is an outrage!" She stared daggers at Freddy. "How could you?"

"How could *you*?" he spat back, mirth fading.

Freddy turned his back on her.

"I didn't mean it, Richard," she pleaded, as they dragged her past his wheelchair. "I was just telling him that so he wouldn't kill us all! I planned to go to you, to go to you both—"

"Spare me, Ava," Richard said quietly.

She stopped fighting. "You fool," she hissed at Freddy. "We could have had it all. You and me."

Her twin slowly turned. The two of them gazed at each other, identical green eyes locked.

"There was never us, Ava," he said. "Only you."

A silent crowd had gathered outside, students and professors. Ava felt their accusing eyes follow her as Tanaka and Ford walked her to the police conveyance. It was humiliating, but not as bad as what waited.

I'm going to prison, she thought in disbelief.

No more parties. No more jewels and pretty dresses. No more maids.

As the weight of that sank in, Ava shed her first genuine tear.

29

THE WEATHER STAYED WARM, though I knew the first hard frost couldn't be far off.

I was chopping wood in the yard. Sebastian lounged on the porch with his feet up, drinking black coffee with an ungodly amount of sugar.

"Makes me tired just watching you," he taunted with a grin.

I wiped perspiration from my brow. "If that arm wasn't in a sling, I'd make you finish the pile."

"I've already chopped enough wood to last a lifetime," he muttered. "Hauled water from wells and churned butter and scrubbed dirty underthings in frigid creeks."

"Your mama made you do laundry?"

"Hell, yes. You know how many brothers and sisters I got? There was nothin' *but* laundry."

I knew he was getting restless. Hardin wasn't made for too much quiet. Even injured, he simmered with pent-up energy, and it wasn't just the gallon of coffee he drank every day. I almost wished some trouble would come along to keep him busy.

Which turned out to be a premonition.

The chickens scattered as Charlie rode up. "You're wanted down at the depot, Ruth."

A goose waddled over my grave. I chunked the axe into the stump and regarded him without expression. "That's what you said last time and look where it got me."

"I'm not fooling. There's a train comin' in." He nodded at Sebastian. "You better come too, Mr. Hardin."

"Which direction?" he asked, thumping the chair down and finishing his coffee.

"Carnarvon City. That's all I know."

Charlie looked tired. We hadn't found Sam Bowdre. I kept hoping he'd turn up, but after searching for three weeks we'd all started to lose hope. It was a strange and terrible thing. If he was dead, he deserved a funeral, but that would have to be Charlie's call. I spent my mornings out at the farm, keeping him company. The thought of him in that big house all alone made me sad.

We followed him down to the charred wreck of the depot. Zippo and her friends had repaired the tracks, though the telegraph had been blown to bits. Jolly's train still lay on its side where Roger's mom kicked it, about a quarter mile off.

Both the Town Hall and general store had been damaged in the fire. We needed lumber to rebuild, but with the telegraph broken, I hadn't been able to wire for supplies. There was so much to do and winter was coming.

Doc had returned long enough to gleefully tell us what happened with Ava. That brightened everyone's day. But then I had to say goodbye for good, which was hard.

Real hard.

Charlie dismounted and took his hat off, blond hair curling around his ears. Sebastian watched the train approach with a resigned expression.

"Mr. Beach killed a marshal," he said quietly, for me alone. "Jack Dubbs. I'll tell 'em I did it."

I shot him a look.

"It's the least I can do to make amends," he said firmly.

The train drew to a halt. Freddy Carnarvon bounded down the steps, then turned to offer a hand to Richard. His older brother wore metal leg braces and made his way slowly, but on his own steam. Both were dressed to the nines, in expensive-looking suits and shiny shoes. I had no idea where I stood with the remaining Carnarvons. Last time I saw Freddy, I'd been a pointing a gun at him.

"Deputy," Richard said, his dark eyes solemn. "Marshal."

"This is Charlie Bowdre," I said. "The sheriff's son."

Charlie nodded, looking a bit starstruck.

"Good to see you all." Richard's shrewd gaze swept the ruined depot. "Doc told us what happened here. You have our personal promise it'll all be rebuilt."

A weight came off my shoulders. "Thank you, Mr. Carnarvon."

"We're heading up to the N.T.," Freddy added. "We thought we'd better go personally." He looked at Sebastian, uncertain. "We hoped you might come back. I understand if you don't want to, but—"

"He does," I said.

Sebastian frowned. "Do I get a say?"

"No," I replied firmly. "You were born for that job and we both know it."

He cleared his throat. "Well, I'd like to take some leave first. Heal up while I think about it."

"Of course," Richard said quickly. "How does a month sound?"

Sebastian brightened. I covered a smile. After a month in Lucky Boy, he'd be ready to run for the hills. Somehow, it all felt right. We'd figure it out.

"Hey, sir!" Faces appeared in the windows of the train. They'd come with a dozen marshals. Hardin climbed aboard and was greeted enthusiastically. He'd always been popular among the men and women of Special Services.

"We have another proposal," Freddy said to me. "A big one. But we need to talk to father first. Merriweather, too, if he's still here."

"He is," I said. "So's Ned Carver. We'll send for them."

The boys were staying out at Miss White's place, doing work in exchange for a couple of horses. She'd taken a shine to them both, and clearly felt proud that she'd been the one to take Lee's gag off and help him banish the phantoms.

"I'll go," Charlie offered. He swung up to his horse and galloped off.

Richard gazed at Jolly's derailed train and the colossal footprints leading off into the prairie. He looked thoughtful. I wondered what exactly their big proposal was.

"What happened to Dean Rodriguez?" Freddy asked me. "Doc mentioned that you found him hiding out in Jackpot. Is he here?"

I hesitated. "The dean saved my life," I said at last. "Mr. Cage killed him, but I wouldn't have gotten away if he hadn't sacrificed himself."

Freddy looked shocked. "My Lord."

"He knew too much about Miss Carnarvon's dealings," I said. "She had a hold over him. But he was a good man. Maybe you can organize a nice memorial for him at the school. Name a building after him or something." I thought he would have liked that.

"Absolutely. He'll be sorely missed."

We stood in silence for a moment. I remembered the dapper, bow-tied man I'd met the day I went to the Academy with Ava. Cheerful and efficient—when he wasn't sneezing into handkerchief. I'd have to make sure Lee kept his mouth shut, too, but I didn't think he'd object. He'd obviously liked the poor dean.

"So that's Lucky Boy," Freddy remarked at last, eyeing the town. "I haven't been through here since I was a kid."

"You never went back to the Northern Territory?" I asked in surprise.

"Not after what happened the first time," he said dryly. "Grandmother wouldn't let me."

"I'm very sorry for your loss."

"Thank you. So am I." Freddy seemed different. Older, somehow—not to mention sober. He cast me a sidelong glance. "Ava's pleading insanity. She hired a team of lawyers, but I'm not sure it'll do her any good. We tried to keep the story quiet, but the students saw her get arrested. Everyone knows what she did. The papers are calling for a life sentence."

"Must be hard," I said carefully. "I know you were close."

"She wasn't always like that. Money does things to people." He looked terribly sad. "But I knew, Ruth. I knew right away when you told me. I just couldn't admit it to myself. And I protected her for way too long. Maybe if I hadn't, things would have turned out differently."

"Could have been worse," I said.

"It could," he agreed. "But you stopped it here. And we plan to pay you back." He grinned and I saw the old Freddy for a minute. "How about a quick tour while we wait for Merriweather? By God, I'm tired of sitting on that train!"

I walked the Carnarvons through the damage on Main Street. Folks were out and about, and soon enough we had a crowd following us around. Freddy and Richard shook hands with everyone and listened patiently to their various complaints, which frequently spilled over into achy joints and indigestion. They were looking a bit weary by the time Charlie returned. He'd brought Lee and Ned—and Miss White, of course. My dad and Abel Beach were already there, both having been warmly greeted by the Carnarvons.

"Is there some place private where we can meet?" Freddy asked me.

"Depends," I said. "Is this idea of yours something that affects the whole town?"

"Well, yes—"

"Then we ought to invite everyone, don't you think?"

He glanced at Richard, who gave a helpless shrug.

"How about the library?" I said, pressing my advantage to Sebastian's obvious amusement. "It's still standing and it's warmer than the feed store."

Before the Carnarvons quite knew what was happening, I'd herded everyone into the library. Charlie and my dad pushed the reading table out of the way. Once folks had settled down, Richard cleared his throat.

"We've given a lot of thought to the question of the phantoms," he said. "In light of what we've learned about them, it seems critical to establish diplomatic relations with the adults of the species."

"The Z's, you mean?" Miss White called out.

"I suppose you could call them that. We were fortunate Ruth had a personal bond with one of the, uh, adolescents." I could tell Richard was still struggling over that one. "But we need to make a concerted effort to ensure that such misbehavior is checked in the future, before it gets out of hand."

"Can't argue with that," Mr. Grady muttered.

"We've decided to found a second Academy. A graduate school. We'll take the most promising students and train them to communicate at a higher level."

"And it seemed like a good idea to locate it outside the city," Freddy put in. "Not stow all our eggs in one basket."

People were nodding. I had to admit, it made sense.

"So we were hoping you'd agree to host the new Academy right here in Lucky Boy."

I figured that was coming, but the statement was met with suspicious silence.

"Two of our finest professors are already here," Richard

said, looking at Gael and Abel. "We thought they might agree to run it."

"Well, I don't see why not," my dad replied, looking a bit stunned. "It's been a while, but I do miss my students. What do you think, Abel?"

Professor Beach grinned. "If you're willing, I am. I wouldn't mind some peace and quiet."

"Mr. Merriweather?" Freddy asked hopefully. "We'd give you tenure."

Lee glanced at Ned. "That's a kind offer, but I'm not ready to settle down. I thought I'd help Mr. Carver look for his family. After that I just don't know—"

"Now, hang on," Miss White said. "What do we get out of this?"

Heads bobbed in agreement.

"Whatever you ask for," Richard said simply.

People started murmuring. It quickly turned into a clamor, as they all started shouting out demands and concerns. I watched with a little smile. They'd come around in the end. It was too good an offer to turn down. And it meant young people would be coming to Lucky Boy. We wouldn't die out after all.

I was glad for my dad, too. He looked happier than he had in years.

The Carnarvons seemed disappointed at Lee's staunch refusal, but they took it in stride. Richard started organizing a committee. Mrs. Johanssen immediately nominated herself as chairwoman.

"Now, the schoolhouse needs a new roof. That's a top priority," she said, pencil scribbling furiously. "And the Berrys lost their silo. Pipe down, Lucas, I know all about your outhouse." She cast me a quick, severe look. "I still have my reservations about all this, but if Gael's running it, you have my support. Long as it's one of our own."

We shared a tiny smile.

"You're welcome to ride north with us," Freddy was saying to Lee and Ned. "A lot of people ended up in Devil's Hopyard. It's a good place to start the search."

Ned seemed cheered by this.

I was, too. I listened to my dad and Mr. Beach chatting excitedly about their plans for the school. Hardin drew Freddy and Richard aside, talking to them in a low voice. They beckoned Charlie over. I wondered what was going on.

"Did you catch any of those phonemes?" my dad asked Abel. "It's a whole new lexicon to master."

They were talking about the Class Z.

"The communicative modalities are different," Abel replied. "But the underlying structure shares similarities with the lower orders. Now, the question is whether we can mimic the acoustics. Our airstream is pulmonic, but the Z is using another organ entirely—"

I gave up trying to make sense of the conversation as Charlie walked over.

"This belongs to you, Ruth," he said, handing me Sam's badge.

I shook my head. "He'd want you to have it, Charlie."

Charlie pressed the tin star into my palm, closing his big hand around mine. "Well, I just got a better offer. They're buying the farm for the new Academy and hiring me for the marshals." He smiled for the first time since his dad disappeared. "Besides which, we both know if there was a vote, you'd win hands down."

I gave him a hug. "I'm so happy for you, Charlie."

Mr. Grady dragged out his cider press and Amos Butler grabbed his fiddle. The town had a little impromptu celebration in the library.

"I nearly forgot." Freddy pulled me aside. "Doc said he left something for you in the jail."

"The jail?" I frowned.

"That's what he said."

Hardin twirled Miss White past the encyclopedias. The man moved light as a feather on his feet. He winked at me as I headed out the door. "Next dance is yours!" he called.

I hurried down to the jailhouse, so full of mixed-up feelings I wasn't sure whether to laugh or cry. Everything had turned out even better than I'd hoped, but there was a hole in my heart. I kept imagining all the rude, sarcastic comments Doc would have made if he'd been there.

But my haint—and yes, he *was* my haint, whether he liked it or not—clearly knew me better than I thought.

When I got to the jailhouse, I found a red telephone sitting on Sam Bowdre's desk. I picked up the receiver. There was a minute of hissing static. I heard ringing on the other end and a series of clicks.

"*Hello*?" A dry, nasty voice.

"Doc!"

"Who is this?"

"Quit fooling. It's me."

He chuckled. "You figured out to work the telly-phone. I'm proud of you, Ruth."

"I just picked it up and it started ringing."

"Yeeeesss. I thought I'd better keep it simple."

"So I can call you whenever I want?"

"Within reason. I do have a life, you know."

"Well, that's dandy." I twirled the cord around one finger. "How's Roger's detention going?"

"They're making him write *I will not break my toys* six thousand times on the blackboard."

"They aren't!"

"Oh, that's just the first part."

"Hey, can you ask him where he left the sheriff?"

"I'll try." Doc laughed. "He's not really talking to me right now."

"Well, try soon." I tipped Sam's chair back. "I feel funny wearing his badge if he's still alive. And Charlie just sold his farm."

There was a commotion in the background. It sounded like a crate of eggs falling into a thresher. "Look, classes are getting out. I have to go. You can call me if you get into trouble." A pause. "Or to say hello, if it's not too frequent."

"Thanks, Doc."

"And Ruth?"

"Uh-huh?"

His voice grew serious. "I really am proud of you."

I smiled.

"We never had the talk, but you're a woman now. I'm not blind. And I suppose you could do worse than Sebastian Hardin, so here goes." Doc mimicked taking a deep breath. "Sometimes, Ruth, when two people love each very much, physical changes occur in the male of the species. It's nothing to be alarmed about—"

I hung up the phone.

When I stepped outside, the sky had darkened. The party was breaking up as everyone headed home before the rain started.

"We're leaving some phantoms to fix the telegraph," Richard said. "I believe you already know Marshal Tanaka?"

"Sure do." I felt fondly towards her, since she was the one who loosened my restraints when Roger locked me in the infirmary with that evil nurse.

"She'll be the liaison for Lucky Boy. Eleanor Johanssen is making up a supply list, just wire it to Carnarvon City when it's ready."

Sebastian and I walked them all down to the depot. We said our goodbyes. I hugged Ned and Lee. Neither owned much more than what they were already wearing, and they'd decided to just get on the train. Charlie had insisted on staying until Lucky Boy was in better shape, which surprised me but probably shouldn't have. He was more like his dad than I gave him credit for.

"Stop back sometime," I said to Lee. "In the summer. We'll have a potluck."

"You can count on it." A little smile played on his face. "Remember when you told me I didn't care for anyone but myself?"

"I didn't mean it."

"Yeah, you did. And you were right." He leaned down and kissed my cheek. His breath tickled my ear as he lowered his voice to a deep register. "But I ain't that man no more, Cortez."

I laughed at the thick N.T. twang. "You never were, Merriweather. Just took you a while to realize it."

We waved goodbye to the train as it headed north. Lee stood on the caboose, waving back. I watched until his tall, skinny form faded into the distance.

"I never got my dance," I remarked to Hardin.

"And I never got my holster."

"Hmmm. How long do you think my dad'll be?"

He'd gone with Abel to Mrs. Johanssen's house.

"Least an hour or two," Hardin said fervently. "God willing."

It started to rain. We ran back to my house, getting soaked to the skin on the way. He grabbed me on the porch and wrapped his arms around my waist.

"I never finished what I wanted to say before," he said, looking insufferably handsome. "So here it is. I love you, Ruth."

"That's Sheriff Cortez," I corrected.

He grinned. "I love you, Sheriff Cortez. Body and soul."

"And I love you back," I said, laughing. "Is that the Colt, or are you just—"

A peal of thunder drowned out my words. I pulled him into a kiss.

"Don't like the look of that cloud," Hardin muttered when we finally broke free.

I glanced out at the prairie. The sky was black as pitch. "Oh, that's nothin'. Don't worry, I'll tell you when it's time to go into the storm cellar."

"You people are crazy," he murmured, kissing me again.

30

Two months later found me walking arm in arm with Hardin to the Nickelodeon Theater on Ash Street.

Snow dusted the sidewalk, gathering on his dark hair. It was nearly Christmas and the holiday shoppers were out in droves, toting packages and the occasional fir tree. I had to admit it was a pretty sight, all the street lamps decorated with little white lights powered by Class A haints and festive wreaths hanging in the yellow shop windows.

They were all so accustomed to having phantoms around that not even the evacuation scare was enough to put people off using them again. I guess they didn't have much choice, since all their machines relied on grims, though Richard was working on some new inventions. Sebastian said he was determined to have back-up systems in place for when Roger got out of detention—even if was forty years from now.

We'd asked my dad to join us, but his cheeks had colored and he said he wanted to watch Rose's show. Apparently, she'd left a ticket waiting for him at the box office.

The new school was almost ready to open its doors. Abel Beach had stayed in Lucky Boy to supervise the final arrangements. It would start with just twenty-five students, which made me secretly relieved. I was happy to get some fresh blood—and so were the folks earning money to keep them fed—but I didn't want my hometown to change *too* much.

As for Sebastian, he'd rented himself a real apartment for when I came to stay. Some might see it as a peculiar arrangement, but we'd decided that even though he'd rather get a root canal from a drunken dentist than live in Lucky Boy, and I felt the same about Carnarvon City, we wouldn't let our differences keep us apart.

That's what trains were for.

I paused under the marquee. My first picture show was a double creature-feature: *Phantom Without a Face* and *The Fiend From Beyond.*

"How scary's it gonna be?" I asked dubiously.

He smiled. "Don't chicken out on me now, sheriff."

"I ain't chickening out." A gang of rowdy teens pushed past us, laughing. "I just don't like too much blood."

"It's black and white anyway."

I jammed my hands into the pockets of the new leather jacket he'd bought me. "What if get nightmares?"

He leaned in and lowered his voice to a whisper. "Bet I can fix that."

I chuckled, feeling unaccountably better. "Well, I bet you can."

Hardin handed over the tickets and we waited on line at the concession. He ordered a big bag of popcorn. I opted for Turkish Taffy. Once we'd settled in our seats, I turned to him.

"Got you an early Christmas present."

I'd snuck off while he was browsing for new sheets at a big department store. Hardin lifted an eyebrow as I handed him a paper-wrapped package. He opened it and laughed.

"Go on, try 'em out," I said.

He slid the sunglasses on. "You sure these are regulation eyewear?"

"Oh, I'm sure." I kissed him. "They look mighty fine on you, marshal."

The lights dimmed and the first picture started. It was a little hard to follow, but soon enough I found myself jumping in my seat and hooting with the rest of the audience. The story revolved around some mysterious element called phantomite and a mad scientist who overdosed on the stuff and went on a killing spree.

Up on the screen, Dr. Scott Nelson paced back and forth, square jaw clenching.

"That's what he's done with the force field. He's compressed the energy of years into a moment!"

His girlfriend Linda went pale. *"But . . . that's like . . . the fourth dimension."*

Captain Rogers: *"I don't believe it. I'm a cop. I work with facts. Now I have to start looking for something that saps the life out of a man like juice out of an orange!"*

I nudged Hardin in the ribs. He nearly choked on his popcorn.

"Fourth dimension," I said with a giggle. "They're still one short of the truth."

"Hush over there!" a lady scolded.

I slunk down in my seat, thinking of Doc and all the strange things in the universe.

That sobered me.

If there were haints, why couldn't there be other things, too?

Maybe even . . . a Fiend From Beyond?

AFTERWORD

The research for this book was arguably even more fun than writing it. While my own characters are all entirely fictional, many were inspired by real people and places in the Old West. The omission of Native American culture, and the many heroic icons of the Western and Southern Tribes, is simply because this is a parallel world that was *not* settled by white Europeans who displaced the Indigenous people so it didn't seem to make sense.

Now, a few tidbits: Sheriff Bose Cahill is loosely based on Judge Roy Bean, the notorious "Law West of the Pecos," who once fined a corpse for carrying a concealed weapon and frequently lit his cigars with the Revised Statutes of Texas.

The newspaper advert Elmira Poole took out for prospective husbands was drawn from the one used by Belle Gunness, who poisoned dozens of husbands and boyfriends—and even her own children.

As for Wyatt, I'm related to him on my father's side, the Berry Earp Stapps. My great-grandfather was a pharmacist in Las Vegas, New Mexico, at the foot of the Sangre de Cristo Mountains, where my grandad grew up. It wasn't as well-known as Dodge City, Tombstone or Deadwood, but some say it was the "worst of the worst" of the Old West. It was during these notorious days that Las Vegas was called home or visited by the likes of Doc Holliday, Big-Nose Kate, Jesse James, Billy the Kid, Bob Ford, Wyatt Earp, Rattlesnake Sam, Cock-Eyed Frank, Web-Fingered Billy, Hook Nose Jim, Stuttering Tom, the Durango Kid, and Handsome Harry the Dancehall Rustler.

Bass Reeves is another legend, escaping slavery to become the first Black deputy U.S. marshal. Reeves arrested more than 3,000 outlaws during his long and illustrious career and may well have been the inspiration for the Lone Ranger.

The Gypsy Arcade in Virginia City, Montana, is the last place where you can play Old West arcade games, some at least a century old. Collectors have bid as high as $2 million to buy the arcade's extremely rare Gypsy fortune-teller device, but the owners refuse to sell.

Other wonderful resources were Bob Bose Bell and his True West website, *Outlaws and Peace Officers: Memoirs of Crime and Punishment in the Old West*, Edited by Stephen Brennan, *Dodge City: Wyatt Earp, Bat Masterson, and the Wickedest Town in the American West* by Tom Clavin, and *Black Cowboys of the Old West*, by Tricia Martineau Wagner.

ACKNOWLEDGMENTS

Huge thanks as always to my trusty betas, Laura Pilli and Leonie Henderson. To mom, for her sharp editorial eye, and to Nick for making me laugh.

ABOUT THE AUTHOR

Kat Ross worked as a journalist at the United Nations for ten years before happily falling back into what she likes best: making stuff up. She loves to hear from readers, so drop a line anytime! She lives in Connecticut with her son and lots of rescue cats.

www.katrossbooks.com
kat@katrossbooks.com

facebook.com/KatRossAuthor
instagram.com/katrossauthor
bookbub.com/authors/kat-ross
pinterest.com/katrossauthor

ALSO BY KAT ROSS

The Fourth Element Trilogy

The Fourth Talisman Series

The Fourth Empire Series

Nightmarked Series

Lord of Everfell Series

Lingua Magika Trilogy

Gaslamp Gothic Collection

Some Fine Day (dystopian YA standalone)

www.ingramcontent.com/pod-product-compliance
Lightning Source LLC
LaVergne TN
LVHW091024080826
845145LV00002B/351

* 9 7 8 1 7 3 4 6 1 8 4 8 8 *